PENGUIN BOOKS

LAST CHANCE SALOON

'One of the most successful writers of contemporary fiction'
Daily Express

'Snappy writing and Keyes' sharp eye for the absurdities of life make
cracking entertainment' *Woman & Home*

'Keyes is a rare writer in the popular fiction genre in that most of her
characters are as strong as her plot lines and the dialogue sparkles
and rings true' *Irish Times*

'She is a talented comic writer . . . laden with plot, twists, jokey
asides and nicely turned bits of zeitgeisty observational humour . . .
energetic, well-constructed prose delivers life and people in satisfying
shades of grey' *Guardian*

'(She) gives popular fiction a good name, no easy feat in a field
dominated by overpaid imitators and charlatans'
Independent on Sunday

'Keyes has a gift for zippy prose which means reading her is like
delving into a delicious soufflé' *Image*

'Keyes has taken over Binchy's crown as the Queen of Irish Fiction.
[She] is a superior storyteller who seamlessly combines style and
substance, humour and pathos, and thoroughly deserves her
bestselling status' *Irish Independent*

'Her writing sparkles and the world is a better place for her books'
Irish Tatler

LAST CHANCE
SALOON

Marian Keyes

PENGUIN BOOKS

PENGUIN BOOKS

Published by the Penguin Group
Penguin Books Ltd, 80 Strand, London WC2R ORL, England
Penguin Group (USA) Inc., 375 Hudson Street, New York, New York 10014, USA
Penguin Group (Canada), 10 Alcorn Avenue, Toronto, Ontario, Canada M4V 3B2
(a division of Pearson Penguin Canada Inc.)
Penguin Ireland, 25 St Stephen's Green, Dublin 2, Ireland
(a division of Penguin Books Ltd)
Penguin Group (Australia), 250 Camberwell Road,
Camberwell, Victoria 3124, Australia (a division of Pearson Australia Group Pty Ltd)
Penguin Books India Pvt Ltd, 11 Community Centre,
Panchsheel Park, New Delhi – 110 017, India
Penguin Group (NZ), cnr Airborne and Rosedale Roads, Albany,
Auckland 1310, New Zealand (a division of Pearson New Zealand Ltd)
Penguin Books (South Africa) (Pty) Ltd, 24 Sturdee Avenue,
Rosebank 2196, South Africa

Penguin Books Ltd, Registered Offices: 80 Strand, London WC2R 04L, England

www.penguin.com

Published by Michael Joseph 1999
Published in Penguin Books 2000

50

Typeset by Rowland Phototypesetting Ltd, Bury St Edmunds, Suffolk
Printed in England by Clays Ltd, St Ives plc

For Kate

For yesterday is but a dream,
And tomorrow is only a vision:
But today well lived
Makes every yesterday a dream of happiness,
And every tomorrow a vision of hope.

Look well, therefore, to this day.

SANSKRIT PROVERB

Acknowledgements

Thanks to all at Michael Joseph and Penguin. Especial thanks to my editor Louise Moore, for her vision, enthusiasm, praise, friendship and meticulous, tenacious, painstaking editing.

Thanks to everyone at Poolbeg for their hard work, support and endorsement. I must make special mention of editor Gaye Shortland's guidance.

Thanks to my agent Jonathan Lloyd and all at Curtis Brown.

Thanks to the 'hardcore' who've stuck with me since the first book and who read this book as I wrote it, and who with their suggestions, comments and encouragement persuaded me to continue – Jenny Boland, Caitriona Keyes, Rita-Anne Keyes and Louise Voss.

Thanks to Tadhg Keyes for advice on what groovy young men are wearing.

Thanks to Conor Ferguson, Niall Hadden and Alex Lyons for the information on the world of advertising.

Thanks to Liz McKeon for advice on toning tables.

Thanks to Dr Paul Carson, Isabel Thompson of HUG, Barry Dempsey and AnneMarie McGrath at the Irish Cancer Society and all at the Terrence Higgins Trust for the time and information they so generously and patiently gave.

Thanks to Mrs Mary Keyes for the County Clare sayings and for making me take lots of bad language out.

Thanks to Emily Godson for enlightening me on the world of acting in Los Angeles.

Thanks to Neville Walker and Geoff Hinchley for information on how the gay young man about town entertains himself. (I never knew!)

Many others have helped with practical advice, encouragement and support. I'm very grateful and would like to thank them all. I sincerely hope I haven't left anyone out, and if I have, I'm really sorry. Suzanne Benson, Suzie Burgin, Paula Campbell, Ailish Connelly, Liz Costello, Lucinda Edmonds, Gai Griffin, Suzanne Power, Eileen Prendergast, Morag Prunty and Annemarie Scanlon.

Thanks to my beloved Tony for everything, for all the support, both practical and emotional. For reading the book as it's written and holding my hand and telling me I'm not a complete failure. For running up and down the stairs bringing me cups of tea. For giving me feedback on characterization, plot development, spelling, grammar and anything else you care to think of. I couldn't do it without him.

And finally, thanks to Kate Cruise O'Brien who worked on this book with me until March 1998, when she died, tragically and unexpectedly.

1

At the chrome and glass Camden restaurant the skinny receptionist ran her purple nail down the book and muttered, 'Casey, Casey, where've you got to? Here we are, table twelve. You're the –'

'– first to arrive?' Katherine finished for her. She couldn't hide her disappointment because she'd forced herself, every fibre in her body resisting, to be five minutes late.

'Are you a Virgo?' Purple Nails swore by astrology.

At Katherine's nod, she went on, 'It's your destiny to be pathologically punctual. Go with it.'

A waiter called Darius, with dreadlocks in a Hepburnesque topknot, pointed Katherine in the direction of her table, where she crossed her legs and shook her layered bob back off her face, hoping this made her look poised and unconcerned. Then she pretended to study the menu, wished she smoked and swore blind that the next time she'd try to be *ten* minutes late.

Maybe, as Tara regularly suggested, she should start going to Anal Retentives Anonymous.

Seconds later Tara arrived, uncharacteristically on time, clattering across the bleached beech floor, her wheat-coloured hair flying. She wore an asymmetrical dress that glowed with newness, sang money and – unfortunately – bulged slightly. Her shoes looked great, though. 'Sorry I'm not late,' she apologized. 'I know you like to have the moral high ground, but the roads and the traffic conspired against me.'

'It can't be helped,' Katherine said gravely. 'Just don't make a habit of it. Happy birthday.'

'What's happy about it?' Tara asked, ruefully. 'How happy were you on your thirty-first birthday?'

'I booked ten sessions of non-surgical face-lifting,' Katherine admitted. 'But don't worry, you don't look a day over thirty. Well, maybe a day . . .'

Darius bounced across to take Katherine's drink order. But when he saw Tara a look of alarm flickered across his face. Not her again, he thought, stoically preparing for it to be a late one.

'Veen-ho?' Tara asked Katherine. 'Or the hard stuff?'

'Gin and tonic.'

'Make it two. Right.' Tara rubbed her hands together with glee. 'Where's my colouring book and crayons?'

Tara and Katherine had been best friends since the age of four, and Tara had a healthy respect for tradition.

Katherine slid a colourful parcel across the table and Tara tore the paper off. 'Aveda things!' she exclaimed, delighted.

'Aveda products are the thirty-something woman's colouring book and crayons,' Katherine pointed out.

'Sometimes, though,' Tara said, pensively, 'I kind of miss the colouring book and crayons.'

'Don't worry,' Katherine assured her. 'My mother still buys them for you for every birthday.'

Tara looked up in hope.

'In another dimension,' Katherine said quickly.

'You look fantastic.' Tara lit a cigarette and wistfully checked out Katherine's claret Karen Millen trouser suit.

'So do you.'

'In my arse.'

'You do. I love your dress.'

'My birthday present to myself. D'you know something?' Tara's face darkened. 'I hate shops that use those slanty forward mirrors, so you think the dress makes you look slender and willowy. Like a poor fool I always reckon it's because of the great cut, so it's worth spending the debt of a small South American country on.' She paused to take a monumental drag from her cigarette. 'Next thing you know, you're at home with a mirror that *isn't* slanty forward and you look like a pig in a frock.'

'You don't look like a pig.'

'I do. And they wouldn't give me a refund unless it had something wrong with it. I said it had plenty wrong with it, it made me look like a pig in a frock. They said that didn't count. It needed something like a broken zip. But I might as well wear it seeing as I went up to my Visa limit to buy it.'

'But you were already up to your Visa limit.'

'No, no,' Tara explained earnestly. 'I was only up to my *official* limit. My real limit is about two hundred quid above the one they set me. You know that!'

'OK,' Katherine said, faintly.

Tara picked up the menu. 'Oh, look,' she said in anguish. 'It's all so delicious here. Please, God, give me the strength to not order a starter. Although I'm so hungry I could eat a child's arse through the bars of a cot!'

'How's the no-forbidden-foods diet going?' Katherine asked, although she could have guessed the answer.

'Gone,' exhaled Tara, looking ashamed.

'What harm,' Katherine consoled.

3

'Exactly.' Tara was relieved. 'What harm indeed. Thomas was raging, as you can imagine. But really! Imagine a diet that tells a glutton like me that nothing is forbidden. It's a recipe for disaster.'

Katherine made murmury soothing noises, as she had every time over the past fifteen years when Tara had fallen off the food wagon. Katherine could eat exactly what she liked, precisely *because she didn't want to*. From her glossy exterior she looked like the kind of woman who never had struggles with anything. The cool grey eyes that looked out from underneath her smooth dark fringe were assured and appraising. She knew this. She practised a lot when she was on her own.

Next to arrive was Fintan, whose progress across the restaurant floor was observed by the staff and most of the clientele. Tall, big and handsome, with his dark hair swept back in a glossy quiff. His bright purple suit had buttonholes punched all over both sleeves, through which his lime-green shirt winked and twinkled. A plane could have landed on his lapels. Discreet murmuring of, 'Who's he . . . ?' 'He must be an actor . . . ?' 'Or a model . . . ?' rustled like autumn leaves, and the feel-good factor amongst the Friday-night diners experienced a marked surge. Truly, everyone thought, this is one stylish man. He spotted Tara and Katherine, who'd been watching him with indulgent amusement, and gave a huge smile. It was as if all the lights had been turned up.

'Gorgeous whistle.' Katherine nodded at his suit.

'A noice, clarssy set of freds,' replied Fintan, trying and completely failing to sound like a Cockney. There was no disguising his rounded County Clare accent.

Though it hadn't always been that way. When he'd arrived in London, twelve years previously, fresh from small-town

4

repression, he'd set about reinventing himself with gusto. The first port of call had been the way he spoke. Tara and Katherine had been forced to stand by, helplessly, as Fintan had peppered his conversations with camp 'Oooohhh, you screaming Mary!'s and 'Meee-yow!'s and wild talk of dancing with Boy George in Taboo.

But in the last couple of years, he'd gone back to his Irish accent. Except with some modifications. Accents were all fine and dandy in his line of work, the fashion industry. People found them charming – witness J.P. Gaultier's, ''Ow har you, my leetle Breetish chums?' But Fintan also realized the importance of being *understood*. So nowadays the brogue he spoke in was a kind of Clare *Lite*. Meanwhile, the twelve years had effected a mild-to-moderate urbanization of Tara and Katherine's accents.

'Happy birthday,' Fintan said to Tara. They didn't kiss. Although Tara, Katherine and Fintan kissed almost everyone else they met on a social basis, they didn't kiss each other. They'd grown up together in a town that didn't go in much for physical affection – the Knockavoy version of foreplay was the man saying, 'Brace yourself, Bridie.' All the same, that hadn't stopped Fintan trying to introduce the continental-style, two-cheeked kiss into their Willesden Green flat, in their early days of living in London. He even wanted them to do it to each other when they came home from work. But he'd met with strong resistance, which deeply disappointed him. All his new gay friends had indulgent fag-hags, why hadn't he?

'So how are you?' Tara asked him. 'You look like you've lost some weight, you lucky thing. How's the beriberi?'

'Playing up, taking it out of me, it's in my neck now,' sighed Fintan. 'How's your typhoid?'

'I managed to shake it,' said Tara. 'Spent a couple of days in bed. I'd a mild bout of rabies yesterday, but I'm over it now.'

'Making those kind of jokes is downright evil.' Katherine tossed her head in disgust.

'Can I help it if I always feel sick?' Fintan was outraged.

'Yes,' Katherine said simply. 'If you didn't go out and get slaughtered every night of the week, you'd feel a whole lot better every morning.'

'You'll feel so guilty when it turns out I've got Aids,' Fintan grumbled darkly.

Katherine went pale. Even Tara shuddered. 'I wish you wouldn't joke about it.'

'I'm sorry,' Fintan said humbly. 'Blind terror is a divil for making you say stupid things. I met this old pal of Sandro's last night and he looks like a Belsen victim. I hadn't even known he was positive. The list just keeps on growing and it scares the living bejaysus out of me . . .'

'Oh, God,' Tara said quietly.

'But *you've* nothing to be scared of,' Katherine interjected briskly. 'You practise safe sex and you're in a stable relationship. How is the Italian pony, by the way?'

'He's a beeyooootiful, beeyooootiful boy!' Fintan declared, in a boomy, theatrical way that had the other diners looking at him again and nodding in satisfaction that he was indeed a famous actor, as they'd first suspected.

'Sandro's grand,' Fintan continued, in his normal voice. 'Couldn't be better. He sends his love, this card . . .' he handed it over '. . . and his apologies, but as we speak he's wearing a jade taffeta ball gown and dancing to "Show Me The Way to Amarillo". Maid-of-honour at Peter and Eric's wedding, do you see.'

Fintan and Sandro had been going out with each other for years and years. Sandro was Italian, but was too small to qualify for the description of 'stallion'. 'Pony' just had to do. He was an architect and lived with Fintan in stylish splendour in Notting Hill.

'Will you tell me something?' Tara asked carefully. 'Do you and the pony ever have rows?'

'Rows!' Fintan was aghast. 'Do we ever have rows? What a thing to ask. We're *in love.*'

'Sorry,' Tara murmured.

'We never *stop*,' Fintan continued. 'At each other's throats morning, noon and night.'

'So you're cracked about each other,' Tara said wistfully.

'Put it this way,' Fintan replied, 'the man who made Sandro did the best day's work he'll ever do. Why are you asking about rows, anyway?'

'No reason.' Tara handed him a tiny parcel. 'This is your present to me. You owe me twenty quid.'

Fintan accepted the parcel, admired the wrapping, then handed it back to Tara. 'Happy birthday, doll. What credit cards do you take?'

Tara and Katherine had an arrangement with Fintan where they bought their own birthday and Christmas presents. This came about after Fintan's twenty-first birthday party when they'd nearly bankrupted themselves buying him the boxed set of Oscar Wilde's work. He'd accepted his present with fulsome thanks, yet a peculiarly expressionless face. And some hours later, when the partying was more advanced, he'd been found sobbing, curled in a foetal ball on the kitchen floor, amongst the ground-in crisps and empty cans. 'Books,' he'd wept, 'fucking books. I'm sorry to be ungrateful, but I thought you were going to get me a rubber T-shirt from John Galliano!'

After that night, they'd come to their current arrangement.

'What did I give you?' Fintan asked.

Tara ripped off the paper, and displayed a lipstick within. 'But this is no ordinary lipstick,' she said excitedly. 'This one really *is* indelible. The girl in the shop said it'd survive a nuclear attack. I think my long search is finally over.'

'About time,' said Katherine. 'How many fakes have you been persuaded to buy?'

'Too many,' Tara said. 'With their promises of lip-staining and colour-fastness, and the next thing there they are all over the side of my glass or on my fork, just like an ordinary lipstick. It'd make you cry!'

Next to arrive was Liv, in an I-might-have-to-murder-you-for-it Agnès b coat. She was very label-conscious, as befitted someone who worked in the world of design, albeit as an interior decorator. Liv was Swedish. Tall, with strong limbs, dazzling teeth and waist-length, poker-straight, white-blonde hair. Men often thought they recognized her from a porn film.

She'd arrived in Tara and Katherine's lives five years previously when Fintan left to move in with Sandro. They'd advertised for a new flatmate but weren't having much luck in persuading someone to take the tiny bedroom. And didn't hold out any hope that this Swedish woman would. She was just too large. But the moment Liv had realized they were Irish – better still that they were from rural Ireland – her blue eyes lit up, she reached into her bag and handed over the deposit.

'But,' Katherine said in surprise, 'you haven't even asked if we have a washing machine.'

'Never mind that,' Tara said, badly shaken. 'You don't even know how far away the off-licence is.'

'No problem,' Liv said, in her slight accent. 'Such things are not important.'

'If you're sure . . .' Tara was already wondering if Liv had any Swedish men friends living in London. Tanned, blond giants that she'd bring around and introduce.

But a few days after Liv moved in, the reason for her enthusiasm became clear. To the alarm and consternation of Tara and Katherine, she asked if she could accompany them to Mass, or join them for the evening rosary. It turned out that Liv was searching for some kind of meaning to her life. She'd temporarily run aground on the rocks of psychotherapy, was hanging all her hopes on spiritual enlightenment, and hoped that the girls' Catholicism might rub off on her.

'Sorry to disappoint you,' Katherine gently explained, 'but we're lapsed Catholics.'

'Lapsed!' Tara exclaimed. 'What are you talking about?'

Katherine looked surprised. She certainly hadn't seen any signs of a recent renewal in Tara's faith.

'Lapsed isn't a strong enough word!' Tara finally elaborated. 'Collapsed would be more like it.'

Liv eventually got over her disappointment. And although she spent a disproportionate amount of time discussing reincarnation with the Sikh newsagent, in most other ways she was perfectly normal. She had boyfriends, hangovers, threatening letters from her credit-card company, and a wardrobe full of clothes that she bought in the 70-per-cent-off sales, then never wore.

She shared the flat with Tara and Katherine for three and a half years until she decided to try and banish her existential ache by buying a place of her own. But she'd spent every evening of her first six months as a home-owner around at Tara's and Katherine's, crying and saying how lonely it was living by herself. And she'd still be at it, if Katherine and Tara hadn't moved out of the flat and gone their separate ways.

2

'So is it just the four of us?' Fintan sounded surprised.

Tara nodded. 'I'm too fragile for a wild celebration. I need to be comforted by a small group of good friends on this sad day.'

'What I actually meant was, where's Thomas?' Fintan had a glint in his eye.

'Oh, he felt like a quiet night in,' Tara said, slightly shamefaced.

There was a chorus of protest. 'But it's your birthday! He's your boyfriend!'

'He never comes out with us,' Fintan complained. 'The grumpy bollocks should have made an effort for your birthday.'

'But I don't mind,' Tara insisted, earnestly. 'And he's taking me to the pictures tomorrow night. Give him a break. I admit he's not the easiest man in the world, but he's not nasty, just emotionally scarred –'

'Yes, yes, yes,' Fintan interrupted. 'We know. His mother abandoned him when he was seven, so it's not his *fault* that he's a grumpy bollocks. But he should treat you better. You deserve the best.'

'But I'm happy with my wash,' Tara exclaimed. 'Honest to God. Your vision of me is too . . . too . . .' she pawed around for the right word '. . . too *ambitious.* You're like those parents

11

who want their child to be a brain surgeon when all they're good for is being a bin-man. I love Thomas.'

Fintan was mute with frustration. Love is blind, there was no doubt about it. In Tara's case it was also deaf, dumb, dyslexic, had a bad hip and the beginnings of Alzheimer's.

'And Thomas loves me,' Tara said firmly. 'And before you start telling me I could do a lot better than him, might I remind you that I'm in the Last Chance Saloon. In my decrepit, thirty-one-year-old state, I'd probably never get another man!'

Liv handed Tara her card and present. The card was covered in hand-painted silk and the present was a slim, sleek, cobalt-blue glass vase.

'It's gorgeous. You're so stylish it *hurts*,' Tara exclaimed, hiding her disappointment at not getting the Clarins anti-cellulite serum she'd hinted at so heavily. 'Thanks!'

'Are you ready to order?' Darius had arrived, pen in hand.

'I suppose,' they all mumbled. 'Someone else go first.'

'OK.' Tara smiled up from her menu. 'I'll have the pan-seared Mars Bar served with a Weetabix coulis, and the parsnip cappuccino.'

Darius stared at her, unamused. She'd done this the last time too.

'Sorry.' Tara giggled. 'It's just that it's a bit funny, all these mad combinations.'

Darius continued to eyeball her stonily.

'Please,' Katherine muttered at Tara, 'just order.'

'I'm sorry.' Tara cleared her throat. 'OK, I'll have the beef brûlé with coriander pesto, curried shoestring beetroot and a side order of chocolate mash.'

'*Tara!*' Katherine exploded.

'No, it's all right,' Fintan hurriedly reassured her. 'That really *is* on the menu.'

Katherine looked down. 'Oh, so it is. Sorry. In fact, make that two.'

After the food arrived – each plate more elaborate than the last – the conversation turned to matters concerning age. After all, it was someone's birthday.

'Despite what everyone says,' Katherine insisted, 'it's not wrinkles that depress me. It's the fact that over the past ten years my entire face has –'

'*Dropped*,' chorused Tara and Liv. They'd played this game many times before.

'I know exactly what you mean.' As smoothly as a relay-race runner, Tara took up the theme. 'If you look at my passport photo that was taken nine years ago my mouth was up around my forehead, but now my eyes are totally droopy and down on my chin – *Which* chin? I know you're thinking – and my temples have dropped nearly as low as my waist.'

'How lucky we are to have the plastic surgery,' Liv said passionately.

'I don't know,' Fintan said thoughtfully. 'I think it's wonderful to grow old gracefully, to let nature take its course. An aged face has so much character.'

The three women looked at him sourly. Obviously he couldn't visualize what it was like to see his looks literally falling away from him. But what were they to expect? Even though he was gay, he was still a man. Blessed with such high levels of collagen he thought he was Dorian Gray. But give him another ten years and *then* let's hear his nonsense of growing old gracefully. He'll be begging for the surgeon's knife, they thought in grim satisfaction.

'"An aged face has so much character,"' Tara mimicked. 'That's good coming from the man who nearly had to move into a bigger flat to house his Clinique collection. A curator is what your bathroom needs. You could nearly open it to the public.'

'Mee-yow!' Fintan laughed. (Some phrases had survived his re-reinvention.)

Then the conversation moved inexorably on to the ticking of their biological clocks.

'I would love to have a baby,' Liv said wistfully. 'I hate having a womb on hold.'

'No!' Katherine chided. 'You're only looking for fulfilment and all you'll get is misery.'

'Don't worry. It's not going to happen,' Liv mourned. 'Not while my boyfriend is married to someone else. And lives in Sweden.'

'At least you *have* a boyfriend,' Fintan said cheerfully. 'Not like Katherine here. How long is it, Katherine, since you did the nasty?' Katherine simply smiled mysteriously and Fintan sighed. 'What are we to do with you? It's not like you don't get offers from sexy men.'

Katherine smiled again, this time slightly more tightly.

'You know, I'd love a baby,' Fintan admitted. 'It's my one big regret about being a pouf.'

'But you can,' Tara cheered. 'Find an obliging woman, do a rent-a-womb contract and away you go.'

'Too true. What about one of you? Katherine?'

'No,' Katherine said shortly. 'I'm never having children.'

Fintan laughed at her disgusted expression. 'The love of a good man, that'll change your mind. What about you, Tara?

Feel the old womb twang at the thought of some baby-carrying action?'

'Yes, no . . . I don't know, maybe,' Tara dithered. 'But, let's face it, I can hardly take care of myself. Having to wash, feed and dress someone else would be the undoing of me. I'm just too immature.'

'Look at what happened to poor Emma,' Katherine agreed. Emma, an old friend, had been the goodest of good-time girls, until she had two babies in quick succession. 'Once upon a time she was *fabulous*. Now she looks like an eco-warrior.'

'The loss of a good woman,' said Tara. 'No time to wash her hair because she's busy wiping bums. But she's happy.'

'Think of Gerri,' Katherine reminded. Gerri was another erstwhile party-girl who'd had a baby and promptly turned into one herself. 'She's completely lost the ability to speak like an adult.'

'But she's potty-trained and can count to ten,' Liv said. 'She's happy too.'

'Then there's Melanie,' Katherine said, darkly. 'Used to be so liberal. Now she's turned into a right-wing Fascist who'd give the National Front a run for their money. That's what having a child can do to you. She's so busy signing petitions against suspected paedophiles that she's forgotten who she is.'

'But think what it would be like to hold your own little baby in your arms,' Liv said, softly. 'The joy! The happiness!'

'Mush alert!' Tara giggled. 'She's going all mushy. Stop her, someone.'

'What did Thomas give you for your birthday, Tara?' To stop Liv from bursting into broody tears, Katherine spoke before thinking.

'A ten-shilling note?' Fintan suggested.

15

'Ten shillings?' Tara scoffed. 'Have sense. He'd never be that flash,' she added. 'A farthing would be more like it.' She banged her fist on the table and, in a Yorkshire accent, announced, 'I'm not mean, I'm just careful.' She sounded uncannily like Thomas.

'A flowerpot covered in Polyfilla, with shells stuck to it, that he'd done himself? A used biro?' Fintan pressed.

'He gave me a Thomas Holmes special.' Tara reverted to her normal voice. 'A jar of magnolia hand cream and a promise of liposuction when he wins the lottery.'

'Isn't he hilarious?' Fintan said sarcastically.

'Was it a *new* jar of hand cream?' Katherine kept her tone expressionless. 'Or did he steal it from the ladies' toilets at work?'

'Please!' Tara was disgusted. 'Of course it wasn't new. It's the same one he gave me last Christmas. I just threw it in the bottom of the wardrobe and he obviously found it and recycled it.'

'What a meaner!' Liv couldn't stop herself exclaiming.

'He's *not* a meaner,' Tara objected.

Liv looked surprised. Usually Tara was the first person to say what a tightwad Thomas was, beating everyone else to it, to show how much she didn't mind.

'He's a mean*ie*,' Tara finished. 'Come on, Liv, say it.'

'Thomas is a mean*ie*,' Liv parroted. 'Thank you, Tara.'

'Anyway, you can see his point,' Tara said. 'They *are* all moneymaking rackets – Christmas, Valentine's Day, birthdays, all that lark. I admire him for refusing to be manipulated. And it doesn't mean he never buys me presents. A few weeks ago, unprompted, he bought me a lovely furry hot-water bottle for my period pains.'

16

'Too stingy to buy you Solpadeine every month, more like,' Fintan scorned.

'Ah, don't.' Tara half laughed. 'You don't see what I see.'

'So what do you see?'

'I know he seems very gruff, but actually he can be very sweet. Sometimes,' she looked slightly sheepish at this, 'he tells me lovely bedtime stories about a bear called Ernest.'

'Is that a euphemism for his willy?' Fintan asked suspiciously. 'Does Ernest do a lot of hiding in dark caves?'

'I can see I'm wasting my time here.' Tara giggled. 'Have you any gossip? Come on, tell us a scurrilous story about someone famous.'

In Fintan's job, as right-hand man to Carmella Garcia, a coke-fiend Spanish designer who'd been hailed simultaneously as a stunning genius and a mad bitch, he was privy to all sorts of startling information about the rich and famous.

'OK, but first will we get another drink?'

'Is the bear a Catholic?'

A long time and several French coffees later, Katherine became uncomfortably aware that Purple Nails wanted to cash up and go home. Or, at least, cash up and go out and take lots of drugs somewhere. 'I suppose we'd better pay,' she said, cutting into the drunken, raucous laughter.

'I'll get this,' Fintan offered, with the magnanimity of the pissed person. 'I . . . absolutely . . . insist.'

'No way,' said Katherine.

'You're offending me.' Fintan slapped his credit card on the table. 'You're insulting me.'

'How are you going to get your overdraft down to eight figures if you keep paying for other people's dinners?' Katherine admonished.

'She's right,' Tara urged, emotionally. 'You told me you'd be arrested if you put any more on your card. That the men in uniforms will arrive with their truncheons and handcuffs . . .'

'Great!' Fintan and Liv exclaimed, nudging each other and sniggering.

'. . . and they'll take you away and we'll never see you again. "Stop me before I spend again," you said.' Tara skittered his card back across the table at him.

'That's good coming from you,' Fintan complained.

'Two wrongs don't make a right.'

'How come I'm so skint?' Fintan demanded. 'I earn a decent wedge.'

'But that's why,' Tara consoled, with drunken logic. 'The more I earn the poorer I become. If ever I get a rise, my spending expands to absorb the new money, except it expands at a far bigger rate. Dieting makes you fat? Forget that – pay rises make you poor!'

'Why can't we be more like you, Katherine?' Fintan wondered.

Katherine had once confessed that when she got a pay rise, she set up a standing order to a savings account for the exact net amount of her monthly increase, working on the principle that because she'd never had it, she wouldn't miss it. She looked up from dividing the bill. 'But I need people like you so I can feel smug.'

Finally, they left.

Darius, the waiter, watched Katherine as she glided across the floor. She wasn't his type, but there was something about her that intrigued him. He'd seen how much she'd had to drink, but she wasn't stumbling across the floor, screeching and holding on to her friends, like the others were. And he was impressed by the way she'd behaved when she first arrived. He was an expert on women who nervously faked insouciance while they waited on their own, and he was fully certain that Katherine's poised unconcern had been genuine. He searched his head for a label for her. (He wanted to be a DJ and words weren't really his forte.) Enigmatic was the word he was searching for, had he but known it.

'Where now?' Tara asked eagerly, as they shivered outside. Though it was only early October it was chilly. 'Anyone know of any parties?'

'No, not tonight.'

'Nothing at *all*? Usually someone can scare something up.'

'We could go to Bar Mundo?' Katherine suggested.

Tara shook her head. 'Because we go there on Wednesdays I associate it with work.'

'The Blue Note?'

'Too packed by now. We wouldn't get a table.'

'Happiness Stans?'

'The music was crap the last time.'

'Subterrania?'

'Please!'

'I'll take that as a no.' Katherine had almost exhausted their list of regular haunts.

'How about the Torture Chamber,' Fintan offered cheerfully. 'Lots of lovely boys there, being led around on leads.'

'No, don't you remember?' Katherine reminded him. 'They wouldn't let us in the last time because we're girls.'

'Is that why?' Liv exclaimed. 'I thought it was because our heads weren't shaved.'

'You know, I don't think I could be bothered going to a

club,' Tara admitted. 'I'm not really in the mood for mayhem. I'd like to chill, sit on a comfortable seat, not have to fight to get a drink, be able to hear our conversation . . . Oh, God!' She clutched herself in horror. 'It's happening already. Thirty-one less than a day and I'm acting old. I'll *have* to go clubbing just to prove I still want to.'

'I don't really want to go to a club tonight either,' Liv consoled. 'But at thirty-one and a half, I've come to terms with it.'

'No!' Tara was appalled. 'Bad enough to not want to go, but to come to terms with it! I hate the ageing process, I really do.'

'Next you'll start feeling that you'd rather lie in bed and watch telly than do anything else.' Katherine sparkled with wickedness. 'You'll find yourself making excuses not to go out. There's even an official name for the syndrome – cocooning. You'll get really fond of your remote control.

'I love mine,' she confided. 'And you'll stop buying *Vogue* and start buying *Living Etc.*'

'That's an interiors magazine?'

Katherine nodded devilishly and Tara winced. 'Eeee-oooh.'

'Let's go to someone's flat.' Fintan sought to get the festivities back on track. 'We can pretend it's a club.'

'How about mine?' Tara suggested, thinking of Thomas and hoping they said no. She was drunk, but not that drunk.

'Or how about mine?' Katherine suggested, also thinking of Thomas.

'Katherine's!' Liv and Fintan said hastily, also thinking of Thomas.

'Have you drink in?' Tara asked.

'Of course I have,' Katherine said huffily.

'Truly we are grown-up,' Tara murmured thickly.

Katherine flagged a taxi, to the annoyance of two men fifty yards up the road who'd been waiting longer.

'Gospel Oak,' she told the driver.

'You could walk that,' he grumbled.

'*I* couldn't,' Tara said brightly. 'I'm pissed!'

'D'you remember,' she reminisced, when the four of them had clambered in, 'the way alcohol wouldn't last candlelight when we lived together? Whenever we went to Ireland,' she indicated Katherine and Fintan, 'or *you* went to Sweden,' she pointed at Liv, 'and brought back freety-due, I mean duty-free, we'd have it drunk before it was barely in the door.'

'It was our poority,' Liv said.

'Poverty,' corrected Tara absently. 'And it wasn't just that. We were young, we had fire in our bellies!'

'Now we're old,' Liv said mournfully.

'Don't!' Katherine commanded. 'It's too early for you to slump. You still have about an hour to go.'

3

While Fintan and the girls had been in the restaurant, two minutes down the road there'd been a party in progress. Of course, there were several going on because it was London, it was Friday night and it was in the Camden area. But this particular party contained Lorcan Larkin.

Lorcan Larkin was a man who had almost everything going for him. In fact, the only thing that didn't really work was his name – rough work at the font. He was six foot two, with a broad-chested, flat-stomached, long-legged, narrow-hipped body which he maintained by eating, drinking and smoking copiously. He had a mane of shoulder-length, dark-red hair, narrow sherry-purple eyes and one of the most beautiful, sensuous mouths in the Camden catchment area around the close of the twentieth century.

Thousands of women were thrown into great confusion when they met Lorcan and fell immediately in lust with him. 'But I don't find red-haired men attractive,' was a common refrain. 'This is so embarrassing!'

Lorcan was a very special redhead. Not for Lorcan the cries of 'Would you look at the ginger fuck!' following him up the road. Entranced gazes were more likely in his wake.

And in the rare cases when someone wavered on the brink of being mad about him, instead of diving straight in, he revealed his secret weapon. His Irish accent. This was no bogtrottery brogue that people imitated when they wished to pour scorn on the Irish, all 'Dis's and 'Dese's and 'Yer honour's. Lorcan's soft-spoken voice was mellow, lyrical but, above all, educated. And he had no fear of dropping the odd quotation or line of poetry into the conversation, if he reckoned it was called for. Women were hypnotized by Lorcan's voice. Because he made damn sure they were.

At the exact moment that Tara ordered two desserts ('Well, it *is* my birthday!' she said, defiantly), Lorcan decided he was going to screw his hostess's sixteen-year-old daughter, Kelly. She was obviously gagging for it, had been coming on to him all evening, giving him meaningful looks with her big doe eyes and brushing her high firm tits against his arm whenever she passed him. OK, so Angeline, her mother, might be pissed-off, but it wasn't the first time a mother and daughter had come to blows over him and it wouldn't be the last. He eyed Kelly, entertained by her glorious adolescent lushness. Her legs were long and slender, her bottom high and round. He could tell she was the type who'd put on weight quickly. In a couple of years she'd have gone to hell entirely, spare tyres, rolls of fat and all the rest. Wondering how everything had gone so wrong. But right now she was perfect.

'Time to go, mate,' Benjy reminded Lorcan, trying to keep the anxiety out of his voice. Lorcan had been due at his girlfriend Amy's birthday party several hours ago.

Lorcan waved Benjy away. 'Not just yet.'

'But . . .' Benjy protested.

'Get off my case,' Lorcan bit.

Benjy was Lorcan's ex-flatmate and unofficial social secretary. He hung around with Lorcan in the hope that Lorcan's tremendous success with women would rub off on him. In the event of that failing, he hoped to be on hand to help Lorcan's cast-offs – and they were legion – pick up the pieces, preferably in bed.

Lorcan stood up, unfolding himself from the sofa with easy grace. His face gleaming, he made his way over to Kelly, who dropped her eyes coyly, but not before Benjy had seen their spark of triumph. He couldn't hear what Lorcan said to Kelly, but he could guess. Lorcan had once, out of the goodness of his heart, shared some of his chat-up lines with him.

'Try murmuring very close to their ear, "You're a terrible woman, tormenting me with those eyes of yours,"' he'd advised. 'Or – and you've got to say this one in a stammering, halting way, like you're dead nervous – "Sorry to interrupt, I just had to tell you that you've got the most beautiful mouth I've ever seen, sorry again to have bothered you, I'll go away now." That'll increase your success rate by a hundred per cent,' he promised Benjy.

But a hundred per cent increase on nothing is still nothing. And the lines that were so successful for Lorcan earned Benjy either blank stares or scornful laughter. And, once, a belt across the face that gave him tinnitus in his right ear for three days.

'What am I doing wrong?' Benjy had demanded in despair, when his hearing was back to normal. It might have helped if he wasn't five foot eight, tubby, with sandy, thinning hair, but Lorcan didn't say that. He was enjoying playing benefactor.

'OK,' he'd grinned, 'listen to the master. You find two girls, one a babe, the other not so hot, that's often the way. You home in on the dog, right – all over her like a cheap suit and ignore the good-looking one. The dog is delighted to be picked over her babe mate. The babe is pissed-off at being ignored, tries to get you interested in her. You get your pick of the two!'

Benjy was suffused with hope. Lorcan made it sound so reasonable. 'Got any other tips?'

Lorcan thought about it for a moment. 'Every woman likes one thing about herself,' he said. 'Every woman has what she calls a "best feature". All you have to do is find out what it is – and believe me, man, it's always obvious – then compliment her on it.'

Benjy nodded hopefully. 'Anything else I should know?'

'Yeah. Fat girls try harder.'

Seconds after Lorcan and Kelly disappeared, Angeline, an attractive woman who worried about the size of her stomach, rushed up to Benjy. 'Where's Lorcan gone?' she asked worriedly. 'And where's Kelly?'

'Er, I don't know,' Benjy stammered. 'But don't worry, I'm sure they've not gone far,' he added, wondering why he bothered.

Indeed, they *weren't* far, in Kelly's pink and fluffy bedroom, the view of the duvet almost obscured by the plethora of cuddly toys piled on to it. Kelly might look like a woman, but the rest of her hadn't caught up yet.

Things with Lorcan were going way too fast. She'd wanted him to kiss her so she could triumphantly say to her mother, 'You see, you pregnant-looking old slapper, I told you I'm better-looking than you.' She hadn't yet decided whether to let him feel her tits – through her clothes, of course – but she thought probably not. So when Lorcan began unbuttoning his jeans it came as a big shock. When he pushed the jeans down to mid-thigh and stroked his large, angry-looking erection in Kelly's face, it came as an even bigger shock.

'Let's go back to the party,' she said, terrified.

'Not yet,' Lorcan said, with a dangerous smile, placing his hand firmly on the back of her silky-haired head.

Benjy looked up in a mixture of admiration and jealous hatred when Lorcan strutted back into the room, all but doing a lap of honour. 'You jammy bastard,' Benjy muttered.

'I didn't screw her.' Lorcan's eyes were limpid with his own goodness. 'Her honour is still intact.'

'Yeah, right! You didn't lay a finger on her,' Benjy scorned. 'And what about Amy? It's her birthday.'

'I can't help myself,' Lorcan grinned, with a shrug that would have reduced several grown females to begging. 'I love women.'

'No, you don't,' Benjy said, in an undertone. 'Seems to me like you hate them.'

'Come on,' Lorcan said. 'Time to go. Move it, man, we're late.' And off he swept, all business, ignoring the weeping and humiliated Kelly, who sat hunched on the bottom step of the stairs.

'Why do you always treat women like dirt?' Benjy demanded, when they got outside into the chilly October night and stood, waiting for a taxi. 'What did your mother do to you? Breastfeed you too long? Not breastfeed you enough?'

'My mother was grand,' Lorcan said, his soft, mellow voice contrasting with Benjy's high-pitched rage. Why were people always looking for stupid Freudian reasons for his short attention span with women? It was really very simple. 'It's the old joke, Benjy, isn't it?'

'What old joke?' Benjy shouted and, when Lorcan didn't answer, followed his gaze and found him looking at three women and a man outside a nearby restaurant.

'What old joke?' Benjy again bellowed, his rage exacerbated by the sight of the four people clambering into the taxi he'd earmarked as his.

'Why do dogs lick their balls?' Lorcan replied.

Benjy looked in sullen silence.

'Because they can,' Lorcan said, almost wearily. 'Because they can.'

4

Liv, Tara, Fintan and Katherine drank gin and tonic, danced to Wham! and annoyed Roger, Katherine's downstairs neighbour.

'Isn't this great?' Tara demanded, her face aglow. 'Do you remember dancing to this that summer we were fifteen? D'you remember, Fintan, d'you remember, Katherine?'

'Yes,' Fintan said awkwardly. 'But don't go on about it, you're making Liv feel left out.'

'No, no,' Liv said, as jovially as she could. 'It's OK, I always feel left out.'

'Except with people you know very well,' Fintan reminded her gently.

'No, *especially* them.'

Eventually, at the appointed hour, Liv was overwhelmed by a wave of melancholy and decided she'd better go home.

'Will you be OK?' Katherine asked, as she saw Liv to the door.

Liv nodded miserably. 'I will eat twelve bags of crisps, sleep for eighteen hours, then I will feel better.'

'God love her,' Tara sympathized, when she'd gone. 'I know I get the odd bout of depression, but you could set your watch by hers, couldn't you?'

'I think I'll head home as well,' Fintan said.

'What? They'll strip you of your title of Oldest Swinger in Town,' Tara warned.

'But I'm tired,' he said, 'and I've an awful pain in my neck and where my liver used to be.'

The head of steam went out of things after that, to Roger's acute relief. 'I think I've danced myself sober,' Tara said. Wham! were told to shut up, Tara's taxi was summoned and Katherine got ready for bed.

'You big girl's blouse,' Tara said, in jealous admiration, as she looked around Katherine's neat, fragrant bedroom. The duvet cover crisp and spotless, plants emerald-green and flourishing, dust an infrequent caller. The many, many tubes of body lotion on her dressing table were full and new-looking. There were no old, grungy ones with half a millimetre left in the bottom that had been there for five years. And if you cared to look in her sparkling bathroom you would find that for every flavour body lotion on her dressing-table, there would be a matching soap or shower gel knocking around on the shelf in there.

Katherine was a great girl for *sets*. She didn't really enjoy things on their own. But the minute they came with something else she fell in love with them. So scarves had to have matching gloves; talcs had to be flanked by similarly scented soaps; a small ornamental bowl was scant comfort unless it had an even smaller, otherwise identical, ornamental bowl as its comrade. Indeed, Tara often joked that Katherine's ideal man had to have good looks, a great body and an identical twin brother.

Tara continued to survey the bedroom. 'You make me feel so inadequate,' she said, wistfully, 'having your bed made when you didn't even know you'd be having visitors.'

She'd forgotten how much of a homemaker Katherine was because it was a year since they'd finally stopped sharing a flat. Katherine had bought her own place and Thomas had let Tara move in with him. And, while she was at it, pay half his mortgage.

Unable to help herself Tara looked in the drawers. Everything within looked organized, fragrant, pressed, pristine, tended. Katherine was that rare creature: the woman who had regular clean-outs when all her grey, saggy underwear got thrown in the bin.

'Do I have double vision from all the drink?' Tara wanted to know. 'Or do you really have two of every pair of knickers?'

'That's right,' Katherine confirmed. 'Two pairs to every bra.'

Tara just didn't get it. She didn't care about underwear. She only cared about what went on on the outside, what people could see. Of course, Thomas got to see her antediluvian pants and bras, but they'd been going out with each other for two years. Sustaining mystique for longer than three months was too exhausting. Besides, he was no great shakes in the underpants department himself, she reminded herself, and waited for the guilt to abate.

Tara opened another drawer and found a selection of little outfits specially for bed. Although they were sweet, rather than sexy. Not for Katherine a see-through black polyester baby-doll nightdress with matching crotchless panties.

'You're so cool,' Tara said, 'spending so much time and money in Knickerbox.'

'Doesn't everyone?'

'Maybe. But no one else I know *buys things for herself.*'

Tara lay on the bed and enviously watched Katherine's legs – taut and muscled from tap-dancing classes – as they climbed into a cute pair of blue and white polka-dotted jersey shorts. Then came a matching little vest. She'd put the vest on back to front and inside out, so that the washing instructions flicked up and down under her chin, but otherwise you'd never have known how drunk she was.

'It's about time you got a fella so that he'd get the benefit of your lovely underwear,' Tara suggested.

'I'm fine without one.'

'But so many lovely knickers,' Tara said, 'and no man to see them. I think it's sad.'

'I don't think it's sad,' Katherine replied. 'And they're my knickers.'

'But I do.'

'Then you should get help for it.'

'I don't need help,' Tara said, dizzy with gratitude. 'I have a boyfriend.'

'But what if it ended . . . ?' Katherine stirred, with quiet mischief.

'Stop!' Tara declared, in passionate horror. 'What would I be like?' She thought about it for a moment. 'I'd become such a weirdo.'

'Here we go again.' Katherine sighed.

Tara feared that boyfriendless women in their thirties became eccentric, more and more so as they continued further into their single state. Developing odder and odder habits, coiling ever more tightly in on themselves. And if the perfect man eventually came along, Tara reckoned they'd be too trapped in themselves to be able to reach out and accept the hand that was stretched in liberation.

'I'd probably become one of those fruit-loops who collect rubbish,' Tara said. 'Who hoard everything from potato-peelings to decade-old newspapers.'

'You're nearly that way as it is,' Katherine said.

'I'd never open my door to the health visitors,' Tara went

on, locked into her apocalyptic vision. 'And you'd be able to smell my flat a hundred yards away. That's what I'd become without a man.'

'Just as well you have one, then,' Katherine said.

The bell rang, indicating Tara's taxi had arrived.

'Cripes, I'm sorry, Katherine, if I've offended you.' Tara was suddenly mortified. 'You're my best friend and I love you and I wasn't implying that *you'd* become a weirdo . . .'

'No offence taken, now off you go. I've got a date with my remote control. But before that,' Katherine added, 'I've got to wash my hands fifty times and iron all my tights. Us single women! Martyrs to Obsessive Compulsive Disorder.'

5

Tara sat in the taxi, smoked, stared into the middle distance and felt guilty. Not only was she a despicable, needy-for-a-man wimp, but there was a chance – admittedly small – that she had upset Katherine. Katherine was so well balanced and independent that Tara sometimes forgot she had emotions at all.

But when the taxi turned into Alasdair's street, Tara forgot about Katherine. Instead she sat up and paid attention. She couldn't help herself. Searching for a glimpse of him, she stared up at his windows. They were in darkness, and the taxi passed too quickly for her to establish whether it was because Alasdair and *his wife* were in bed or out on the tiles.

I'm nuts to keep doing this, Tara realized. Besides, he mightn't even live here any more. Once people got married they had a tendency to move out of their stylish flats in central London, away from the good bars and restaurants, to a three-bedroomed semi with a garden on the far side of Heathrow.

Her stomach twanged with displeasure. Tara loved Thomas, but she still had a strange proprietorial interest in Alasdair. It pained her to think of him making big life changes without her knowing about them. Alasdair had been the boyfriend before Thomas. And very different from Thomas. Generous, spontaneous, reckless, affectionate, convivial. Fond of meals out and he never once looked at the menu and said, 'Ten quid, ten bludeh quid for a piece of chicken. I could buy that int' supermarket for twelve bob,' the way Thomas did.

Tara had met Alasdair after a chain of unserious boyfriends led her to the age of twenty-six. She was enchanted by his Scottish accent, his close-cropped black hair and his slightly mental eyes sparkling behind wire-rimmed glasses. She even found his name seductive. It hadn't taken long for Tara to decide that he was the man she was going to marry. All the signs were auspicious.

She reckoned she was the right age to get married. As he was two years older than her, so was he. They both had good jobs and came from similar rural backgrounds. But most importantly they wanted exactly the same things in life – lots of fun and meals out. Despite all the restaurants they went to, she was less overweight than might have been expected.

They were the balsamic-vinegar generation – a handsome couple in their twenties, having dinner parties, getting great use out of Alasdair's cappuccino machine, driving around London in his red MG, drinking champagne at least once a week, shopping on Saturdays at Paul Smith or Joseph. (Sometimes they even bought something. Like a pair of socks or a tie-pin.)

When Tara went home to Ireland for a week one summer, Alasdair came with her. Suddenly she saw Knockavoy through his eyes. The magnificence of the crazed Atlantic, taking lumps out of the cliffs, the vast expanse of empty golden sand, the air so soft and clean you could almost see it. Up until then she'd hated her home town. A tiny rural backwater where nothing ever happened, except for a few months in the summer when the tourists came.

Tara's mother had loved Alasdair. Her father hadn't, of

course, but he disliked everything about Tara, why would Alasdair be any different? Next, Alasdair took Tara to meet his family in Skye, which Tara found immensely reassuring. She often feared that the people she met in London weren't giving her the full picture. That to some degree they'd reinvented themselves. Simply because they could – almost no one was actually *from* London so they hadn't any annoying family hanging around to give the lie to whatever fantasy they fed people. And even though it took her a week to recover from the excessive partying Alasdair's family made her do, at least now she knew where and what he came from.

Shortly after their return from Skye, it was their two-year anniversary and Tara thought it was about time things started to move in the direction of marriage. Or, at the very least, living together. She practically lived in Alasdair's flat anyway, and she reckoned making it official was merely a formality.

However, when she put it to him, he surprised her by looking terrified. 'But . . .' he said, his dancing eyes sitting this one out. 'But we're fine as we are, no need to rush things . . .'

Badly shaken and denying how hurt she was, Tara backed off. 'You're right,' she reassured him warmly. 'Things *are* fine as they are, and there's no need to rush things.' Then she settled in for a war of attrition. All things come to those who wait. The only thing was, at twenty-eight, she knew time was a commodity she no longer had a surfeit of.

She calmed her hysteria by telling herself he loved her. She was certain of it. She gripped on to this knowledge as if her life depended on it.

Things continued for another six months or so, ostensibly the same. Except they weren't. Alasdair had a faint hunted air about him that permeated everything, tainting it, dousing fun.

35

And Tara had become watchful and anxious. Conscious that she was no longer in her mid-twenties, conscious that everyone she'd been to school with, with the exception of Katherine, was married and had children, conscious that there were fewer men around than there used to be, conscious that she was hurtling towards thirty. She'd invested a lot of time and hope in Alasdair – *all* her time and hope – and the idea that she'd backed a loser was unbearable to contemplate.

I'm too old to start again, she often thought, gripped with nauseating panic when she woke in the middle of the night. I haven't got *time*. This one has got to work.

Eventually, patience not being her strong point, she couldn't help but ask him again what his long-term intentions towards her were. She knew she shouldn't. That if it was good news, he'd have let her know. And that trying to force his hand would only bring things to a head, to the conclusion she didn't want.

She was right. Brusquely, because he was angry with her for ruining something good with her unreasonable demands, he told her that he didn't want to marry her. He loved her but he just wanted to have fun, and wasn't interested in the tedium of domesticity.

Tara had to take a week off work with shock.

'Cut your losses,' everyone advised her, as she ricocheted around, crazed with disbelief and pain. 'Leave now, don't throw good time after bad.' But she couldn't. Just couldn't say goodbye to two and a half years. Couldn't admit that there was a possibility that she might have to consider a future without him.

She kept trying to salvage it, first by pretending that the issue had never been raised, and that everything was as it had always been. And then, when living with the forced normality became too taxing, she once again tried to change Alasdair's mind, by calling his bluff and threatening to end the relationship entirely. She'd heard of other cases like hers: when the man was faced with the reality of doing without the woman he suddenly saw that making a commitment was a wonderful idea. But nothing doing. Instead Alasdair said sadly, 'Go, if you must. I don't blame you, no one would.'

'But don't you love me?' she demanded breathlessly, her voice high-pitched with horror, as she realized how badly she'd misjudged things. 'Won't you miss me?'

'Yes, I love you,' he replied, gently. 'And of course I'll miss you. But I've no right to hold you if you want to go.'

Mortified, Tara quickly shut up with her dramatic, It's-all-over talk. That ploy had backfired good and proper. A swift U-turn had her re-embracing the status quo, hoping no one had noticed. However, the relationship that had been wonderful a year before no longer seemed charmed and charming. It was a making-do, a half relationship, she thought bitterly. But it was better than nothing.

Except it wasn't. At least, not for Alasdair. 'It's no good any more,' he told Tara, about a month later. She stared at him in terror, the much-derided, half-assed relationship suddenly flaring up into a highly desirable one, now that it was under threat.

'But nothing's changed,' she stammered, confused because she was supposed to have the moral high ground. She was allowed to hold the threat of ending the whole thing over him, because he'd hurt her. Not the other way round. 'I'm sorry I brought up the getting-married thing again, and I'm sorry I've been such a pain about it, but forget it, let's just carry on as we were.'

But he shook his head and said, 'We can't go back.'

'We can,' she insisted, hysteria in her voice, wondering why bad things insisted on happening when you were already beaten and broken.

'We can't,' he repeated.

'What do you mean?' she asked, knowing, but defiantly refusing to let herself find out.

'It's time to call it a day,' he said quietly. And for a second Tara pretended he hadn't said anything, refusing to move from life as it was to life as it is.

'No,' she said frantically. 'There's no need, things are fine as they are.'

'They're not fine,' he said. 'You deserve someone else, someone who'll give you what you want. Go on, there's no good in staying with me, you're wasting time.'

'I don't want anyone else,' she promised desperately. 'I'd rather have you the way things are than be married to someone else.'

But no matter how much she tried to tell him she was happy as things stood, he wouldn't have it, becoming more and more intractable as the conversation went on. Until she realized that there was no hope of convincing him, that, in fact, there never had been. His mind had been made up before she uttered a word.

Tara nearly lost her reason. For weeks she was demented and hysterical. Her grief was so agonizing that she lay in bed and howled like an animal. So loudly that the upstairs neighbours called the police one night.

She moved the CD player into her room and, roaring, crying, played Roy Orbison's 'It's Over,' incessantly. Every time the last bars of it faded she sobbed even harder and pressed the replay button. Liv and Katherine counted it twenty-nine times in a row one night. Sometimes she half howled, half sang along with it, getting particular relief from the part where it moved up an octave. 'It's *ooooh-ohhhh-verrr.*' Up an octave. 'IT'S OOOOH-OHHHH-VERRR!' The upstairs neighbours talked about calling the police again.

She had to take another week off work and when she went back her colleagues wished she'd stayed away. Every program she was supposed to have tested was flawed, sending systems crashing all over London. Her department's workload doubled for a couple of months, their manpower stretched to capacity cleaning up Tara's messes. She only managed about three hours' sleep a night and wandered the flat smoking cigarette after cigarette. She lost the ability to function normally. Forgetting to rinse conditioner out of her hair. Going to work on a Saturday and wondering why the building was all locked up. Driving to work, taking the tube home, then thinking her car had been stolen when she couldn't find it outside her flat the following morning. Taking the lid off a carton of yoghurt, throwing the carton in the bin and staring at the lid, trying to figure out what she'd done wrong. In calmer moments, she talked, her knuckles clenched translucent, of evening classes. Pottery, Russian, cake-icing.

Every week or so, when the pain got too much, she rang him and begged him to meet her. He always did and, naturally, they slept together. Frantic, tearful sex, scratching the clothes off each other, bruising each other with the relief of their familiarity.

This happened so often she began to think that maybe there was a chance they'd get back together. It was obvious that he was as torn apart by the break-up as she was, that he still loved her.

Until one night he wouldn't let her come over.

'Why not?' she asked. He'd always been keen before.

She heard him take a breath, and in the pico-second's pause between the end of that breath and the start of him speaking, she got a very bad feeling. Before he even said it, she knew.

'I've met someone else.'

Tara calmly hung up the phone, got into her car, drove around to Alasdair's, let herself in with the key she hadn't yet returned, found him in the kitchen boiling the kettle and, with her forearm, hit him such a blow in the skull that his glasses fell off.

Before he had a chance to recover, she slapped his head and face repeatedly with the palms of her hands. 'Bastard,' she gasped. 'You bastarding bastard.' But slapping him wasn't expending the hatred or stopping her pain quickly enough so she punched him in the stomach, surprised by how weak her arm felt.

Although it seemed to do the trick all right, she thought dispassionately, as she watched Alasdair choking and retching.

'Ali?' someone asked, and Tara turned to the kitchen door to see a plump blonde girl standing there.

'What's going on?' the girl gasped in horror, as she took in the scene.

Tara came out of her trance. Pausing only to give Alasdair a violent shove that sent him toppling into her usurper, she left.

When she got home and told Katherine and Liv what had happened, they couldn't hide their shock. Too late, they tried to make her feel better about it. 'The bastard,' they consoled. 'Good on you. I hope you broke a couple of ribs.'

'Stop,' begged Tara. The red mist had evaporated, leaving

her sickened and frantic with self-loathing. 'I beat him up,' she moaned, rocking backwards and forwards, her face in her hands. 'Now I'll never get him back.

'I thought I couldn't possibly feel worse than I have been for the past seven weeks, four days and . . .' she paused to look at her watch '. . . sixteen and a half hours, but I was wrong.

'I have to lie on my bed and howl like a dog,' she said brokenly, and made for her bedroom. Katherine and Liv braced themselves for Roy Orbison. But to their surprise and relief instead they heard 'Somebody Else's Guy'. And then they heard it again. And again. And again. And again. And again. And again.

Later that night Tara re-emerged. 'I'm going to call him,' she announced.

'Don't!' Katherine commanded, diving on the phone and confiscating it. 'You'll only make things worse.'

'Worse,' Tara said miserably. 'How could they be worse? Jehovah, Jehovah, Jehovah!'

'A film called *The Life of Brian*,' Katherine explained hurriedly to Liv's perplexed face. 'No, Tara, no calling him.'

'Let me just apologize,' Tara begged. 'If you don't let me, I'll wait until you've gone to bed, and it'll be far worse if I phone him in the middle of the night.'

Eventually Katherine agreed. 'But if you start shouting at him or making threats, then I cut you off.'

'Thanks,' Tara said miserably, and dialled Alasdair's number.

'Hello,' she said hurriedly, when he answered. 'It's me, I'm sorry, please don't hang up, you wouldn't believe how sorry I am, or how ashamed I am.'

Instead of slamming the phone down, he said, 'It's fine, I understand.' Actually, Alasdair was quite relieved. He'd been

41

feeling guilty about his involvement with Caroline, but every slap that Tara had given him had changed the balance of sympathy in his favour. Now, instead of it being 'Poor cuckolded Tara', it would be 'Poor beaten-up Alasdair'.

'You know, you pack one hell of a punch,' he added, with an attempt at a laugh.

'Sorry,' she whispered. 'Please forgive me.'

'I forgive you,' he said.

But all the same, when he rang her six weeks later to tell her he was getting married, he took the precaution of getting the locks changed first.

That was the night when Tara met Thomas.

They were at a party given by Fintan's assistant, Dolly. Tara, dancing like a woman possessed, absentmindedly took Thomas's cigarette from his mouth and stuck it in her own. Not in a deliberate attempt to be provocative – she didn't even *see* Thomas. She was simply dying for a smoke and couldn't find her own. Since she'd heard of Alasdair's impending nuptials she'd been losing *everything*.

Despite the theft of his cigarette, Thomas was instantly besotted with Tara. He mistook her lunacy for vivacity and decided that her forwardness was an indication that she'd be uninhibited in bed. And he was most impressed with the slim figure she'd achieved by throwing all those cartons of yoghurt in the bin. For a few moments, he dithered, trying to decide what his chat-up line should be. But Thomas was a plain-spoken man, so he went for the obvious.

'Can I have me fag back?' Tara heard, and ceased her frantic dancing. She turned and saw a man standing four-square and smiling at her. Not bad-looking. Not *good*-looking, either, mind. Not compared to Alasdair.

But once she took a closer look she saw that he had shiny brown hair and a reassuring stockiness that made her yearn to lean against him.

He continued to smile, washing her with his warmth and admiration. 'You're a cracking bird,' he told Tara, with an endearing combination of shyness and sureness. 'Keep the fag.'

Under normal circumstances Tara would cross the road to avoid a man who called women 'birds' but she'd been through a lot. Thomas's brown eyes held hers, and Tara was astonished to see devotion and respect in them. After what Alasdair had done, she'd thought she was as worthless as the Russian rouble. In amazement it hit her that maybe this man could redefine her, revalue her.

Though he wore a bit more brown than she considered ideal (any brown *at all* was more than she considered ideal), she felt strangely drawn to him. When she realized he was hers for the taking, the joy was like a heroin rush.

'Come and dance with me,' she invited cheekily, and took his hand. Even though Thomas's dun-coloured clothing seemed to stay in the one place while the rest of him attempted to dance, Tara's world instantly became a sparkling, magical place. An alternative future had opened up for her. Alasdair was going to marry someone else, but there were other men who liked her. Who cared more about her than she cared about them. Who might eventually marry her. Her pain had stopped and she'd thought it never would. Thomas was her saviour. 'There's a Chinese proverb,' she murmured, 'that says, if someone saves your life, they own you.'

Thomas nodded blankly, then nudged his mate Eddie and said, 'She's more pissed than I thought. I'm on a winner tonight.'

They spent from Friday night to Monday morning in Tara's

flat, mostly in bed, but occasionally they got up to watch telly, Tara draped all over Thomas, snogging passionately, as Katherine and Liv tried to watch *Ballykissangel* and tune out the slurping noises.

'They keep making the sound of a horse's hoof being levered out of thick mud,' Katherine said, when she rang Fintan to complain.

Liv grabbed the phone from her. 'There's a thing in the bathroom, that has suckers, and it sticks to the washbasin. It's to keep soap on,' she told Fintan. 'When you pull the suckers off the basin, *that's* the noise Tara and this man are doing. Can we come over to your flat?'

But Tara was thrilled with Thomas. 'I'm mad about him,' she announced to everyone.

'Mad is right,' Katherine muttered, scathingly eyeing Thomas in all his brown glory.

'She is on the refund,' Liv said, sagely.

'Rebound,' Katherine corrected. 'And you're right.'

6

The feelings that bubbled up after passing Alasdair's house had Tara dying to see Thomas. She almost ran from the taxi to the front door, but between her enthusiasm and all the alcohol still washing around in her system, she found it difficult to get the key in the lock. It took four attempts before she finally managed to stumble into the hall. Righting herself, she called, 'Thomas?'

He was in the living room, four empty Newcastle Brown cans and a Fray Bentos steak and kidney pie tin on the floor beside the sofa. 'About bludeh time,' he grumbled good-naturedly.

'Have you missed me?' Tara asked, hopefully. She was so glad to see him.

'Maybe I have.' He gave a tantalizing, crinkle-eyed smile. 'And maybe I haven't. But I've had Beryl for company.'

Beryl was Thomas's cat, upon whom he lavished attention, affection and admiration. Tara was wildly jealous of her and of the slinky, careless, ungrateful way Beryl received Thomas's love, draping herself along him, then, on a whim, abandoning him as though it cost her nothing.

'Good night?' Thomas asked.

'Yes.' She didn't say it was a pity he hadn't come. Her friends and her boyfriend just didn't get on, it was a common enough situation, only exacerbated when people tried to force it. 'I didn't have a starter and wait till I show you my presents! Look at my lipstick, isn't it magnificent?'

' 'S all right.' He shrugged.

She noticed something on the coffee table. 'Oh, Thomas, you've filled in my car insurance forms. Thanks. You know how much I hate doing it.'

'Don't say I never do owt for you.' He grinned. 'And while we're on the subject I booked the flicks for tomorrow night.'

'What film?'

'*Lock, Stock and Two Smoking Barrels.* About gangsters. Looks good.'

'Oh.' Her face fell. 'I said I wanted to go to *The Horse Whisperer.*'

'I'm not going to that bludeh girly weepy.'

'But . . .'

Thomas looked hurt and before he did one of his quick about-turns of mood, Tara said quickly, 'Well, never mind. I'm sure the other thing will be good.'

Thomas was terribly sensitive. It all went back to one Sunday morning when he was seven and he'd found his mother in the hall with a suitcase. When, in surprise, he'd asked where she was going, she'd laughed and said, 'Don't talk daft. You know.' He'd protested that he didn't, so she'd said bitterly, 'We're splitting up, me and your dad.' It was the first Thomas had known about it and he told Tara that even now, twenty-five years later, it still pained him that his mother had been about to leave without saying goodbye to him.

'Don't come if you don't want.' Thomas looked wounded. 'But seeing as I took trouble to book . . . ?'

'I want to come,' she assured him. 'Honestly, I do. Thanks for doing it. Who wants to see Robert Redford with his old face hanging off him, anyway?' She noticed the bag of peanuts that Thomas was practically lying on. 'Yummy.'

'Oi!' He slapped her hand away.

'Aw, it's my birthday.'

'I – am – your – conscience,' he boomed. 'You'll thank me for this.'

'I suppose I will,' she said sadly.

'Cheer up, Tara.' He chided. 'It's for your own good.'

'You're right.' She rummaged in her bag. 'Oh, no, I'm out of fags. How did that happen? Have you any?'

There was an infinitesimal hesitation before he tossed her his packet of cigarettes. As he leant over with his lighter, he said, 'We have to give up, Tara.'

'We really must.'

'They cost a bludeh fortune.'

'They do.'

'Three quid a day, Tara. Each.'

'I know.'

'That's twenty-one quid a week. Each.'

'I know.'

'That's eighty quid a month. Each.'

'I know.'

That's a thousand quid a year. Each. Think what we could buy with that, Tara, Tara said in her head.

'That's a thousand quid a year. Each.' Thomas said. 'Think what we could buy with that, Tara.' *And it's OK for you. You're a computer analyst. You earn twice as much as me.*

'And it's OK for me,' she said, cheekily. 'I'm a computer analyst. I earn twice as much as you.'

There was a moment's edgy pause, then Thomas grinned ruefully.

In a sombre documentary voiceover, Tara intoned, 'He was the meanest man I had ever met.'

'Like I've any bludeh choice!' Thomas declared hotly.

All his friends from college had landed fabulously well-paid jobs, where their quarterly bonuses were often more than Thomas's annual salary. But as Thomas was too blunt to charm prospective employers in industry, he'd ended up becoming a geography teacher in a west London comprehensive. He worked very hard, got paid a pittance and his bitterness was legendary. But not as legendary as his stinginess. 'I should get paid as much as a government minister because teaching kids is one of the most valuable jobs anyone can do,' he often said. ('Sorry, I've forgotten my wallet, you'll have to pay,' was another regular.) People spoke of him as having short arms and deep pockets, of him having a padlock on his wallet, of him being first out of the taxi and last to the bar, of him pinching a penny till it begged for mercy.

But he didn't do himself any favours. Instead of at least pretending to be generous, he compounded his reputation as a tight-fisted leech by not letting his change rattle around in his trouser pockets like normal people did. Instead he kept it in a purse. A little brown plastic old-ladies' purse that snapped closed at the top. Katherine had once wrestled it out of his hand and managed to open it before Thomas tore it back from her. She'd *insisted* that a moth had flown out.

'I hate us being skint, Tara,' Thomas whined. 'You won't stop spending and I've nowt to spend. The fags'll have to go.'

'The start of the month is always the best time to quit smoking,' Tara humoured him.

'Happen you're right.'

'And we've missed the start of October. So we'll both give up on the first of November.'

'You're on!'

Then they both promptly forgot about it.

'Time for bed.' Thomas heaved himself out of the couch, where he was slumped surrounded by aluminium. 'Come on, birthday girl, I've a present for you.'

Tara's face lit up. Until Thomas glanced down at his crotch. Oh, *that* kind of present.

Wistfully she remembered her birthday two years ago. She'd been going out with Thomas less than a month and because it was her twenty-ninth birthday he'd given her twenty-nine presents. Granted some of them had been tiny – one had just been a box of multicoloured matches. And more of them had been crap – like the jar of pink sparkly nail varnish and the earrings that infected her ears. But the time and thought and effort he'd put into buying each thing and wrapping them individually had touched her to the heart.

She sighed. The first flush couldn't last for ever. Everyone knew that. In the darkness she wrapped her arms around him and pressed herself against his snuggly warmth, a blissful hum in her veins. She was safe and loved, in bed with her man.

7

Even though the following day was a Saturday, Katherine had to go to work. Before she left she rang her grandmother because it was her ninety-first birthday. She was reluctant to make the call. It was no reflection on the birthday girl – Katherine loved her granny. But as she dialled the number and waited for it to ring in Knockavoy, she prayed, as she always did, that her mother, Delia, wouldn't answer the phone.

'Hello,' Delia's breathless voice said.

Katherine felt the familiar surge of irritation. 'Hello, Mam,' she managed.

'Katherine,' Delia gasped. 'As I live and breathe! I was talking about you not five minutes ago. Wasn't I, Agnes?'

'No,' Katherine faintly heard her granny say. 'Indeed'n you were not. Unless 'twas to yourself you were talking, and if you were, it wouldn't be the first time.'

'I *was* talking about you,' Delia stalwartly insisted to Katherine. 'I knew the phone was going to ring and I knew it'd be you. I always know these things. I have the gift, the sight.'

'You wish,' Katherine scorned. 'You know I always ring on Granny's birthday.'

'Don't call her Granny, her name is Agnes. And haven't I been telling you since the day you were born not to call me Mam. I'm Delia.'

Katherine's family was an unusual one. At least, in Knockavoy it was. It centred around Delia, Katherine's mother, who'd been a wild and beautiful young woman in her time. She'd been very forward-thinking, and spent her teenage years in the sixties berating anyone who'd listen (precious few in Knockavoy) about the stranglehold the Catholic church had on Ireland. She had no fear.

One day when she was seventeen she arrived in the kitchen, her hands dirty, her black hair more tousled than usual, an air of barely contained glee bringing a sparkle to her silvery eyes.

'What were you doing?' Agnes, her mother, feared the worst.

'Pegging lumps of turf at the curate when he went past on his bicycle.' Delia snorted with laughter.

Agnes rushed to the window and in the dip of the road she could see young Father Crimmond cycling away furiously, a clod of turf still attached to his big black coat.

'Conduct yourself! You'll get us all into terrible trouble,' Agnes objected, alarmed yet shamefully exhilarated.

'Trouble is what this place needs,' Delia said darkly. 'Trouble would do them no end of good.'

When news of the turf-throwing antics got out, the townsfolk were in uproar and two stout matrons purported to faint clean away. They'd never heard the like. Father Crimmond made oblique reference to the assault in his sermon and urged prayers for the poor deranged creature who'd attacked him. 'More to be pitied than scorned,' he concluded, which disappointed the congregation because they'd been looking forward to a good bit of scorning.

Delia became the most talked-about person for several parishes. People shook their heads when they saw her coming, saying, 'That young girl of the Caseys has a bit of a lack,' and, 'That Casey child isn't all there.'

Austin, Delia's father, a dangerously mild man, suspected she was a changeling. Others with a bit more nous simply suspected that Agnes had strayed.

Delia continued to rebel. But no one else would join in, they were all too frightened. And as it isn't much fun by oneself, Delia left Knockavoy in 1966 and went to London, where she found many other ways of railing against the establishment than throwing combustible fuel at mobile clergymen.

She channelled the bulk of her rebelling through the medium of sex and drugs, enjoying copious quantities of both. In case anyone doubted the sincerity of such rebelliousness, Delia put their minds at rest by getting pregnant. Better still, the man responsible was married and had no intention of leaving his wife.

But suddenly, to her great surprise, Delia became very frightened. She felt young, alone and scared. Rued the day she'd left Ireland. Sorry she'd ever heard of London. Cursed her contrary nature. Why couldn't she have behaved herself like the girls she'd been at school with? A fifth of them had gone into the holy orders. Why hadn't she been afraid of hellfire and damnation like everyone else?

Her poor father. He'd feel obliged to take his belt to her; it was the done thing. He'd hate having to do it because he was such a gentle soul, but rules were rules.

As it happened Austin was spared because a week after Delia realized she was pregnant he had a heart attack and died. (He'd been out getting turf for the fire. As Agnes said, turf brought nothing but sorrow to the Caseys.)

On the train home for the funeral, Delia practised her justification. 'A new life in place of the old. Dada is gone, but a new person will be born in his stead.' She was nervous. Being impregnated and ditched had knocked the stuffing out of her.

The free-spirited principles that had seemed so worthy and true in London became less and less convincing the closer she got to Knockavoy.

But she had to wait until the mourners and freeloaders had eaten all the ham sandwiches, drained the barrel of porter and finally left, before breaking the news. 'Mama, I'm going to have a baby.'

'I suppose you are, *alanna*,' Agnes said. She had expected nothing less. She knew the high jinks they got up to in godless places like London and she was stoically prepared to accept the consequences. Her only regret was that she wasn't able to spend some time in London herself. She hadn't had any excitement in a long time. Not really since the civil war, once she thought about it.

The child was born in late August 1967. As it was the Summer of Love, Delia was keen to saddle her with a name like Raindrop or Moonbeam but Agnes intervened. 'She's the town bastard,' she pointed out equably. 'Would you not give her a decent name so that she won't be the town laughing stock into the bargain?'

Everyone expected Delia to return to London, but she didn't. She stayed in Knockavoy and no one could understand why, least of all herself. She knew it had something to do with the terror she'd felt when she found out she was pregnant. Fear wasn't something she was familiar with and she wasn't keen to renew the acquaintanceship. She lived with her mother, in the house she'd been brought up in, and reared her child. She got piecemeal jobs. Barmaiding during the summer months, driving the school bus – the regular driver was a martyr to the drink – and helping her mother with the hens, cows and crops on their smallholding.

Beautiful, but with still too much of the basket case about her, no local man was interested in taking her and her daughter on. She remained outspoken and difficult, more of an outsider than ever. She practised radical politics from afar. She organized a mass rally against US intervention in Vietnam, to be held one Saturday at four o'clock outside Tully's Hardware – she targeted Tully's because Curly Tully had lived in Boston for eighteen months in the fifties. But the only people who turned up were herself and the two-year-old Katherine. (Agnes said she'd love to lend her support, but she was busy milking the cows.) At about five to five, just as Delia was getting ready to call it a day, she saw a crowd of six or seven people heading up the street towards her. Instead of throwing a snide remark and passing her by, as everyone else had done all afternoon, they stopped. Delia was ecstatic. Until it transpired the whole seven of them were there to help Padraig Cronin buy a ladder.

Next, Delia started a petition against apartheid, and nabbed people outside half-twelve Mass to make them sign. She managed seven signatures – her own, her mother's, her daughter's, Loony Tommy Forman's, a Mr D. Duck, a Mr M. Mouse and a Mr J. F. Kennedy.

In the late seventies she became fixated with the Sandanistas, and held a sale of work to raise money for them. Which four people came to, generating takings of two pounds elevenpence.

She dreamt of having a drop-in centre. Sometimes she made noises about setting up a rape crisis centre in Knockavoy, even though no one had been raped for several decades.

She tried to teach yoga, except no one came. She tried to set up a craft-shop, but the crafts were crap.

She dressed in smocks, clogs and wooden jewellery and claimed to have psychic powers. She urged Katherine to call her Delia, told her she didn't have to go to school if she didn't want and that she *certainly* didn't have to go to Mass if she didn't want. Katherine ended up knowing the ins and outs of the reproductive system before she'd mastered the ins and outs of tying her shoelaces.

Naturally Katherine rebelled. Which she did by being neat, tidy, quiet, respectful, diligent and devout. She was meek, questioned nothing, did exactly what the nuns told her, knew her catechism backwards (the best way), and told everyone that her first holy communion was the happiest day of her life.

Delia was devastated. 'Wait'll that child hits adolescence,' she wept, hopefully. 'Genes will out, she's her mother's daughter.'

But she was also her father's daughter.

True to her libertarian principles, Delia never fed Katherine a pack of lies of how her daddy had been killed tragically in a war or car crash or bizarre ploughing accident (tick as preferred). From an early age, Katherine knew that her father was a snivelling, bourgeois coward called Geoff Melody, who had got Delia into bed by a mixture of drugs and empty promises that he'd leave his wife.

Although there was no contact – or love lost – between Delia and Geoff Melody, Delia repeatedly impressed upon Katherine that if she ever wanted to contact her father she'd do her best to facilitate it. But she wasn't taken up on it until Katherine was nineteen. Of course Katherine's fatherless state was cause for scorn in the school playground. At least, on the rare occasions when Tara wasn't hovering protectively by her side. But Katherine responded with admirable aplomb whenever her classmates – one anxious eye out for Tara's return – started up their chant of, 'You've no dada, you've no dada.'

'How can you miss something you've never had?' she'd ask calmly. Then she'd give an enigmatic smile, while the others faltered in confusion, their chant dying away. Why wasn't she crying like she was supposed to? Why did *they* feel like the stupid ones? And where did Tara Butler learn to do such a good Chinese burn?

When, finally – her heart having recently been broken for the first time – Katherine said she wanted to contact her father, Delia willingly supplied his last-known-at address. 'Though it's twenty years old, he'll probably still be living there,' she said. Adding spitefully, she couldn't help it, 'He was that type.'

Agnes came to the phone and spoke to Katherine. Said she was having a grand birthday and thanked her for the two matching silk scarves she'd sent. 'I'm getting great use out of them,' she said. Which was the truth. They'd come in extremely handy the evening before when the hinge fell off the hen-house door, and something was needed to re-tether it to the post. How's London?' Agnes asked wistfully. 'Still godless?'

'Absolutely, Granny,' Katherine said enthusiastically. 'Worse than ever. Why don't you visit me, and you can see for yourself?'

'Ah, no,' said Agnes. 'It mightn't be as bad as you say and I'd be disappointed. No, I'm better off here with my imagination.'

8

Katherine swung out of the red-brick, converted house in which she had her first-floor flat and a passing motorist nearly mounted the pavement while he gazed intently at her. In her grey suit, she looked fresh and crisp, and not a single hair on her head was out of place – it wouldn't have dared. At the gate she paused and feasted her eyes on her pride and joy, her powder-blue Karmann Ghia. Katherine loved her car very much and would have kissed it if she hadn't been afraid that one of her early-rising neighbours might see her.

People were often surprised that Katherine owned such a stylish car. But what they didn't realize was that Katherine was the type of person who aimed high. When she chose to aim at all.

People were also surprised that Katherine owned such an *unreliable* car. The Karmann Ghia was the one reckless thing in her almost entirely careful life. Though her heart and her bank balance were nearly broken by it, Katherine remained devoted. So frequently was she round at the VW garage, that she joked with Lionel, the mechanic, that she'd call her first-born after him. He was charmed and she felt he didn't need to know that she had no intention of ever having children.

Katherine didn't normally drive to work, but as it was Saturday, and the streets were clear, she did. To her amazement, she was able to park right outside Breen Helmsford, the advertising agency where she was the accountant.

'Praise the Lord,' she muttered. 'It's a miracle.'

As with the car, people were often surprised to discover that Katherine worked in advertising. They didn't think she was dynamic and gung-ho enough. She was too serious and reserved. Luckily, as an accountant it wasn't part of her job description to be wildly enthusiastic all the time, or to bandy around phrases like, 'Let's run this one up the flagpole and see if the cat licks it!' On the contrary, her job was to douse the worst excesses, to be awkward about people's expenses, to insist on taxi receipts, to question why a bill for a weekend in a double room at a country hotel with nine bottles of champagne was being claimed or to point out that putting through a restaurant bill and the credit-card slip for the same meal constituted claiming twice and might be just the smallest bit fraudulent. Even though, as accountant, she was supposed to be above such mundane tasks, she didn't trust her assistants to weed out swizz-masters.

'Morning, Katherine,' Desmond, the porter, called, as she made for the lifts. 'Bunch of tossers getting you to come in on the weekend, eh?'

But instead of receiving the bitter tirade of agreement that he'd got from the other employees who were already in, Katherine just smiled noncommittally and said, 'I suppose someone's got to do it.'

Desmond was baffled. 'An odd fish,' was how he described her. 'And no young man waiting for her, that's plain to see. Else why'd she be happy to come to work on a Saturday? It's no life,' he'd say, with a heavy sigh, 'for a young girl.'

Breen Helmsford was small by most advertising agency standards, with only about seventy employees, crammed into two huge, open-plan floors, with occasional glass boxes as offices for the higher-ups.

When Katherine walked in, lots of people were already there. As well as Katherine's assistants, Breda, Charmaine and Henry, there was a clutch of 'creatives', who considered themselves to be the *real* staff, not like that crowd of awkward bureaucrats who withheld expenses for no good reason. The creatives – a bunch of elaborately trendy New Lads who looked like they'd bought up the entire stock of Duffer of St George – were putting the final touches to a presentation they were giving on Monday to a tampon company. Lots of images of beaming girls landing on the moon and on a yellow landscape that was supposed to be the planet Venus, overlaid with George Michael's 'Freedom'. The hook lines they were proposing to use were 'I bet she drinks Carling Black Label,' and 'Possibly the best feminine hygiene product in the known universe.'

Two hard and fast rules existed for tampon ads: the product is only ever referred to euphemistically; and the colour red must *never* appear.

Everyone automatically looked up at Katherine. Then looked away again when they saw who it was. Katherine wasn't terribly popular with her colleagues. She wasn't *un*popular either. But because she didn't go on the piss several nights a week or sleep with all her male co-workers, she didn't really exist.

Sex was very high on the list of activities at Breen Helmsford. As the staff regularly found themselves in the position of having slept with all their colleagues of the opposite sex, the arrival of a new temp caused more excitement than the landing of a new account. Luckily, the creatives were sacked and replaced at dizzying speed, so there was always new blood being brought into the company, fresh bodies to sleep with.

Katherine was called the Ice Queen. She knew about this,

and her only objection was that she thought an advertising agency might have had a bit more imagination.

The tampon-account director, Joe Roth, was in the thick of the five lads, who were passionately saying things like 'Everyone *knows* you can do a bungee jump while you're wearing a tampon,' and 'Yeah, bungee jumps are yesterday's news,' and 'Space-landings are so now!' He watched Katherine as she walked over to her desk and switched on her PC. 'Nice piece of work, boys,' he praised his team. 'Personally speaking, I'd buy these tampons. Hell, I nearly wish I got periods.

'Now, if you'll excuse me,' he said, his sights on Katherine, 'it's time for my daily knock-back.'

Joe Roth was intrigued by Katherine. He'd only been at Breen Helmsford three weeks – in other jobs this would mean he had barely started, but advertising years were like dog years. Three weeks was usually long enough to win a major account, be promoted twice, written up in *Campaign*, caught in bed with the MD's wife, lose a major account and get fired. Certainly Joe thought that three weeks was long enough to have made some progress with Katherine, but he wasn't sure if he was getting anywhere.

On Joe's first day, Fred Franklin, the overweight, fortyish, heavy-drinking Lancastrian who was to be his boss, had taken him aside. First he'd established what football team Joe supported – Arsenal – then gave him some words of avuncular wisdom on his new post. Where the coffee machine was, how to fiddle his expenses and, most importantly, the best women to pursue. 'Martini, there,' Fred told Joe, indicating a tall, toothy redhead. 'Goes like the clappers.'

'I thought her name was Samantha,' Joe said.

'Aye, technically speaking it is,' Fred admitted, 'but we call her Martini, because anytime, anyplace, anywhere, she's up for it.

'She's great,' Fred said, with a fond smile. 'She'll do anything. *Anything*. And she never wants those daft things women always want.'

'You mean flowers and chocolates?' Joe asked.

'I mean phone calls, remembering her name, that kind of thing. She's just in it for the sex. She'll even let you watch the footie while you're at it.'

'She's great,' Fred said again, then delivered the highest praise he could give any woman. 'She's like a bloke with tits.'

'Now Flora there,' Fred indicated a little woman with blonde bubble curls. 'Does a great stunt with a bottle of baby oil and a cold flannel, but she's a bit of a handful, rang my wife and told her –'

'I thought her name was Connie,' Joe interrupted.

'Oh, it is,' Fred agreed. 'It is, but we call her Flora because she –'

'– spreads easily,' Joe finished drily.

Fred gave Joe a face-splitting beam. 'Got it in one! I think you're going to like it here, son.'

Joe wasn't so sure. 'What about that . . . er . . . Katherine, the accountant?' he asked casually.

'Who?'

'You know, the skinny cute one who wears the suits.'

'Cute?' Fred was perplexed. 'Skinny? Do you mean Lolo?' He pointed at a dark-haired girl, who was so emaciated her legs were nearly as narrow as her arms. 'Don't fancy yours much. But get her to do the thing with the toothpaste when she's sucking your knob. She won't swallow, though, I'm giving you fair warning now. She's too afraid of getting fat.'

'I thought her name was Deirdre,' Joe said.

'It is,' Fred confirmed. 'We call her Lolo because she's always depressed. Moany cow. But at least when she's got your knob in her gob she can't go on much.'

'I see,' said Joe. 'But I don't mean her, anyway. I mean the little Irish girl.'

Fred was so shocked he could barely speak. 'Her!' he finally managed. 'That dried-up old bag.'

'She's gorgeous,' Joe said, in surprise.

'Gorgeous is as gorgeous does,' Fred retorted. 'And she doesn't *do* anything! I wouldn't waste your time with her, son. Not when you've all these great goers to pick from. I reckon that Katherine lass is a lesbo.'

'So she wouldn't go out with you?' Joe asked, sympathetically.

'Not just me,' Fred roared. 'She won't go out with anyone. She's just a pigging waste of space. And take a look at her clothes. She's like a frigging nun!'

Katherine always came to work decked out in slim, professional suits and crisp white blouses. Some of the other women at Breen Helmsford also wore suits, but with heavy irony. Theirs were sexy, fashionable ones, in bright colours, with short skirts. By contrast, Katherine played it very safe, with her skirt invariably ending just above her knee.

But Joe had noticed giveaway signs of the woman underneath. A slight bunching under her tailored skirt that indicated she was wearing stockings and suspender belt, rather than boring tights. The absence of the little seam up her belly that confirmed his suspicions. Or sometimes, as he sat in front of her, being bollocked for not keeping restaurant receipts, he caught a glimpse of something lacy under her neat white blouse, and resolved to lose even more receipts. So for the eleventh working day in a row he strode over and perched on the edge of her desk.

He was very tall – about six one – and lean with it. But the consensus was that it suited him. Clothes kind of hung on his lanky frame, looking languid and stylish. Today he wore black combats and a long-sleeved T-shirt. To see him properly Katherine had to lean back so much that her face was almost parallel with the ceiling.

'Morning, Katie,' he said, a huge smile on his thin face. 'What's got you in on a Saturday?'

Katherine was stunned at the 'Katie' bit of 'Morning, Katie.' At work she cultivated a definite, deliberate distance. No one called her Kathy or Kate or Katie or Kath or Kit or Kitty. She was always Katherine. In fact, she'd have liked it to be Ms Casey, but she knew she was pushing her luck. Breen Helmsford was too contrivedly informal to stand for surnames. Even the managing director Mr Denning insisted on being called Johnny. (Although his name was actually Norman.)

Only the cleaner was addressed by her surname. A hard-faced chain-smoker, afflicted with a hacking cough, who complained bitterly about the mess. Everyone was terrified of her, and wouldn't dare get over-familiar. She had probably been *born* Mrs Twyford.

Katherine gave Joe her Scary Look, grade four. This was a terrifying glare that flooded men with unexpected, shocking fear. It was only a couple of grades below the Medusa Look, and she'd sometimes nearly frightened herself as she honed and perfected it in front of her bedroom mirror. But before she could tell him in icy tones that no one was allowed to abbreviate her name, Joe asked, a twinkle in his friendly brown eyes, 'Ooh, toothache? Nasty! Or have you got something in your eye?'

'Um, neither,' Katherine muttered, liberating her face muscles from their narrow-eyed, teeth-baring rictus.

'And why are you here today?' Joe asked.

'I don't normally work weekends,' she said politely, looking up at him, 'but it's the end of the accounting year so I'm very busy.'

'I love that accent of yours,' Joe said, with a sunbeam smile. 'I could listen to it all day.'

'I'm afraid you'll never get that opportunity.' Katherine gave a chilly smirk.

Joe looked mildly shocked, then soldiered on. 'Is there any point asking you to have lunch with me, then?'

'None,' she said, shortly. 'Why don't you leave me alone?'

'Why don't I leave you alone?' Joe mused. 'I'll tell you. As a very wise man once said, let me see, what was the exact phrase . . . ?' Joe stared thoughtfully into the middle distance. 'Oh, yes!' he said. ' "I've got you under my skin." '

'Is that right? Well, in the words of one of my heroes, the great humanist Rhett Butler . . .' Katherine retorted crisply ' . . . "Frankly, my dear, I don't give a damn." '

'Ach, she's cruel, so cruel,' Joe gasped, staggering around in front of her desk, as though he'd been stabbed.

She looked at him with steady contempt. 'If you'll excuse me, I've got work to do,' she said, turning to her screen.

'How about a drink after work, then?' he suggested, brightly.

'Which part of the word "no" is it that you don't understand? The N or the O?'

'You're breaking my heart.'

'Good.'

64

He stared, in admiration. 'You're the most intriguing woman I've ever met.'

'You'd want to get out more.'

Joe, an intelligent man, knew when he was wasting his time. 'No further questions,' he said crisply, like a young, keen, cross-examining attorney. He'd hoped Katherine would laugh. She didn't. Joe took his leave. 'I ought to go and see a man about some tampons. But as the great savant and philosopher Arnold Schwarzenegger once said . . .' he paused for emphasis, leant close to Katherine, then whispered hoarsely '. . . *I'll be back* . . .'

With a twinkly smile, he walked away. Yes, she was definitely loosening up. Much more chatty, no doubt about it. At this rate of progress, in another ten years she might smile at him.

Katherine watched him go. She knew she'd been gratuitously cruel. But she had to admit she'd enjoyed it. Guiltily, she thought about having a quick drink with him. But, no, she decided. Look at what happened the last time she'd gone out with someone. And the time before that.

'You go, girl!' Katherine heard Charmaine say. 'He's a babe!'

She turned to berate her.

'I know.' Charmaine beat her to it. 'Shut up and get back to breaking rocks on the chain-gang.'

Later that day, Joe saw Katherine approach a Karmann Ghia, open it, swing her little bottom into it and drive away. He stared after her, transfixed, his admiration increased tenfold. A woman with a good body was a thing of beauty, but a woman with a good car, well . . .

9

'Wear your red dress,' Thomas coaxed, 'you look right sexy in that.'

'But we're only going to the pictures.' It was a while since she'd last worn it and Tara strongly suspected she'd put on a lot of weight since then.

'Ah, go on.'

'After we've eaten,' she promised, hoping he'd forget about it. 'Dinner is served!'

She ushered him to the candlelit table.

'Shepherd's pie?' Thomas asked suspiciously.

'The surprise,' Tara said happily, 'is that mine is 127 per cent fat-free and yours is the standard issue fat-bastard one.'

'Champion.'

'Turn off the telly, please.'

'But it's *Gladiators*.'

'So it is.'

With the candles flickering, they watched *Gladiators* and silently ate their dinner. When Thomas didn't grumble wistfully, 'That Ulrika Johnson, she's right fit,' it was safe for Tara to beam, 'This is romantic. We should do it more often.'

After their individual blackcurrant cheesecakes (Tara's 210 per cent fat-free, Thomas's the normal one), Thomas once again asked Tara to put on her red dress. With mild foreboding, she went to the bedroom where she discovered that, as she'd feared, she'd expanded somewhat since the last time she'd worn it. Pulling in her stomach and holding her breath, she displayed herself to Thomas.

'Let's have a look at you,' he said proudly.

His eyes flickered over her, and Tara noticed that he lingered slightly too long on her stomach. She glanced down and saw that the dress was ruched across her too-big belly. But she couldn't suck in any further. Desperately she hoped that Thomas wasn't going to go into one of his troughs on account of her weight. Tara's size depressed her, but it depressed Thomas even more, and Thomas in a good mood was fine, but in a bad mood, he was very bad indeed.

'It looks different,' Thomas declared, confused and annoyed.

Two years before, when he got off with Tara, he hadn't been able to believe his luck. Top marks for her blonde hair, generous bosom and slim waist, hips and legs. Like many tabloid-indoctrinated men, he had high standards and rigid ideas about what 'qualities' his ideal girlfriend should have.

But as soon as Tara settled back into being someone's girlfriend, the horror of Alasdair's rejection receded, and she began to eat again. She'd put on weight much more quickly than she'd lost it, and Thomas was bitterly disappointed. Why did women always let him down? In an attempt to recreate that perfect era, he spent a lot of time and energy trying to streamline Tara. Urging her to go running, suggesting that she join a gym, making her feel guilty whenever she ate something. Although he was no Twiggy himself. 'Watch him,' the dinner ladies at his school warned each other. 'Especially on a Thursday.' (Jam roly-poly day.) 'He'd have the kids' share if he thought no one would notice.'

But despite his own tubbiness, his initial frantic devotion to Tara had waned as her size had waxed. 'Aw, Tara,' he grumbled, as he surveyed the red dress from all angles. 'You look like you've a bun in the oven. When I first met you, you were right sexy.'

'I wouldn't go that far.' She laughed.

'You bludeh were, but if I saw you now, I'd have nowt to do with you.'

'I wouldn't blame you,' she said lightly. 'I'd have nowt to do with myself if I'd any choice.'

'Six months gone,' he said, nodding at her stomach. 'That's what you look like.'

'Seven, more like,' she suggested, with a rueful grin.

But when he didn't chuckle, she upped the ante by suggesting, 'Wouldn't it be hilarious if we found out that I *was* with child. What would we do?'

She was hoping to jolly him out of his black mood. She usually managed to. She certainly wasn't expecting him to say, '*We?*' as if he'd never heard the word before in his life.

'We?' he said again, even more surprised. 'What would *we* do?'

'Yes, we.' Laughingly she rolled her eyes at his denseness. 'You know, the two people responsible.'

Thomas retorted, with a dismissive snort, 'I'd have nowt to do with it.'

'Sleepless nights, dirty nappies.' She winced playfully. 'Who'd blame you? The poor child would probably die of neglect.'

And that, she hoped, would be the end of that. But the conversation wouldn't lie down and play dead because Thomas repeated, in the same confrontational tone, 'I'd have nowt to do with it.'

She knew she shouldn't, but she couldn't stop herself asking, in a voice much diminished, 'What do you mean?'

'I mean what I said. I'd have nowt to do with it.'

Tara was assailed with a creeping sense of dread. The whole thing was only meant to be a joke, but Thomas wasn't laughing.

Let it alone, her head urged her. Let it lie. Don't open any doors you can't close. He's not serious. And if he is, you don't want to know. 'You mean, you wouldn't . . .' She stopped, just before she said the words 'Marry me?' She'd scared Alasdair away with that concept and she'd sworn she wouldn't make the same mistake with Thomas. Instead she said, 'You mean, you wouldn't stand by me?' And belatedly managed a very brittle, unconvincing smile.

Thomas sat down on the couch and stared at her. Tara was very, very sorry that she'd ever opened her mouth. She had a horrible sensation of déjà vu, and an awful presentiment of what was coming.

'I don't know,' he said, flatly.

Tara's heart plummeted through her body, carried on a waterfall of cold fear. 'Surely you'd stay with me and make a go of things?' she asked, desperately. Her voice sounded muffled, as if her ears were blocked.

Again he stared at her. 'I don't think I'd want to,' he said, as if he'd just undergone a revelation.

It's not surprising, she breathlessly reminded herself. *How can he believe in families? After what happened to his parents.*

This was scant comfort.

'But you love me,' she protested.

'Aye, but . . .'

'Would you give me money for the baby?' Tara croaked, feeling as panicky as if there really was a baby.

'Tara, you earn twice as much as me,' he said bitterly.

'I suppose,' she admitted, ashamed.

Silence fell, a taut thread of tension stretched between them.

Horrible questions clamoured in Tara's head. What did all this mean? What kind of future had they?

'But, if you wouldn't –' Tara started and abruptly stopped. Why lever the lid off a can of worms? 'This discussion is mad, because I'm not pregnant,' she exclaimed, forcing a grin, as she frantically worked on patching up the rip. Quick, quick, before he noticed. Quick, quick, before *she* noticed. 'Fat, certainly, but not pregnant. There's nothing to worry about!'

Thomas was looking at her differently. In confusion, almost. As if questions were occurring to him, too. He opened his mouth to say something.

'Let's go,' Tara blurted, in an attempt to stop him. 'We'll be late for the film.'

He wavered on the brink, his breath drawn to speak. But between the breath and the utterance, the lethal light in his eyes died. 'OK,' he said, putting his arm around her. 'Let's go.'

No more was said about it. But after the pictures, instead of going out to a party or club as they often would, they came home instead, and watched telly, smoked and drank a bottle of wine in silence. When the wine was finished, Tara went to the kitchen and had a huge, secret gin and tonic. Then another, and another. She drank enough to fell an elephant, but couldn't get happy.

Later that night, as Thomas snored beside her, she made drunken plans. Though she wasn't going to examine it, she knew she'd been given some sort of warning tonight. She simply must try harder to make this tormented, scarred man of hers happy.

It was within her power to do so. He'd been mad about her at the start. *Mad* about her. God, how she yearned to return to those wonderful days when he smiled all the time and told her what a cracking bird she was. When they had sex around the clock. When he said she had the best figure of any girl he knew. When she felt adored and cherished and powerful.

She couldn't say when they'd slipped into their current baddish patch. But it was only temporary. Good times were just around the corner. All she had to do was try a little harder.

She gritted her teeth as she swore blind that she really was going to lose weight. And because her extravagance annoyed him she was going to stop spending money. She would buy lots of sexy underwear. *Cheap* sexy underwear, obviously, if she was going to stop spending money. She'd become a complete raunchbag, and tackle him to the floor as soon as he came in from work, and have sex in the hall. She'd cook lovely meals for him. And nothing for herself.

She stared into the darkness, racking her brain, as she tried to think of something really special to do for Thomas. What was the nicest thing anyone had ever done for her? Actually, as far as Tara was concerned, the nicest thing anyone had ever done for her was when she was nine years old. She'd begged her mother to buy her a denim skirt and waistcoat like the one she'd seen in *Jackie*, but perpetually skint Fidelma Butler couldn't afford to. However, what she did instead was go to Ennis on the bus and buy a pattern and enough brushed denim to hand-make the skirt and waistcoat. Which she did exactly to Tara's specifications, right down to where she explained, 'There's got to be two lines of orange stitching around the edge,

Ma. And you've got to be able to see it.' And even though Fidelma was mortified by the idea of sewing a hem that was visible to the naked eye, she bit the bullet and went right ahead and did it, because that was what Tara wanted. *That* was the nicest thing anyone had ever done for her, Tara decided. Even when her father looked over his newspaper and sneered, 'You can dress a goat in silk, but it's still a goat,' nothing could have ruined her joy in her new outfit.

All the same, she couldn't imagine Thomas being terribly thrilled at the suggestion that Tara hand-make a brushed denim skirt and waistcoat for him. But the idea of making something to clothe him appealed to her, and suddenly it was very clear what she would do. She was going to . . . going to . . . going to . . . *knit him a jumper!*

10

The following morning Tara woke very early. Something was wrong. Hangover time. I'm too old for this, she thought, as she swallowed a handful of painkillers. I can't hack it any more. Yet even though the pain lifted, faint sensations of impending doom draped themselves around her, like will-o'-the-wisps, and followed her from the bedroom to the bathroom to the kitchen.

Despite her night-time vow to go on a diet, Tara was viciously hungry. It was how hangovers affected her. They made some people so sick they couldn't face food all day. But they made her feel as though she'd never eaten anything ever before in her whole life. A stomach-growling, head-lightening hunger that was almost primal. She craved carbohydrates. At the thought of toast, she felt a rush of adrenaline that almost lifted her off the floor.

Surreptitiously, she closed the kitchen door so that Thomas wouldn't smell what she was doing, and put on two slices of toast. Frantic with impatience, she stared at the toaster, willing it to work faster. Hurry up, she passionately urged, put your back into it. If she didn't get something to eat *right now, this exact moment* she'd make a start on her own foot. But all there was in the cupboards was dried pasta, tinned tomatoes and cat food. Thomas had long since purged the kitchen of biscuits and crisps in a self-sacrificing attempt to remove temptation from Tara's way.

Her toast popped up and her hands shook as she covered one slice with cheese, the other with jam. While she crammed them into her, she put on two more slices. Then two more. An orgy of toast and she was in heaven. Toast with peanut butter, toast with cheese, toast with jam, toast with Marmite.

Covered in crumbs, she practically inhaled each slice whole, as she leant against the kitchen door, listening for Thomas.

A face appeared at the kitchen window and she jumped guiltily out of her skin. Until she realized it was Beryl, her green eyes contemptuous and condemnatory in her black little face. Tara stuck two fingers up at her, then turned her head from the window and back to her toast. Until she went to put on two more pieces and found there was no bread left.

Oh, God! She'd finished the sliced pan! Thomas would notice, he'd wonder where it had all gone. She had a moment of panicky fear before she calmed down. What's the problem? she asked herself. You're being silly. You can simply go out and buy another, under the guise of buying the Sunday papers. If the Pakistani grocery wasn't open yet – although she'd never known it not to be, day or night, as they slaved to make a living – then she'd go to the twenty-four-hour garage. She quietly got dressed, desperate not to wake Thomas, then went out into the damp misty morning, watched suspiciously by Beryl. She wouldn't put it past that bloody cat to tell on her.

The grocery shop wasn't open so Tara went to the garage and bought bread and newspapers. She also found herself buying three doughnuts – a chocolate one and two custard ones, how she loved custard – which she ate on the deliberately slow walk back, disposing of the wrapping in a dustbin in someone else's front garden. Vigorously brushing telltale crumbs away, running her tongue around her teeth to dispose of any lingering evidence, she braced herself for a return to the flat.

Thomas still wasn't up, which meant she was free to eat more if she wanted. But the frenzy had passed. I'm only eating like this because of my hangover, Tara soothed herself, lighting a cigarette. I'll be starting the diet proper tomorrow, but I'm going to try hard for the rest of today also. She sat at the kitchen table, smoking and trying to read the paper. Wasn't it dreadful to wake up too early on a cold, damp Sunday morning in October? she asked herself. She supposed she could go back to bed with the paper, but she was afraid of waking Thomas. With that she finally let herself see what was in the sack of doom on her back. It was what he'd said to her last night.

Instantly she felt another pang, of something like hunger trying to fight its way through the food and emerging as nausea.

With a firmness born of terrible fear, she spoke common sense to herself. So what if he didn't want her to get pregnant? She didn't want to get pregnant either – the mere thought! She and Thomas had had a meaningless, hypothetical discussion. Big banana.

This was nothing like the Alasdair situation. She was *living* with Thomas. And it was he, not she, who'd suggested she move in with him. Proof positive that he loved her – even if she'd suspected his eyes had lit up with pound signs rather than the light of love.

She'd played it so safe for the past two years, never putting pressure on Thomas, never even mentioning marriage, that things *couldn't* fall apart, the way they had with Alasdair. If she continued to play the waiting game as well as she already had, it would all come right in the end. There was no need for her to be worried, he loved her and this one would work. Lightning didn't strike twice.

She rang her mother because she wanted to talk to someone who loved her, but instead she got her father.

'Your mother isn't in,' he said, grumpy as ever.

'Where is she at this hour of the morning?' Tara asked.

'Where do you think, you pagan?' he replied.

Still desperate for comfort, she rang Katherine. No fear she'd be at Mass. 'Sorry,' she apologized. 'I hope I didn't wake you.'

'It's OK,' said Katherine. 'I've to go to work anyway.'

'On a Sunday? You advertising whizz-kids.'

'End-of-year accounts, it wouldn't usually happen.'

'I feel terrible,' Tara said.

'Vitamin C and a bracing walk.'

'I'm eating Disprin like they're Smarties, in fact I wish they *were* Smarties. But anyway, I'm not talking about my hangover, mammoth though it is.'

'What is it, so?'

'Not now, I don't want to make you late for work. Just tell me one thing. Lightning never strikes twice, does it?'

'You know it does,' Katherine reminded her. But gently, sensing this was important. 'Remember, the thatch on Billy Queally's roof was set on fire during one storm, then two years later he was electrocuted and thrown across the kitchen when he put on the toaster during another.'

'I didn't mean it *literally*,' Tara said miserably. 'But thanks anyway.'

'I'm sorry,' Katherine comforted. 'Tell me what's wrong.'

'It mightn't be anything,' Tara said heavily.

'Come over tonight when I get home from work.'

'Thanks, you're a sweetheart.'

Katherine had guessed what it was about. She'd never thought Thomas would last longer than a couple of weeks so she'd been poised for Tara and him to end for nearly two years.

She hadn't been keen on Thomas right from the very first night. Of course, she was delighted that Tara had met a new bloke – witnessing her pain after Alasdair had finally given her the slip had been excruciating. Not to mention that, with the best will in the world, sharing a flat with someone who's recently had their heart broken becomes a small bit tedious after the first three months of hysteria and bizarre behaviour.

But some instinct had screamed at her that Thomas wasn't Tara's Mr Right, or even Mr Keep The Wolf From The Door.

'Looks like she's made a new friend,' Fintan had murmured to Katherine, as Tara and Thomas ate the faces off each other in Dolly's kitchen, oblivious to everyone around them.

'Mmmmm,' Katherine said noncommittally.

'What is it?' Fintan asked.

'I don't know. Maybe it's his brown jeans.'

'Brown is the new black.'

'But they're horrible. And look! His shirt is brown too.'

'Don't be brownist,' Fintan advised. 'And he's probably a dead nice person.'

But later on, when Thomas came home with Tara, Katherine and Liv, he wouldn't contribute to the taxi-fare. 'No,' he said bluntly. 'If I weren't here, you'd have to pay what you always pay. It's daft if you profit from me being here. I speak as I find.'

Katherine burst out laughing. Maybe Thomas was OK, after all. ' "I speak as I find?" That's a good one.' In a poor Yorkshire accent she'd continued, '"Better wi' nowt tekken out. Where there's muck there's brass. Tetley's make teafolk make tea. I'm made up for our kid. You don't get owt for nowt." I love those Northern sayings. Any more?'

Suddenly she realized that Tara, Thomas and Liv had gone very still. At the exact moment that Tara hissed, '*Katherine!* Close your fat yap,' Katherine realized that Thomas hadn't been joking.

In grim silence Tara paid the taxi-man. And as Katherine watched Thomas swagger into the flat, and be led straight to Tara's bedroom, she thought she'd explode with injustice.

'I speak as I find,' was Thomas's favourite phrase. And what he found was rarely to his liking.

And then he spoke about it.

The day after Tara first met him, when they were all strewn about the living room, Katherine decided it was time to do some tidying, though she knew there would be objections.

'I've something to get off my chest,' she began.

'You call that a chest,' Thomas interrupted.

Tara screamed with laughter, so much so that even Thomas began to look alarmed. And when Katherine recovered from her shock and tried to object, he interrupted loudly, 'But it's TRUE, in't it?'

'That's not the point,' Katherine said coolly. 'It's very bad manners –'

'BUT IT'S TRUE, IN'T IT?' he said again, louder. 'You haven't got tits. It's a fact and I'm not going to lie to you.'

'No one asked you to say anything at all,' Katherine said.

'You can't tek the truth, can you?' He shrugged. 'You're too bludeh soft. I speak –'

'– as you find,' Katherine finished. 'I know.'

In a matter of days, Thomas had managed to insult all of Tara's friends. He called Liv a giantess, and as soon as she'd looked it up in the dictionary she was very upset. When he was formally introduced to Fintan, the way he hesitated about shaking hands, and the speed with which he wiped his palm on his jeans straight afterwards, made it abundantly clear that he didn't approve of homosexuals.

However, when he turned his plain-speaking on Tara, in a subtle attempt to change the balance of power back in his favour, the others *really* took against him. But by then Tara was in too deep. Thomas had rescued her when she'd thought she was facing into forty-five years of spinsterdom. She'd become addicted to his devotion, and if he had any criticism of her, she'd do her best to address it.

She'd been going out with him about a month the first time she let slip that he was annoyed about her weight gain.

'How dreadful,' Liv said, in shock. 'He is supposed to love you for *you*.'

'But he's only telling me because he cares about me,' Tara insisted. 'And he's right. I have put on a few pounds. Which I'm going to lose.'

Liv clenched her hands in frustration. 'After what Alasdair did you have the self-esteem of a gnu.'

'You mean a gnat,' Katherine interrupted, gently.

'Thomas is merely a bully, don't surrender to him,' Liv urged.

'Ah, now,' Tara said softly, 'I know you're upset by what he said about your height. And, Katherine, I know you're upset about what he said about your chest. But, in fairness, he was just being honest. Isn't it refreshing to be around someone who lets you know exactly where you stand?'

Katherine had decided there and then that she was going to move out and buy her own place.

'I love his strong views,' Tara admitted, dreamily. 'I love the way he'll take a stand and not back down. Don't you think his confidence in himself and his own rightness is very sexy? Speaking of sexy, he's like a madman in bed, day and night . . . Are you OK, Katherine? You've gone very red in the face.'

'I'm fine,' Katherine muttered. If she had to listen again to how great Thomas was in bed, she'd scream.

'Besides,' Tara said, returning to the matter in hand, 'if Thomas sometimes hurts people, it's not his fault.'

At their sceptical expressions, she launched into the story of his mother leaving him. 'Maybe if our mothers had left us at such a formative age, we'd be going around speaking as we find too.'

Though Fintan, and to a lesser extent Liv, tried to talk sense to her, they were wasting their time. Soft-hearted Tara was on a mission to love Thomas better. Even at his most hard-to-please – and he became progressively more hard-to-please as, over the months, he retrieved all the power he'd given to Tara in their early days – Tara couldn't help but forgive him.

She saw the abandoned boy in the adult Thomas. Was it any wonder if he occasionally lashed out after that ultimate betrayal?

And there was a consolation prize. Loyalty was very important to Thomas. He demanded fidelity, but he also promised it.

11

When Tara got off the phone from Katherine and ventured back into the kitchen, Thomas was up. Staring into the *faux*-rustic bread-bin that he'd bought at King's Crescent market for 99p.

'This bread . . . but it was open last night.'

Tara was clutched by the cold hand of fear and began pawing for her cigarettes. Why had she just put the bread into the bread-bin as it was? Why hadn't she recreated the scene as she'd found it when she got up this morning?

'Is this a new sliced pan?' he hooted incredulously.

'Yes,' Tara said. She couldn't manage the energy to lie or to say something funny.

'And where's the other one?'

Tara thought she might say that it had gone off and she'd thrown it out but she was too depressed to bother. 'I ate it.'

He looked at her, goggle-eyed, open-mouthed. He was so shocked he could barely speak. 'Nearly an entire loaf?' he stuttered. 'But why?'

Tara felt a merciful bout of flippancy. 'It was there, I was lonely,' she quipped.

'It's nothing to laugh at, Tara,' he exploded.

'Ah, come on.' Tara grinned. 'I'm starting right now. Starvation for me. And I'll do a step class after work tomorrow.'

*

All day a malaise lay on them. As if the damp grey morning mist had found its way into the flat, curling itself around them, lacing the air with doom. Dissatisfaction radiated so strongly from Thomas, Tara could almost see it. He was like a chimney belching grey clouds of negativity.

The atmosphere in the front room – depressing at the best of times with Thomas's brown sofa and brown carpet tiles – became more and more oppressive. Both of them were smoking more than usual and the cigarette fug further leadened the atmosphere. Tara was desperate to defuse the weirdness some-how, to say something light-hearted to put a smile on his face and make everything all right again. But she couldn't think of a single thing. When she pointed something out in the paper he just grunted or plain ignored her.

They'd sat this way countless times, over countless Sundays, and it had always been comfortable. As far as Tara could see, nothing was different. There was no reason for this stomach-knotting... *anticipation*. Yes, that was the right word. Anticipa-tion. But what was she waiting for?

'I'd really like to go and see that play about Woodstock,' Tara said, breaking an hour's worth of silence. She actually didn't give a damn about that play about Woodstock, but she couldn't endure any more absence of sound. She felt she needed an excuse to talk to him and she wanted a promise of some kind of intimacy, a suggestion that he'd come to the play with her.

Thomas looked at her over his paper. 'Well, why don't you *go* to that play about Woodstock, then?' he barked, as if he'd never heard anything so stupid in all his life. Then gave his paper a paternal shake and redisappeared behind it, missing Tara's stricken face.

Beryl trotted into the room, gave Tara a disdainful, superior body-swerve – *I saw you eating all that toast, you fat cow,* she seemed to say – and hopped on to Thomas's lap.

'Have you come to see your daddy?' Thomas crooned, all lit up like a Christmas tree. 'Who's a beautiful girl? Oh, who's a beautiful girl?'

Tara watched Thomas's hand curving along Beryl's back and tail, then saw Beryl staring smugly at her, snuggled on Thomas's lap, and felt as if she was in a love triangle. She longed to be that bloody cat. To get a tenth of the affection that Thomas lavished on it. To have her tummy tickled. To be bought a scratch-pole. To be fed rabbit chunks in jelly.

Beryl hung around for just as long as it suited her then, with the take-it-or-leave-it independence that Tara yearned to emulate, got down off Thomas and stalked out. Thomas's gloom reappeared immediately.

'I'm going to have a shower,' Tara muttered, when the walls of the room began to move closer to her. The pounding water and the fresh, clean smell marginally uplifted her. But when she went back into the front room to Thomas, her anxiety greeted her at the door and reattached itself like a wraith. 'Is something wrong?' she asked. And that seemed to annoy him even more. After a while she couldn't bear it any longer. 'Come on,' she said, gaily, 'let's do something. Instead of sitting here like a pair of slugs, let's do something.'

'Like what?' he sneered.

'I don't know,' she floundered, her confidence shaken by his hostility. 'Go out. We live in London, for God's sake. There's millions of things we could do.'

'Like what?' he repeated.

'Er . . .' Frantically she searched her head, desperate to come up with something interesting. 'We could go to an art gallery. The Tate! That's a nice one.'

'Bugger off,' he said bluntly. And Tara had to admit she was relieved. Bad and all as it was trapped here in the living room, traipsing round a bloody art gallery would be immeasurably worse. Fighting through busloads of rowdy tourists and those terrible people who 'understood' art, then having to queue for an hour in the café for the obligatory slice of carrot cake didn't appeal.

'Shopping, maybe?' she suggested. 'It's the new rock and roll.'

He curled his lip derisively at that. 'You're overdrawn, you're up to the limits on all your cards, and even though mine is one of the most important jobs anyone can do, I've no brass either.'

'I know,' she declared wildly. 'We'll go for a drive.'

'A drive?' Thomas had failed three driving tests, so he tried to make driving sound like a form of deviance. 'A drive where?'

Her mind went blank. 'The seaside!' she suggested, her enthusiasm laced with desperation.

But suddenly that seemed like a great idea to Tara. The brisk, bracing sea air would blow away the stagnation that cloaked them. A little spontaneity would do them no end of good.

'The seaside? On the fourth of October?' He looked at her as though she were mad.

'Why not? We'll wrap up warm.'

'Go on, then,' he conceded, grumpily.

After the toast débâcle Tara was afraid to have any lunch before they left. Which meant that for the entire journey to the coast she smoked constantly and obsessed about food. Everything she drove past looked like something she could eat. Trees became heads of broccoli. Hay bales turned into giant

Shredded Wheats or – even better – baklava, bursting with honey and sugar. When they passed a field full of sheep, her breathing quickened as she thought of a bursting bag of marshmallows. The cliff face of a chalk quarry reminded her of a lovely big slab of nougat. Her mouth began to water when they drove by a slick, muddy field. A two-acre chocolate fudge cake, she thought, smothered in chocolate icing. The other vehicles on the road tormented her more than anything. Not just because their tyres looked like liquorice wheels. But those cars with a shiny metallic finish put her in mind of chocolates, as if each car had been wrapped with coloured tinfoil, then a layer of Cellophane. Quality Street on wheels. A red car passed her going the other way. Strawberry Supreme, she thought. A purple car passed. Hazelnut in Caramel. A yellow car passed. Toffee Deluxe. A green car passed. Noisette Triangle. A brown car passed. Coffee Crème.

This happened to her a lot. When Liv wore her green-coloured contact lenses, Tara could never look at her without instantly being put in mind of lime Jelly-tots. When Tara went to Italy and was flying over whitish mountains covered with brown scrub, all she could think about was tiramisu. She'd once visited a friend's flat and from across the room saw a bowl of sweets. Wine gums, she'd deduced, and promptly asked if she could have one. But they weren't wine gums. They were crystals, and Tara had had to spend the next half an hour pretending to admire them.

'I suffer from a food analogy,' she muttered at Thomas, but he was too busy smoking in the passenger seat and staring out of the window away from her. She hadn't wanted him to hear her anyway.

After they'd been driving for over an hour Thomas stabbed

a finger and said, 'Look!' in the general direction of a Little Chef. Tara's heart leapt with hope. Maybe she'd be allowed to eat something. But, as it turned out, Thomas was pointing at the first sighting of the sea. They went to Whitstable in Kent, and had the pebbled beach entirely to themselves. The day was as damp and misty as it had been early that morning. The unmoving sea was a sludgy colour between brown and grey, and the sky looked as if it had been concreted over. The emptiness and greyness depressed Tara further. Coming here had been a mistake. The two hours they'd spent trapped in the car with each other, smoking their heads off, had been even more electric with tension than their morning in the front room. Despite the uninviting weather she insisted that they get out and walk, hoping that the fresh air would perform miracles. Heads down, they trudged along the gravel and, when they got to a breakwater, stopped. They sat on the damp gravel and stared out at the stagnant sea. As beneficial as looking at a switched-off television. No birds sang.

After fifteen silent minutes they slogged back to the car and returned home. On the drive back to London it started to rain.

12

Fintan and Sandro were having a far nicer day than Tara and Thomas. They'd had a lively, chattery lunch with a crowd of friends at Circus, and now they were at home reading the Sunday papers. Fintan was stretched full-length on their so-hip-it-hurts tan leather sofa, his feet in Sandro's lap.

Perfectly in tune with each other, they barely needed to speak to communicate.

'Did you read –'

'– Michael Bywater?'

'Mmmmm. Funny.'

'Mmmmm.'

A long comfortable silence followed.

'Do you think –'

'– a shag-pile rug? I do. We could look –'

'– next weekend. We will.'

Another blanket of hush.

Sandro folded up the Culture bit of the *Independent* and opened his mouth to ask Fintan to pass the Real Life section, but Fintan had beaten him to it and was already proffering it.

Fintan and Sandro had met six years previously when Fintan was sharing the flat in Kentish Town with Tara and Katherine. Sandro had literally been the boy next door.

The day Sandro had moved into the flat across the hall,

Fintan took one look at his small, jaunty frame, his elfin face, his shaved head and round glasses, and fell in love. He was ripe for it. For about a year he'd been complaining, 'I'm tired of playing the field. I'd like to settle down. I want a significant other.'

They knew from his mail that the new boy's name was Sandro Cetti. He was always smiley and friendly if he met any of them in the hall, so one morning Tara brazenly questioned him and established that he was an architect, originally from Rome.

'An Italian stallion.' Fintan said later.

'Hardly a stallion,' Tara said. 'An Italian pony is more like it.'

And the name stuck.

'I just don't know if he's gay,' Fintan agonized. 'I'm not picking up any signals.'

'But neither am I,' Tara said. 'I'm not sure he's straight either.'

'Maybe he's an alien,' came Katherine's voice from the bathroom.

'He's going out, he's going out,' Tara yelped, and Fintan rushed to the window and discreetly watched Sandro walk buoyantly down the road, neat and dinky in his trendy little suit and shiny Doc Martens.

'Isn't he gorgeous?' Fintan sighed. 'As cute as all get out?'

As the weeks passed, everything Sandro said and did simply served to increase Fintan's devotion. One night there was a car crash outside their house and Sandro was full of dancing-eyed excitement by the front door the following morning.

'I was lying in my sleep and BOOM!' He lifted both hands as if conducting an orchestra. 'I hear a big, big noise so I run to my window and I see glass in all the places!'

Later Fintan repeated every word that Sandro had said. '"I see glass in all the places." How could anyone resist that? "I was lying in my sleep." The boy's an angel.' He sighed, love-sick. 'This is getting worse.'

Time went on and Fintan continued with his high-octane life: pubs, partying, clubbing, always with one eye out just in case Sandro showed up in any of the gay clubs. But he didn't and the vitality continued to drain out of Fintan, until he began to remark, 'Life has lost its taste.'

The crunch came late one night when Fintan was on his way home, wearing his white Katherine Hamnett neo-bondage trousers. He hobbled off the night-bus, taking tiny little geisha-girl steps on account of the fact that his legs were strapped together, when he was set upon by a crowd of thugs, over-burdened with prejudice and too much free time. Fintan tried his best to escape. Because he was unable to run, he began hopping frantically, like a person in a sack race, all the while trying to undo the straps. But it was too late and he was beaten into unconsciousness. It had happened before, but never as badly.

After three days in hospital he arrived home, and that was when Sandro came into the picture. He said he would call in on Fintan when the girls were at work during the day. Fintan looked like a train crash but was so weepy and depressed after being attacked that he couldn't be bothered with vanity.

Sandro made Fintan tea and soup and in order not to disturb his dislocated jaw, helped him drink them through a straw. Then, because Fintan could barely see through his black, puffy eyes, Sandro offered to read to him.

'Yes, please. If you could pick a magazine from that pile there.'

Fintan flailed his hand, and Sandro tentatively made his approach, wondering what kind of magazines they were. They were travel brochures.

Fintan's depression lifted as he lay in delicious torment, within touching distance of the object of his desire, who poured sweet words into his ear. '. . . a swim-up bar, landscaped gardens, air-conditioning, tea and coffee facilities and a supervised play area.'

'Half board?'

'Room only. But it say there is three restaurants. "The casual beachside grill, the child-friendly Harvey's and the more formal Cochon Gros."'

'Not that I'll ever get to go to any of these places,' Fintan murmured. 'But it's nice to dream. What's the average temperature this time of year?'

Sandro consulted the chart at the back of the brochure, then suddenly flung it on the floor. 'I am so angry with these peoples, these *animals*, that do this to you,' he said fiercely.

'Are you . . . really?' Fintan choked.

'I am angry that they do it to the gay man and I am angry that they do it to you!'

But what did that mean? Fintan wondered. Was Sandro just a bleeding-heart liberal? A *straight* bleeding-heart liberal?

Luckily, no. Sandro was as gay as the next man. (Fintan.) When pressed it all came out, and Sandro admitted that two years previously his boyfriend had died of 'the virus'.

'And I feel I can never again care for anyone. But I see you coming in and out of your flat,' Sandro ducked his head in embarrassment – not that it made any difference because Fintan was still, to all intents and purposes, blind, 'and I think, he's . . . he's good-looking. Then you bring me my letters and the leaflet about pizzas and window-cleaning and I think you're very kind.'

Very gently, taking care not to dislocate Fintan's jaw any further, they had their first kiss and Fintan experienced such a surfeit of happiness that he thought his heart would split open – just like his lip had. From that day forth, Sandro and Fintan were an item and it was a match made in Heaven.

They were mad about each other. Sandro was overwhelmed with happiness at falling in love again and Fintan had met his long-awaited Mr Right.

'I understand now why they talk about your "other half",' he admitted. 'That's what Sandro is to me.'

Both had been wounded – Fintan by the trauma of being beaten up and Sandro by the death of his previous boyfriend – and they were tender and mindful of each other. At the same time they both had bags of energy, an enormous circle of friends and a great love of socializing. Sandro's English improved greatly. The only thing was he now spoke with an Irish inflection and peppered his conversation with 'grand' and 'feck'.

Six months later they bought a top-floor flat in Notting Hill and Sandro used his architectural skills to take out so many ceilings and walls and put in so many mezzanines, portholes and polished concrete floors that it appeared in *Which House?* and *Elle Decoration*.

'Up we get.' Fintan heaved his feet out of Sandro's lap. 'Things to see, people to do. Do you want to go to Katherine's later?'

Sandro nodded enthusiastically. That was another reason that Fintan and Sandro worked so well. Fintan came as a package deal with Tara and Katherine – love me, love my friends – and Fintan had once dumped a potential love interest because he'd taken violently against Katherine, exclaiming, 'She's so *anal*.'

'After Katherine's will we go out for a drink and a dance?' Sandro asked.

'Sure. So we'd better get you organized for Norwich now, because you'll be too tired in the morning.' Fintan bustled: the following day Sandro was going to Norwich for a week, doing major work on a house there. 'Bring me your shirts to be ironed.'

'You know you don't have to do that,' Sandro protested. 'I could try.'

'Pah, no. You never make them as nice.'

'Okay,' he said shyly. 'Thanks.'

Fintan got out the ironing-board and Sandro gave him five shirts.

'What do I need to pack?' Sandro called from the beige Japanese-style bedroom, his case flung open on the raised platform bed.

'Five pairs of knickers, five pairs of socks, toothbrush, smellies, charger for your mobile, you forgot that the last time . . .'

'Can I have your jean jacket?'

'If you don't mind it being too big.'

After Fintan had lovingly removed every crease from Sandro's shirts, he carefully laid them in the case, smoothing them flat. 'Right, you're all set. Now I'd better ring my mother.'

Every Sunday without fail he rang his mother. For a seventy-something, Irish-Catholic mother JaneAnn was pretty cool. She knew Fintan was gay and seemed to have no great problem with it. The only fly in the ointment was the question of Fintan's 'flatmate'. Fintan had never quite known how to bring the conversation around to the fact that he was living with his boyfriend, and as time had gone on, and no mention had been made, it had seemed harder and harder to broach the subject. Fintan picked up the phone and he and JaneAnn chewed the fat for ages, JaneAnn doing most of the talking. For a small town, Knockavoy had an awful lot of drama. Three heifers had escaped from Clancy's bottom field and destroyed a shrub in the parish priest's garden, and now the priest's housekeeper was refusing to speak to Francie Clancy. Delia Casey was organizing a benefit gig for Rwanda, 'whatever the heck a benefit gig is. Might it be something like a sale of work?' And the hottest news of all – they were after getting Pop-tarts into the Spar.

When Fintan hung up he suggested to Sandro, 'Why don't you come to Ireland with me at Christmas?'

Sandro giggled nervously. 'I am afraid. What if they didn't like me? Your mother and your brothers?'

'They would. Ah, Sandro, five years is too long to not have met each other's family. It's time we dealt with it.'

'You're right, and we could go to my family for New Year's Eve.'

Fintan paled. 'Or we could forget the whole idea and go to Lanzagrotty.'

'Again?'

'We'll see. Let's get ready for Katherine's.'

'Did you take your vitamins today?'

'Oh, I forgot. I'll take them now.'

'Fintan, you must stop forgetting. It's important that you take them.' Sandro sounded annoyed.

'Sorry, Mum.'

13

That evening Tara was almost afraid to go out, reluctant to leave Thomas while things were still tense and weird. It felt like an admission of failure. But once she was out of the front door and in her car, she found she was nearly hyperventilating. The relief of being out of that flat! Away from that terrible claustrophobic atmosphere of tension and fear.

'Are you OK?' Katherine asked, when she opened the door.

Tara nodded, lighting a cigarette. 'Sorry about the SOS phone call at the crack of dawn. I'd my morning-after-the-night-before head on me, where the world seemed . . . ominous, I suppose. That'll teach me to drink too much gin.'

'Whatever,' Katherine said. Tara wasn't telling – yet.

'Oh, no,' Tara exclaimed, demonstrating her cigarette, which had a ring of lipstick around the filter. 'My new indelible lipstick isn't indelible after all! The girl said I'd need paint-stripper to budge it.'

'Typical,' Katherine condemned.

'Why do they always lie to me?' Tara demanded, sadly. 'Why do they always let me down?'

'Have a drink,' Katherine consoled. 'Beer or wine?'

'Beer. I'm going to knit Thomas a jumper.'

Katherine had an instant of being utterly nonplussed. Quickly she managed to say enthusiastically, 'Good girl yourself!'

'I was good at knitting at school, j'remember?' Tara pointed out. 'Remember the lovely pink scarf I knitted for Fluffy the cat?'

'Yeeess,' Katherine said, faintly. 'And does it matter that it was twenty-six years ago when you were only five?'

'Ah, knitting's like riding a bike,' Tara pointed out. 'Although,' she said, suddenly anxious, sucking at her cigarette and inhaling down to her toes, 'do you remember the way Fluffy pulled and tore at the lovely scarf until he got it off? He didn't have a moment's peace until he'd got rid of it.'

'That's cats for you.' Katherine smiled encouragingly.

'That's cats for you, indeed,' Tara agreed, bitterly. 'Ungrateful swine. Dogs, now. They're a different kettle of fish, they're affectionate and loyal. But cats would sell you down the river, eat your last Rolo, double-cross you just for the fun of it. They'd shop their own granny if they thought it would be to their advantage, blacken your good name –'

'Maybe pink just wasn't Fluffy's colour.' Katherine felt she'd better interrupt.

Tara looked at Katherine as if she didn't quite recognize her. 'Er, maybe it wasn't,' she muttered. She looked around as if she wasn't sure where she was. 'Oh, Katherine, what's *wrong* with me?'

Your hideous boyfriend? Katherine refrained from asking.

'It could be hormones,' Tara answered herself. 'It's a bit early but it would account for a lot of how I've felt today. All I needed was to fall down a flight of stairs and spend a month's salary on a cute yellow corkscrew for the full complement of symptoms to be present. PMT gets worse as you get older, doesn't it?'

Katherine agreed. 'Except it's PMS now,' she corrected.

'I didn't know how lucky I was in my twenties,' Tara said dreamily. 'All that happened then was that for ten days a month

I ingested a four-stone sack of sweets and cried if anyone so much as asked me the time, but in my thirties it's mutated into full-blown *psychosis*! Roll on the menopause.'

'You're fine,' Katherine told her compassionately. 'And don't forget I've a spare room if you ever need somewhere to sleep . . .'

Tara felt dreadful again. And she'd just been starting to feel better. Oh, well.

'I rang Fintan,' Katherine was saying, 'and he said himself and the pony will come over.'

Tara's spirits leapt. Fintan could always cheer her up and she felt her own personal dense grey cloud, which had dogged her all day, move away from being so close to the crown of her head.

'I rang Liv too,' Katherine said, 'but Lars is in town. He arrived unexpectedly.'

Lars was the Swedish married man who Liv was walking out with. Or, rather, staying in with. He came to London every couple of months, always keeping the gap between visits just the right length to drive Liv mad with loneliness, yet not quite long enough for her to get over him. On account of the brevity of his visits, they spent most of their time in bed.

The bell rang, indicating that the boys had arrived. Katherine buzzed them in through the front door, then waited at the open door of her flat. Fintan thumped up the stairs, decked out in a horrifically expensive-looking pistachio-green sheepskin coat. He was all of a dither. 'Come on, come on,' he commanded, refusing to step into the flat. 'Quick, girls! Just outside the gate I was nearly knocked to the ground by the *über*bloke to end all *über*blokes. Striding along like a Viking. Sandro's keeping watch.' He grabbed Katherine's hand and tried to drag her towards the stairs. 'He was huge,' he related, 'like a brick

shithouse with – and I know you'll find this hard to believe –
gorgeous red hair. Red hair! I ask you. But he was delish . . .
what's up with you, Katherine? You've a face on you like a
robber's dog chewing a wasp.'

'Nothing's up.'

'Come on out for a gawk at your man, so. Before he's gone.'

'But it's raining.'

'Have it your way, you miserable Margaret. Come on, Tara.'

'Not tonight, Josephine,' Tara said. She loved Fintan but she
couldn't be bothered to go out into the cold night and admire
some fool with red hair. 'Settle yourself. Come in and show us
your fantastic coat!'

'*Et tu, Brute?* I don't know what's up with you pair of moaning
Minnies,' Fintan complained. But he realized his Viking was
probably out of sight by now, so he stuck two fingers in his
mouth and gave a piercing whistle. There was the sound of
running feet and Sandro appeared up the stairs.

'The love-god is escaping,' he said, breathlessly. 'If we don't
hurry –'

'Forget it, Sand,' Fintan said. 'They're not interested.'

Sandro stared in horror and Fintan murmured, 'I know.'
Then Sandro threw his eyes to heaven and Fintan murmured,
'I *know*.'

Then Sandro said, 'Girls!' and Fintan murmured, 'I *know*.'

Katherine scolded, 'Get in here, the pair of you,' and both
men jumped with fright.

Meekly, they did so.

'So, what are you doing chasing after men in the street and
you two practically married?' Tara interrogated Sandro and
Fintan as they sat on the sofa, Fintan still wrapped in his
pale-green coat.

'What problem is there to look?' Sandro grinned. 'We didn't kidnap him.'

'Only because we'd left our big net at home.' Fintan nudged Sandro and they both gave big, dirty laughs, leaning into each other.

'Benders,' Tara sighed. 'You're dead lucky. Don't you ever get jealous or insecure?'

'No.' They looked at each other and shrugged.

'How come?' Tara asked.

'Why go out for a hamburger when you've steak at home?' Fintan said, in a sing-song voice.

'That's so sweet,' Tara squeaked, on the verge of tears. A rosy glow crept around the room, until it got to Katherine. Where it lost its nerve, turned tail and ran.

'Except,' Sandro broke the quiet by saying shamefacedly, 'sometimes it's nice to have a hamburger.'

'There's certainly no harm,' Fintan nodded carefully, 'in just looking at them.'

'If Thomas tried to throw a net over a good-looking woman in the street, I'd cut his balls off,' Tara admitted. 'And I know you all hate him, but –'

'We don't all hate him,' Katherine interrupted.

'I do,' Fintan said baldly.

'And so do I,' Sandro added. 'And so does Liv.'

'And so do I,' Katherine admitted. 'Sorry, Tara, you're absolutely right. We *do* all hate him. Carry on.'

Tara looked bleakly as the other three killed themselves laughing.

'I'm joking,' Katherine backtracked hastily. Unlike Fintan, Katherine usually managed to hide her contempt for Thomas. She walked a narrow line – while it was her duty to let Tara know that she deserved better than Thomas, it was also her duty to be Tara's sounding board. If Tara realized how much Katherine despised Thomas, she'd never tell her anything, and that wouldn't be good. At least, not for Tara. On the other hand it would be very good for Katherine – her blood-pressure soared sky-high every time she heard What Thomas Did Next.

'I know you all hate him,' Tara reiterated. 'But you don't see what I see.'

'Of course,' Fintan murmured, unable to look at any of the others in case they all started laughing again.

'I know he's sometimes . . . difficult. But that's only because of his mother leaving him. He loves me and he'd never be unfaithful,' Tara said. 'That counts for a lot. Especially after . . .'

Everyone waited.

They knew the script.

'Especially after . . .' Tara gave an ominous little hiccup.

'Especially after . . .'

'. . . Alasdair left you . . .' Fintan supplied gently.

'. . . and married someone else . . .' Katherine finished.

Tara looked at them suspiciously. 'Have I been going on about it too long or something?'

'Ah, no,' Fintan said, kindly. 'Two years is nothing.'

'If you're sure.' Tara brightened up.

'Sure we're sure,' they chorused.

It was time to inspect Fintan's clothes.

'May I touch the coat?' Tara asked, reverentially. 'Is it really yours or just a loaner?'

'I borrowed it from the stockroom. Carmella would have my guts for garters if she knew.'

'Clothes look beautiful on you.' Tara sighed enviously. 'Even better since you lost the bit of weight.'

Fintan always dressed in character. As the coat was part of the Manchester look, he also wore baggy jeans, a baggy top and cobalt desert boots. 'I feel nostalgic tonight,' he said, just in case anyone might think that he thought the Manchester look was still in. His finger was superglued to the pulse and he was keen that people knew it. 'I thought we'd go a bit retro. Have a nineteen-ninety-seven revival.'

'The only thing I'm missing is . . .' Fintan said slowly, eyeing Sandro's spectacles.

Sandro adopted a defensive position. 'No! I won't give them.'

'Five minutes, that's all I ask,' Fintan beseeched. 'I feel naked without them. You can't do the Manchester look without John Lennon glasses. Pleeeeeeeease.'

'OK.' Sandro reluctantly handed over his little round glasses, and Fintan put them on.

'There!' he said. 'Finally, I feel fully dressed. Holy Jesus, though, they're strong.' He tried to focus on the others. 'God, this is great. I wish I'd known about them before. Talk about hallucinations! I could have saved myself a *fortune* in drugs over the years.'

'Can I have them back now?' Sandro begged. 'Without them I'm blind.'

'But you go out and get blind drunk every Sunday night, anyway,' Fintan pointed out. 'Consider this a head start.'

Tara waved away Fintan's offer of a 'go' of Sandro's glasses. 'When I wear glasses I look like an owl.'

'An oul' what?'

'An oul' eejit.' Tara laughed.

'So how do you manage? Contact lenses?'

'Yip,' said Tara.

'How about you?' Fintan asked Katherine. 'How's your eyesight?'

'Twenty-twenty,' she said.

Everyone erupted into laughter, even Katherine.

'Yours would be,' wheezed Tara. 'Little Miss Perfect.'

'Sometimes I even make myself sick,' Katherine agreed, her face contorted with mirth.

'Bumlickers Anonymous,' Tara advised. 'That's where you need to be going.'

'Ouch, ouch,' Fintan complained, putting his hand beneath his ear. 'Oh, damn it, ouch. My glands! I've an awful pain in my neck.'

'That's no way to talk about Sandro,' Tara said.

'Ah, no, it's not funny. My neck, my stomach, I'm a crock! That bloody E-coli. I was grand all day, thought I'd shaken it.'

Katherine opened her mouth to scold, then shut it again when she saw the worried look that Sandro gave Fintan.

Fintan turned to Tara. 'How are *you* this weather? What ails you today?'

'Malnutrition,' Tara sighed. 'I'm at the stage where your stomach bloats up from no food. I've a very advanced form of the disease, where my thighs and bum and the rest of me has blown up too.'

'Speaking of which,' Katherine said smoothly, 'are we ringing for pizzas?'

'Food?' Fintan said airily. 'Never touch the stuff. Us fashion types never eat.'

'But you have to have something.'

'I couldn't!' Fintan shrieked, pawing his stomach. 'I had an Anadin last Tuesday and I put on a gram. I'm almost four stone now. That's what I have to listen to every day at work, you know,' he said gloomily. 'They'd make you boke. OK, give me a large Four Seasons with extra cheese, tomatoes, mushrooms, pepperoni, ham . . .' Everyone waited for him to say, 'Feck it, make it *two* large Four Seasons, and be done with it!' Like he always did. But he didn't, and when Katherine reminded him, he said, 'I'm not that hungry. One will do.'

'A large deep-dish *Quattro Formaggio* for me,' Sandro said firmly. He was one of those whippety little men who ate like a pig, and never put on weight.

'I'm so hungry I could eat the hind leg of the Lamb of God,' Tara said. 'But I can't have anything, I'm on a diet.

'You know,' she continued, 'when I'm on a diet I eat as much as I usually do, the difference is that I think about food incessantly. Although I think about food incessantly, anyway. I'm always hungry. Stand on my toe and my mouth opens!' Her voice began to increase in pitch. 'When I'm nervous I want to eat. When I'm excited I want to eat. When I'm worried I want to eat. Even when I feel sick, the only thing that settles my stomach is *food*. My life is a NIGHTMARE.' She finished on a shrill note, her words reverberating into sympathetic silence.

Then Katherine said, 'So, the usual, then?'

'How about some extra garlic bread with cheese?' Tara suggested.

Katherine made the phone call, then all four of them settled down to watch *The Ambassador*.

'This is great,' Fintan observed, when the first lot of ads came on. 'Good, clean, old-fashioned fun. Just like the old days.'

'I really shouldn't have ordered all that food,' Tara interrupted, in a low voice, talking to herself. 'I really shouldn't.' Her voice was getting louder. 'I wish I hadn't. Oh, God, I really wish I hadn't.'

'You don't have to eat it,' Katherine offered half-heartedly.

'I have no choice,' Tara hooted, hysteria putting in an appearance. 'I have no bloody choice. Now that I've ordered it I won't be able to stop myself from eating it. I haven't an iota of willpower. But my entire future depends on it. Oh, my God.' She choked. 'What's going to become of me?'

With that she burst into face-in-hands, shoulder-shuddering tears.

The pizza-delivery boy chose this moment to arrive, so while Tara was comforted by Katherine and Sandro, Fintan went down and dealt with pizzas and their payment. He couldn't resist going to the gate to have one last quick look for his Viking. But Lorcan was long gone.

As soon as it had started to rain, he'd hurried home. Lorcan was always reluctant to be out when it was drizzling because, despite the beauty and silkiness of his hair, it invariably puffed up into a big, frizzy ball within seconds of encountering precipitation. He was afraid of looking undignified by running, so by the time he reached his flat twenty minutes later, he could have doubled for Ronald McDonald. He had to wash his hair. As luck would have it, it was his night for doing a deep-conditioning treatment anyway. Even as Fintan was giving one last rueful look up and down the road, Lorcan was about to wrap a hot pink towel around his head. He rubbed the last of the conditioner into his ends. Because I'm worth it, he told himself smugly, smiling into the imaginary camera. Because I'm worth it.

*

Fintan went back in.

'I'm sorry about this,' Tara sobbed. 'I'm just finding it a bit hard at the moment. What with Thomas and my birthday and being a fat cow and the awful day at the seaside and my indelible lipstick not being indelible! But everything will be OK when I've lost a bit of weight and knitted Thomas the jumper . . . I'm sorry.'

'You don't have to be sorry,' Fintan shushed her.

'Of course you don't,' Sandro comforted.

'Not with us,' Katherine assured her.

'We're your friends!' they said in unison.

14

While Tara and Katherine had been best pals since their first week at school, Fintan was a relative newcomer to the friendship. They hadn't bonded until they were both fourteen and he was fifteen. Of course, they knew him: it was a small town and you knew almost everything about your neighbours. Especially because Fintan had always been 'different' from the other boys. His kindness to his mother, his dreadful hand-to-eye co-ordination and his lack of enthusiasm for pulling the legs off frogs were testament to that.

But it wasn't until 1981 when he discovered the New Romantics that Fintan's 'specialness' got out of hand altogether. (The New Romantic phase had arrived in the rest of the civilized world some time previously but Knockavoy was in a different time zone, about six to nine months behind.) Suddenly he was parading the two streets of Knockavoy draped in shiny yellow fabric. (Even then he was calling material 'fabric', a sure sign that a career in fashion awaited him.) He wore a silk headband around his asymmetrical bob, purple lipstick and earrings that he'd made himself by stealing feathers from his brother's fishing kit, and dying them red and blue.

'Fintan O'Grady's had his ears pierced!' The rumour spread from house to house like wildfire. There hadn't been so much excitement since the last time Delia Casey had done something mad. There was great disappointment when it turned out the earrings were only clip-ons.

Despite that, Fintan continued to intrigue the townsfolk. 'Look at him,' they muttered from the dim, low-ceilinged interiors of bars, shops and the sub-post office. 'Strutting up and down like a paycock. And is that JaneAnn O'Grady's good tablecloth he's wearing? Jeremiah O'Grady must be twirling in his grave.'

In the normal course of events Fintan could expect to be beaten to a pulp by the other young men of the town. Certainly there was bitter hostility. A couple of corner boys were moved to shout, 'Ah, yuh maggot, yuh,' at him, as he floated past in his saffron silkiness. One of them even went so far as to yell, 'Yuh durthy bindher, yuh.'

But when Fintan replied, 'Oh, Owen Lyons, you weren't saying that last Sunday up behind Cronin's cowhouse. Or you, Michael Kenny,' the crowd of lads abruptly ceased their accusations. Despite the flurry of panicky denials from Owen Lyons and Michael Kenny – 'I don't know what he's talking about, the lying bindher' – suspicion and fear of each other were cast into their midst.

Fintan had a sharp and scathing tongue. He was tall and well-built. He had four older brothers who were also tall and well-built, *and* very protective of him. All in all, the lads of the town nervously decided, best to leave him be.

Because he'd chosen the position of outsider, or had it thrust upon him, Fintan had no friends. Which tore lumps of anxiety out of Tara. 'It's desperate,' she told Katherine, as they watched Fintan making his way up Main Street, assailed by daggers' looks and an undercurrent of muttered insults. 'He must feel awful lonesome.'

A lightbulb sprang into life above Tara's head. 'I know! *We'll* be his friends.'

Katherine and Tara had recently emerged from the wilderness years of loathing and despising boys (traditionally between the ages of seven and twelve). At fourteen they were quite partial, at least Tara was and Katherine didn't have any objection to them, though Fintan wasn't a boy in Tara's conventional interpretation of the concept – in other words, she needn't hold out any hopes of getting off with him.

'What do you want to be friends with him for?' Katherine asked in a little voice, a cold lump of jealousy in her stomach. 'Is it because he's . . .' she hesitated over the taboo word '. . . gay? Is it because the Limerick girls laughed at your sandals last summer?'

Katherine yearned for Tara's motives to be suspect. These were the days when a gay friend still carried kudos and novelty value. Having Fintan by one's side was bound to impress visiting Limerick girls – possibly even Dublin girls. More so, even, than a sweatshirt with a pattern picked out in glitter *and* a pair of white tukka boots with fringes and beads.

Tara was shocked by Katherine implying that Fintan was merely a fashion accessory. 'No. It's because he hasn't any friends.'

Katherine didn't want to be convinced. 'Anyway.' There was a sour taste in her mouth. 'He's not gay at all. Sure, how could he be gay when there's no one in Knockavoy for him to be gay with?'

To her dismay this piece of astonishing information *still* didn't put Tara off, and Katherine had to endure a couple of agonizing weeks while their alliance with Fintan was cemented. Mute with fear and misery Katherine was sure that the minute

Fintan and Tara were officially pals they'd abandon her. With a rigid smile on her face, she yearned for reassurance from Tara, but didn't know how to ask. 'You and me will always be best friends,' Tara had a murky inkling of Katherine's distress, 'but we can't leave poor Fintan on his own.'

'Poor Fintan, my foot,' Katherine mouthed, with silent sarcasm. But to her surprise, she and Fintan hit it off like a house on fire. So well that Tara almost felt left out.

Of course, both Katherine and Fintan had been brought up without a father – Fintan's had died when he was six months old. And Fintan loved the way Katherine looked as though butter wouldn't melt in her mouth yet could back-answer with the best. He had great plans to make her over as Holly Golightly in *Breakfast at Tiffany's*. 'You've that small, neat Audrey Hepburn look about you,' he told her. Tara tried to quell her envy.

While Katherine was a bit doubtful at talk of wide-brimmed hats and Givenchy gowns, she was giddy with relief that Fintan approved of her. Now she had not just one friend but two!

Although her friendship with Fintan didn't go down so well with her granny. 'Who were you out with?' Agnes asked, one evening in early spring, when Katherine came in, her cheeks red with the cold.

'Tara, and Fintan O'Grady,' she said, unable to keep a hint of pride out of her voice.

'Fintan O'Grady,' said Agnes. 'Tell me now, why does he dress up in JaneAnn's dressing gown?'

'Because he's gay,' Katherine explained.

'Gay!' Agnes objected angrily. 'Well, how do you like that? Gay, no less.'

Katherine and Delia were astonished because Agnes was usually such an easygoing old woman.

'I'll give him gay where he'll feel it,' she threatened.

Delia was appalled and already planning a Cake Sale Against Homophobia. 'Mama . . . I mean Agnes, you've got to learn not to be so bigoted. Fintan's entitled to express his sexual preferences . . .'

'I'm not talking about his sexual preferences,' Agnes exploded. 'I couldn't give a fiddler's about his sexual preferences. For all I care he can do it with the hens and good luck to him! They might lay better. I'm talking about "gay". It used to be such a lovely word.' Her face took on a dreamy expression. 'When people visited my mother, God be good to her, she'd be sitting there in the corner by the fire and they'd say to her, "Wisha, Maudie, but you're right gay. As gay as the feather of a hearse." Meaning she was looking well and happy, like. But you couldn't say that now, of course, you'd be shot!'

However, Tara's mother, Fidelma, was charmed by Fintan. When he arrived with Tara and Katherine after school, he'd sit on the settle-bed, girlishly tuck his legs up under him, smoke Woodbines through an ebony cigarette holder and discuss films with her. While Tara's three younger brothers, Michael, Gerard and Kieran, stuck their heads into the room and sniggered at the strange, exotic creature, Fidelma and Fintan held forth on *Gentlemen Prefer Blondes* and *La Dolce Vita* and other films that Fidelma had seen when she worked in Limerick, before she married Frank and moved home to Knockavoy.

Tara's brain usually glazed over during the interminable reminiscences, but it was worth it to see her father wigging out. She loved it when he came into the room and hissed furiously at Fidelma, 'Is that gombeen allowed to smoke? I'm sure JaneAnn O'Grady doesn't let him.'

And she loved it even more when Fidelma replied equably,

'I'd say there isn't much that JaneAnn O'Grady doesn't let him do.'

Frank Butler was a very bad-tempered man. He was an autocrat and a patriarch and everyone was afraid of him. Nothing made him happy. He and his brother had a tiny business where they worked cutting and selling turf. With the result that whenever there was a mild winter, and everyone else was thanking God for it, Frank Butler was railing against it in fury. 'Lovely day,' he mimicked, when he overheard his wife talking to someone about the unusually clement elements. 'Lovely day. Well, you wouldn't think it was so fecking lovely if you saw our order book.'

'I still have the geese and the turkeys,' Fidelma soothed him.

'That's your money,' he pointed out, wildly. 'That's supposed to be your money. Have you any sewing jobs?'

'A few,' Fidelma said mildly.

'What?' Frank demanded. 'Who? It'd be a godsend if you could get something big like a curtains job for the hotel.'

'It would,' Fidelma agreed. She didn't want to tell him about Fintan arriving at the house, with a bolt of shiny magenta lining under his arm and a request that Fidelma sew him a kind of cloak-type effort, to a pattern he'd drawn up himself.

Despite his phenomenal unpleasantness, Katherine secretly idolized Frank Butler. With all his rules and intractability he was a man after her own heart. Frank Butler was particularly non-negotiable on the question of homework. One of Katherine's biggest worries about losing Tara was that she wouldn't be able to go to Butler's every afternoon after school to bask in the atmosphere of tension.

She often lay awake at night, *dreaming* of a father shouting at her for not having done her exercise. Of a patriarch questioning her on her homework every evening: 'How many yards to a mile?', 'What year was the proclamation of the Republic?', 'What's the capital of Lima?' Although she had been very embarrassed for Mr Butler when Tara had finally managed to get him to understand that Lima couldn't have a capital because it *was* a capital.

Delia, Katherine's mother, defiantly refused to check that Katherine had done her homework. 'That's no way to teach children,' she said repeatedly. 'Instilling fear and trepidation into them, getting them to parrot stuff by rote. If they're interested in something they'll learn it, and if they're not interested, then there's no point in forcing them.'

Katherine begged her to reconsider.

15

Something roused Lorcan Larkin from a deep sleep. Automatically, he did the first thing he did every morning as soon as he woke up – he grabbed his penis to make sure it was still attached.

It was, and he sank back with familiar relief.

The room was in darkness, and his body was telling him it was the middle of the night. What had woken him up?

There was no one he could ask because, unusually for Lorcan, he was in bed alone.

On Friday night, when he'd turned up at Amy's birthday party so late that almost everyone else had gone home, she'd been hysterical with fury. He'd grinned, given her his what-can-I-say? shrug, said, 'I'm starving,' and shoved one of the few remaining by now curling-at-the-edges sandwiches into his perfect mouth. To his surprise she'd had the temerity to screech at him to put it down, that he'd got all he'd ever be getting from her, that she'd never been so humiliated and that she never wanted to see him again.

'And you,' she shrieked, turning her attention to Benjy, who'd been sampling the remains of a tray of canapés, 'leave my food alone and get the fuck out!' Benjy paused, a mini-quiche the size of a tenpence piece hovering three inches from his mouth. Should he risk it? Perhaps not, he thought, on reflection. Amy wasn't in her right mind, there was no knowing what she might do.

'Sure, if that's what you want.' Lorcan gave her a huge, white-toothed smile. He was very angry, but he was damned if he was going to show it.

'Will we be off?' he asked Benjy, making it sound as if he was choosing to leave. Benjy stared like a rabbit at Lorcan, not knowing the right answer. He tried a very tentative nod. Luckily that was the correct response.

'Come on,' said Lorcan, and marched through the room, grinding torn streamers into the carpet, kicking withered-looking balloons out of the way, Benjy scurrying behind him.

Of course, a few hours later Amy had changed her mind and when Lorcan woke up on Saturday morning his answering-machine was full of ever-more-desperate messages from her.

'I'm sorry.'

'I'm *so* sorry.'

'*Please* call me.'

'Where are you?'

'Please, please call me!'

'Listen to this,' he said scornfully to Benjy, who'd slept on the couch. 'Grovel, girl, grovel!'

Benjy, who'd spent the night two feet from the phone and answering-machine, had already heard every one of Amy's messages. 'Are you going to call her?' he asked, uncomfortable with the agony in Amy's voice.

Lorcan looked as disgusted as if Benjy had just asked him to eat his own spleen. 'Ring her? After what she did to me?'

'It was her birthday,' Benjy pointed out, in a small voice. 'You were very late.'

'Whose goddamn side are you on?' Lorcan asked coldly, and Benjy shut up.

The messages continued over the next thirty-six hours and,

on Sunday night, while Lorcan deep-conditioned his hair, Amy rang repeatedly. Sometimes she hung up and sometimes she left a message. 'If you're there, please pick up the phone,' she begged, trying to tamp down her hysteria. 'You must have got my messages by now. And if you haven't, where are you?'

Lorcan heard the terror in her voice and he nodded in grim satisfaction. That would teach her to shout at him in front of everyone. To attack him and tell him it was over. To upset him so much that he couldn't let Benjy go home until Sunday afternoon.

Over the weekend his anger had become even more defensive and his position as the wronged party got further and further entrenched. By the time he went to bed on Sunday night he felt like the most maligned person in the universe. Wrapped in a pink towel and a cocoon of sanctimonious self-righteousness, he slept deeply.

But now he was awake.

He looked at his alarm clock: it was ten past four. What had woken him? It certainly wasn't the guilty whisperings of his conscience. Because he hadn't got one.

As he lay in the dark, holding on to his penis, he was surprised to hear his doorbell ring. It was then that he realized it had already rung a few minutes before. That was what had woken him up.

Who could it be? Let's see, he thought sarcastically, might it be Amy? Or on the other hand, of course, it might be Amy. It wouldn't be the first time a woman had arrived in person in the middle of the night, deranged and demented from him refusing to take her calls. Well, she could wait, Lorcan decided. Why should he put her out of her misery? She'd told him she never wanted to see him again. She'd *hurt* him.

But the doorbell rang again and Lorcan began to think about answering it. She was obviously sorry and maybe she'd suffered enough. When it rang once more he got up.

To his surprise, he could hear strange sounds outside his front door, on the communal landing. Voices. In the plural. At least one of them was male, so it wasn't just Amy talking to herself, insane with heartbreak. Then he heard a burst of static, as if a pizza-delivery person or a taxi-driver was outside. Then more voices, tinny and muffled. Very weird.

Lorcan jumped as a very sharp ratatat-tat hammered on his front door. An officious, imperious ratatat-tat, not the apologetic knuckle-grazing of a broken woman.

'Mr Larkin,' a man's voice commanded. 'Can you hear me? Can you open this door?' Another burst of static followed.

'He doesn't appear to be responding,' the voice said.

'We'd better go in,' replied a woman's voice. Not Amy's.

Lorcan was more intrigued than frightened. Not frightened at all. If they were trying to rob him they were making an awful job of the discretion that was the hallmark of a good burglar.

'We'll try to remove the lock,' the man's voice said.

You will in your eye, Lorcan thought in alarm. Locks cost lots of money. He marched to the door and flung it wide.

To their great consternation, Constable Nigel Dickson and Constable Linda Miles came face to face with a very large, very annoyed, very naked man wearing a pink towel around his head and holding tightly on to his penis.

'Er, Mr Larkin, sir?' Constable Dickson asked, when he'd recovered his aplomb.

'Who wants to know?' Lorcan replied cagily, taking in the burly twosome, the uniforms, the hats, the walkie-talkies, the hefty truncheons, the fluorescent overjackets, the black and white squares on everything.

'A Mr Lorcan Larkin has been reported missing by a Ms Amy . . . What's her second name?' he asked his colleague.

But Constable Linda Miles wasn't really paying attention. She couldn't take her eyes off Lorcan. She'd never seen ginger pubes before. Although, she thought, these weren't so much ginger, as a beautiful, reddy-gold colour . . .

'A Ms Amy Jones.' Nigel had to consult his notebook as it became clear his colleague couldn't tear her eyes away from Lorcan's pubic area. 'She was concerned when you didn't answer her telephone calls, even though she could see lights on in your flat. She feared that you may have injured yourself, either accidentally or . . . deliberately.' His voice faded away when he saw the fury on Lorcan's face.

'Where is she?' Lorcan hissed, letting go of his willy.

'In the squad car.' Nigel swallowed anxiously. Maybe it was one of those ones that didn't get much bigger when they were erect. 'We said we'd radio her when we'd gained entrance.'

'Before you arrest her for wasting police time,' Lorcan menaced, 'tell her I've got an audition tomorrow. If I don't get the part, it'll be her fault.'

Lorcan slammed the door in their faces and Linda narrowed her eyes at Nigel. 'You know, I suspected that woman was a time-waster.'

'You fancied him,' Nigel threw jealously at Linda.

'Nige, I never!' she exclaimed, defensively.

'You did, I saw you looking at his todger. I bet you wish mine was as big as his.'

'Nige, I never!'

Constable Nigel Dickson and Constable Linda Miles had

116

been having an affair for the previous four and a half months. This was their first row.

'Anyway,' Nigel said, a mite tearfully, 'he's a Paddy, probably in the IRA.'

'Oooh, was he Irish, Nige?' Linda said, in disappointment. 'I don't like the Irish.'

Lorcan slammed the door and returned to bed. Not as angry as he'd pretended to be. Very relieved, actually. For one heart-stopping moment he'd thought his past had finally run him to ground and that he was going to be arrested. For one of those ridiculous crimes like having sex with a minor.

Instead a woman had used the boys in blue in a desperate attempt to make him talk to her. It was a first and he had to admit he was flattered.

16

On Monday morning when Tara woke up she was starving. But she was filled with a great determination not to eat. Hunger is my friend, she repeated over and over again as she lay in bed and drank the black coffee Thomas had left for her. Hunger is my very best pal.

She'd had a bad night's sleep, jerking awake at some godforsaken hour, seized with terrible fear. What if Thomas stopped loving her and dumped her? What if he'd realized on Saturday night that he didn't want to be with her any more? What would become of her? Now that she was thirty-one she *really* didn't have any time left to start again. She'd thought it was bad when Alasdair gave her the slip. But at only twenty-nine, she hadn't known how lucky she was. Single men in their thirties were like gold-dust – it could take her *years* to meet someone else. Then, if she ever did, she'd have to bide her time and pretend she wasn't serious for at least twelve months. By which time she could be thirty-four or thirty-five. Oh, God! That was ancient. When Tara began to get dressed, she was glad Thomas had already left for work. Watching her struggling into clothes that were too small for her would make him cross again. Despite the cold morning, she was sweating, her hands slipping as she tried to do up the button on her skirt.

She'd been wearing a size fourteen for some time now, but it was only ever meant to be a temporary measure, until she'd lost weight and gone back to being a size twelve. Mind you, wearing a size twelve was only meant to have been a temporary measure also, until she slimmed down and went back to her correct weight, her true size, her spiritual home of size ten. But now, with the waistband of her skirt so tight it was crushing her internal organs, she reluctantly began to face the fact that maybe she'd better buy some size sixteens. Just so she could breathe. It wouldn't be a long-term measure, of course. Only until she'd lost a bit of weight, and then she'd be back to size fourteen.

But size *sixteen*, she thought, appalled at how far she'd come. Size *sixteen*. After that came size eighteen, and then size twenty. Where would it all end?

By the time she'd got her jacket buttoned, the sweat was pouring off her and she was exhausted enough to go back to bed. She hated her body, how she hated it. Having to lug all that lard around with her, she felt as though it didn't belong to her.

It *didn't* belong to her, she reminded herself. It was simply an uninvited visitor that had overstayed its welcome. Its days were numbered.

She forced herself to look in the mirror before she left. She looked awful, she conceded miserably. Her smart jacket was stretched and splayed across her midriff, the round ball of her belly poking out where the jacket's two seams no longer met.

I'm fat, she realized, in cold horror. I'm actually officially fat. I'm no longer just slightly overweight or pleasantly plump or a bit tubby. I'm fat. The real thing.

She felt herself hurtling headlong towards utter marginalization. I won't be able to go upstairs on buses. I'll have to pay excess baggage on planes, just for my bottom. Small boys will throw stones at me. I'll break people's chairs when I go to their house for dinner. I'll be demoted because everyone knows that fat people can't do their job as well as skinny people. Once I'm in my car I won't be able to get out again without a winch. People will think I'm a failure because superfluous weight is a sure sign of terrible unhappiness. I'll have to lie and say I have trouble with my glands.

I'm not worthy to be out in the world, she told herself. I'm so ashamed of myself.

She caught lean, slinky, I-can-eat-what-I-want-and-never-put-on-an-ounce Beryl smirking at her and yearned to give her a kick. Then, very reluctantly, Tara left the flat. So great was her self-loathing, she half expected people to hoot their horns and shout, 'Look at the fat cow,' as she walked to her car. It was pouring with rain, and for that Tara gave thanks. People looked at each other less in wet weather. Tara's car was a bright orange, noisy, backfiring, second-hand Volkswagen. It was a mobile skip, which stank of cigarette smoke and had tapes and cassette cases spilt all over the floor. The seats were strewn with maps, old newspapers, sweet wrappers, empty drink cans and a pair of knickers, which she used when the window steamed up.

Her windscreen wipers were broken so at every red light she had to jump out of the car and wipe the front window with a piece of scrunched-up newspaper, at the same time as fighting off aggressive youths armed with cloths and buckets of soapy water who were intent on cleaning her windscreen and extracting a pound for their trouble. The drive from the Holloway Road to Hammersmith was a long one and by the time she got to work she was soaked and exhausted, having shouted the word, 'No!' twenty-eight times en route and 'Go away, I've no change,' eleven times.

When she arrived at her small open-plan office only Ravi was there. As usual he was eating. 'Morning, Tara,' he brayed, in his cut-glass accent. 'Care for some double-chocolate cheesecake? Twenty-seven grams of fat in every slice. Superb!'

'How could you at this hour of the morning?' Tara asked. She liked to pretend that she had an appetite like a normal person's.

'Up at five,' he bellowed. 'Rowed twenty miles. Bloody starving!'

Ravi did huge amounts of exercise. As well as belonging to a rowing team, he went to the gym at least four times a week and wouldn't leave until he'd been told by the computerized machines that he'd burned off a thousand calories. His prodigious exercising was matched only by his prodigious eating. Not a morning passed that he didn't arrive at the office weighed down with Marks and Spencer bags full of goodies. 'Perhaps you'd like to keep the wrapper and lick it later?' He waved a wedge-shaped piece of plastic, which she accepted. 'How's the new lipstick Fintan gave you? Do the trick?'

'No, Ravi, another disappointment.'

'Aw, boo. So the search continues.'

'Certainly does.'

'See Real TV on Friday night? Bloke goes up in a hot-air balloon, comes down through a skylight into a bathroom. Breaks his leg, nearly bloody drowns. Sooo-perb!'

'Please stop. Have you updated the football-league stuff?' Tara switched on her PC.

'Absolutely.' Ravi nodded, letting a thick lock of glossy black hair fall across his forehead. He looked like an Indian version of Elvis.

Ravi organized a football league for the employees of GK

Software. At the start of the football season each person predicted where they thought all the teams in the Premiership were going to be placed. After each weekend, Ravi updated the results, so everyone could keep an eye on their interim progress. People had been overheard saying that it was the only thing that got them out of bed on a Monday morning.

People began to drift in. Evelyn and Teddy arrived. Evelyn and Teddy were married. They lived together, drove to work together, worked side by side, ate lunch together and went home together. 'Morning,' they said, simultaneously.

'Have you . . . ?' Evelyn asked Ravi.

'Of course.' He smirked.

Evelyn and Teddy both keyed frantically until they found the updated table.

Vinnie, Tara's boss, arrived, a nice man in his forties, with four young children and a receding hairline. He entertained dreams of being a dynamic businessman who barked things like, 'I've put my cock on the block on this one, lads,' but whenever he tried, everyone just laughed at him and patted his fast-disappearing hair. 'Morning all,' he called. 'Good weekend?'

'No,' everyone replied automatically.

'Have you updated the . . . ?' he anxiously asked Ravi, and when the answer was in the affirmative, raced to his terminal and switched it on.

Despite working in a computer company, Tara's colleagues weren't geeks. They were normal people whose conversation in the office mostly revolved around holidays and food. Just as it should.

Tara's phone rang. It was Thomas. Her heart leapt, half with anxiety, half with joy. But he didn't want to talk to her, he said, more brusquely than Tara considered necessary. He was simply reminding her to pay the cable-television bill. *Don't take it personally*, she tried to soothe herself. *It's just his way.*

On Monday lunchtimes, it was traditional for everyone from Tara's section to go to the Italian greasy-spoon caff. It was a nod to the weekend, an assumption that everyone was nursing a hangover. From ten thirty onwards, as soon as the breakfast bacon sandwiches were out of the way, people began to plan what they'd have at the greasy.

'Fried bread, scrambled eggs, mushrooms, tomatoes, sausages, a KitKat and a glass of Coke,' Teddy announced, without looking up from his screen.

'Chips, two fried eggs, bacon, beans, a slice of bread and butter and an Aqua Libra,' Vinnie replied, also remaining glued to his screen.

'Toast, two sausages, a cheese and onion omelette, a fudge finger and a cup of tea with three sugars,' came slim Cheryl's voice from behind a partition. Slim Cheryl had been on Vinnie's team for over a year, and although she'd been moved to Jessica's team, she never broke the link with Vinnie.

'Four sausages, four fried eggs, mushrooms, tomatoes, bacon, a double portion of chips, six slices of bread and butter and a Lucozade Sport,' Ravi said.

At twelve thirty, regular as clockwork, everyone always surrendered to their screensavers, put on their coats and marched as a single body to Cafolla's. One person had to stay behind to man the help-desk and field calls from hysterical customers whose entire system had just crashed. The position rotated and this Monday Sleepy Steve was the help-desk misfortunate. (Known as Sleepy Steve for his habit of getting drunk after work, falling asleep on the train home to Watford and waking up at the end of the line in Birmingham.) Hollow-eyed, he watched the exodus, and asked in a little voice if someone would fetch him a sandwich.

'Come on, Tara,' Ravi ordered, loud as a sergeant-major. 'Off we go!'

'I don't think I should go.'

'Ah, boo,' Ravi said, in disappointment. 'Your bloody diet? You daft girl. OK, carry on without me, men, I'm staying behind with Tara.'

Tara felt guilty. Ravi mightn't have been the sharpest knife in the drawer, but he had a heart of gold. It wasn't fair to deprive him of his mammoth fried lunch.

Besides, she hadn't eaten a thing since she woke up, and all she'd planned for dinner was a big plate of vegetables. And let's not forget, she reminded herself, that you're doing a step class after work, you'll faint if you don't eat something now. 'It's all right,' she told Ravi. 'I'll come.'

Sitting squashed into a plastic booth, before a Formica table, in a clattery, steam-filled caff, eating a plate of chips and beans, drinking strong tea from a thick white cup, always cheered Tara up. But not today. Thomas had been cold and impatient on the phone and the feeling she was carrying around was impending doom revisited.

After the fry-up it was customary for the menfolk to retire to the pub next door for a quick pint and for the ladies to remain behind to have a bun. Mr Cafolla took the confectionery orders as he cleared away the greasy plates.

Evelyn ordered an apple slice. 'Apple-a slice,' Mr Cafolla called behind the counter to his wife.

Slim Cheryl asked for a fudge finger. 'Fudge-a finger,' Mr Cafolla called.

'And you, hyong lie-dee,' he asked Tara, when it looked like she wasn't going to order anything, 'what would-a you-a like-a? Custard-a pie?'

She winced. Oh, the bastard. He certainly knew her weak spot. She shouldn't. She'd never be skinny if she ate custard-a pies. But there was no way she couldn't.

As she gazed at the bright yellow swirl of custard, so thick it could stand by itself, an appetizing sprinkling of nutmeg peppering its glossy surface, sitting in its little circle of pastry, all supported by its tinfoil container, she knew true bliss for a moment. Seconds later, when the pie was a mere memory, guilt arrived. How she hated herself for her weakness. Briefly she thought about asking Mr Cafolla for the key to the bathroom and trying to make herself puke, but whenever she'd tried it in the past it just hadn't been a success. Hardly worth the effort. She had no idea how bulimics managed it. She took her hat off to them. Maybe there was some trick of the trade that she didn't know about.

17

Back at work, Tara nipped into the ladies' for a quick fag. There she bumped into Amy Jones, who worked on the floor above her, in Procurements. They'd only been on nodding terms with each other until the previous Friday lunchtime, when they'd discovered they shared a birthday. They'd both been in the pub, celebrating with their respective departments. And although the two groups hadn't known each other well enough to merge, they'd acknowledged each other and the synchronicity of the occasion with smiles, nods and the raising of pints in each other's direction.

On Friday, with four gin and tonics under her belt, Tara had thought Amy seemed very nice. But now, as Tara inhaled so hard her ears almost met in the middle, she watched Amy glide a comb through her long, strawberry-blonde, ringlety hair and decided that she hated her. Maybe she was a good person, but with all that gorgeous hair and tall, slender beauty, she couldn't have known a day's hardship in her life, ever. How could two people who shared the same birthdate look so different? Explain *that*, Mystic Meg.

'Nice birthday?' Tara politely asked Amy. She thought she'd better, otherwise Amy might guess Tara hated her for being so thin and for her hair being in such even ringlets.

'Um, OK,' said Amy, with a wobbly smile. She looked very ropy, obviously had a high old time of it over the weekend,

Tara reckoned. 'The only thing was,' Amy said, her voice becoming thin and high, 'I . . . er . . . had a row with my boyfriend and ended up . . . like . . . getting arrested.'

Tears began to cascade down Amy's perfect white skin, as she spilled out the whole story of the birthday party; the huge embarrassment of her boyfriend's non-arrival, his eventual appearance, the sandwich-eating, the order to leave, the hellish hours that followed, the myriad phonecalls, the longest Saturday and Sunday in history, the hysterical desperation, the call to the police . . . Tara rearranged her shocked expression and made the appropriate comforting platitudes, like 'It was only a row,' and 'You know what men are like, just give him time to get over his bad mood,' and 'Maybe you should leave him alone for a couple of days,' and 'Yes, I know how hard it is to do that, really I do,' and 'You'll look back on this and the pair of you will laugh,' and 'You know, this'll probably make the two of you closer,' and 'Men, can't live with them!' and 'Er, sorry for asking, but what exactly is police bail, just out of curiosity?'

Back in the office, Tara itched to ring Thomas. Usually she felt no need to call him at work, especially as it involved getting him out of a classroom. Besides, as her office was open-plan, it was impossible to have an intimate phone conversation – Ravi, in particular, took great interest in Tara's life. But because she was afraid something was out of kilter with herself and Thomas, she craved reassurance. She wanted to know if she'd imagined his hostility on the phone this morning.

However, after she'd steeled herself to make the call, Lulu, the school secretary, wouldn't fetch Thomas. She always acted as if she owned him. 'I'll tell Mr Holmes you called,' she lied.

'Thick tart,' Tara muttered, putting down the phone.

'Who? Lulu?' Ravi bellowed.

'Who else?' said Tara. She spent a short while consoling herself that at least she hadn't set the peelers on Thomas. She shuddered with horror at the thought. He'd never forgive her for that, never. Still upset, she rang Liv for a moan. She got her answering-machine, so tried her mobile.

'Hello,' Liv said.

'It's me. Are you busy?'

'I'm in Hampshire with a terrible woman who wants everything in her house to be gold,' Liv wailed.

'Yuk. Like bathroom taps and door-handles?'

'No, like kitchen units and garden sheds.'

'Oh, no. Anyway, how are you getting on with Lars?'

'Very good.' Liv sounded uncharacteristically optimistic. 'He says he's really going to leave his wife this time.'

'Brilliant!' Tara forced herself to say. She'd believe it when she saw it. She didn't like Lars. Just because he was tall, blond and craggy it didn't give him licence to string Liv along for fifteen months with his spurious talk of wife-leaving. 'When's he going back?' Tara asked.

'Saturday.'

'Right, I'll be round then for the mopping-up operation.'

'I must go,' Liv hissed. 'Midas Woman is returning.'

'Has he left his wife yet?' Ravi asked, when Tara hung up.

'He says he's just about to,' she said, and they rolled their eyes at each other. Next, Tara dialled Fintan's number. Vinnie gave her a sharp look. 'If I don't ring people, I'll e-mail them,' Tara thought it only fair to point out to him.

'Oh, don't do that,' Ravi objected. 'How else will I know what's going on?'

'Just as well you're both good at your jobs,' Vinnie grumbled.

Fintan wasn't in work. Sick, allegedly. Tara knew what was up with him. At twelve o'clock, the night before, as she was leaving Katherine's, Fintan and Sandro had been on their way out. The evening was only beginning for them. 'I'm going to get off my *mong*,' Fintan had declared.

Tara rang his home number.

'Fintan hung over, eh?' Ravi asked.

'I'd stake my granny's life on it,' she replied. The phone rang and rang for ages before Fintan finally answered. 'What's up with you, you piss-head?' Tara asked cheerfully.

'There's something wrong with my neck. I've an enormous lump on it.'

'God, you're so vain.' Tara sighed. 'Everyone gets spots.'

'No, Tara, it isn't a spot. It's a swelling that makes me look like the Elephant Man.'

'I'd an awful turn myself with my Black Death this morning,' Tara empathized. 'The boils!'

'Tara, really,' Fintan insisted. 'I'm serious. I have a lump the size of a melon on my neck.'

'Go on. What kind of lump?'

'The lumpy kind!'

'But it's hardly the size of a melon?' She smiled at how much of a drama queen Fintan was. 'A grape, maybe?'

'No, much bigger. Tara, I swear to you, it genuinely is the size of a melon.'

'What kind of melon? A honeydew? Galia? Cantaloup?'

'OK, maybe not a melon. But a kiwi fruit, certainly.'

'Try putting Savlon on it.'

'Savlon! It's drugs I need.'

'You'd better go to the doctor, so.'

'Oh, no,' he said sarcastically. 'I just thought I'd lie around here waiting for my neck to return to its correct size of its own free will.

'I've an appointment for this evening,' he added.

He sounded upset, and she half regretted her jokey response. 'Do you want me to come with you?' Then she muttered, close to the phone, 'Vinnie'll let me off if I say I've my period, that always embarrasses him. Some months I have two or three and he's too shy to mention it.'

'Ah, no, I'll be grand.'

'What time will you be home?'

'I don't know how long it'll take, but say about eight to be on the safe side.'

'OK, I'll give you a shout then. Good luck, but I'm sure it's nothing.'

As soon as she hung up, Ravi gasped eagerly, 'What's happened to Fintan?'

'Swollen glands or something.' Tara shrugged. 'He's such a hypochondriac.'

Next she rang Katherine, but she wasn't back from lunch yet. At three thirty? Tara thought. That's not like Miss Diligent.

'Right, Vinnie, I've rung everyone.'

But as Tara settled back to work, she found herself thinking about Fintan. What if he wasn't just being a drama queen attention-seeker? What if there really was something wrong with him? Something serious? That was the problem whenever a gay friend became sick. The A-word always cropped up. Then she felt uncomfortable with her train of thought – did she think gay people and Aids were uniquely linked?

Her worry about Fintan moved smoothly on to worry about Thomas. What was the weirdness that was hanging between them? Perhaps it was only in her head. But she was brought back relentlessly to what he'd said on Saturday night and couldn't decide whether she should be freaking out with worry or if she was better off ignoring it in the hope that it would go away.

She couldn't do any work, so at four o'clock she prepared to leave.

'Excuse me, where are you going?' Ravi asked suspiciously.

'Thought I'd try a soupçon of retail therapy.'

'No!' Ravi tried to block her path, as instructed. 'You must stop spending money.'

'Thank you, Ravi.' Tara tried to skirt past him. 'I appreciate your vigilance but I don't *want* to be stopped today.'

'You said even if you begged I was to take no notice.' Ravi squared up to her fiercely.

Tara made a leap to the side of her desk to try and get through the gap there, but quick-as-a-flash Ravi had her marked. There was a brief skirmish.

'Vinnie, call him off!'

'He's only doing as you asked.' Vinnie shrugged wearily. No wonder he was losing his hair.

They faced each other – Ravi bent at the knees, his many muscles tensed and ready for action, his hands crossed, poised to do a kung-fu chop. Tara bitterly regretted ever enlisting his help. 'Can we start tomorrow?' she wheedled. 'Please?'

In disappointment, Ravi dropped his *en-garde* stance. 'Off you go, then.'

So Tara went shopping and tried to pretend that she wasn't starving. She had high hopes that looking at clothes would take her mind off things, but found she couldn't wrap her head around the idea of being size sixteen. Shopping for clothes was a pleasure that no longer belonged to her; instead it had become an exercise in damage limitation.

There were so many clothes that she was automatically disqualified from; sleeveless tops, fitted macs, knitted dresses, anything involving jersey, Lycra, pleats or no bra. She couldn't *tell* you the last time she'd worn trousers.

The only consolation lay in looking at sexy, funky shoes. Shoes were the fat woman's friend. Shoes still looked beautiful when all else had gone to hell in a handcart.

Hair mascara also struck her as a good idea – she always had an eye out for diversionary tactics. Interesting jewellery, mad handbags and technicolour make-up were all part of the look-over-there factor. A blue fringe was as good as anything to distract people from her rotund belly.

By the time she'd bought a strawberry-flavoured tree air-freshener for the car, a pair of high black dolly shoes, blue hair mascara, purple hair mascara and the knitting pattern, knitting needles and wool for Thomas's jumper, she'd missed her step class.

She pretended she felt let down. She had the option of going circuit training, but that was always full of beefy men doing one-handed press-ups and grunting a lot. She couldn't take it, not in a pink leotard. I'll start tomorrow, she vowed.

18

On the way home, on impulse, she called in on Katherine. She hadn't been able to get her on the phone all afternoon and she felt like having a chat with her.

Visiting Katherine unexpectedly wasn't something she normally did. They'd been affected by the ethos in London, where it was considered the height of rudeness to drop in on someone unannounced. The words, 'I was just passing . . .' were considered to be as much of a social gaffe as 'You've a really big nose.' Many Londoners, used to being able to screen their telephone calls with the aid of an answering-machine, were sent into a flat spin by an unexpected ring on their bell. A person! In the flesh! On their doorstep!

If they were sure it wasn't the postman, Londoners often simply refused to answer the door. The usual drill was to flatten themselves against the wall and try to peek out the window, like someone in a police shoot-out. Not with the idea of letting anyone in, but simply to get some notion of who this social deviant was and cross them off their Christmas card list forthwith.

Katherine was having a shower, but Tara thought she was being ignored because she hadn't made the requisite appointment. She pulled out her mobile to ring Katherine and order her to open the door but she'd forgotten to charge the battery.

'It's me,' Tara called, stepping back from the intercom and

standing in the tiny front garden, looking up at Katherine's front window.

'Let me in.

'You hairy-arsed eejit,' she yelled in frustration. 'I know you're up there, I can see the light.'

'Hello,' said a voice. 'Looking for Katherine?'

Tara turned around and someone, who must have been poor Roger, was advancing towards the front door with a key.

'Yes.' Tara could barely look at him, considering the other occasions they'd had contact – Roger banging his ceiling with a broom handle and Tara screeching drunkenly, 'Lighten up, would you, you young fogey?'

'Thanks,' Tara gasped to Roger, running away from him and up the stairs to Katherine's. While Tara pounded with her fist and shouted, 'Let me in!' Katherine calmly opened the door. She was wearing a short, silky white nightdress and a longer, matching robe, which swung open, showing off her lean little legs. She radiated feel-goodness, but Tara was too agitated to notice.

'Hello.' Katherine treated her to a smile. 'How did you get up here?'

'Roger the codger let me in.'

'Poor Roger,' Katherine said. 'I must apologize to him some-time for all the noise. What's wrong? Why were you trying to batter the door down?'

'I thought you were ignoring me.'

'Why would I do that?' Katherine asked, with another wide smile. Katherine had lovely feet. Small and dainty, her toenails painted iridescent. Although why she went to the fuss of painting her toenails was beyond Tara. She wouldn't bother her barney if she didn't have a boyfriend. In fact, even when she *did* have a boyfriend!

Tara found a strange comfort in watching Katherine's pretty little feet move nimbly about the thick carpet as she led Tara into the living room and asked her if she'd like a cheese sandwich.

'Get thee behind me, Satan,' Tara said. 'I'll just have a cup of tea. Even though I could eat a nun's arse through a convent gate, I beg of you, don't give me any food.'

She was safe with Katherine. There was scant danger she'd be planning to have a high-calorie, high-fat meal, which Tara would be forced to join in with. Most nights if you asked Katherine what she was going to have for her dinner, she'd say vaguely, 'I don't know, toast or something.' Whereas Tara would have known since the previous Wednesday.

'I'll boil the kettle,' Katherine said.

The bag of Hula Hoops on the shelf in the living room had been there from the night before. Tara distinctly remembered seeing it. How could Katherine have left all those lovely Hula Hoops there overnight without eating them? She wouldn't have got a wink of sleep herself. As it was, she was going to eat them now. Being face to face with food melted her resolve. Besides, she'd missed her exercise class, the damage was already done. She launched herself on the bag just as Katherine came back.

'No,' Katherine yelled, and Tara jumped.

'Put. The Hula Hoops. Down,' Katherine bellowed across the room. She cupped her hands to form a megaphone. 'I repeat. Put. The Hula Hoops. Down.'

Tara froze, taken aback by Katherine's uncharacteristic rowdiness.

'Down,' boomed Katherine. 'On the floor. Slowly now. Don't try anything funny.'

Tara found herself placing the red bag carefully on the ground beside her feet. Katherine isn't normally like this, she thought, in confusion.

'OK,' said Katherine. 'Place your hands on your head.'

Tara obeyed.

'Now kick the Hula Hoops over to me.'

The red Cellophane pack skittered across the carpet and Katherine grabbed it when it arrived, a huge grin on her face.

'Thanks,' Tara said, as they both laughed – Tara mildly hysterically and Katherine brimming over with *joie de vivre*. 'That was a close call.'

'You shouldn't be buying these things if you're worried about your weight,' Katherine scolded good-humouredly.

'I didn't. They're yours. How come you don't see these things?' Tara moaned. 'The minute I walked in the bag started to glow like a beacon. Demanding my attention. Parading itself in front of me. Cavorting licentiously. If it wore clothes it would have taken them off . . .'

Katherine laughed and Tara noticed vaguely that she was looking extraordinarily well.

'I bought the wool for Thomas's jumper,' she announced.

'Hot news.'

'It is, actually. It's me taking control of my life. Knitting, dieting and not spending money. The new me.' Tara drew a mental veil over the thirty-five-minute-old shoes that were almost throbbing with illicitness on the back seat of her car. 'So where were you today? I rang you at half three and you were still at lunch.'

Katherine didn't answer.

'Where were you?' Tara repeated.

'Hmmmm? Sorry?' Katherine asked dreamily.

What the hell is up with her? Tara wondered. Something was different. A glitteriness about the eyes, a knowingness about the mouth. She was giving off suppressed-excitement vibes. 'For your long lunch, where were you . . . ?' Tara paused and said falteringly, 'Are you listening to me?'

'Yes,' Katherine declared unconvincingly.

Tara looked at her again. Her skin was flushed and peachy-looking and she had that cocooned air of someone with a pleasant secret. 'You haven't been . . . have you . . . You've been having sex with someone, haven't you?' Tara demanded.

'I have not!'

'Well, there's something doing you good. Do you fancy someone?'

'No.'

'Does someone fancy you?'

'No,' Katherine said, but Tara had picked up on the tiniest little hesitation.

'Aha,' she sang. 'Ahaaaaa. Someone is after you, who is he? Tell me.'

'There's nothing to tell,' Katherine said stiffly.

Tara was excited. Glad that something was going right for one of them. 'I bet he's magnificent,' Tara urged. 'Your fellas always are.'

On the rare occasions that Katherine had a boyfriend, they were usually extraordinarily beautiful. Total hunks. Real stunners. Way out of Tara's league. Mind you, they never lasted long, but however.

'It has to be someone at your work,' Tara surmised. 'Where else would you get to meet a man?'

'Behave,' Katherine said.

'What's up with you? What's wrong with fancying someone?'

'I don't.'

'Well, what's wrong with someone fancying you?'

Katherine didn't reply. But all her glow had faded and she now wore a face that would stop a clock.

'Katherine,' Tara said gently, 'I know we've had fights about this before, but being in love is nice, it's a good thing. And I know you don't like to relinquish your famous control, I know you don't like being vulnerable, but sometimes you've got to take a chance.'

'Relationships are misery from start to finish,' Katherine said coldly.

'Not at all,' Tara spluttered, and opened her mouth to say, 'I mean, look at me and Thomas, see how unmiserable we are,' then found she couldn't.

'I'm perfectly happy on my own,' Katherine said, her face like stone. 'Being alone doesn't mean lonely.'

'You can't duck and dodge for ever,' Tara said in exasperation. 'Falling in love is part of the human condition. Without it you're only living a half life. Everyone needs a partner, it's a basic human need.'

'It's not a need,' Katherine said. 'It's a want. And what I *want*, more than a person to argue with over who loves who the most, is absence of pain. Falling in love leaves you open, relationships mean pain.'

'Relationships aren't all about pain,' Tara protested, alarmed at Katherine's intransigence. She seemed to have become more entrenched since the last time they'd had this row.

'So relationships aren't all about pain?' Katherine interrupted. 'You're hardly in a position to say that. Look at how miserable you are with that *shithead* Thomas.'

'I'm not miserable,' Tara said stoutly.

Despite her anger, Katherine couldn't help noticing that Tara hadn't denied that Thomas was a shithead. 'Well, if you're happy,' she told Tara, 'then I'm fine as I am.'

They stared, their faces close together, furious looks hopping from one to the other.

'I'm going to ask you one more time,' Tara said menacingly.

'What?' Katherine hissed.

'Is he someone from work?'

Katherine's eyes popped with rage. She opened her mouth to begin a tirade of abuse, working her mouth silently as she tried to find the right words.

'Yes,' she finally said.

19

'Tell me,' Tara ordered.

But actually, Katherine decided, there was very little to tell. First thing that morning Joe Roth had ambled over to her desk, as he had done every morning for the previous twelve working days. Maybe it was the icy-green of the shirt that he'd worn in honour of the tampon-account presentation, or the way his cobalt-blue suit followed the lines of his long, rangy body that made Katherine admit that he was particularly easy on the eye that day. Automatically, her expression became harder, more inscrutable.

'Morning, Katie,' Joe said, with a huge smile that filled his entire face.

'Mr Roth,' Katherine said icily, with Scary Look grade three – she felt there was no need to go to a four or a five because the tone of her voice was a weapon in itself. 'My name is Katherine and I don't answer to abbreviations of it.'

Katherine waited for him to slink away, cowed and beaten. Instead, when he leant on her desk and laughed and laughed, she had an unexpected premonition of disaster. She looked at his teeth, arrayed like white flags on a washing-line, and felt for herself. Be afraid, be very afraid.

He stopped laughing. 'Mr Roth,' he parroted, his brown eyes looking at her with what seemed to be affection. Unmoving, she faced him, doing her best to exude the patience of a very busy but long-sufferingly polite woman. 'Mr Roth,' he repeated. 'I love it. You know, Katherine, you're wonderful. You're simply wonderful.'

When she continued to stare at him stonily, he said, 'I'm sorry if I've offended you by being over-familiar. It'll be Katherine from now on. Unless you'd prefer to be called Ms Casey.'

The fraction of a second that it took before she began to protest was too long. Joe roared with laughter again. 'You would, I see. Very well, Ms Casey it is.'

'Now, Ms Casey,' he said, suddenly businesslike. 'We need to have a meeting about the overspending on the Noritaki beer account. But the Geetex executives are due shortly for the presentation, so why don't we discuss it over lunch?'

'Lunch?' she asked coolly. 'On whose budget?'

Katherine Casey was not to be bought. Though she didn't often get taken out for expensive, trendy lunches in the course of her work – in advertising, the accountant is a Cinderella-figure – she refused to get excited by the thought of a free goat's cheese salad. On the contrary. She was far more likely to lose the run of herself at the thought of a campaign coming in under budget. 'After all,' she continued, 'if it's overspent it's hardly appropriate that we discuss it while spending more money from it.'

'I'll pay for lunch myself,' Joe offered.

Katherine laughed. Joe was not encouraged by its timbre. 'Nice try, Joe,' she said. 'But I see all the expenses claims.'

The account directors never paid for anything. They kept receipts for everything they ever bought and attempted to claim them. Not just restaurant or hotel bills, but everything from shaving foam ('I had a presentation, I had to look my best,') to ties (ditto) to birthday cards to the weekly shop at Tesco.

Once someone had slipped in a receipt for an Armani suit, another time a home Jacuzzi. Katherine had seen it all.

'You have my word,' he insisted. 'I'll pay for lunch out of my own pocket.'

'No.'

'Come on,' he joked. 'Lunch. With Joe Roth. Accept no substitute.'

'No.'

His expression became serious. 'This isn't a come-on. I genuinely need to talk to you about the overspending on the budget.'

'I'm sorry,' Katherine lied. 'I'm up to my eyes doing the end-of-year accounts.' She'd managed to get most of the work done by coming in the previous day, but she wasn't telling him that. 'Why don't you talk to my assistant, Breda?' she suggested. 'She'll be able to help you and I'm sure she'd appreciate a nice lunch.'

'OK,' said Joe desolately and moved away.

It wasn't the kind of thing he would normally do, but he was in despair as he faced into his fourth week of rejection – he went to Fred Franklin to ask him to pull some strings. Fred was in his little glass office with Myles, a young would-be-wide-boy copywriter. 'Fred, I need you to do me a favour,' Joe said, dispensing with pleasantries.

Fred knew what Joe wanted because he'd been watching him talking to Katherine. Fred understood the international language of rejection. In fact, he was *fluent* in it, having had no luck with women until he got promoted at the age of thirty-five. And from Joe's body language while talking to Katherine – the pleading, outstretched arms, the earnest expression on his face – it was clear that he was being given the bum's rush.

'You're a sick man,' said Fred.

'Are you?' asked Myles eagerly. 'How sick? We cater for most tastes here, mate. How about Chain in printing, if it's kinky you're after?'

'Jane?'

'Not Jane. *Chain*. She'll sort you.'

'What's her real name?' Joe asked wearily. He'd inadvertently called several of the women by their nicknames since he'd started at Breen Helmsford. Most of them hadn't seemed to mind, but he had.

'Pauline,' Myles said. 'We call her Chain, because . . . Well, if I say the words "furry handcuffs", I think you'll know what I'm on about . . .'

'He fancies the frigid Paddy,' Fred said bluntly.

'Who? The Ice Queen?' Myles said in astonishment. 'Didn't know you were into masochism.'

'I'm not.'

'You are, mate. You're banging your head against a brick wall.'

Myles had liked Joe Roth, had thought he was a good bloke, who was game for a laugh. He decided he might have to reconsider.

'What about May in the post room?' he suggested, desperate to save Joe. 'You know her – nipples you could hang your coat on, arse you could park a bike in. Up for it? Not half. Just because she's on a care-in-the-community back-to-work scheme, don't let that put you off. Nothing wrong with a bit of mental illness, I always say. Blinding!'

'What's her real name?' Joe asked, feeling depressed.

'May,' Myles answered simply. 'Though I don't know why, there's no *may* about it. She's a definite and no mistake!'

Both Fred and Myles burst into raucous, macho laughter and Joe began to consider a career change. Was the misogyny worse here than at his last employer's, or was he just getting old?

He cut into the hilarity by saying, 'Apart from anything else, I genuinely need to discuss the Noritaki budget with Katherine.' The guffaws came to an abrupt halt.

'Do you think I was born yesterday, son?' Fred scoffed. 'Talk to Heavy Breda about it.'

'Go on,' he encouraged, when Joe didn't reply. 'At least Heavy Breda has tits.'

'Have a word with Katherine,' Joe pressed. 'And I'll owe you.'

Fred considered. Joe was a good-looking lad, he featured a lot in the conversations of the female employees. If he ever got anywhere with the frigid Paddy he'd immediately lose interest in her. By which time, she'd probably be very taken with him. And *that* would be worth seeing.

'All right,' grumbled Fred, heaving himself out of his leather chair.

As Katherine watched Fred lumber across the floor towards her, she knew what was coming. Part of her was deeply contemptuous of Joe for running to the boss. But against her deep instincts of self-preservation, her interest was piqued by how hard he was trying. Although men had tried that hard before and it had still ended in tears . . .

'Now, listen to me,' Fred barked at Katherine. He hated talking to her. She always made him feel as though he'd just crawled out from under a rock. Ever since, three years before, in her first week at Breen Helmsford, when he'd asked her out for a drink, and she'd said, 'I don't go out with married men.'

Though Fred had puffed and blustered and said, 'I'm only being friendly, trying to make you feel welcome,' she'd given him a scathing, knowing look and when he'd finished hating himself, his hatred had come to rest on her.

'You're to go out for lunch with Joe Roth and discuss bloody budgets.'

'Is this an order?'

'Aye, I suppose it is.'

'You're not my superior.' She smiled. Then she said to herself, In fact, you're barely on the same evolutionary scale as me. And turned up the volume on her fake smile.

'I know I'm not your direct boss,' Fred admitted, utterly hating this, 'but the lad is worried about the account. Breda is a grand lass, but Joe wants it straight from the horse's mouth.'

'A double-breasted white suit,' Katherine said thoughtfully, 'with a fur coat thrown over your shoulders, a Panama hat at a rakish angle, and a ho' in a short, tight red dress on each arm.'

'You what?'

'Isn't that what pimps usually look like?'

'A pimp!' Fred was aghast. 'I'm not a pimp! He only wants to have lunch with you.'

The air zinged with animosity, and briefly Katherine wished she was like other people. Why couldn't she be a party animal? Why couldn't she have gone out with Fred Franklin? Even had a quick fling with him? An affair with a married man wouldn't kill her, she knew that only too well. And it would certainly have made her work life a lot easier. She knew she wasn't popular and sometimes it got to her. Like today.

'It's only *lunch*,' Fred repeated loudly, his eyes bulging with outrage. 'To discuss work.'

It *was* only lunch, Katherine acknowledged. 'OK.' She sighed.

Fred lumbered triumphantly back to his goldfish-bowl office. 'You're in, son,' he said to Joe's anxious face. 'Don't forget to come back and tell us all about it.'

The phone on his desk buzzed. 'The Geetex boys have arrived,' he said.

Joe's elation helped him deliver a dazzling presentation to the Geetex deputation. So powerful was his oration that they almost began to believe in the tampons themselves.

'I reckon it's in the bag,' Myles said, as he watched the entranced Geetex men take their leave.

Usually, after a pitch that had gone well, the team went for a lengthy, boozy lunch. However, that day Joe declined to join them. But he urged them to go with his blessing, after first checking which restaurant they were planning to descend on. He intended to take Katherine somewhere far away from it.

In the meantime Katherine had spent the morning knee-deep in accruals. She'd switched her head off from Joe Roth completely. Not for her the spurious excuse about having to go to the bank/stationer's/chemist, followed by a frantic dash to Oxford Street to buy a toothbrush and toothpaste, new lipstick, extra foundation, body spray, sheer stockings, high heels and a new suit with a short skirt in honour of the impromptu breaking of bread.

She refused to let herself get excited. Years of practice ensured that fighting back anticipation wasn't even an effort.

Of course, work was a great help. The exquisitely ordered world of figures, where there were no loose ends. If it balanced you knew you were right; there was simply *no room* for doubt.

And if it didn't balance you went back into it until you found where you'd made your mistake, *and then you fixed it.*

Katherine considered the double-entry system of bookkeeping to be one of the great achievements of mankind, on a par with the invention of the wheel. She wished the world was run along the same principles. Debits on the left, credits on the right, so that you always knew where you stood. Beautiful.

At one o'clock, Joe sheepishly materialized by her desk, his earlier rush of euphoria dissolved by the embarrassment at having pulled rank on her.

'Oh, right, the Noritaki discussion lunch,' she said ungraciously, keeping him hovering awkwardly while she finished a calculation. It could have waited, but why should it?

As she switched off her calculator she found she was dying to go to the loo, but felt too embarrassed to tell him. Perhaps she could go to the ladies' at the restaurant. But why shouldn't she go now? After all, he was nothing to her. In the dim and distant past, when she had fancied someone, it had been a different matter. Any bodily functions would have to be dismissed and denied, written out of the picture. But not with Joe Roth. 'I must go to the ladies' first,' she said, brazen as could be. She deliberately left her handbag on her desk so that he needn't flatter himself that she was going to brush her hair and put on lipstick for him.

20

The restaurant he took her to was within walking distance. Katherine thanked God. The thought of being trapped with him in a taxi made her feel like she was suffocating. Although walking wasn't pleasant either. She felt awkward and couldn't look at him. And they both kept going at different speeds, trying to second-guess the other's natural velocity. Because Joe was very tall, Katherine decided he probably walked at high speed. She didn't want to be found lacking, so she began by racing along. Then she realized she was probably going *too* fast, so she slowed down dramatically. Meanwhile, he'd noticed her decrease in speed and, angry with himself, deduced he'd been forcing her to keep up with his long legs, so he ground almost to a halt. Then Katherine noticed how deliberately slowly he was going, how unnatural it seemed for him, so she revved up again. So did he, thinking he'd slowed down too much for her. And in this miserable, stop-start, jerky fashion, they arrived at the Lemon Capsicum.

It was an expensive, trendy, noisy restaurant, enjoying its fifteen minutes of popularity. With its curved front wall made of glass bricks and its surfeit of blond wood, it wasn't unlike the place Katherine had gone to on Saturday night with Tara. She didn't even have to look at the menu to know what was on it. She'd have staked her life on mahi-mahi appearing somewhere.

Joe had taken the precaution of reserving a booth. Once they were installed the noise lessened and Katherine began to relax. To the point of ordering a glass of wine. 'Don't look at me like that,' she said, patronizingly. 'I may be diligent, but I'm still human.'

'I'm not looking at you "like that",' he said, with one of his sunbeam smiles. 'If you want a glass of wine, you have a glass of wine. Have as many as you like.'

He looked at her with such warm appreciation that she said crisply, 'Let's get down to business. On the Noritaki account, the main areas of expenditure to date have been –'

'Katherine,' he interrupted gently, and the way he said her name – almost sadly – made her want to get up and leave. 'Let's order first.' And suddenly, she decided to lay off herself, to give herself a break, just for an hour. She'd had three weeks of deflecting him and she was momentarily out of ammo. To hell with it, she thought. I'm only human. Why shouldn't I let someone be nice to me? Just for an hour. And the smile that she turned on Joe was, for the first time, devoid of sarcasm or disdain.

'What starter are you having?' he asked, nodding at her closed menu.

'Probably the chanterelle risotto with truffle shavings,' she said, with a twinkle in her eye. 'How about you?'

'The coriander and lemongrass soup. Hey!' he exclaimed, examining his menu. 'But there's no chanterelle risotto with truffle shavings.'

'Ah, there must be.' She smiled. 'I mean, look at this place.' She waved a hand at the obligatory textured lemon walls, the two-foot-square Zen gardens, the round metallic spotlights inset in the ceiling. As Joe laughed, she watched herself blossom in his eyes. But when Katherine opened her menu, she burst out, 'There's no coriander and lemongrass soup either.'

'Ah, there must be,' Joe echoed. 'I mean, look at this place.'

Then, to Katherine's discomfort, it was her turn to watch Joe blossom.

But she couldn't fit him into one of the usual categories. Most men who pursued her this relentlessly had an ego the size of a continent. They *had* to have – if there were any chinks in their armour of self-belief, her disdain found them, and administered mortal wounds. But if he wasn't a crazed egotist, he had to be as thick as a plank, or as naïve as Forrest Gump. And she didn't think he was that either.

The waitress arrived. 'Let me tell you about today's specials,' she said. 'As a starter we have chanterelle risotto . . .'

Katherine didn't hear the rest. She'd erupted into a huge smile at Joe, who – briefly taken aback by her warmth – returned the beam in kind. Katherine had just remembered how much fun this kind of thing could be. As she watched his long, sensitive fingers fiddling with the stem of his wine-glass, she felt an almost-forgotten plucking sensation low down in her body. Like some elastic had snapped. Oh, no!

She ordered tagliatelle. No surrender. She refused to have a manageable date-like meal that left no room for unsightly accidents. So what if the tagliatelle hung in unruly strands from the fork as she raised it to her mouth? So what if some of it swung against her chin, coating it in Cashel blue and porcini sauce? It showed she didn't care. She'd have ordered spinach with a view to getting it caught between her teeth but, sadly, it wasn't on the menu.

As they ate their starters conversation naturally veered towards the one big thing they had in common: work. But Joe talked easily about himself, which made Katherine suspect that he wanted her to respond in the same way. He mentioned something about having gone 'home' a few weekends ago. Then said, 'I was thirty in July and my mum has decided that because I'm not married by now I must be gay.' But when he didn't leave a long silence and stare at her eagerly, like a dog hungry for his dinner, she relaxed. Maybe this wasn't a ruse of his to try and find out what age she was and if she was spoken for.

'Where's home?' she asked.

'Devon. I'm a country boy at heart.' Like it was something to be proud of, she thought scornfully.

But then she found herself saying, 'I'm from the countryside too.'

And in response to his questions she told him a bit about Knockavoy. At least, about its scenery. The huge waves of the Atlantic, the way they were sometimes so high they came in people's windows. The air that was so potent that 'My friend Tara says you could eat it with a knife and fork.' Poor Tara, Katherine thought. She's right, she *is* obsessed with eating. 'I sound like an ad for Ireland.' She smiled.

'It must have been hard to leave.'

'No. I couldn't get away fast enough,' she admitted. 'I like the anonymity of London.'

'It's an urban wasteland,' Joe teased, 'where people don't care enough about each other.'

'Maybe. But it has great shoe-shops,' she quipped.

He laughed, and looked at her with open admiration. He really was good-looking, she thought. This annoyed her.

Their main courses arrived. Joe's was an awesome vertical affair. 'How do they do it?' he asked in admiration, deconstructing it with his eyes. 'I see. A layer of bruschetta, a layer of chicken, a layer of basil, a layer of sundried tomatoes and a layer of mozzarella. Repeat as necessary. Blimey, don't try this at home, viewers!'

'Can you cook?' She didn't know why she'd asked. What did she care?

'Oh, yes.' He twinkled. 'I make a great Thai green curry. Would you like to hear how?'

Winding her tagliatelle, she nodded, her spirits starting a slow slide. Now he was going to try and impress her with his New Man ability to cook. Oh, the tedium.

'Well, first off you go shopping for the ingredients – any Marks and Spencer's will do. Go to the chilled section – this is important, Katherine,' he wagged an admonishing finger, 'because lots of people make the mistake of going to the frozen section – and pick up a ready-made Thai green curry. Then when you get home take the cardboard off and prick the plastic cover with a fork, four times. No more.' He paused, then continued meaningfully, 'And no less. Then – and this is my well-kept secret – though it says on the back to microwave it for four minutes, *just do it for three and a half.*' He nodded sagely at Katherine. 'Then take the plastic cover off and put it in for another thirty seconds. You get a lovely, what we experts like to call, *caramelized* effect.'

He finished with a grin, and she actually laughed, entertained and relieved.

'Well, it goes a bit hard,' he admitted, 'which is nearly the same as caramelizing. Then serve with rice, which can be delivered by any Indian takeaway. Now, you tell me one of your recipes.'

'OK,' she said, slowly getting into it. 'Let me have a think. Right, this is a good one. Ideally you need a phone book, although of course leaflets dropped through your letterbox will do at a stretch. Pick up the phone, dial a number, ask for a twelve-inch, thin-crust marinara with extra tomatoes, then – and this is the vital bit – tell them your address. And there you have it – a delicious meal served in under half an hour! Delivery boy's moped permitting, of course.'

'That's useful to know,' he said, thoughtfully. 'I might try that some night when I have my husband's boss to dinner.'

'Do you *ever* cook?' She sensed a kindred spirit.

'No.' His brown eyes were sincere. 'Never. Do you?'

'Do you hate people who make a big fuss about cooking?'

'I don't exactly hate them. I just don't understand them.'

'I know what you mean.'

'If God meant us to bake cakes why did he invent Pâtisserie Valerie?'

'Quite.'

They eyed each other in companionable silence.

'We could co-author a cookery book,' he suggested, suddenly. 'For people who hate cooking.'

'We could. I know loads of recipes.' Katherine's face took on a gleam. 'I've a lovely one for humous. Go to Safeway, buy a tub, tear off the cardboard and Cellophane, serve!'

'I love it.' He dazzled her with a smile. 'Let me tell you my one for a fuss-free roast dinner. Instructions: go and stay with your mum for the weekend.'

'And we could do glossy colour photos,' Katherine said, enthusiastically, 'of the microwave and the pizza-delivery boy and people eating things out of plastic containers.'

'It would make a change from the usual gastro-porn.' Joe's face was alight with amusement. 'Delia Smith, your days are numbered.'

Katherine had to admit Joe was nice. Or, at least, he *seemed* nice. Which meant he was probably a mad axe-murderer. They usually were. A silence followed, and they noticed for the first time that it had started to pour with rain outside. 'Rain.' Katherine sighed.

'I like rain.'

'You seem to like everything,' Katherine was washed with sudden sourness. 'Is there a male version of Pollyanna? Because you're it!'

Joe laughed. 'I just happen to think that most things can be turned to your advantage. Take the rain, for example. Imagine the scene,' he invited, waving his hand with a vague grace. 'It's pouring down outside, and the rain is rattling at the windows, but you're indoors, with the fire on, lying on the sofa, with your duvet, a bottle of red wine –'

'You're wearing thick socks and sweatpants,' Katherine interrupted, astonished at her eagerness.

Joe nodded. 'A Chinese is on its way . . .'

'A lovely film on the telly . . .'

Joe's eyes were bright with enthusiasm. 'A black and white one . . .'

'Of course . . .'

'*Philadelphia Story . . .*?'

'*Casablanca . . .*?'

'No,' they said simultaneously. '*Roman Holiday!*'

They stared at each other. A bolt of connection shot between them, so intimate that Katherine felt he'd frisked her soul. Positively goosed it. When the waitress chose that moment to shove her face between them and ask if they were finished, Katherine could have kissed her, while Joe could have happily bludgeoned her about the head and neck.

In an effort to stave off the time when they had to go back to work Joe energetically encouraged Katherine to have pudding. 'How about a tri-chocolate terrine?' he suggested, reading from the menu. 'Or a fudge and caramel praline?'

Katherine's lips tightened. What did he think she was? A woman? 'Are you having something?' she asked.

'No, but . . .'

'Well, then,' she replied coldly. And he wondered what he'd done wrong. It had been going so well.

But Katherine had looked at her watch and seen that the hour was up. In fact she'd let it go way over the hour and she was cross with herself and cross with him.

Her mask was back on. She ordered a double espresso and began barking out the Noritaki fixed and variable costs. Just to show him that the fun and games were well and truly over she took a printout from her bag. Then – and there was no other reason except to be cruel – placed her portable calculator on the table.

'How about a liqueur?' Joe suggested, when she was done. 'Just one and then we'll go back.'

She shook her head, her face closed.

'Go on. As a very wise man once said, "Won't you stay, just a little bit longer?"'

'And in the words of one of the greatest minds of the twentieth century,' Katherine replied coldly, dropping her calculator into her bag, '"That's all folks!"'

She stood up.

She let him pay the bill, trampling her feelings of guilt into the ground. After all she hadn't wanted to come. But as he got up to leave, she said, archly, 'Don't forget the receipt, so you can claim it back.' The look he gave her – hurt and disgust at her gratuitous unpleasantness – almost made her wish she hadn't said anything.

It was nearly four o'clock when they got back to the office. This shouldn't have happened. Well, it wouldn't happen again, she'd make damn sure of that. Anyway he was bound to be given the boot before the month was out. He was already into extra time by Breen Helmsford standards. And calculating his redundancy package would give her the greatest of pleasure.

The only problem was that he was good at his job and people liked him a lot. That gave her an unpleasant fluttery feeling of fear.

But by the time she'd got home that evening, her bad humour had been overwhelmed by a warm glow, which she wasn't even aware of. Until Tara noticed and pointed it out to her. Then she wasn't one bit pleased.

21

As Tara pushed open the front door, trying to hide her shopping, Thomas was in the hall, Beryl lacing herself possessively through his legs. 'How was your step class?' he demanded.

It took her a moment to realize what he was on about.

'My step class? Oh, tough,' she managed to lie. 'Hard.'

'Good.' Thomas smacked his lips in satisfaction.

Perhaps it was her hunger, perhaps it was unexpressed anger over what Thomas had said to her on Saturday night, but it must have been something because Tara rounded on Thomas in a sudden, inexplicable fury. 'Good? *Good*? Are you going to give me a gold star? Or grade me? What do I get? Eight out of ten? B minus? C plus? For God's sake!'

Thomas's eyes bulged with shock and he opened and closed his mouth without saying anything.

'You look like a goldfish,' she snapped. 'I'm going to make a phone call.'

She slammed into the bedroom, flung her purchases on the floor, lit a cigarette with one hand and tapped out Fintan's number with the other. 'So what did the doctor say?'

'I didn't go,' Fintan soothed. 'Just after I spoke to you today, you'll never guess what happened.'

'What happened?'

'The lump disappeared.' Fintan laughed. 'Like letting air out of a balloon. One minute it was a kiwi fruit, the next a grape and the next a raisin!'

'I was slightly worried, you know.' She felt like an eejit. 'Maybe you should have gone to the doctor anyway. At least to find out what caused it.'

'No need,' he countered. 'Crisis averted. It was just a blip on the screen, and now we can all forget about it.'

'Was it really the size of a kiwi fruit?'

'Close enough.'

'People don't get big lumps on their neck just for the fun of it,' she insisted, sucking hard on her cigarette. 'Something is wrong and you should find out. What if it happens again?'

'It won't.'

'It might.'

'It won't.'

'What does Sandro think?'

'Sandro *doesn't* think, or at least he does so as little as possible, as well you know.'

'Fintan, please be serious.'

'Oh, no.'

There was a long pause. Eventually Tara was compelled to voice her worry. 'Fintan, I have to ask you something. It's none of my business, but I'm going to ask anyway. Have you had an HIV test recently?'

'Tara, you're overreacting.'

'Look me in the eye,' she interrupted forcefully, 'and tell me that you've had an HIV test recently.'

'I can't do that.'

'So, you mean you *haven't* had a test?' Anxiety made Tara's voice thin and high.

'I mean we're on the phone.'

'You know what I'm getting at.'

'Have *you* had an HIV test?' Fintan surprised her by asking.

'No, but . . .'

'But what?'

She paused delicately. How could she say this?

Fintan interrupted, 'Do you always use a condom with Thomas?'

In different circumstances Tara might have laughed as she remembered the song-and-dance Thomas had made on their first night when Tara had tried to get him to wear a condom. 'Like eating sweets with the wrapper on,' he'd whinged. 'Like going paddling in your shoes and socks.' She'd never suggested it again. Luckily she'd still been on the pill from the Alasdair days.

'Well, no, we don't always, but . . .'

'And has Thomas had an HIV test?'

As if, Tara thought. He'd be the last man on earth to have one. 'No, but . . .'

'Then please shut your clob,' Fintan said, pleasantly but very firmly putting her in her place. 'Thank you for your concern, but it was probably just a mild dose of myxomatosis. Or maybe diabetes. How are your diseases at the moment?'

But Tara, red with censure and shame, didn't want to play.

'Any sign of the rabies recurring?' he asked.

She said nothing, damning her misplaced, knee-jerk concern. There was probably more chance of *her* being HIV positive than Fintan.

'Or the malaria?' he inquired politely.

Still she said nothing

'I hear there's a bad dose of anthrax going around at the moment,' he said, 'so wrap up warm!'

'If you're sure you're okay,' she said humbly. 'I must have my dinner. Talk to you tomorrow.'

'I'll be away all week,' he said. 'Working in Brighton. See you at the weekend.'

Thomas was listening at the door. She pushed past him and banged into the kitchen. She was angry with herself, stung by Fintan, very hungry, and fresh out of any resolve to stick to her diet. 'Is there anything to eat?' She threw open a cupboard door and looked, with disgust, at the Weight-watchers soup, tinned tomatoes, dried pasta and cat food within. 'It's like a famine zone,' she muttered. 'A Third World kitchen. If we're not careful the World Health Organization will start airlifting in crates of maize and flour. If we set up a donations line, we'd make a fortune.'

Thomas watched her in shock. He'd never seen her like this before. Another cupboard revealed Thomas's stockpile of tinned steak and kidney pies.

'You could always have one of them,' he suggested, surprised at the nervous tremor in his voice.

'I'd rather eat my *own* kidney,' she retorted. 'What time is it? Safeways is still open, I'm going out to buy food.'

'Hang on a mo', I'll come with you.'

'No, you won't,' she said, gathering her car keys.

'Get plenty of vegetables,' he called after her.

Tara turned around, walked back in and put her face very close to his. 'Why don't you shut it?' she suggested, then left again, leaving him staring in confusion as she got into the car and screeched away. The worm had turned. The worm was positively gyrating.

*

There were a couple of cast-iron rules that Tara lived her life by. 'Do unto others as you would be done by' was one. 'Don't go to the supermarket when you're hungry' was another.

But she was in a rule-breaking mood. Trolley or basket? Basket or trolley? How much damage was she planning on doing?

Trolley, she decided.

She blitzkrieged her way through the fruit and vegetables department, casting disdainful looks left and right. Not a single piece of fresh produce would be coming home with her tonight. Then some carrots caught her eye. Carrots are my friend, she remembered. Many was the time that raw carrots had kept the spectre of hunger at bay. But not today. Not unless they were chocolate-coated.

'Carrots can shag off,' she muttered.

A young man, two days off the bus from Cardiff, overheard her. It was true what his mother said: London *was* full of mad people. Great!

Tara caught him looking at her speculatively and a thought struck her. They did singles nights at some London super-markets. Could it be that she'd stumbled upon one? She glanced shyly and found that the boy was still looking at her. She was surprised and not displeased. Vaguely, she thought about smiling at him and then decided not to bother.

Who needs a man when you can have food?

And food she would have.

Usually a trip to the supermarket took Tara a very, very long time. It was like walking through a minefield. Temptation on all sides. Every purchase was deliberated and agonized over. Assiduously, the back of each packet was examined to see how many calories and grams of fat it contained. Nothing with more than five per cent fat was allowed into the trolley. 'None Shall Pass!' was her motto.

Unless Thomas wasn't looking.

Sometimes she trailed a finger wistfully along the forbidden Indian meals or frozen pizzas, wishing things were different. But she'd long stopped going into the biscuit aisles, because the sense of loss was too great. Best to just close the door on that part of her. It had been a passionate love affair, *too* passionate, and she knew they could never be just friends. But sometimes she couldn't help but remember the good times.

Memories can be beautiful, but still . . . A pink, fuzzy-bordered picture of her laughing and twirling in slow-motion, her hair flying, her arms wrapped around a packet of Jammy Dodgers. Or of her running downhill through a cornfield on a beautiful summer's day, holding hands with a packet of orange Viscounts. Or of her giggling happily, cheek to cheek with a chocolate ginger nut. Ah, the way we were . . .

But this night was different. Tara bulldozed through the aisles, like an Iraqi tank invading Kuwait, hidebound by none of her usual reticence. Instead it was Access All Areas. With one sweeping gesture she tipped a large part of a shelf of crisps into her trolley. Without an atom of guilt she threw in a couple of fat-bastard sandwiches for the journey home.

But it was hard not to make a start on what she was flinging into the trolley. Eventually, hoping not too many people were looking, she broke open a bag of Monster Munch. Then another. Then a pork pie. And then she reached the biscuits.

Unable to stop herself, she picked up a packet of Boasters and looked at it. *Maybe I shouldn't*, she thought. But an evil little voice suggested, *Says who?*

She hovered on the brink, trembling with desire and possibility. Then, with a rumbling in her ears, a tidal wave of adrenaline whooshed through her, carrying along everything in its path, and she was tearing open the packet with shaking fingers.

It was like a dogfight, the hand-to-mouth action a blur, as crumbs, chocolate chips, stray nuts and the torn wrapper went flying. She was transported, almost ecstatic, though she barely tasted anything she put in her mouth – it wasn't there long enough for her taste-buds to get a grip on it. Strictly through-traffic only.

But, so quickly, it was all over. Sanity returned, and with it came shame. Although her acute anxiety and hunger had been sated, she felt wretched. She slunk to the checkout, horribly ashamed of the empty packaging in her trolley, mortified as the girl bipped it over the electronic reader. But if she'd tried to dispose of the evidence by hiding the wrappers, she might have been done for shoplifting. She was just the type who'd be caught.

What had she been thinking of? she wondered miserably. Had she gone mad? A whole day's attempted starvation wiped out in a ten-minute frenzy. Look at the amount of saturated fat she'd just consumed. What about her diet? What about her good intentions? All her hard work? Hadn't she nearly gone to a step class that day, and was all that effort to come to naught?

She found the young man staring at her again, and she no longer thought he fancied her. Then she remembered Thomas. And terror arrived.

She'd shouted at Thomas, *and* she'd broken her diet. She was not just fat, but a termagant as well. What had she done? Things were way too delicate to chance telling Thomas he looked like a goldfish. Shaking with fear and sugar-overload, Tara drove home. She had so many additives in her bloodstream that if she'd gone apeshit with a shotgun in a public place there wasn't a jury in the land who'd have convicted her.

Thomas was sitting at the kitchen table, smoking heavily, Beryl crouching beside him in her basket. He looked up with anxiety as Tara came in. 'Hello,' he said, with a sweet, nervous little smile.

'I'm sorry I shouted at you.' She prostrated herself, so conditioned to him having all the power that when it fell into her hands she assumed it was a mistake and returned it immediately to its rightful owner, as if it was a wallet she'd found in the street. 'If you're furious with me I don't blame you. I'm extremely sorry, and you have my word that I'm starting a very strict diet tomorrow.'

With each contrite word, Thomas's subdued air evaporated and his swaggery arrogance returned. His chest visibly expanded, and his meek, hangdog face became just a distant memory. By the time Tara told him about Fintan's kiwi-neck, Thomas was once more sure enough of himself to say, 'With all his carry-on, he's lucky it's just his neck that's giving him grief.'

22

Lorcan Larkin was an actor. It was what he purported to do for a living, as well as how he conducted his private life.

In his twenties and early thirties he'd been extremely successful in Ireland, the equivalent to a superstar. He'd set the stage ablaze in *The Playboy of the Western World* and *Juno and the Paycock*, eclipsing the rest of the cast. He'd been unpopular with other actors anyway, and after that they hated him.

For a few years he'd starred in an Irish soap, playing a philandering rake. Which was extremely handy because he was able to excuse his appalling behaviour off-screen by saying he was a method actor. Despite the capriciousness of his television character (which was only a watery imitation of the real thing) Lorcan was a huge sex-symbol. Fêted and drooled over. He met the Taoiseach and the President and it was a poor day that he didn't receive a pair of knickers in the post. Even when the tabloids published a bitter tirade from the wife who'd supported him through the lean years and whom he'd abandoned as soon as the good times began to roll, adulation for him didn't waver. But, for Lorcan, it wasn't enough – nothing ever was. He felt uncomfortable about his success with the Irish. They hadn't a clue, he suspected. OK, so they're one of the most articulate and literate nations on earth, but he needed to be endorsed by people who really, you know, *mattered*.

So, about four years earlier, amid a media circus, he took

his leave of Ireland. 'I'm not getting any younger,' he joked with the journalists. Although he didn't mean a word of it – he thought he was immortal.

Then off he went to Hollywood to show them how it was done. He reckoned it would be only a matter of days before he was lounging beside his very own azure-blue swimming-pool, drowning under scripts, beating off directors with sticks.

However, it came as a very unpleasant shock to discover that Hollywood had reached its quota of sexy Irishmen. Three was reckoned to be enough. Pierce Brosnan, Liam Neeson and Gabriel Byrne did the trick nicely, thanks very much. Apparently Scottish actors had become the current flavour of the month, with Hollywood unable to get enough of them. Briefly, Lorcan considered changing his name to Ewan.

Undaunted, he accepted the part of a gay cyber-vampire biker in an art-house movie where the walls fell over every time someone closed a door. And for which he was never paid, as the money ran out less than half-way through shooting. Hot on the heels of that success he was offered a part – the starring role, actually – in an adult film when a director noticed in a men's room that Lorcan had the right credentials for the job.

Then he was no longer undaunted. Then he was very daunted indeed. The only azure-blue swimming-pools he'd come within an ass's roar of were the ones he ended up cleaning for a living.

The day finally came, during his fourteenth month of 'resting', when he was forced to admit that things hadn't worked out – he just couldn't bring himself to use the word 'failed'. He was living in a roasting hot, airless, twelve by twelve room with a 'window effect' – no window but a closed plastic blind hanging on a square of the bare concrete wall – in Little Tijuana. Marshmallow Cheerios had been his breakfast, lunch and dinner for the past week. His car had been reclaimed, so that he had to ride the bus three hours across town to get to auditions. Not that there were many auditions – Lorcan was such an undesirable in Hollywood he probably wouldn't have been able to get *arrested*.

Up until then, success had followed him, magnet-like. Realizing it had abandoned him caused excruciating agonies of terror and insecurity. His ego was so big yet so fragile that he always needed more than everyone else did just to tick over. More success, more acclaim, more money, more women. It was imperative to leave this place where he was a nobody.

He had just about enough money for his plane fare back to Europe. But there was no way he was going home to Ireland. Not after the way they'd lied to him, telling him he was a star when he clearly wasn't. Instead he went to London, hoping to hide his humiliation in its vastness. He moved into a tiny, dingy room in Camden, where his flatmate was an affable, tubby man called Benjy who earned his living processing parking fines.

Then Lorcan desperately set about trying to recover lost ground and his sense of self by making disdainful noises about the trash being made in Hollywood. 'The stage has always been my first love,' he insisted in the *Guardian*. That was the *Camden Guardian*, the only paper interested in the fact that he was making a home in London. (And then only because he lived next door to their office.) 'No, really, it has.' Lorcan's confidence had been badly dented in Hollywood, but he got an agent and began going to auditions in London. However, the world of acting is incredibly sensitive and can spot the merest whiff of loserism at a thousand paces. Astonishingly good-looking, almost threateningly sexy, there was nevertheless the faintest aura of the has-been about Lorcan. Some unkind people went even further and identified it as the scent of the never-was.

No one wants to be associated with that. It might be catching. So while the casting girls were perfectly happy to sleep with Lorcan, they weren't so keen on giving him a part in their production. Pride kept him going. That, and the fact that he was equipped for nothing else. He had no choice but to pick himself up after every knockback and try again.

So far, during the two years he'd been in London, he'd auditioned for *Hamlet*, *King Lear*, *Macbeth* and *Othello*. After ten months of rejection, he finally got a part. In *The Bill*. Imaginatively cast as an IRA bomb-maker, and the only line he got to say was, 'Jaysus, dey're on to us. Run, Mickey!'

Much to his disappointment this *tour de force* didn't open any further doors and beneath his smart-arse, arrogant exterior, he was in torment. He hated not being the most admired, the most sought-after, the most in-demand. Yet all wasn't lost – he might have been without the roles or the money or the kudos but there was no doubt that he still got the girls. It was the only area of his life that still worked, a microcosm of how he wished everything else to be.

With women, Lorcan could wield his beloved power with a free hand. Of course it wasn't much of a *challenge* making girlies cry but it was better than nothing. It was safe and he'd always be the winner. As the months passed without another part, it became very difficult to make ends meet. In fact, ends were barely on nodding terms with each other. Bitterly, resentfully, he got a job as a waiter. He, the great Lorcan Larkin, reduced to dishing up spaghetti carbonara to peasants. How are the mighty fallen. Luckily he was sacked within the week for having an attitude problem. (The manager just couldn't get Lorcan to understand that if someone asked for a second cup of coffee, the correct response was 'Certainly, sir, coming right up,' and not 'What did your last slave die of? Get it yourself.')

He had no choice but to look for an alternative form of income.

He could have gone the gigolo route. There were enough rich older women in London who would keep Lorcan in a style to which he could quickly become accustomed. While he, in return, would provide sexual services. But he just couldn't stomach it.

He had no objection to sleeping with them, but only on his terms. However, six months ago came a week where three good things happened for him. First, he got a job doing voice-overs for the Irish tourist board, which wasn't exactly 'smell-of-the-greasepaint-roar-of-the-crowd' territory but it put beer in the fridge. The following day, he managed to get a housing-association flat in Chalk Farm – his own place. (Benjy was heartbroken.)

And then he met Amy.

He and Benjy were at a party when they first saw her.

Benjy took one look at her long, willowy limbs, her pure, radiant face, her tendrils of red-blonde hair, and thought she was the most beautiful girl he'd ever seen. 'Look,' he gasped, and elbowed Lorcan.

'I thought you were a tit-man.' Lorcan sounded unimpressed.

'Not really. I'm an anything-man,' Benjy said mournfully. 'An anything-I-can-get man.'

'Well, may the force be with you. And remember what I've told you. Act shy. Be bashful.'

'I can't possibly go and speak to her.' Benjy was horrified.

'Why not? You fancy her.'

'That's exactly why.'

'Go on, my son,' Lorcan urged, giving Benjy a little push in the back.

So, with quaking legs, Benjy crossed the room and made his pitch. Lorcan leant against the wall and watched the girl through almost-closed eyes. What's sauce for the goose was sauce for the . . . other goose.

All too soon, Benjy was back, red with mortification. Acting shy only worked when the man was extraordinarily handsome. Otherwise he just seemed like a geek.

'How did you get on?' Lorcan patronized him by asking.

'She patted me on the head and told me I was a pet.'

'I think we'll both agree that that wasn't the desired response,' Lorcan said. 'OK, now watch how it *should* be done. Look and learn. Because I'm a woman whisperer.'

'What the hell's that?' Benjy demanded angrily, terrified that Lorcan was going to snatch Amy effortlessly from under his snub nose.

'Like the horse whisperer, except instead of getting messed-up horses eating out of my hand, it's messed-up women.'

'She's not messed-up,' Benjy said hotly.

'Oh, but she is. That sweet face, all that niceness, she's just a bit too eager to please,' Lorcan said thoughtfully.

'Not to me, she isn't,' Benjy retorted bitterly.

Timing was everything. So Lorcan waited until every other man in the room had made his move. He knew she'd seen him. He was so tall it was hard to miss him, and he'd caught her glancing at him once or twice.

He didn't march straight up to her and demand attention – a good-looking man who's arrogant often scares the girls away. But a good-looking man who's vulnerable is on the home stretch. So the contact he made with her was seemingly accidental, under the guise of helping the host collect glasses and empty cans. 'Sorry to interrupt, but do you know if this is an empty?' Lorcan asked, his purple eyes intense with contrived vulnerability.

When she nodded, he said haltingly, 'You know . . . I mean, you've probably heard it before . . . No, no, nothing, sorry. Forget I said anything.' And he made to move away but by then he had her interest.

'No, please, say what you were going to say,' she said.

'Ah, no.' He shuffled in a triumph of gawky body language. 'It's nothing.'

'You can't just start saying something then stop.' Her blue eyes pleaded up at him.

Lorcan looked away, swallowed, then blurted out, 'OK. You're probably sick hearing it, but can I just say that you've the most beautiful hair I've ever seen.' He had the handy gift of being able to blush on cue.

'Thank you,' Amy said, also blushing.

'I'd better . . .' he made an awkward gesture with the empty glasses, followed by a shy smile '. . . you know, put these in the kitchen.'

Ten minutes later, when Amy put a cigarette into her mouth, Lorcan belted through the crowds in a great display of clumsy haste. He fumbled for his special lighter, and clicked it under her nose. When – as planned – the lighter didn't work, he allowed a brief spasm of horror to cross his face. Then, holding Amy's gaze, burst out laughing. Ruefully, he lied, 'It was working five minutes ago.' It hadn't worked for two years.

'Isn't it true,' he sighed, 'these things always let you down when you're trying hardest to make an impression?' Then he shrugged, 'Sorry,' and moved away, leaving Amy staring longingly after him. A short time later, as expected, she came after him. He was home and dry. Elation tingled through him. God, he loved this! No one could touch him. He was the master, truly the master!

The following day Amy called an Extraordinary General Meeting of all her friends. 'I felt terribly embarrassed for him,' she exclaimed. 'The look on his face! He actually *blushed*. It meant ever so much to him to light my cigarette. And he's so drop-dead gorgeous it hurts, when you see him, you simply won't believe what a babe he is. How about it? A good-looking man who's also thoughtful and vulnerable. I know it's very soon and perhaps I'm ever so slightly jumping the gun, but I honestly think he might be . . .' she paused and exhaled shakily '. . . The One.'

A few days later when Benjy realized that Amy was to be Lorcan's girlfriend he went into a decline. 'I thought it was just a case-study,' he said, reeling from shock and jealousy. 'I thought you only slept with her to show me how it's done.'

'Really, Benjy.' Lorcan tutted in disapproval. 'What a thing to say. That's no way to treat people!'

23

The first summer that Fintan, Tara and Katherine were pals was a magic time – though Frank Butler declared Fintan O'Grady was a very bad influence. He declared it long and loud to anyone who'd listen in O'Connell's snug. Not that he drummed up much support for his cause.

'Sure, what harm is he doing?' Tadhg Brennan asked, visualizing Fintan in batwing sleeves and harem pants. 'He livens the place up. Anyway, 'tis only a phrase he's going through.'

'And when he's finished going through his phrase, *phase*, he'll have my daughter well and truly corrupted.'

Frank's buddies fell silent. It wasn't fair to blame Fintan O'Grady. Tara Butler would have been corrupted sooner or later. Even aged fourteen she had that look about her.

She was highly popular with the local gurriers, who made a full-time job of wearing flares and leaning against the corner of Main Street and Small Street – professional corner boys, who could probably put it on their CVs.

'Here's my chest, the rest is coming.' They'd nudge each other, when they saw Tara approaching.

'You're a fine hoult of a woman,' they'd shout, as she swept past, curvy and sexy, her nose in the air. 'I wouldn't mind having you in my herd. Will we go away and find a gable end?'

'Romance Knockavoy style.' Katherine laughed.

No one suggested that straight-up-and-down Katherine was

a fine hoult of a woman. In fact the corner boys sometimes shouted after her, 'G'wan, yuh dhroopy dhrawers. I'd sooner coort a shtick.'

Tara was worried about her. 'Do you mind . . . ?'

'Do I mind what?'

'That they don't say . . .' Tara faltered 'that they'd like you in their herd.'

The look Katherine gave her redefined the concept of scornful.

'No? Good,' Tara murmured nervously.

As a fourteen-year-old Tara was very interested in lads, though she'd have nothing to do with the locals. She lived for the summer months, when the famine became, if not quite a feast, then certainly a square meal, with a fresh batch of boys arriving at the caravan park every week. Tara and – to a lesser extent – Fintan had their work cut out to get around to everyone.

'No one goes home disappointed!' Fintan was fond of saying.

During the evenings that went on for ever, Tara, Katherine and Fintan sat for hours on the sea wall in the pinkish light, until the sun finally got around to setting far out to sea.

'Over there's America,' they were fond of saying. 'Next stop New York.' Then they'd strain their eyes, in case, shimmering on the horizon, they could see the top of the Statue of Liberty.

'Some day.' They'd sigh. 'We'll go there some day.'

'What do they do?' Frank Butler demanded angrily of Fidelma. 'Just sitting there all that time. I drove past at half past five and they were there and when I was coming home again at ten o'clock they were *still* there, not a budge out of them.'

Fidelma sighed. She knew how easy it was to spend four hours on a damp wall, unaware of time passing, building castles in the air, then moving into them. She remembered being young, certain that a wonderful future awaited you, like a flower ready to blossom. 'Maybe they're admiring the view,' she suggested.

Frank snorted, and with good reason. Tara, Katherine and Fintan never even noticed the vast expanse of sky and sea, except as something to escape over. The only view they were interested in was that of the crowds of boys who gravitated to the sea wall most evenings. There was a flourishing social scene with up to twenty there on any one night. Visitors from Limerick, Cork, Dublin, even Belfast.

To Tara's dismay, visiting girls also appeared, in their sophisticated, trendy city clothes. Even when they realized they were wasting their time with Fintan they still kept coming. But at least none of the locals tried to muscle in. Sometimes girls from school hovered on the edge, but when no one welcomed them into the privileged inner-circle, they drifted away again, disappointed.

Nightly, the air was thick with adolescent longing. To facilitate which, fixed courting rituals were in place. You knew someone fancied you if they tried to trip you up or if they threw a jellyfish at you. People were forever up and down the steps to the sand, picking jellyfish up on to pieces of driftwood, then firing them at the object of their desire.

Tara had more jellyfish thrown at her than anyone else. Katherine had a few pelted at her by a twelve-year-old boy, until he realized that Katherine was fourteen, then he was very apologetic. Fintan had none thrown at him.

Until darkness fell, and then you'd have been surprised.

If the person you threw the jellyfish at squealed, 'Oooooh, you big meanie! I hate you!' you knew they fancied you. But if they ran away and returned five minutes later with their father and pointed you out, saying, 'That's him, Dad. The one who tried to kill me,' you realized you'd badly misjudged the situation.

Another sure-fire method of announcing your amorous intentions was by holding up a piece of seaweed and saying, 'Guess what this is? It's your hair.' Likewise if someone found an old, decrepit pair of knickers that had been washed in by the tide, and asked you, 'Are these yours?' you knew you had an admirer.

Tara spent June and half of July with constant anticipation churning in her stomach. It was the most wonderful time of her life. She kept declaring, 'I'm in love,' and Katherine would say indulgently, 'Again? Who is it this time?'

Most nights, as the sun finally sank below the horizon, Tara repaired to the sand dunes for a courting session with her current squeeze. Katherine waited on the wall, talking shyly to the runners-up. She had no interest in going to the sand dunes to snog boys.

And they weren't terribly interested in her either. She was too skinny and plain, with no hint of the sleek, mysterious woman she'd eventually become. They said of her, 'She has a nice personality,' which was just adolescent-speak for 'She has no diddies.'

Tara spent most Friday nights in tearful goodbyes and promises to write, while Saturday afternoons were used to check out the new arrivals, the cars low in the ground as they rumbled into the caravan park, laden with people and roof racks. Life couldn't have been better.

But Fintan wanted more than just sea walls and sand dunes for the three of them. He had vision. Around mid-July, he shocked Tara and Katherine to the core by suggesting casually,

'Let's go to the disco.' For the past three summers, there had been a disco for the over eighteens on Saturday nights in the community hall, with an extra one on Wednesday nights in August when the trickle of tourists became a slightly bigger trickle. The local clergy had given their reluctant approval to the disco in the hope that it might lure tourists away from the fleshpots of Kilkee and Lahinch, further along the coast. This, only after they'd tried and failed to raise money to buy bumper cars.

The disco was an occasion of sin. Even though Father Neylon patrolled the slow sets with a big stick, the confession box was overrun with people afflicted with impure thoughts. It wasn't good to encourage depravity. Except if money could be made from it.

'The disco!' Tara and Katherine swallowed. 'But we're too young.'

'Says who?'

'Everyone,' Katherine pointed out. 'Our birth certs, for example.'

'Rules are made to be broken.' Fintan smiled.

'Have you been before?' Tara asked.

'Er, ah, yes, of course,' Fintan said, airily. 'Last year and the year before.'

'Would we get in?' Tara asked, feeling a rush of delicious, fearful excitement. She'd never even *thought* of going to the disco. She just assumed she'd have to be at least sixteen. But suddenly it seemed possible.

'I'd say so,' Fintan said, with confidence. 'If you wear the right clothes and make-up. Leave it to me.'

'My father is right,' Tara said in admiration. 'You *are* a bad influence.

'Just as well. Let's face it,' she said fondly to Katherine, 'if I was waiting for you to lead me astray, I'd be waiting till the Day of Judgement.'

Preparations for the visit to the disco were frantic. Katherine took money out of her post-office account and lent it to Tara. Who hitched a lift with Fintan as far as Ennis, where she bought a pair of pink stretch Sasparillas, the most beautiful item of clothing she'd ever possessed. An order for a tube of hair-gel was placed in the Knockavoy chemist, who promised to pull strings to get it in by Saturday. A Day-Glo pink lipstick that had come free with *Just 17* summer special was called into active service, and Fintan said it could be used as blusher and eye-shadow too.

'I can't get ready in my house,' Tara said, fearfully. 'If my father sees me all done up he'll kill me.'

'Get ready in my house,' Katherine said.

'But won't Delia mind? Won't she tell?'

'For Cripe's sake.' Katherine sighed. 'She's been annoying me all summer to go to the disco. I'm only afraid she'll want to come with us.'

'Janey Mackers!' Tara exclaimed. 'You are so flipping lucky.'

'No, I'm not.'

'What does *your* mother think?' Tara turned to Fintan. 'Will she be cross if she finds out?'

'If my mother heard that I'd gone to a dance with two girls she'd burst with happiness,' Fintan reminded them.

On the big day Tara bought four lemons, as instructed by *Just 17*, squeezed the juice over her hair, then prepared to spend six hours sitting in the sun, waiting for her mousy hair to turn blonde. Unfortunately, the sky clouded over, then it began to rain, so that was the end of that. Fintan arrived just as Tara was about to start rinsing her hair with beer to make it shine. (Another *Just 17* tip.)

'What are you doing?' Fintan sounded apoplectic. 'Don't tell me you're rinsing your hair with *beer*?'

'Is it bad for my hair?' Tara asked anxiously.

Fintan might have been camp, but he wasn't that camp. 'Who cares if it's bad for your hair? It's bad for your sobriety,' he exclaimed. 'You're wasting good Smithwick's!'

'But I want my hair to look nice for the disco,' Tara said.

'Believe me, your hair will look far nicer if you drink the beer,' Fintan replied. 'At least, it will look far nicer to *you*.'

Tara arrived at Katherine's with a plastic bag full of her clothes, her make-up, and two pint bottles of porter that she'd stolen from her father's stash. Delia was out, working in the pub. Agnes, hunched, grey and lonely, looked up suspiciously from Delia's copy of *Spare Rib* as Tara clinked past.

Fintan swept Tara into Katherine's bedroom. 'I need to be alone with my client,' he said pompously, as he closed the door on Katherine. 'Genius at work.'

When Tara re-emerged some time later, Katherine was mesmerized with admiration. 'You look . . .' for once she was speechless '. . . so old.' She paused, unable to express herself. 'You look *seventeen*. Like the girl from Bananarama, or something.'

Tara was dressed in the pink jeans, a white ruffly shirt, with a blue T-shirt underneath, crammed to capacity with her generous bosom. She had blue kohl around her eyes, Day-Glo pink lipstick on most of the rest of her face, and her hair was backcombed and gelled into sticking up in all the right places.

'Right,' said Fintan to Katherine. 'Now you.'

'But I'm ready.'

Katherine had on baggy black non-stretch jeans, a roomy white T-shirt and not a scrap of make-up. She only wanted to wear make-up if there was a chance that someone might tell her to take it off. She longed for a father to shout at her, 'Wash that muck off your face! No daughter of mine is going around the town of Knockavoy like a painted whore,' the way Frank would to Tara.

'But we've got to look older, else we mightn't get in,' Fintan said anxiously. 'Would you not even pad your bra?'

'I have,' Katherine said, in a little voice.

As Tara emerged into the kitchen, Agnes was aghast. 'Holy Mother of sweet divine suffering Jesus on the cross with six-inch nails through his hands and feet!' she declared. 'Comb your hair, child! How did you get so many knots in it?'

'This is the way it's supposed to be. It's the fashion.'

'But it looks like a furze bush.'

'Thank you.' Fintan and Tara smiled shyly at each other.

'I'm with you now.' Agnes began to understand. 'Hair like that is all the go, is it?'

'It is.'

'Well, would it be nice on me?'

There was a nonplussed pause, until Fintan rallied. 'Agnes, it'd be *divine* on you.' And the career-guidance God smiled down and thought, This young man will go far in fashion.

'I might have to cut it,' Fintan warned.

'Cut it all you like!'

As Agnes unfurled her grey bun, she reached for the bottle of whiskey and said, 'Ye're welcome to drink Frank Butler's porter, but I'm having a proper drink.'

When Delia came home several hours later, she found her

mother sitting in the chair where she'd left her, blind drunk, smeared in shocking pink lipstick and with a mass of sticky, backcombed, spiky grey hair.

'Look at me,' Agnes screeched. 'I'm the height of style!'

The corner boys were dubious about Tara's transformation. 'Don't like the war-paint.' Bobby Lyons watched her go past.

'And her hair looks like a hay reek,' Martin O'Driscoll complained.

'A pile of silage,' said Pauley Early.

'But the pink pants are nice,' Michael Kenny admitted.

'Oh, yes.' There was a chorus of agreement. 'We like the pink pants.'

Despite the porter, Tara, Katherine and Fintan were nervous wrecks at the community-hall door. 'Remember,' Fintan muttered, 'you were both born in nineteen sixty-three.'

But there was no need to be frightened. The only details that Father Evans was interested in checking was that they had the money to pay in.

They'd been to the community hall hundreds of times, but this night the dusty wooden floor, the tiny little stage, the orange plastic chairs, the diagrams for the Order of Malta classes, the posters for Delia's abortive yoga classes – the lotus, the Smirnoff – all looked magically different.

Even though it was only half past seven and still bright outside, the atmosphere was charged. A strange machine put moving pictures of coloured bubbles on the walls. The bubbles expanded, then split into two, changed from blue to green to red. It reminded Katherine of biology at school, looking through the microscope as cells split and grew. They were the first people there. Nervously, they sat on the edge of the plastic chairs, tense with expectation, as they waited for people to come. And waited. And waited.

'Should we dance?' Katherine eventually asked. She had a keen sense of duty.

'Wait a while,' Fintan urged, looking anxiously at the door, willing someone, anyone, to come in. It became clear to Tara and Katherine that, for all his talk, this was Fintan's first time too.

They sat in silence, the dust motes spinning in the silvery evening light.

'I think I'll go to the toilet to see if my hair's still OK,' Tara said, after some time had elapsed.

'It is,' Katherine said.

They sat in silence again.

'I think I'll go anyway.'

At about half past nine as the songs were going around for the third time, one or two people arrived. Then as the sun finally set outside, more people came, then still more.

Mute and nervous, Tara, Katherine and Fintan sat, amazed at how relaxed and confident everyone else seemed, how very comfortable they were in this wonderful place. Would they ever be that blasé?

Katherine kept half an eye on the door. She knew that her mother was supposed to be at work, but she wouldn't put it past her . . .

24

Joe Roth watched Katherine walk up to her desk and his heart lifted. There were at least twenty other women in the office, so what was it about this one that the mere sight of her had all his senses on full alert? Was it the face? The accent? The self-possession? The challenge . . . ?

After the limited success of the lunch the previous day, he was working himself up to asking her out for dinner. And this time he'd do it without the help of Fred Franklin or the pretext of discussing work. Subterfuge and manipulation weren't Joe's usual methods. Though the lunch had been partly work-related, he was ashamed he'd brought pressure to bear on her. But he just hadn't been able to stop himself.

As he watched her carefully hang her jacket on the back of her chair, he was trying to decide where to take her. Somewhere so new the paint was still drying? Or somewhere old, mellow and out of town? Which would she prefer?

Katherine sat down, switched on her computer and opened a file. Then closed it and opened another. Then closed it again. She couldn't decide where to start. Momentarily, she didn't *care*. Then, as she watched Joe walk over to her desk, she realized she'd been waiting for him. He looked extremely good today. That made four days in a row. He wore a beautiful navy suit, with a turquoise weave, and the pale, pale green of his shirt made his dark eyes and hair look even darker. The clothes maketh the man, she told herself, firmly. It was the cut of the suit that made him look so elegant and graceful. It was the soft texture of his jacket that made her want to touch his arm.

He stood in front of her. She looked at a button midway down his shirt and, to her surprise, thought, I could just open that and slide my hand in. In the split second that she imagined the touch of his skin – taut, silky beneath his chest hair – she had a hot flare of sensation. He sat on the edge of her desk, and she found she was watching the way the front of his trousers bunched and gathered. What would happen if she inched down his zip and slipped her hand in . . . ? Once more her nerve endings prickled with heat. Mesmerized, she forced her eyes from his flies to his face. She felt frightened. Then angry. He smiled at her as he'd done every morning, but today it was different. All the intensity had moved from his mouth to his eyes. Less sweetness, more tension. Less sunniness, more breath-holding anticipation.

'Morning, Katherine.'

'Morning,' she said, shortly.

He paused and managed to make eye-contact before saying, 'Thank you for coming to work today. You've made an old man very happy.'

Katherine coldly quirked an eyebrow. 'Is that so?'

'Yes, it is. As a very wise man once said.' Joe paused, rubbed his chin thoughtfully and said, 'What was it exactly? Oh, right! "You are the sunshine of my life." '

'That's interesting,' Katherine replied slowly, 'because another very wise man – he's a judge, actually – once said, "Sexual harassment in the workplace is a crime." '

There was a split second of stillness, then Joe twitched as if she'd hit him. As his face flooded with colour, he was already moving off her desk, sickened by shock and sudden self-loathing.

Sexual harassment! She said he was sexually harassing her. Him! Joe Roth. He'd always thought that sexual harassment was done by older men, who held a position of power and abused it for sexual favours. Like Fred Franklin. It had never occurred to Joe that his enthusiastic wooing of Katherine might be viewed in such a light. He'd just thought he'd been *flirting* with her. He felt dirty and disgusting – and rejected.

'Sorry,' Joe said, his face aghast as he backed away. 'I didn't mean to . . . it wasn't my intention to . . . I'm terribly sorry.'

Savouring her sour triumph, Katherine turned her attention to the figures on her desk. To be fair, she thought, it wasn't exactly *harassment*, as such. He hadn't ever accidentally-on-purpose grazed her nipples under the guise of passing her an expenses claim. Or suggested she sleep with him if she wanted a pay rise. Or while she was photocopying in the eight-foot-wide corridor, he hadn't rubbed up behind her, making sure she felt the full benefit of his erection, saying, 'Whoops, excuse me, just trying to squeeze past you. Tight fit, this eight-foot-wide corridor,' the way Fred Franklin did to some of the other girls.

But he had bullied her into going to lunch with him. Even if it was work-related. And he had smiled at her a lot, an awful lot, and that *wasn't* work-related. Not to mention all that irritating stuff about wise men saying things. It'd get on your nerves!

She stuffed down the unpleasant feeling that true victims of sexual harassment wouldn't have been one bit impressed with her accusations. But at least she'd managed to get rid of him. Right, then. Opening balances!

*

185

Joe went back to his desk and Myles, who'd been watching the exchange – him and most of the Breen Helmsford payroll – murmured sympathetically, 'Kicked you to the kerb?'

'Yes,' Joe said hollowly.

Instantly it was mass-exodus time, as all the other men gave him the widest possible berth. Sometimes a man's just got to be alone, they reasoned.

If it was a woman who'd been blown out, she'd have been besieged by other women, laden down with chocolate and comforting platitudes. 'That pig!' 'Plenty more where he came from.' 'Bet he had a tiny willy, anyway.'

But because he was a man, Joe's desk immediately became a tiny raft marooned in a very big sea. All morning, any men on the right-hand side of the office who wanted to talk to anyone working on the left-hand side went to the back of the office, down five flights of fire escape, out the back by the bins, around the block, back in the front door, up in the lift, into the office and over to the desk of the person they wanted to speak to, rather than pass in front of Joe.

Fred Franklin was the sole source of human contact and then only because he couldn't be arsed walking down five flights of stairs. As he lumbered past, he placed his hand awkwardly on Joe's shoulder and suggested in wise-and-kindly-elder-giving-advice-to-raw-youth fashion, 'Shag someone else, son.'

Katherine ignored it all, she had work to do. Besides, she thought, he might be back. And if he is, I'll know he's a pathologically arrogant wanker. And if he doesn't come back, he couldn't have handled me anyway. Either way, I can't lose.

Then she had an unexpected, unwelcome throb of loss. Maybe he wasn't that bad. But, no, there was no scope for thinking that. Because they all were. Sooner or later.

Usually just after they'd slept with her.

Joe got through the morning, not quite a broken man but definitely badly bent out of shape. He went over and over his behaviour during the past three weeks and had to admit he'd been very persistent with Katherine. He'd always been can-do and practical. If you want something – or someone – you do your best to get them. But he'd never meant to be pushy.

Or to *sexually harass* her.

The thing was he was fairly sure he *wasn't* guilty of sexual harassment. Which almost made it worse. She'd flung an extreme accusation at him, not because it was true but because she loathed him so much she had to find a good way of getting rid of him. The pain of rejection was acute. Especially when he'd thought he'd noticed a tiny thaw.

At lunchtime Myles looked deep inside himself for some words of comfort to offer Joe. Something profound and healing. Finally he hit on it.

He walked over to Joe, placed his hand on his shoulder, looked at him with immense compassion and said, 'Fancy a pint?'

A tiny light appeared in Joe's dazed, dead eyes. 'Sure.'

They took a long lunch, even by advertising standards. In other words, they didn't come back until three o'clock. The following day.

By the fifth pint, they'd exhausted their usual topics of conversation – Arsenal, cars, Arsenal, breasts, what pricks all their clients were, Arsenal, England's chances of hosting the World Cup in 2006 – and were buffered enough to skirt around their feelings. In the middle of a discussion on Manchester's public transport system, Joe blurted out the sexual-harassment charge.

'I shouldn't have forced her to come for lunch with me yesterday,' he admitted, with shame and regret.

'Worth a try, mate,' consoled Myles, ever the wide-boy.

'I pushed her too far, she's obviously very fragile.'

Myles muttered something to the effect that Katherine was about as fragile as a Sherman tank

'You don't see what I see. She's so . . .' Joe stared dreamily into the middle distance '. . . sweet sometimes.'

'She's accused you of sexual harassment and you say she's sweet. You're pissed, mate.'

'Now that you mention it, I am.'

'When you're sober again, you'll have gone right off her.'

'I won't.'

'You'll 'afta. 'Cos she don't want you, mate.'

Joe winced. 'I'm going to apologize to her.'

Myles was appalled. 'You're bleeding radio.'

Joe looked puzzled.

'Radio rental – mental!' Myles expounded. 'Cockney rhyming slang.'

'I know,' Joe said. 'But you're not a Cockney.'

'Nah. From Surrey. The poor bit, though. Now, listen, mate, you can't apologize to her. That's as good as admitting you're guilty. Do you want the sack? You work hard, you're ambitious. Leave it, mate!'

'But I don't think she meant it. I think she just wants me to shove off . . .'

'Then do!' Myles said, simply. 'Now listen to Uncle Myles. What you need is to get up-close and personal with a totally pukka bird. That'll sort you.'

'No. It's too soon.'

'By the weekend?'

'No.'

'Sorry, mate. Forgot you're going to the footie.'

'No, I mean it would still be too soon.'

'All you have to do is pretend it's her.'

'I can't. I'd know. She wouldn't be Katherine.'

'Who looks at the mantelpiece when they're poking the fire?' Myles smirked triumphantly. He had an answer for everything.

'Myles, you're depressing me,' Joe said wearily.

'Cheer up, mate. You've been kicked into touch before, right?'

'Well, I went out with Lindsay for three years, then she moved to New York –'

'And you're still up for it with other girls, right?' Myles interrupted.

'I suppose. I mean, it took a while, we'd kind of run out of steam anyway, but it wasn't easy and though it was amicable it was still –'

'Blinding,' Myles cut in. 'Very interesting. Not. What I'm trying to say here is that you win some, you lose some. You'll get over it.'

Drunken hope filled Joe. Through the fuzz of alcohol, it seemed eminently possible to stop caring about Katherine. Even to meet another girl. He felt better already. 'You're right!' he agreed. 'Life's too short.'

'That's it,' Myles urged. 'And who wants to go where you're not wanted?'

'Not me. I'd make a bad obsessive,' Joe admitted.

'Why's that, mate?'

'Dunno. I'm just not obsessive enough, I suppose.'

'Yeh, 'sa problem, innit? Right, so this Kathy –'

'Her name's Katherine,' Joe interrupted. 'She doesn't answer to abbreviations of it.'

'Ooooooooh, excuse *me*,' Myles hooted, grabbing the handbag of the woman at the next table and thrusting it at Joe. 'The award of the handbag!'

He looked angrily at Joe. 'Don't take it so serious, wouldja?'

'Sorry,' Joe said, slumping back into his pit of gloom. 'It's just that I just thought I was finally getting somewhere with her.'

'Snog ya?'

Joe snorted. 'No.'

'Take my advice, mate, you weren't getting nowhere if you haven't even snogged her.'

Joe sighed. In his crude way, Myles was right.

'Give the woman back her handbag,' he said, wearily.

25

Tara staggered into the office, laden with carrier-bags, which she dumped on her desk. 'I don't know why they call it forbidden fruit,' she complained. 'Fruit is about the only thing that *isn't* forbidden.'

Ravi, tearing open a Marks and Spencer's ploughman's roll, which boasted thirty-six grams of fat, watched with interest as she unloaded apples, satsumas, pears, nectarines, plums and grapes and arranged them like amulets around her desk. 'Care for half my roll?' he offered, in his public-school voice.

Tara made her two index fingers into a cross.

'It's got extra mayonnaise,' he tempted.

'Bad magic. Keep it away from me.'

'You're absolutely barking.' Ravi jumped up, thrust his hands on Tara's head and bellowed, 'Out, out, demons, leave this poor child.'

'That feels *spectacular*.' Tara sighed, as Ravi massaged her skull. 'I love it when you exorcize me.

'Oh, don't stop,' she begged, as Ravi abandoned her, to cram eight hundred calories of sandwich into his mouth.

'No choice,' he mumbled through mouthfuls. 'Nothing like a good exorcism for working up an appetite.'

A highly harassed Vinnie rushed in. A sleepless night with his three-month-old had had him pulling his hair out, and as soon as he saw Tara's desk, he felt his hairline recede another inch or so. What kind of office was he running? 'What's going on here? It's like Albert Square!'

'Are you subcontracting?' Teddy and Evelyn, the his 'n' hers couple, had arrived.

'Opening a fruit stall?' Teddy inquired.

'What a great idea,' said Evelyn. 'Can I buy a banana?'

'Bananas aren't welcome round here,' Tara said curtly.

'Too fattening?'

'Too fattening.'

'Bananas aren't fattening.' Vinnie knew he should maintain managerial distance, but couldn't help himself.

'That's right. Nothing is fattening,' Teddy insisted. 'Look at me. I eat whatever I want, as much as I want of it, and I'm like a stick insect.'

'Women talking about how many calories things have – *that's* what makes them fattening,' Vinnie decreed. 'Women ruin food for themselves.'

'Did you see the documentary last night about the blokes up Everest?' Ravi brayed. 'Bloody freezing. One of them, his thumb completely froze and fell off. Nothing to eat but snow . . .'

'Maybe I should try that,' Tara said, thoughtfully. 'The Everest diet. Right, Ravi, Evelyn, everyone gather around, we're going to have a credit-card-cutting-up ceremony.'

'Another one?' Vinnie exclaimed. 'It's only six months since the last time.'

'I know, but I got my Visa bill this morning. Stop me before I spend again,' she intoned darkly. 'Ravi, scissors!'

Ravi dutifully passed the office scissors.

'Bin!'

Ravi already had the wastepaper basket in his hand: he knew the drill of old. Tara took out her purse and held her Visa card aloft, swivelling from the right to the left. 'Everyone looking?' Then, fighting a pang of loss, she pushed the scissors through the unwieldy plastic. As everyone except Vinnie burst into applause, Tara murmured, 'I am cleansed, I am pure. Now for my Access card.'

Everyone stood in respectful silence as the Access card was neatly snipped in two, then clapped again.

'Your Amex?' Ravi suggested, and after a slight hesitation, Tara took it out and reluctantly bisected it.

'Sears card?' Ravi then said, and Tara said irritably, 'Look, I'll need something. What if it's an emergency?'

'You'll still have your cashpoint card and your Switch card.'

'O . . . K.' Sadly, Tara cut her Sears card in two and let it fall into the bin.

'I'll give it a week before you're on the phone saying your purse has been stolen and that you need replacement cards.' Vinnie sighed. Maybe it was time he went on another course to learn how to manage staff. 'Can you all please do some work now?' he urged, belatedly trying to act like the boss he was.

News of Tara's fruit stall spread, so much so that people from other departments came to look and snigger. She was embarrassed, but unbowed. Something had to be done, especially after the frenzy in the supermarket the previous night. If she was surrounded by fruit, there was no excuse for eating anything else.

But fruit just never seemed to hit the spot, no matter how much she ingested. She ate an apple, a plum, a couple of satsumas, three nectarines, another satsuma, four more plums, a handful of grapes, one more satsuma and was still starving. So she started into a pear and nearly broke a tooth. She sighed.

She knew about pears. There was a one-and-a-half-minute period during which pears could be eaten. Until then they were as hard as concrete. Thereafter they were rotten mush. If you caught them during the short window, they were delicious, but the chances of that happening were slim.

They had a brainstorming session that morning as they formulated a game plan for the MenChel project they'd just been allocated.

Vinnie marched up and down in front of the office whiteboard, drawing grids and time scales and anxiously rubbing his thinning scalp.

'I've put my cock on the block with this one, lads,' Ravi muttered to Tara, as Vinnie did his spiel.

'We're talking a two-thousand-person-day project and we've got to do it right because we've got the ruddy quality auditors breathing down our necks,' Vinnie urged.

'What do you think that white stain on Vinnie's sleeve is?' Ravi whispered to Tara.

'Baby puke.'

'We've a very tight deadline,' Vinnie galvanized, 'no room for slippage, so we've got to really pull together as a team on this one and . . . and what on *earth's* that funny, squelching noise?'

Ten people turned to look at Tara.

'It's Tara,' Teddy said triumphantly.

'That was hardly team-spirited.' Tara was wounded. 'Fingering me like that. Sorry, Vinnie, it's my stomach. The different fruit acids mingling. I think they're having a party in there.'

She longed for some carbohydrate to calm it all down. Something to fill up that liquid hollowness. She felt like her stomach was a great banqueting hall, with forty-foot-high ceilings. Or an enormous conference centre that could hold three thousand delegates. Huge and echoey, cavernous and empty, empty, empty. But she was fired with willpower and wouldn't give in. Not even when Sleepy Steve did a doughnut run to oil the wheels of the think-tank.

She rushed to the smoking room the minute the meeting was adjourned. 'God bless these babies.' Tara waved her pack of cigarettes at the small cluster of diehards in the tiny smoke-filled chamber. 'Think of how huge I'd be if Nick O'Teen hadn't kept a lid on the great hunger over the years. The fire brigade would have to cut me out of my house with a chainsaw.'

In the hour before lunch, whenever someone passed Tara's desk, they broke off a couple of her grapes and popped them in their mouths.

'What's wrong?' Ravi saw her distressed face.

'My grapes,' she complained. 'Everyone thinks they're fair game. But they're not. They're my lunch. I mean, I don't go up to you and just help myself to one of your sandwiches.'

'You do,' he gently reminded her.

'Well, maybe I do,' she admitted. 'But I'm different. *Normal* people don't go around eating other people's lunches uninvited.'

At one o'clock Ravi approached Tara. 'How's about you and me strolling up to Hammersmith? Doing some aimless wandering around the shops, maybe partaking of a scratch-card or two?' he suggested suavely.

They often did this when Ravi didn't go to the gym.

'No, thanks.' Tara whipped out her wool and needles. 'I'm going to knit my hunger away!'

He stared in amazement. 'What's that?'

'A jumper for Thomas.'

'I hope he knows how lucky he is.'

'Don't worry. He will.'

Ravi lingered, reluctant to leave without her. 'How about I fetch you some more fruit from the shops?'

'Don't bother, Ravi,' she said. 'The fruit is just making me hungrier. I suspect utter starvation is the only way, because if I eat a little bit the floodgates open and I want more and more.'

'I don't know why you do this to yourself,' Ravi said.

Tara looked scornfully at him. 'Blind, are you?'

'I think you're a top girl,' Ravi said.

'No you don't. Now go away, I've to knit myself a happy relationship.'

'Aw, please, Tara,' he wheedled. 'It's no good going around the shops without you.'

She indicated her knitting.

'We can stand in the newsagent's and read the magazines,' he tempted.

She shook her head.

'They might have a new lipstick in Boots that really doesn't come off,' he said, wickedly. 'It could be just in.'

'Do your Elvis impersonation,' she conceded, 'and I'll think about it.'

'I'm taking requests.'

'"Hound Dog".'

Ravi shook a lock of hair over his forehead, curled his lip, held up his arms and did some serious hip action. '"You ain't nothin' but a hound dog,"' he began.

'You see!' Tara yelled. 'I knew you didn't fancy me.'

Tara survived the trip to Hammersmith, with all its temptations, without breaking out. First they went into Marks and Spencer's and half-heartedly looked around, Ravi checking to see if any new lines in cakes or buns had been introduced since that morning. Tara bought three pairs of stomach-flattening tights because she wanted to leave with *something*. Then they went to Boots where Ravi checked out their sandwiches and Tara looked at all the lipsticks that claimed to be virtually irremovable, but which she knew through bitter experience were very much the reverse. Unable to muster much enthusiasm she purchased some face capsules.

'Thalidomide?' Ravi said in alarm.

'Biomide,' she corrected him.

Next they went into the newsagent's where Ravi flicked through *Top Gear* and Tara read *Slimming*. For a grand finale they bought a scratch-card each. Ravi passed her a twopence piece and they flaked away aluminium ink in companionable silence. Neither of them won anything.

'How long have we been gone?' Tara asked.

'Forty-five minutes.'

'S'pose we'd better go back,' Tara said.

'S'pose.'

After lunch, back in the office, as conversations drifted over to her, everyone seemed to be talking about food.

Vinnie described the new project to Evelyn as 'a Marathon task', and Tara instantly thought of peanuts, caramel and thick milk chocolate.

'Don't be chicken,' Evelyn gently teased, and Tara almost fainted at the idea of a big bucket of KFC.

Ravi was on the phone to Danielle, his girlfriend. 'You can't have your cake and eat it,' he advised. What kind of cake, Tara wondered dreamily. Moist, sticky banana cake? Dark, rich chocolate fudge cake? Sweet, delicious carrot cake? Dense and heavy Dundee cake?

'Join the club,' Ravi laughed affectionately into the mouth-piece, as Tara visualized tearing off the yellow wrapper and the gold foil and biting through the thick chocolate and the biscuit underneath. God, this was torture.

'. . . cast your bread upon the waters . . .' drifted over to Tara, from yet another conversation. What kind of bread? Ciabatta? Focaccia? Baguette? Batch loaf? But did anyone other than Bible-bashers talk about casting bread upon the waters? Was she hearing things? Hallucinating from hunger?

Just then a dark, elegant woman appeared at the office door. 'Hello,' she said. 'I'm Pearl from Technical Support. I heard I could buy an orange here.'

Everyone turned and looked at Tara.

'You heard wrong,' she said bluntly.

'Sorry,' said Pearl from Technical Support, edging back to the door. She suspected she'd put her foot in it.

'Oranges put up too much of a fight,' Tara explained. 'Juice everywhere except in the orange. I can do you a satsuma, though. Far more convenient.'

After work Tara did a step class, and was delighted when she almost fainted. She had to sit on the bench for fifteen minutes before she could stand up without her knees buckling. When she got home, Thomas smacked her on the bum and said, affectionately, 'You're not bad, for a fat lass.'

That night, she went to bed trembling with hunger and overexertion. All in all, it had been a very good day.

26

Katherine was interested to see that the day she implied Joe was sexually harassing her he didn't come back to work after lunch. He'd obviously gone to the pub, and she couldn't help a slight thrill at her power to hurt him.

At work the following morning, she was mildly curious. Joe would have had time to recover from her accusation, so would he revert to being charming and familiar? Would the morning chats continue? Would the desk-sitting continue? Would the flirting and persuading continue?

Would her cruelty continue?

To her surprise, she was inclined finally to give him a break. He'd been so persistent, it was only fair. Perhaps she'd go for a drink with him – acting as though he had a gun to her head, of course.

She kept watching the door, not exactly anxious yet not quite at peace. But he didn't appear. She turned her attention to a trial balance but by lunchtime realized there was a part of her that had been on the alert all morning for him.

Finally, at three o'clock, he arrived, Myles in tow, carrying a bottle of Lucozade. Both men looked pale and sheepish.

'Gentlemen! Glad you could join us today,' Fred Franklin said, sarcastically.

Joe muttered something about having been on a shoot for an ad.

'So they shot it in your bedroom, did they?' Fred scorned.

'No,' Joe said defensively. 'In the bathroom, actually,' he added, with a rueful, hangdog smile, and moved across the office.

Instantly, Katherine assumed her smooth, enigmatic expression. Here we go!

Joe came towards her, right up to her desk – and kept going. To the coffee-machine. Seconds later, on his return, Katherine once more poised herself. But he bypassed her completely. In fact, he didn't even look in her direction as he went to his own desk.

Katherine gave him a few minutes to check his calls and e-mails, and expected him to come over then. But he didn't. She waited a bit longer while he dealt with any urgent work, and still her desk remained unsat on. Perhaps he had too much catching up to do after his twenty-six-hour lunch. She watched him covertly. He didn't *look* like a man snowed under with work.

After an hour passed, Katherine had to acknowledge that Joe wouldn't be visiting her today. That it seemed he'd given up on her. Relief clashed with disappointment. He's a wimp, she thought. What's an accusation of sexual harassment to a real man?

With an effort she switched her focus back to work, but her concentration was patchy. To the outside world she looked like a woman immersed in amortization calculations, but her head was full of exclamation marks. I can't believe he's just given up on me! Just like that! He was cracked about me yesterday! I was the sunshine of his life, he said!

She kept flicking glances, checking on him. In case he'd changed his mind. She happened to be watching when, across the office, Joe took off his jacket, tugged his tie loose and rolled up his sleeves. Though she didn't want to, Katherine stared hard. At the hair on his forearms, the skin silky underneath, the muscles bunching and lengthening every time he picked up the phone or clicked his mouse. His chrome watch sat heavy on his wrist. There was nothing wimpy about his arms.

That really irritated her. He presented himself as Mr Safe, Mr Too-Thin-to-Be-Macho. But, lean though he was, he had strength. Those arms were the arms of a sexy man . . . Oh, no! Back in your box, she admonished her recalcitrant feelings, back behind bars.

As she finished for the evening, Joe and his team were making noises about going to the pub. Hair of the dog, and all that.

Joe called, 'Hey,' and Katherine looked up. At long bloody last, she thought. And prepared to play hard to get. No point giving anything away too easily. But Joe's eyes skimmed over her and moved further along the office. 'Hey, Angie,' he called again. 'Coming for a drink?'

Katherine's stomach contracted. Angie was a copywriter. She was dainty, dark-haired, pretty and so new she hadn't yet been rechristened with regard to her sexual propensities.

'Why not?' Angie smiled.

Katherine waited for Joe to suggest that she come too, but the air resonated with his silence.

She shoved in a disk to back up her day's work and deliberately, with cold pleasure, hardened her heart. Joe Roth was an asshole. To think she'd felt sorry for turning him down! It hadn't taken him long to get over her. Clearly, small and skinny was his type, and he'd moved on to the office's *new* small and skinny woman.

He'd just been playing games with Katherine, and the minute she'd become interested, he'd have run off and left her with reopened wounds. He only wanted her because she was unavailable. Men were such children, their grass was always greener.

She'd had a lucky escape.

She finished backing up and threw the disk into her drawer with force. When she got to the lift, they were all there, Joe laughing at something Angie had said, his head close to hers. Katherine wanted to turn back, but that would have been even more excruciating. Stiff-faced, she went down with the merrymakers, all of whom kept saying that they could murder a pint.

'Why don't you come with us?' Myles suggested to Katherine, in the hope of cheering Joe up. Then he immediately regretted it. What if she accused *him* of sexual harassment?

'No, I don't think so,' she murmured, and waited for Joe to weigh in and try to persuade her. But he said nothing and she brimmed over with rage. Shallow swine. As she got out of the lift, she threw, 'Have fun,' over her shoulder and wondered how it hadn't choked her.

On Wednesday evenings, Katherine usually went tap-dancing. Losing herself, clattering along to 'Happy Feet' with six other women with flared shorts and fantasies of a happy childhood, while everyone else en route to the normal aerobics classes looked into the studio and sniggered.

Then after the class she often went out with Tara, Liv and, sometimes, Fintan and Sandro. But today she just wanted to go straight home. Too distressed to feel guilty, she flung herself into the tide of office workers making for Oxford Circus tube. And she couldn't bear that either. So she flagged a taxi and prayed for the driver not to be loquacious. The odds were stacked against her. Sure enough, she had to endure a forty-minute rant from a xenophobic Fascist called Wayne, who kept a photo of his three fat, ugly children on the dash, and said, of every nation on earth, 'Fing is, lav, they're filfy, in't they?' The French, Bosnian, Jamaican, Algerian, Greek, Pakistani and, of course, the Irish, were all, according to Wayne, filthy. As she rang the others from her mobile, and left messages to say she wouldn't be going out, she could barely hear herself think.

Finally Katherine got home but her elation was short-lived. Her clean, sparkling flat seemed sad and sterile. Too clean. *Neurotically* clean. She thought vaguely about eating, except she couldn't be bothered. She switched on the box, but couldn't find anything she wanted to watch. Her life, which she usually found so satisfactory, was unaccountably lacking. Everything in it, from her job to her flat, seemed dull, inadequate and only half alive. She popped a few blisters of bubble-wrap, but even that had lost its charm.

Apart from the one enormous worry hanging over her – and that was so big she sometimes didn't even see it – she'd been perfectly content with her lot even a couple of days before.

She hated Joe for doing this to her. She'd made the mistake of starting to see herself through his eyes, and she'd liked the view. Now that he'd withdrawn his admiration she had to go back to seeing herself through less rose-coloured eyes – her own. The adjustment was always painful.

She couldn't ring Tara, Fintan or Liv to spill her guts and seek comfort. It just wasn't what she did. She'd always coped on her own. And she knew it'd upset the others if she dissolved into a gooey mush. Everyone thought that she was capable and emotionless.

Eventually she decided she'd better eat something but, as usual, she had nothing in. Listlessly she traipsed to the corner shop and uninterestedly picked up some things. But as she went to pay she was drawn to look at the paltry items languishing in the bottom of her basket. A frozen lasagne. Serves one. A single apple. The smallest carton of milk in existence. How pathetic. What a massive advertisement that she was alone. How the checkout man would pity her.

Angrily, she heaved up a two-kilo bag of mucky potatoes and threw it in the basket, nearly dislocating her shoulder and stretching her arm to twice its length. There! That'd teach people to think she didn't have a bloke. No single person would buy a two-kilo sack of potatoes. *Especially* ones still covered in earth. They were the preserve of mothers – standing at the sink, their knuckles chapped, scrubbing the dirt off with a nailbrush, before boiling a huge big pot of them for their demanding family.

High colour on her cheeks, Katherine smiled challengingly at the assistant. See. I'm a real person. But he didn't even make eye-contact with her. Then she lugged the spuds home, wondering what on earth she was going to do with them.

She ate her lasagne, her apple, and had a cup of tea, but the evening was long and she was agitated by its emptiness.

She ran herself a Philosophy bath, choosing the 'I know' bottle because the label promised 'self-worth, confidence, empowerment and a sense of achievement'. Then she went to bed and, for the first time in ages, she noticed she was alone.

Never mind, she thought. I've always got my television. She picked up her beloved remote control, determined to find something to lull her to sleep. Who needs a man when you've got Sky Movies?

But she found herself wondering what Joe would be like in bed. What he would look like naked. What it would feel like to circle her hands over his pearly-beautiful skin, to feel the muscles in his back. Despite all his boyish friendliness, he was sexy, Katherine conceded miserably. When he had been actively pursuing her, she wouldn't let herself think about how attractive he was. Only now that he was probably no longer available was it safe to.

At four in the morning she bumped awake and found herself cuddling the remote. Foreboding hung over her and it took a few seconds to identify exactly what it was. Then she remembered. Joe going out. Angie going too. In a flash she realized that he could be in bed with her right now. *Right now.* Somewhere across town, Joe Roth could be in bed, his arm around a naked woman. Katherine had fallen into the trap of thinking that she should be that woman. That his ardour belonged solely to her.

Flat on her back, she looked anxiously at the ceiling. It was a long time since she'd had interrupted sleep, and she didn't like what it meant. Old, old feelings were upon her, twisting and tormenting her.

Suddenly she was nineteen again, the pain of having her heart smashed into smithereens for the first time as fresh as ever. She'd been working as a trainee accountant in Limerick, but just couldn't bear to stay there any longer because she associated it with her lost love. She felt she'd go insane if she didn't get away. So she'd handed in her notice at Good & Elder, which caused consternation because she'd been doing so well. Although not so well *lately*, once her superior thought about it.

Then she went home to Knockavoy, hoping she'd outrun the pain. Unannounced, she arrived on the bus one September afternoon. Everyone was surprised to see her, because she hadn't been home much all summer. They were even more surprised when it transpired that she was back for good. She had been the class of '85's one big success story, the one that got away. Now she was home, and wouldn't say why.

Tara and Fintan's initial delight at her return soon changed to alarm. She'd obviously been very badly burned by the boyfriend she'd had in Limerick. Something to do with the snide way she sneered any time either of them said they fancied a boy gave it away. 'What's the point?' she'd scorn, heatedly. 'They pretend to be mad about you, then as soon as you're sucked in they leave.'

'I wouldn't mind being sucked in.' Fintan laughed, while Katherine glared.

'You're far better off on your own,' she insisted, her face a twisted, pained mask.

She'd always been so sweet and sunny before. Even if she didn't partake of boys herself, she'd never had any objection if they did. What had happened?

'Please tell us,' they asked over and over, with increasing desperation. 'It helps to talk about it. I swear to you, we know what it's like.'

But she wouldn't be drawn. She *couldn't* be drawn.

Meanwhile, locked in her silence, the longing tore her apart. And wouldn't go away.

She'd been brought up in a women-only house, had no male uncles, had never had a real boyfriend before, and she'd always been happy. But now that she'd experienced the presence of intense masculinity in her life everything was different, and she'd tapped into a great well of need. She wanted love and balm – from a man. Though it didn't make any sense to her, she felt that only a man could take away the pain inflicted by another.

But what was she going to do? The idea of falling in love again filled her with terror. Besides, she'd never get over her broken heart. Then, one sleepless night, two weeks after her return from Limerick, she thought of Geoff Melody, her father. And everything fell into place.

Immediately, the desire to meet him was powerful and all-consuming. She wanted to get out of bed, there and then, and go to England to look for him. What baffled her was how she could have left it until now. How could she not have felt this gaping absence before? Why had she wasted so much time?

Fresh, sweet hope swept aside her bitter pain and suddenly Katherine had a reason for living. She'd thought her life was over, that no one would ever love her again, but she'd been given another chance. Instantly her father became the repository for all her dreams and aspirations. He'd understand her – he was probably just like her. He would be her salvation, she was certain of it. It was obvious that everything would be okay now.

What would he be like? No point asking her mother, she was bound to give him a bad press. The nice thing was, though, that if her mother didn't like him, it meant she, Katherine, was bound to.

Katherine's thoughts ran away with themselves as she saw a bright, happy future unfold ahead of her. She'd go and live in England with her dad. Who needed a husband or a boyfriend when you had a father? He'd put a different spin on her past as well as her future, and she'd never mess up again, because she'd have the guidance of a man.

She lay awake fantasizing about what he was like. She bet he had an allotment. Englishmen of a certain age had allotments. He'd grow rhubarb for her. She'd sit with him, just the two of them, while he tilled the soil, and she'd tell him about her life, and he wouldn't say much but what he did say would be full of wisdom. *Male* wisdom.

Or he might be really lively and cheeky, with a Cockney accent and funny sayings. 'Stroike a loight, Kaffrin, me old choina,' making his living ducking and diving. *Legal* ducking and diving, mind. No funny business. One less-than-respectable pillar of the community was enough in any set of parents.

Or perhaps he'd be a bit of a toff. Call her 'm'dear', his terse delivery not hiding the warmth he felt for her. Maybe he had other children but didn't really get on with them and needed someone to take over the family accountancy business, and she'd arrive at just the right moment.

In her head her father became a combination of Arthur Fowler, Dick Van Dyke and Rumpole of the Bailey.

She barely considered that Geoff Melody mightn't be interested in her. Her need was so great that she couldn't contemplate it not being reciprocated.

It took her a long time to write the letter. She'd learnt that men don't like to be faced with naked need, so she couched her desire to meet Geoff Melody in casual, no-strings-attached terms. She knew he would fix her, but there was no need to scare him away by telling *him*.

I will ask you for nothing, was the subtext.

Ten days after she sent the letter, Katherine received an envelope with an English postmark. Her father had replied! From the stiffness of the expensive cream stationery it seemed that Geoff Melody was more Rumpole of the Bailey than Arthur Fowler.

But the letter wasn't from her father. It was from the executor of his will, informing her that her father had died from lung cancer six months previously.

While the end of her love affair had felt like a bereavement, her bereavement felt like the end of a love affair.

27

In the morning Katherine was anxious to get to work, keen to discreetly inspect Joe to see if there were any signs that he'd been up all night shagging Angie. But by the time she arrived at Breen Helmsford, she'd calmed herself down. He'd really seemed to be besotted with her, and she wasn't convinced that that had entirely evaporated. Besides, he had integrity and decency – not the type to screw someone he barely knew.

And she felt no need to ponder why, if he had that much integrity and decency, she wouldn't go out with him.

All anxiety was gone by the time she breezed into the office. When she saw Joe leaning against the wall by the coffee-machine, she couldn't help smiling at him. Until a closer look showed him to be unshaven, dishevelled and very weary. He looked lots more than a day older.

She swept her eyes over him and noticed, in nightmarish slow-motion, that his clothes were the same ones he'd had on the day before. Could she be imagining it? She forced herself to check again. Oh, God! Exactly the same suit. Same jacket that he'd taken off yesterday afternoon. Same shirt whose sleeves he'd rolled up. Same tie that he'd loosened. A sure sign he hadn't gone home.

A stillness settled on her. Her blood felt like it had stopped flowing, as though the shock had brought it skidding to a halt.

He didn't return her rapidly disappearing smile. His brown

eyes, which usually twinkled with warmth and puppyish good humour when he saw her, remained cold. Grimly he nodded at her, chucked his polystyrene cup in the bin and turned away.

Like a sleepwalker, Katherine took off her coat. Maybe he'd stayed with one of the lads, she told herself. It didn't have to be Angie, small and skinny though she was.

As she switched on her computer, she had a powerful, unexpected flash of dislike for her desk. What was wrong with it? Irritably, she looked at it, trying to identify what was lacking. Then she realized: Joe wasn't sitting on it.

All morning, as she pretended to busy herself with spreadsheets, Katherine perfected the art of looking without seeming to, discreetly checking for any signs of rapport between Joe and Angie. Neither of them approached the other but, as Katherine well knew, that meant nothing. Often when people slept with each other they ignored each other the next time they met. In fact, the more they ignored each other the more *likely* it was that they'd had sex.

Both Joe and Angie were at their desks, busily keying stuff into their computers, but Katherine found no comfort in this – they were probably sending each other erotic e-mails.

Katherine noticed something else disquieting. If you took away Joe Roth's boyish, puppy-like friendliness, what were you left with? A grim, sexy man, that's what. Rough, stubbly and in yesterday's clothes, Katherine had never seen him looking so good.

She kept half an ear on the office banter, mostly to hear if they called Angie a name other than Angie. Something vulgar, which would mean that someone had slept with her. But nothing doing. Just a running commentary on how sick and hungover they all felt. How they were never going to drink again. How they couldn't remember a thing past ten o'clock. How Darren had puked in a doorway. How they'd been asked to leave Burger King.

She was back to feeling bleak and weird, never in the heart of life, always hovering on the edges.

'Excuse me, Icequeen.' Katherine's head shot up to find Angie standing in front of her. For a brief mad second she thought Angie was there to tell her that she hadn't slept with Joe Roth. But just a moment . . .

'*What did you call me?*'

'Icequeen,' Angie said, nicely.

At Katherine's expression, Angie faltered. 'Isn't that your name?' She was now confused. 'But that's what everyone calls you. I thought it was Irish. I've a cousin called Quiveen . . .'

'My name is Katherine, and your colleagues and mine call me the Ice Queen because I happen to respect myself enough not to sleep with people I work with,' Katherine snapped.

'Oh, fu –' Angie looked mortally embarrassed – and slightly ashamed. Ashamed because she *hadn't* respected herself enough not to sleep with a person she worked with?

'Now I understand – *the* Ice Queen. I'm sorry! I just wanted to give you my tax-free allowance for the payroll.' She flung her tax code on the table. 'So that I won't be put on emergency tax.' Then she legged it.

Katherine looked at the piece of paper in front of her. It would be so easy to make a mistake and put Angie on one of the most vicious tax codes in existence, so that her net take-home pay would be a negative figure of several thousand. Of course, it would have to be fixed the following month, but wouldn't it be worth it just to see the look on her face?

I'm a professional, she reminded herself, and the madness

stopped. It had been a lovely fantasy, but that's all it was. With an inaudible sigh she started work again. She'd be OK. It might take a few days for it all to calm down, but she'd be OK.

28

Tara had a good week. Well, she had an abstemious week. Only a couple of slips. Fish and chips for lunch on Wednesday and Friday afternoon buns. (Who was she to fly in the face of tradition?) But the great thing was that her breaking out had been contained. It hadn't unleashed an unstoppable tide of gluttony. Not only that but she'd managed to knit twenty-eight rows of Thomas's jumper and get to the gym four times.

Even though there was no obvious reduction in her size, Thomas seemed pleased with her for trying so hard and he'd been uncommonly affectionate.

On Wednesday night he'd said, 'C'mere, you old baggage,' and held her hand as they watched Real Madrid versus Barcelona. On Thursday night he'd thrown his arm over her in his sleep. She'd savoured being beneath its heavy weight, lying very still, afraid to do anything that might disturb him and make him take it away again.

Then, on Friday morning, he said bluntly, 'Your hair wants doing. Put the yellow stripes in it.' Which sent Tara to work all aglow – she found his Northern, uncompromisingly macho ways so sexy and was touched that he took an interest in her appearance. An interest that, for once, didn't have to do with her size.

She thanked God that the ominous anticipation which had been unleashed the previous weekend seemed to have died away. Briefly, she wondered if maybe she'd just got used to it.

She spent most of Saturday having her hair highlighted, mistakenly thinking that if you improve your hair you can improve your life. Sure enough, when she got home, Thomas was in a foul mood because Huddersfield had lost at home to Bradford.

'Three nil,' he roared, as she let herself in. 'Three bludeh nil.'

'Do you like my hair?' she asked foolishly.

'It looks like a load of bludeh straw,' he thundered. 'How much did that set you back?'

Tara was so angry she felt like crying. He'd wanted her to get it done – he'd practically *ordered* her. She thumped down her bags and strode from the room – she would never let herself cry in front of him. Not since he'd complained about his last girlfriend, Bella, 'She were always bludeh sobbing.' Bella, apparently, had been clingy, oversensitive and demanding, and Claire, the girlfriend before Bella, hadn't been much better. When she'd seen Thomas's contempt for them, Tara had sworn to herself that she'd be totally different. She'd please Thomas by never getting drippy and upset, by being a much better, less irritating girlfriend.

As she hyperventilated with humiliation in the bedroom, she told herself that Thomas didn't mean to be such a prick. He was just angry with life and had to take it out on someone. She shouldn't take it so personally.

That night Tara was under orders from Thomas to go to his friend Eddie's birthday party. As she wasn't exactly wild about Eddie, she rang Fintan to beg him to come and provide her with moral support, but just got his machine. So she rang his mobile and it went straight to voicemail. She hadn't spoken to him since Monday night. They normally spoke to each other daily, but as he'd been in Brighton all week and she'd been so trembly from not eating, as well as slightly stung and mortified by their conversation about HIV tests, she hadn't dwelt on it.

Next she rang Katherine. She hadn't seen her all week either.

'Come to Eddie's party, *please*,' Tara pleaded.

'No,' Katherine said, gently. 'I'm sorry, but I hate Eddie. It would choke me to wish him a happy birthday.'

Katherine regarded Eddie as simply a better-paid version of Thomas.

'But I haven't seen you since last Monday,' Tara said sorrowfully. 'I know it's mostly my fault, spending all my evenings going to the gym, but still. So what will you do this evening? Have a quiet night in with your remote control?'

'I was supposed to be going out with Emma but Leo's got croup.'

'Oh dear. I really must visit Emma . . .'

'Then I was supposed to be going to a party with Dolly but she fell off her new five-inch stilettos and sprained her ankle.'

'Cripes. If Fintan's assistant is wearing stilettos, they really must be back in. I'd better get into training.'

'Anyway, the upshot is, I'm going to the cinema.'

'On a Saturday night? That's a bit sad.'

'Not as sad as Eddie's party is going to be.'

'Who are you going with?'

'On my own.'

'God,' Tara said enviously. 'You're so cool.'

'Tell me what's up with Fintan. I can't get hold of him.'

'Don't ask me, I can't get hold of him either.'

Then Tara rang Liv.

'Sorry,' Liv said, 'but Lars is returning to Sweden so I have to stand in Terminal Two and embarrass both of us by crying and begging him to leave his wife and come and live with me.'

Despite starving herself all week, getting dressed to go out was still utter torment for Tara. Being fat made her feel so much less human, shunted to life's margins, with no outlet to indulge her femininity. She'd love to have wiggled about confidently in a short, tight, flirty little dress, but the best she could hope for was to wall-hug in a wide, baggy top which covered a multitude of sins and sent Thomas into a flinty-eyed fouler.

Cronyless, she had to endure three hours in the pub, drinking diet Coke, lasciviously eyeing the peanuts, and yearning for the day when they invented reduced-fat lager. Then they all went back to Eddie's flat in Clapham for the party. Which, as Tara realized, surveying it in disappointment, wasn't much of a party. There were only about twenty guests and every single one of them *had been invited*. There would have been a bigger turnout, except after the pub multitudes had to leave early to relieve their babysitters.

The music was on too low for anyone to want to dance. People stood and sat in little clusters, discussing the wonders of MDF, door-handles in the Conran Shop, good sofa-shops – and some of these were straight men!

Tara listened in on a conversation between Stephanie and Marcy who, from the sound of things, were trying to get pregnant. Lots of talk of folic acid and how very acceptable it was to have your first child at thirty-seven.

'Is your partner supportive?' Stephanie asked Marcy.

'What partner?'

'Er, the man, the father . . . ?'

'Oh.' Marcy laughed nervously. 'I don't know. I haven't met him.'

'But I thought you said you were trying to get . . . pregnant?'

'Sperm bank.'

Tara hastily made her excuses and went over to Mira, Paul's girlfriend, who wore a short black rubber skirt – no fear she'd be talking about sofas and folic acid.

'It's only small,' she sighed, blissfully, 'but I love it.'

What was she talking about? Tara wondered. Her tattoo? A nose-ring? Paul's penis?

'It's a real sun trap,' she enthused. 'In the summer the rhododendrons along the back wall are *glorious*. They thrive like wildfire . . .'

Jesus! Gardening. Tara was disgusted. I mean, *gardening*.

Aimlessly, she wandered into the kitchen, where Thomas and his circle of pals stood, neçking lager and trading insults. Turning their mouths upwards to show how 'good-natured' it all was. Eddie laughingly belittled Thomas's badly paid job, while Thomas retaliated by calling Eddie 'a flash bastard'. Thomas scorned Paul for supporting a third-division football team and Paul swaggered that at least he had loyalty. Paul doubled over with mirth when he heard that Michael's girlfriend had dumped him. Michael nearly had to be hospitalized when he heard that Eddie had totalled his car during the week.

While they clutched their beer cans and howled with hilarity, Tara retained a polite smile. Making sure Thomas wasn't looking, she flicked a quick look at her watch. One thirty. Hopefully they could go home soon. What a let-down of a Saturday night. She'd nearly have been better off going to the pictures with Katherine.

The merriment continued. Roaring with laughter, Eddie said that Thomas's flat was a dreadful investment and that he was bound to be in negative equity for the rest of his life. In high spirits, Thomas told everyone that Paul's ex-girlfriend said that Paul could do with a course of Viagra. With a great display of amusement Paul grinned at Thomas: 'At least my mother didn't run off and abandon me.'

Tara anxiously realized that things were about to break through the maintenance-level hostility when, luckily, someone put 'One Step Beyond' on the tape deck. Suddenly the living-room carpet was aswarm with thirty-something men dancing for the one and only time that evening.

29

During the week, she'd gleaned a certain pleasure from feeling light and empty, enjoying the sensation of control and moral superiority. But it had started to wear thin. So when Sunday rolled around, Tara had that Friday feeling and was ripe for a major blow-out. She was keenly aware of the danger of her metabolic rate dropping through lack of food. And, of course, she'd endured five days of fruit and deprivation. She deserved a reward. She was vaguely aware that this was her usual pattern, but not aware enough to be able to break it. Washing around in the backwaters of her brain was the idea of going for a lovely, long, alcohol-sodden, six-course lunch.

And her luck was in – Thomas was going to be out for most of Sunday because he was playing football.

Tara rang around and unfortunately Katherine was working, doing the Year Start. 'But you've just done the Year End!' Tara pointed out, disappointed.

'Yes, and with every end comes a beginning,' Katherine said.

'Very profound,' Tara said. 'And something that you'd do well to remember.'

Once more, without success, Tara tried Fintan. Perhaps he and Sandro had gone away for the weekend. But they always told her and Katherine when they were going anywhere. No matter whether it was Marrakesh or Margate, a production was made of it. So where the hell were they?

Lighting a cigarette she rang Liv who, in the wake of Lars' departure, was game for an outing. The only downside was that Liv was utterly miserable. Although even when her life was going fantastically well, she was still utterly miserable.

In Thomas's earshot, Tara agreed with Liv that they'd go shopping. Except Tara intended they'd keep it very brief and, as soon as possible, head for a purveyor of deep-fried potato skins. Her mind was made up, and she didn't care that she was probably about to wipe out five days of weight loss in one sitting.

'I'm on my way,' Liv promised.

Liv tried to time her arrival for after Thomas's departure, but to her distress he was still there. He nodded brusquely as she passed en route to the kitchen with Tara. Though he approved of Liv's long blonde hair and firm golden skin, he was irritated that she had to go and ruin the whole thing by being taller than him.

Liv hated Thomas's flat: it was so depressingly dark and stank of cat. She itched to rip off the brown hessian wallpaper and paint the walls eau-de-Nil, to tear up the carpet tiles and varnish the wood, to rip down the roller blinds and swag and drape with lilac organza. But the kitchen was the worst, she thought, looking around at the mustard Formica cupboards. She longed to . . . to . . . burn the whole sorry mess to the ground.

Tara really should take it in hand. Didn't she know that decorating was the new rock and roll?

Tara closed the kitchen door. 'So Lars has gone back?' she asked gently.

'Yes.' Liv nodded, her face taut with misery. 'I'm very bad this time. Very bad.'

'You're always very bad,' Tara tried to cheer her up. 'Even if he leaves his wife and marries you, you'll still be miserable.'

'But I think I'm too bad to go shopping,' Liv apologized. 'What if I don't find anything nice? I don't think I could cope in my current fragile condition.'

'Think of the joy you'll have if you see a great pair of shoes,' Tara encouraged. She didn't want Liv to abandon her, because then she'd have to go and watch Thomas play football.

'And what happens if they don't have them in my size?' Liv countered. 'It could be dangerous. Jung says – '

'Jung knows nothing about shoes,' Tara said firmly. She refused to be browbeaten by Liv's extensive knowledge of psychotherapy. 'But if Jung won't let you go shopping, what do you want to do?'

Liv stared at her, her blue eyes clear and candid. 'I want to get pissed,' she said.

'Why didn't you say?' Tara exclaimed, wreathed in smiles. 'I just thought you wanted to leave me and go home. Come on, then! We'll go to one of the locals, get mouldy drunk and . . .' she dropped her voice just in case Thomas heard '. . . have a roast lunch.'

'With extra roast potatoes . . .' Liv whispered in excitement.

'The whole thing drenched in gravy . . .'

'Then some apple pie . . .'

'With a bucket of custard . . .'

'Let's just wait for Thomas to go,' Tara said.

Ten minutes later Thomas's lift arrived. Tara and Liv gave him a few more minutes just to make sure he really was gone, then gleefully elbowed each other and said, 'Come on!'

'Shall we take a taxi?' Liv asked, as they stood on the street.

'I've a suggestion to make,' Tara said, staring into the middle distance theatrically. 'It's a long shot, but it might just work. We could walk.'

'Walk? How far is it?'

'Only about fifty yards.'

'OK. Shall we take a taxi?' Liv deadpanned. 'Oh! I did a joke! Did you hear me, Tara? I did a joke!'

'Good girl yourself.'

'It's a French letter day when I do a joke.'

'*Red* letter.'

As they made their way to the Fox and Feather, Liv said, 'I don't do this often.'

'What? Get buckled on a Sunday?'

'No. Walk.'

Three doors down from the pub was the Beauty Spot. It still had the big sign in the window saying, 'TONING TABLES! FREE TRIAL!' With a leap of hope, it crystallized for Tara that there were other ways to get slim, aside from exercise and starvation. Maybe she'd call in next Saturday and find out how much it cost.

The pub was crowded and noisy, with people eating, drinking and playing darts. Good humour abounded.

'What do you want to drink?' she asked. 'Wine? G and T?'

'No,' Liv said, firmly, 'I want a pint of lager.'

'Oooooh, that's my girl.' Tara clasped Liv's shoulders, and shook them affectionately. 'I was hoping you'd say that.'

'Will we eat now or later?' Liv asked.

Tara was torn. Obviously food was always welcome, but alcohol had a strong effect on an empty stomach, and she really wanted to get twisted drunk . . .

'*Exactly!*' Liv agreed. 'So when it's safe and we're very drunk, then we'll eat.'

Tara fought through the crowds at the bar, and came back with two brimming pints of lager. Then immediately went away again, but returned in moments bearing two more pints. 'Might as well. We're on a mission.'

She set them down and produced a selection of savoury snacks from about her person. 'Can't drink pints without crisps to keep them company.'

They clinked glasses, 'That'll put hair on your chest,' Tara said. 'No, no, not literally!' she added, to Liv's appalled face. Liv spoke better English than Tara, but her knowledge of colloquialisms sometimes let her down.

As they caught up on their week, their conversation automatically and comfortably slipped into My Life's More Of A Disaster Than Yours – a game for two or more players.

'Here we are in Self-pity Corner, where I'm fatter than you,' Tara said.

'No, I'm fatter than *you*,' Liv retorted.

'Well, I'm poorer than you,' Tara insisted.

'No, I'm poorer than you,' Liv replied.

'Yes, but I owe more money than you,' Tara elaborated.

'No, I owe more money than you,' Liv countered.

'I smoke more than you.'

'No, I smoke more than you.'

'Liv, you don't smoke.'

'Yes, but if I did, I'd smoke more than you. I'm very self-destructive,' she added proudly.

'Point taken. Now where were we? Oh, yes. My flat is messier than yours.' Tara was adamant.

'No, my flat is messier than yours.' Liv defended herself valiantly.

'Well, my boyfriend is a bigger bastard than yours,' Tara insisted.

'No, my boy – Just a moment, you're right, your boyfriend *is* a bigger bastard than mine,' Liv agreed. 'You win that round.'

'Oh.' Tara was upset. She'd only said it so that Liv would contradict her.

'Was that a bad thing to say?' Liv asked, in a little voice.

'Oh, Liv.' Tara sighed, taking a big swig of lager, then lighting a cigarette. 'Something's wrong with me and Thomas.'

Tell me something I don't know, Liv refrained from saying.

Though she was frightened of talking about it, because it made it more real, Tara found herself blurting, 'We had an . . . um . . . conversation last Saturday . . .'

She paused and Liv remained silent and compassionate-looking.

'. . . and he said that if I got pregnant he wouldn't stand by me. Not that I'm planning to or anything, but it scared the life out of me. I've tried my best not to think about it and I know he loves me. But all week, under the surface, I've been expecting something terrible to happen.' She took a shaky drag from her cigarette. 'It's not like we've had a particularly bad week – in fact, a couple of times he's been lovely to me – but I just have this awful feeling hanging over me. And I'm so narky! I lost my temper with him on Monday night, and I wanted to again when I got home from the hairdresser's yesterday. I can't understand it.'

Liv could think of millions of reasons to be furious with Thomas.

'What should I do?' Tara asked, desperately. 'And please leave your personal feelings out of it.'

Liv took a breath and decided to risk it, 'I think you should leave him.'

'HAHAHAHAHA,' Tara roared, then quickly lit another cigarette.

'I'm serious,' Liv said. 'What kind of future have you? If he says he won't stay if you become pregnant, he's not exactly offering a long-term relationship.'

'I'll just make sure I don't get pregnant,' Tara said grimly.

'Don't you want to have children. Eventually?'

'I'll survive.'

'But, in any case, that's not the point. You want more of a commitment than he wants to give. Cut your losses.'

Now, where had Tara heard that before?

'How the hell can I leave him?' she asked, suddenly tearful.

'Easy, pack a bag, come and stay with me, or Katherine or Fin –'

'I'm thirty-*one*.' Tara's voice was high and hysterical. 'I can't leave him, I'll never meet anyone else. I haven't any time left . . .'

'Nonsense.'

'. . . I'm losing my looks, my flesh is drooping floorwards, my childbearing days are slipping through my fingers like mercury . . .'

'You just said you don't mind if you don't have a baby –'

'And there's nowhere to meet men.' Tara ignored her. 'That awful party I went to last night was so depressing. And, worse again, I've kind of gone off going to clubs.' She paused with dreadful realization. 'It's a disaster, Liv. I'm in the Last Chance Saloon . . . and I want them to turn the music down!'

Liv despaired. Tara was so hard to help. 'So, because you

think you won't find someone else, you will stay with a difficult, selfish man?'

'It's not his fault he's like that,' Tara insisted. 'And, if you don't mind, I prefer to think of him as damaged and sensitive.'

Liv didn't think she could bear another insightful lecture on Thomas's childhood, so she said quickly, 'So you'll stay with a damaged, sensitive man?' Adding under her breath, 'Who behaves in difficult, selfish ways?'

'Certainly, if the alternative is no man at all.'

'We're modern women, *millennium women . . .*'

'Don't even say it,' Tara hissed, scrabbling once more for her cigarettes.

'What?'

'That we don't need a man. Need doesn't come into it.'

'But what about self-respect?' Liv felt compelled to ask.

'Self-respect doesn't keep you warm at night.'

'Self-respect doesn't bring out the bins.'

'Neither does Thomas.'

'Actually, neither does Lars.'

A silence ensued.

'I'm in the Last Chance Saloon also,' Liv had the decency to say.

'No, you're not. Lars has said that he'll leave his wife for you.'

'He's lying,' Liv admitted.

'Well, yes, but at least he had the decency to *say* it. And maybe he'll actually do it one day.'

'A leper can't change his spots,' Liv said mournfully.

'Why are relationships so difficult?' Tara demanded.

It was actually a rhetorical question but, according to Liv, there were explanations for everything. 'We must look to our childhoods,' she said pompously. 'As I've told you many times. For example, Katherine has no man because of the absence of a father-figure in her life when she was growing up.'

'If Katherine was here, she'd make you cry for saying that,' Tara felt she'd better point out.

Liv ignored her. 'We human beings have a design flaw in that we're drawn to the familiar, even when it's not pleasant. You're with a bad-tempered man like Thomas because your father was . . . What's the word? Narky?'

'A narky pig,' Tara supplied, helpfully. 'So you keep telling me.' She'd almost finished her second pint and, miraculously, felt slightly less despairing. 'But knowing why I – allegedly – do it hasn't stopped me from doing it,' Tara said wryly. 'If you want my opinion, psychotherapy is just a big cod.'

Before Liv could start into her usual trip that self-realization is no good without acting on it, Tara said quickly, 'And how about you? Explain to me why you're having an affair with a married man.'

'My mother had a very long love affair with a married man,' Liv explained.

'Did she really?' Tara was amazed and admiring. 'You Swedes. Such goers. I can't imagine my mother doing anything like that. In fact, I still don't believe she ever had sex at all –' Tara stopped abruptly.

'*No, wait a minute*,' she started again, in a suddenly high-pitched tone. 'You've always told me that your parents were the most happily married couple in Sweden! How could your mother have had an affair with a married man?'

'She did,' Liv insisted.

'But happily married people don't have affairs. Or, if they do, they have their happily married badges taken away.'

'She did.' Liv was adamant.

'Weeelll, perhaps if it was only a brief fling at the start of their marriage.' Tara was prepared to compromise. 'How long did it go on for?'

'Let's see.' Liv began to do arithmetic on her fingers and mutter to herself. 'If they got married in nineteen sixty-one and it's now nineteen ninety-nine, they have been together for thirty-eight years.'

Suddenly Tara understood. 'Liv, I don't think it counts as an affair with a married man,' she pointed out, 'if the married man is your husband.'

'Awwww,' Liv said gloomily. 'I like when it all makes sense.'

'More drinks,' Tara ordered.

By the time they'd finished their third pints, even more of the edge had been taken off Tara's anxiety.

'No one's relationship is perfect,' she consoled herself, wrapped in a warm fuzz of self-justification and too much alcohol on an empty stomach. 'It's all about compromise. Myself and Thomas are grand and I'm perfectly normal. Do you know what it is if you kiss a frog and complain when he doesn't turn into a prince? It's immature, that's what it is! If you're grown-up you kiss a frog and you make yourself *like* it.'

'Are you drunk yet?' Liv asked.

'In all bibaprolity, one more pint might do it.'

'Excuse me?'

'I *said*, in all probability, one more pint might do it. Are you deaf?'

At about three o'clock, when they finally decided they were drunk enough, all the food in the pub was gone.

'Oh, no.' Tara put her hand to her mouth and giggled. 'What'll we do?'

'I'm very, very, very hungry now,' Liv warned.

'OK, we could get a takeaway, there's lots of places around here.'

'Chips!' Liv declared. 'If we can't have roast potatoes, we must have chips. We *must* have chips.'

She banged her empty pint glass on the table as she shouted, 'Chips! Chips! Chips! Chips!'

About ten feet away was a man who was within a whisker of winning the darts match. He threw his final dart just as Liv started her chips chant and he was lucky to barely miss skewering someone's ear to the wall.

In search of chips, Tara and Liv lurched out on to the Holloway Road, deeply surprised to find it was still daylight. Into the nearest fast-food joint, which was bursting at the seams with divorced fathers enjoying weekly visitation rights with their children. The noise was deafening.

'Eat-in or take-away?' Tara asked.

Liv looked around at the sea of children wearing cardboard hats. 'Take-away,' she replied. 'Take-far-away. Take-very-far-away. Oh, Tara, I think I did another joke! Am I a gas woman?'

Armed with two very full brown bags, they made their way back out on to the street.

'I'm so hungry I could eat a piebald pony between two bread vans,' Tara warned. 'Come on, hurry back to the flat.

'It's OK,' she said to Liv's aghast face. 'Thomas won't be back for hours and hours.'

But as they hurried past the Beauty Spot, it was open. Suddenly Tara thought how *fantastic* it would be to call in and give the toning tables a go, right there and then. And when she suggested it, Liv clutched her and yelled, 'That's a great idea. I've always wanted to go on them.'

They swung through the doors and Deedee, the beautician on duty, took one look at their red faces and manic eyes and felt a very strong urge to hide below the counter and pretend she wasn't there. 'We're closed,' she attempted.

'You're not.' Tara gave a wolfish grin and drenched her with lager fumes. 'We want to go on the toning tables.'

'I really don't think now is the right time.'

'Is someone else on them?' Tara asked.

'No, but –'

'Are you saying we're drunk?' Liv demanded, her eyes very blue in her puce face.

'Er, no.'

'We're good customers,' Tara insisted. 'I get my wags lexed here.'

'I beg your pardon?'

'I get my legs waxed here. How many times do you want me to say it?'

Poor Deedee had no choice. Reluctantly she led them into a little room that had six big pink plastic beds side by side. Tara and Liv were highly enchanted, in the way a sober person wouldn't be. Ooohing and aaahing and saying, 'So *that's* what they look like,' they hopped up on a bed each, still holding their brown paper bags. However once her ankles were strapped in, Liv declared, 'I'm starving! How long is this going to take?'

Tara looked at her in astonishment. 'But . . . but eat your nosh!' she said. 'Wasn't that always the plan? That's what I'm going to do.'

'Oh, great,' Liv said, delving into her bag. 'Very hungry.'

'I really don't think . . .' Deedee protested helplessly.

'Have a chip,' Liv offered her.

'I'm switching the tables on now,' Deedee said, in tight-lipped response.

'Here we go,' Tara said, as the end of the table lifted right up, taking her legs with it. 'Wehay! This is the business.'

Up and down, up and down went Tara's legs. In and out, in and out, scissored Liv's, while they both lay flat on their backs, eating their chips and cheeseburgers.

'This is wonderful,' sighed Liv. 'I feel so healthy.'

'It's very important to take care of our figures and our bodies,' Tara said, cramming another handful of chips into her mouth. She said something else but it was muffled by the food.

'Excuse me?'

'I *said*, we're worth taking care of. Awww, we're stopping.'

Grimly, Deedee shooed them on to another table and off they went again.

'Hey, my arms are going now!' Tara declared. 'Look, I'm waving at you.'

'And *I'm* sitting up. No, sitting down again. No, just a moment, sitting up, and down again . . .'

When they got off, brushing stray chips and blobs of ketchup off their fronts, they examined each other and declared they could see a definite improvement in their silhouettes.

All smiles, they left, assuring a stony-faced Deedee that they'd be back to book a full course each in a day or so. Then they made a join-the-dots progress home, where they drank every drop of Thomas's Newcastle Brown ale.

30

On Monday morning when Tara's phone rang at work, she braced herself for it to be Thomas, possibly to tell her to pack her bags and move out. He'd been splutteringly angry the evening before and Tara had been so drunk she still wasn't exactly sure why. Was it the theft of all his Newcastle Brown and his bottle of brandy? Or coming home to find Tara and Liv surrounded by pizza boxes? Or the burger wrappers he found in the bin? Or the way Tara and Liv screeched with laughter at him in his muddy knee-length nylon shorts? Or the way they'd neglected to feed Beryl?

Tara was sick with mortification. When she'd woken up that morning, Thomas had already left for work. With a mouth sticky and dry, she sat for ten minutes with her head in her hands, moaning. Then she rang Liv and whispered, 'I can't believe we did that. Say we didn't, tell me we didn't. Tell me I dreamt it, that we ate the burgers. Can you believe that we actually ate our burgers? On the toning tables? The shame, oh, the shame . . .'

'We were horrible,' Liv said, in a strangled voice.

'I'll have to find somewhere else to get my legs waxed,' Tara forced herself to admit. 'I can never go there again. I'll even have to cross the road rather than pass in front of it.'

'Guess what I did when I got home?' Liv choked.

'Oh, no. You didn't . . .'

232

'Ring Lars. Of course I did, I was drunk.'

'And what did you say?'

'The usual, I imagine. I can't exactly remember, but I think I called him a bastard and threatened to tell his wife about us.'

'Well, so long as you didn't tell him you loved him.'

'Oh, no,' Liv gasped, as the dreadful, drunken memory was jogged by Tara's words. 'I did. I told him I loved him. Now, I'll really have to ring and apologize. If he thinks I meant it, he'll dump me.'

On Tara's desk, her phone continued to ring. She was afraid to answer it, but as those around her gave frowning, inquiring looks, she was forced to.

'Hello,' she managed, in a trembling voice, hoping against hope it would be an irate punter.

'Tara?' It wasn't Thomas, it was Sandro.

'Hi!' Tara greeted, delighted to hear from him. 'Where've you and your fella been all weekend? We thought you must have been kidnapped by aliens.'

Just as Tara realized that although she and Sandro were very fond of each other, they never really rang each other directly, Sandro said, 'I have bad news.'

In an instant Tara's head became crystal clear. Seated though she was, the ground tipped beneath her. 'What is it?'

'It's Fintan.'

'What about him?'

'He's ill.'

'*Ill*? How? Flu or something?' But she knew it wasn't.

'We don't know for sure what's wrong with him.' *Yet*, hovered unspoken.

'But what way does he seem? What are his symptoms? Vomiting? Temperature? A pain in his stomach?' Vinnie, Teddy,

Evelyn and Sleepy Steve's heads shot up from their screens. Ravi's didn't. He was already hanging on Tara's every word.

'Weakness, fever and night sweats,' Sandro admitted.

'Weakness, fever and night sweats,' she mouthed, and it took only a second for the words to impact.

Immediately it was as if she'd always known. Ever since the first of Fintan's friends had become HIV positive, this had been one of her worst nightmares. Now that it had happened there was a horrible inevitability to it – how could she ever have doubted it would happen?

She remembered the fun she'd made of the lump on his neck and her breath became short and panicky.

'Also, he's lost a lot of weight,' Sandro said.

'It's only a week since I've seen him.' Tara felt inexplicably angry. 'He can't have lost that much.'

'I'm sorry, Tara,' Sandro said.

'Why didn't you call me? I've been leaving messages all weekend. I've been ringing and ringing.' She had the crazy feeling that if she'd known sooner she'd have been able to stop it.

'I didn't know how ill he was,' Sandro protested. 'I haven't been here – I was working on a house in Norwich until yesterday.'

'So why didn't *he* call me?'

'Tara, he was in the hospital much of the week.'

'The HOSPITAL!'

Vinnie knocked over a cup of coffee and Slim Cheryl, Sandra and Dave poked their heads around the partition to see what all the commotion was. Tara noticed none of it. She was too stunned by Fintan being at the hospital stage already. She began to cry, but didn't know if they were tears of rage, grief, fear or compassion. 'I thought he was in Brighton.'

'He lied to me, also. Told me he had flu.'

'But how could you let him go to hospital on his own?' Tears trickled over her cheeks and she barely noticed Ravi pressing a Marks and Spencer napkin into her hand.

'Tara, I didn't know, I didn't know!' Sandro was distraught. 'He called me in Norwich and said he had flu and not to worry if he didn't answer the phone, that he would be sleeping.'

'So you didn't worry?' Tara asked, tartly. Almost sarcastically.

'Of course I worried,' Sandro replied. 'I have been worried for a long time.'

That was a shock. Tara's anger with Sandro vanished. He hadn't neglected Fintan. He had been worried. This was far worse than she'd realized.

'Maybe he *has* flu,' she said, in a flash flood of irrational hope. 'People get high temperatures with the flu and they feel weak and lose weight. Except if they're me, of course. I must be the only person in existence who puts *on* weight when she's sick.'

'He's been in the hospital,' Sandro reminded her. 'It's not flu.'

The urge to see Fintan was desperate. To know exactly how bad he was and to will him better with her presence.

'We're in the hospital and he's with a doctor,' Sandro said. 'He'll go home later. You can see him then.'

'I don't suppose . . .' Tara's sweaty hand gripped the phone '. . . that you've told Katherine?'

He hadn't.

Tara dialled Katherine's number. Often, bad news is conveyed with an odd glee. Even when there's huge sympathy, there's still an undercurrent of horrified delight at the drama. As well as the macabre kudos that attaches to being the bearer of shocking news.

Tara felt none of that.

Telling Katherine was one of the most appalling things she'd ever had to do. At least she, Tara, had had a warning, an intimation that all wasn't well when Fintan had his kiwi-neck. But, for Katherine, this was a cold call.

'Katherine?'

'Hi!'

'I've bad news,' Tara blurted, quick to sidestep a normal Monday morning conversation – what they did on Saturday night and how Tara wished it was already Friday.

Katherine waited with her customary sangfroid. There was no flurry of panicky inquiries.

'It's Fintan,' Tara said. 'He's sick.'

'What kind of sick?' Katherine's voice sounded cool, measured, thoughtful.

'They don't know for sure yet. But he's been having night sweats, losing weight, is terribly weak . . .'

Pure silence ensued, then a strange noise came over the phone to Tara. Part whimper, part wail. Katherine was crying.

Katherine never cried.

In the afternoon, a request came from Fintan, conveyed by Sandro. Would Tara and Katherine call to see him after work that day?

'Of course,' stammered Tara. 'I'll come now, this minute.'

'Later is better,' Sandro soothed. 'We'll know more then.'

'You mean . . . ?' Tara choked. 'There's something to know?'

'Yes.'

'Good or bad?' she pleaded.

'Oh, Tara.' He sighed, and said nothing more.

'But . . .' she started.

'We'll see you later,' he said firmly.

Even though Tara had to go miles out of her way, she insisted on collecting Katherine from work so that they could arrive at Fintan's flat in Notting Hill together.

At six thirty, when Katherine came out of the front door of Breen Helmsford, Tara waved to attract her attention, then stopped abruptly. Waving wasn't right. Not today.

Katherine climbed into the filthy little Beetle, sat on the window-wiping knickers and didn't even notice. They drove in silence. It was a cold October night and Tara's heater wasn't working, yet both of them were perspiring.

'He had a lump on his neck last week,' Tara said quietly. She was reverberating with shame from the way she hadn't taken that seriously. 'I think this has been going on for some time, Katherine. I'm sorry to shock you.'

'Who's shocked?' Katherine snapped.

'Why?' Tara was amazed. 'Did you know?'

'Of course I knew,' Katherine said angrily. 'He's lost his appetite, been losing weight and had pains in his neck and stomach and various other places. All that talk of rabies and beriberi and anthrax . . .'

'Was I the only one who didn't know?' Tara wondered, appalled. 'Was I the only one?'

When they reached Fintan's road, Tara parked even more haphazardly than usual, and leapt out. She was desperate to see him. 'Come on,' she said, making for the steps. But just before she rang the bell a reluctance came over her. She didn't want to see him at all now. She wanted to run away.

'Oh, Tara,' Katherine said, grabbing her hand and, for a few seconds, squeezing it tight. They could feel the pumping of their blood, pressing against each other's palms.

How could someone get so thin so quickly?

In a week, Fintan's face seemed to have shrunk. Something was weird, Katherine thought, then realized what it was. It was his teeth. They looked too big for his face now. Like an old man whose mouth had become too small for his dentures.

Below his ear, protruding like a bumpy egg, was a large, grotesque lump. Covering part of it was a thick white bandage, cotton wool sticking out raggedly on two sides.

Tara stared at it, horror-struck. 'You told me the lump was gone,' she couldn't stop herself from exclaiming.

'I lied,' Fintan sang, with unexpected levity.

Sandro brooded silently, as though he was sucking the oxygen out of the room. He acted as though he was angry. But Fintan seemed curiously elated. 'Sit down, sit down,' he pressed, his eyes glittering in his skull head. 'And Sandro will get the drinks. Now, I've good news and bad news. Which do you want first?'

'The good news,' Tara clamoured. They already knew the bad.

'Right you are. The good news,' Fintan declared, jauntily, 'is that I've had several tests and I'm definitely, without a doubt, one hundred per cent HIV negative.'

His words dropped into a pool of utter silence.

'Negative?' Tara eventually managed to say. 'Negative? You mean . . . you haven't got Aids.'

'I haven't got Aids.'

'And you're not going to get Aids?'

'Not if I can help it.'

'Oh, my God!' A bubble of joy whooshed up through Tara's body. 'I can't believe it. I was so sure you were a goner. This is great, great news.' She jumped up and flung her arms around Fintan. 'You're not going to die!'

'You've given us the good news.' Katherine's voice was strangled. 'What's the bad?'

Everyone turned to look at Fintan.

'The bad news,' he said, 'is that I have an interesting little condition known as Hodgkin's disease.'

Katherine was chalk-white.

'What the hell's that?' Tara demanded.

'I know what it is,' Katherine said.

'It's a problem with my lymphatic system,' Fintan interrupted.

'It's cancer,' Katherine said, faintly.

31

After Katherine spoke, there was a horrible silence.

'Is it?' Tara asked, rubbernecking from Katherine to Fintan to Sandro. 'Is it?'

'Katherine's right,' Fintan confirmed.

For a moment Tara hated Katherine. Why couldn't she have been wrong, just this once? 'How can they know without doing a biopsy?' Tara asked, with forced scorn. She wasn't quite sure what a biopsy was, but she clutched at anything that might overturn the news.

Fintan chortled. 'Tara, I've *had* a biopsy. What do you think I was up to last week? What do you think this bandage is doing on my neck?'

'I thought you'd tried to cut your throat again.' She smiled weakly. 'You mean last week you were in hospital having that done and you went through it on your own? That's the saddest thing I've ever heard.'

'It happened so fast.' Fintan shrugged. 'One minute I was talking to the specialist about the kiwi fruit on my neck, the next I'm on my way to theatre to have a biopsy. Before I know it I'm lying on an operating table, fully conscious, while they whip out a lymph gland. Then they sew me back up and send the gland to the lab. A veritable whirlwind, my dears!

'I think I must have been in shock,' he added, dazedly. 'Then I had ten thousand blood tests, was poked and prodded by all sorts. And today they called me back in and told me I've cancer!'

Katherine spoke for the first time since her diagnosis. 'So how bad is it?' Her voice was deliberately matter-of-fact. 'How far gone?'

'I don't know.' Fintan lifted and let fall his arms. 'There's different kinds of HD . . .'

'HD?' Tara questioned.

'Hodgkin's disease.'

Oh, God. Already he was speaking a different, sick-person's language.

'. . . and they know I've got it in the glands in my neck, but they've to do more tests to see if it's in other places.'

'Like where?' Tara asked.

'Chest. Bone-marrow. Internal organs. If I've only got it in the lymph glands I'm grand, really. Bit of chemo and I'll be right as rain.'

'And if you have it in the other places?' Tara asked, not wanting the answer.

'It's treatable,' Sandro cut in. 'Wherever it is, it's definitely treatable.'

'So you're not going to die?' Tara cut to the chase.

'We're all going to die.' Fintan grinned suddenly and Katherine and Tara recoiled from his wild eyes.

'The doctor was very hopeful,' Sandro said, in a low voice.

Tara's heart went out to him. No one had forgotten that Sandro's last boyfriend had died – this must be torture for him.

As the first shockwave receded, and a strange, toxic normality set in, questions occurred.

'What exactly is a lymphatic system?' Tara broached tentatively. 'The only thing I know is that lymphatic drainage helps with cellulite.'

'It's a circulatory system, isn't it?' Katherine looked at Fintan for confirmation. 'Part of the immune system.'

Tara turned to Fintan. 'So, have I got this right? If you only have the . . . it in your lymph glands it's not so bad?'

Fintan nodded.

'And what if it shows up in your chest or bone-marrow? Or where was the other place?'

'Internal organs,' Katherine supplied, stiffly.

'Not so good if it's in the chest, even worse if it's in the bone marrow,' Fintan said. 'And if it's in something like a kidney or the liver, you might as well start saying your prayers.'

'Does the lump hurt?'

Fintan shook his head.

'So what happens next?' asked Katherine.

'Tomorrow morning I go into hospital again for two days. And they do stuff to me.'

'What kind of stuff?'

'Oh, you know.' Fintan was flip. 'A bone-marrow biopsy. A CT scan. X-rays à go-go. Us fashion types, it's just non-stop glamour!'

'Are you scared?' Katherine asked gently.

'No,' Fintan said. 'I'm absolutely terrified,' he added, and convulsed with laughter. He abruptly stopped his yelping. 'I'm going to the loo.'

When the door closed behind him, Sandro asked, 'Do you know how they do bone-marrow biopsies?' Tara and Katherine mutely shook their heads.

'It's from one of your hipbones. You get a local anaesthetic to numb the skin and muscle, but it's impossible to numb the bone,' he said, in a monotone. 'When the needle goes in, it's like having your bone broken. Apparently it's agony.'

Katherine's mouth went dry and Tara felt light-headed. They hadn't expected anything like this. Tests, yes. But they'd no idea that they *hurt*.

'I thought he'd be knocked out for it,' Tara whispered.

Sandro shook his head. 'They're very mean with giving general anaesthetics.'

'That's horrific.' Katherine's face was clenched. The thought of Fintan having to suffer unbearable pain was almost worse than him having a life-threatening disease. 'Can't we cause a big fuss? Insist on an anaesthetic?'

'We did our best.' Fintan had come back into the room. 'Shouted. Even *cried*. Hoped to embarrass the doc into giving in. But he just thought I was a big girl's blouse. Which I am, of course.'

'A Chanel one, though,' Katherine said.

'Schiaparelli, do you mind?' he countered, haughtily.

'When will you get the results?' Tara asked.

'The end of the week, hopefully.'

Something occurred to Katherine.

'Have you told your mother about any of this?' she asked.

'No.'

'When are you going to?'

'I have no immediate plans.'

'Fintan,' Katherine rushed to his side, 'you've got to tell her. It's only fair.'

'Yes, Fintan,' Tara insisted. 'You must.'

'That's what I keep telling him.' Sandro glowered.

'I can't,' Fintan said. 'I just can't. It'd kill her.'

'It'll kill her more if she found out and it was too . . .' Tara realized how tactless she was being.

'Your mother's tougher than you think.' Katherine rescued Tara. 'You've got to tell her.'

'I can't.' Fintan put his face in his hands.

'How about if we – I mean Tara and I – told her?' Katherine asked carefully. She thought he'd scorn that suggestion. She certainly wasn't expecting him to take his face out of his hands, look at her hopefully and ask, 'Would you?'

'Sure. We'll do it right now, this minute,' Katherine said. Tara's face was a rictus of horror.

'Would you mind if I didn't listen?' Fintan asked.

'We'll ring from your bedroom, you won't hear anything. Come on, Tara.'

They went into the bedroom, and when they'd closed the door behind them, Katherine said, 'It's OK, you cowardy custard, I'll do it.'

'I'll do it if you want.'

'No, just hold my hand. And remind me of the number. What's wrong with me? I can't even remember the code for Ireland.'

As JaneAnn's suspicious 'Hello' crackled down the line, Katherine was trembling.

'Hello, Mrs O'Grady. It's Katherine Casey here.' Tara gripped Katherine's spare hand so tightly the bones squeaked.

'Katherine Casey,' said JaneAnn's slow, country voice. 'Is it you? How the dickens are you?'

'Grand, thanks. I've something –'

'And your mother? And all belonging to you?'

'They're grand too. JaneAnn, I must –'

'I saw your granny the other evening at the Rwanda Benefit gig. Faith, she's thriving.'

'Mrs O'Grady, I'm sorry, but I've bad news for you. Fintan's sick,' Katherine blurted. She liked her bad news to be delivered quickly. She couldn't bear being kept waiting while the blow was softened.

'Fintan is sick? Sick? Is it serious?'

'Yes, I'm very sorry, he's got –'

'Aids,' JaneAnn interrupted. 'I've been waiting for this. There was a thing in the paper about it.'

'No, Mrs O'Grady,' Katherine forced herself to be gentle, 'he hasn't got Aids.'

'I know all about it.' Her voice was dignified. 'Just because I live in the backs of beyond, don't think I don't know.'

'Mrs O'Grady, Fintan has a form of cancer.'

'I'm his mother. The truth is bitter but tell it out to me anyway. Don't fob me off with talk of cancer.'

'Mrs O'Grady, I swear to you, Fintan really has cancer.'

'And you're not just putting sweet words in my ear?' JaneAnn sounded suspicious. 'Trying to spare my feelings?'

'Hardly,' Katherine said, on the verge of tears.

Fintan got very drunk that night. 'Might as well.' He laughed. 'Could be my last chance for a while.' He glittered with wild and bitter humour.

Tara, Katherine and Sandro also drank heavily in an attempt to escape the horrors, but never managed to get off the ground.

'Jesus, cheer up, would you?' Fintan complained, as three taut, white, miserable faces looked at him. 'I mean, *I'm* the one who's going to die.'

Now and again, the evening seemed almost normal. Almost, but not quite, everything was a bit skewed, tinged with nightmare. They could only think about it for a certain amount of time, before they stopped being able to process it. Like the lights in the hallways of apartment blocks, they worked for a while, then their mechanism just clicked off.

At about midnight, Fintan announced he was going to bed. 'Big day tomorrow!'

'See you in the morning,' Tara promised.

'With a pair of nice pyjamas,' Fintan reminded her. 'Try Calvin Klein.'

'Consider it done.'

'And if you can't get Calvin Klein ones, try Joseph. Just get me something wearable, I have my career to think of. If I'm spotted in those dreadful hospital ones, I could be sacked.'

'It's in hand,' Katherine reassured.

'Do you mind?' Fintan was suddenly anxious. 'Will you get into trouble for taking time off work?'

They both looked at him, mute with exasperation.

Katherine summed it up. 'Feck work,' she said simply.

'My God,' Fintan murmured. 'This *must* be serious.'

Tara and Katherine said nothing to each other as they left and got into the filthy Beetle.

'Are you all right to drive?' Katherine asked, anxiously, as Tara screeched away from the kerb.

'I always drive better when I've a few drinks on me,' Tara insisted.

'You don't, you just think you do.'

They both laughed, then stopped abruptly.

'It's strange,' Katherine said, feeling her way through her thoughts. 'That we can think something is funny at a time like this.'

'I know.' Tara sighed. 'Tonight, in places, we had a laugh. Sometimes – and I feel really ashamed about it – but sometimes I felt almost normal. But in a parallel-universe kind of way.'

'Maybe we're in shock.'

'Could be. It's certainly a lot to take on board. Pity Liv isn't here, she'd be able to explain what's happening to us.'

'Oh, God!' They were both stricken, as they thought of Liv.

'Who's going to tell her?' Tara gasped. 'She'll be devastated, she's so fond of him. Can you do it? You're better than me. Less emotional.'

And, though Katherine wouldn't have agreed, she said, 'I'll ring her tonight. She'll be up. Poor insomniac.'

They drove in silence.

'I can't stop thinking about that bone-marrow thing.' Katherine said faintly. 'It's barbaric. Tomorrow morning's going to be unendurable. Mostly for Fintan,' she added quickly.

'I just wish it was tomorrow lunchtime,' Tara said, 'because then it'll all be over.'

'But it won't be,' Katherine replied. 'It'll only be starting.'

'No.' Tara clasped the steering-wheel tightly and her face lit up with hope. 'We mustn't think that way. Maybe he'll be fine.'

Katherine thought about it. 'Well, maybe he will be,' she admitted.

'Attagirl!'

32

The following afternoon, JaneAnn, all four foot ten of her, flew to London, with a selection of her tall, silent sons.

None of them had ever been on a plane before. In fact, they'd rarely crossed over the Clare borders. In their lumpy, old-fashioned 'good' clothes, amid the bustle and gleam of the airport, they looked as if they'd just landed from another planet.

Even though Tara and Katherine didn't arrive into work until lunchtime, they left again at four to meet the flight from Shannon.

'There they are.' Tara pointed at JaneAnn, Milo and Timothy, standing in a little huddle around their suitcase, like wartime refugees.

JaneAnn was decked out in an ancient black coat with an astrakhan collar. Milo, the eldest brother, wore a borrowed brown blazer over dungarees, while Timothy wore his one suit – a navy, pinstriped, wide-lapelled, flared ensemble that he'd been married in over twenty years before. It was so old it was nearly fashionable again. He'd put on some weight since the last time he'd worn it. Or maybe it was the thick jumper he wore under the jacket that made it bulge so.

Despite their unsophisticated appearance, the O'Gradys were unfazed by the mayhem of Heathrow. Still going at the same slow pace they employed in Knockavoy, they were amused when a young businessman tutted and pushed past them muttering, '*Some* people!'

'It must be a matter of life and death,' JaneAnn remarked.

'Faith, no.' Milo smiled. 'By the looks of him it's far more important than that.'

They drove straight to the hospital, everyone crammed into Tara's Beetle. Milo and Timothy had to squash into the back with Katherine, because even though they were both enormous and JaneAnn was tiny, protocol dictated that the Irish Mammy sat in the front.

The mood was chatty. They swapped gossip from home and even shared the occasional laugh. Then Katherine would remember why she was sitting spooned into a tiny car with Fintan's relations, and was stricken by how unfitting laughter was.

Tara couldn't get the hang of things, either. She kept behaving like the O'Gradys were in London for a holiday.

'That's Kensington Palace,' she pointed out, as they inched through the traffic on Kensington High Street.

'And what goes on there?' Milo asked politely.

'It's where Princess Diana used to live,' Tara faltered.

'Lord, she must've had ferocious heating bills.' Milo winced, leaning forward for a good look as they passed.

Although the hospital looked more like a hotel than a place to house the sick and dying, none of the O'Gradys commented. Neither did they waste time buying sweets or magazines for Fintan. The mood had flipped and they were frightened.

Tension built as they travelled up in the lift, along the wide, linoed corridor and towards the room Fintan shared with five others. Outside the swing door, JaneAnn clutched Katherine. 'How does he look?'

'Fine,' she said, her guts twisting. 'Thinner than he was, and his neck is a small bit swollen, but otherwise fine.'

No need to mention that he hadn't looked too hot earlier when he'd been brought back from having his biopsy. All the muscles in Katherine's legs and the soles of her feet clenched at the memory of Fintan, his face grey, his eyes closed, as he'd whispered, 'The pain was disgusting, I actually saw stars.'

Tara and Katherine hung back as the O'Gradys trooped towards the curtains around Fintan's white, metal bed. Sandro sat meekly on a chair beside him.

'God bless all here,' Milo said, leading the clan.

'Love the blazer, Milo,' Fintan said weakly, as he lay on the flat of his back, in his new peacock-blue silk pyjamas.

'Sure, I'm pure lovely,' Milo laughed wryly.

'Hello, Mammy,' Fintan greeted JaneAnn.

'Aren't you the heart-scald,' she complained affectionately, tears in her eyes, 'worrying us all like this?'

'Fair play to you, though, you picked a good time,' Timothy said.

'You waited till after the hay was in,' Milo finished, 'and before the lambing starts. That's what I call decent.'

Sandro hovered with over-elaborate meekness as the family reunion took place. He was very nervous. That morning he'd waited by the bed until Fintan returned from his biopsy and, as soon as he'd established that Fintan had everything he needed, blurted anxiously, 'What if they don't like me?'

'Who?' Fintan had croaked through a haze of pain.

'Your family. What way should I behave with them?' Sandro laid a beseeching hand on the recently biopsied hip.

'Ow, ow, Christ almighty, ouch!' Fintan twitched in the bed. 'Do you bloody well mind? My poor hip.'

'Sorry, sorry, sorry! My apologies, please forgive me. Anyway, shall I wear this suit or be more casual?' A vision of Sandro draping a jacket over his front swam before Fintan's exhausted eyes.

'Who cares?' he said, weakly. 'Haven't we more important things to worry about?'

'I'm polishing the ashtrays on the *Titanic*,' Sandro had replied.

Now Fintan summoned him from the shadows. 'Sandro,' he said formally, from the bed, 'this is my mammy, JaneAnn, my brother Milo and another brother, Timothy.'

Sandro raised his hand nervously, '*Ciao*, hello, pleased to meet you . . . er . . .'

'Sandro is my . . .' meaningful pause from Fintan '. . . friend.'

'You're doing a line with Fintan?' JaneAnn understood.

Sandro was horrified. 'We never do drugs,' he lied haughtily.

'No, no, no,' Fintan explained. 'She means are you my boyfriend?'

'Oh! Oh, now I understand! Yes, Mrs O'Grady, I'm doing the line with Fintan.'

'And where is it you're from?' JaneAnn pressed gently.

'Italy. Roma.'

'Rome! Have you ever met the Pope?'

'*Mammy.*' Fintan flapped an arm at JaneAnn.

'But I have met *Il Papa*,' Sandro surprised him by saying. 'Well, there were many other people there, but I heard Mass in St Peter's Square with my mother.'

'You're blessed.' JaneAnn stared at him. 'Was it beautiful?'

'Beautiful,' Sandro confirmed, wondering should he expound on the gorgeous purple frock His Holiness had worn, but on second thoughts deciding it might be better not to. Things were going much, much better than he could have expected, so there was no point in blowing it.

Milo cornered the doctor-on-duty, in his office. He spoke so quietly Dr Singh could barely hear him.

'I'm Fintan's eldest brother,' Milo explained, looking at his lap. 'I've nearly been a father to him, I know about Aids. Just because we're a crowd of Paddies from the bogs, don't think we don't know. And what's more we're well able to deal with it.'

Dr Singh was a busy man who had been on duty for thirty-two hours. He wasn't inclined to be patient. By the time Milo returned to the ward, he was quite certain Fintan didn't have Aids.

At about seven thirty, just as all six of them were preparing to leave and let Fintan go to sleep, there came the sound of running feet down the corridor. It was Liv, her long hair flying, her skin pink, her eyes intensely blue. She looked like a warrior queen. When she saw the throng around Fintan's bed, she gasped to a halt.

'Liv,' Fintan called graciously from the bed, 'come in, come in. That's my mammy, that's Timothy, my brother, and Milo, another brother.'

'Hello.' Liv sounded very precise, very Swedish. 'How do you do?' She shook hands with all three of them and when she got to Milo she stared.

'Excuse me,' she apologized. 'I'm startled . . . You look so like Fintan.'

'Faith, no, Fintan's the handsome one.' Milo shrugged, with a slow smile. 'I'm just a poor imitation. I'm a . . . What do you call those things? A bootleg.'

'Not at all,' Fintan croaked gallantly. 'I model myself on you.'

There was certainly a family resemblance – they both had

252

dark-blue eyes and black hair, although Milo's looked like it had been cut by a lawn-mower.

'Any luck?' Fintan asked Liv.

'I got them.' She handed a carrier bag to Fintan, who took out two exquisite goblets in lime-green and turquoise glass.

'What are they?' Tara asked.

'I came here two hours ago and he was upset by the ugliness of his water-glasses,' Liv explained.

'And I'd seen these ones in *Elle Decoration*,' Fintan took up the story. 'So Liv, sound woman, went to the Conran Shop for me.'

'Did you have to go far?' Milo asked.

Liv pinkened. 'They didn't have them in the Michelin building, so I got a cab to the one in Marylebone High Street and they didn't have them there either. But luckily – you've guessed it! – they had them in Heal's.'

Milo, the man who'd barely been east of the Shannon before in his life, nodded knowledgeably. Yes, his nod seemed to say. Yes, but of course, Heal's was the obvious choice, you did *exactly* the right thing.

'Come on, we'd better go.' Tara stood up and looked around at the others.

'Sure, where's your hurry?' Milo teased gently and remained seated.

'But we were on the verge of going . . .' Then Tara understood. The O'Gradys felt it would be bad manners to leave straight after someone else had just arrived.

She sat back down and turned to Fintan. 'What time tomorrow are they letting you out?'

'They're not,' Fintan said bluntly.

'*Whaaat?*' What the hell had happened now?

'It's no big deal,' Fintan said. 'I'm after getting an infection in my neck, where they took out the lymph gland. They want to keep an eye on me till it's better.

'And I'll be very cross if it doesn't get better,' he complained. 'I'll have to have my neck amputated. Then I'll have no neck and I'll look like a rugby player!'

'How long will you be in for?' Katherine croaked. This didn't bode well. National Health beds were rare and elusive creatures. Only if the hospital staff were very worried about you were you permitted to have one.

'Five or six days.' Fintan shrugged, seemingly unconcerned. 'We'll see.'

Thirty minutes later they bade Fintan goodnight and trooped towards the door.

'Katherine, Tara,' Fintan hissed, calling them back. 'Keep an eye on Sandro, will you?' he murmured. 'Not that it's the same, but after what happened to his last boyfriend . . . I worry about him and while I'm stuck in here there's not much I can do.'

Down in the car park Sandro took Katherine and Tara aside. 'We must keep Fintan's spirits happy,' he insisted. 'We must entertain him and keep him from worrying.'

The O'Gradys were to stay in Katherine's flat. It was the obvious choice: she had a small spare room which the boys could just about fit into, a pristine master bedroom fit for an Irish Mammy and a decent sofa bed for her own humble needs. As Tara said, 'They wouldn't stay with me. I'm living in sin.' No need to mention that Thomas had refused to let them.

JaneAnn went into paroxysms of praise about Katherine's flat. 'It's pure lovely! Like something belonging to a fillum star.'

'No, it's not.' Katherine shrugged. 'You'd want to see Liv's flat. *Hers* is like something belonging to a film star.'

'She's a fine, handsome girl,' JaneAnn said. 'All the way from Switzerland.'

'Sweden,' Milo corrected.

'Sweden, if you want,' JaneAnn conceded. 'Wasn't she a grand girl, Milo?'

'She'd a fine set of teeth and lovely manners. Now where will I put these?'

Katherine looked, and to her surprise there was food all over the kitchen table. A boiled ham, brown bread wrapped in a tea-towel, rashers, black pudding, butter, tea, scones and what looked like a roast chicken wrapped in tinfoil.

'Oh, you shouldn't have brought food,' Katherine wailed. That morning she'd gone out and bought acres of food in honour of her guests. They'd never get through it all. Her fridge hadn't seen this much action, ever.

'We can't land in here on top of you and expect you to feed us,' Milo said.

'He's right. We can't.' Timothy spoke. A rare event.

'Will you have a sandwich?' JaneAnn urged.

'No, no, I'm fine,' Katherine said.

'But you have to eat something. There isn't a pick on you. Sure, there isn't, Timothy?'

'Faith, there isn't.'

'Sure there isn't, Milo?'

'Leave poor Katherine alone.'

A few miles away, Tara had just arrived home.

'Poor baby,' she heard Thomas call from the kitchen. 'Come here and be cuddled.'

Tara's heart lifted and relief made her light. Thomas was being nice to her. *Thank God*. Only now that things were OK could she admit how tense and weird they'd been since – well, since they'd had that dreadful conversation about her getting pregnant. But what a shame that it took a crisis to fix things.

She rushed into the kitchen, just in time to see Beryl snuggle into Thomas's chest. 'Where were you?' he demanded brusquely.

'At the hospital.' She was confused. What about her cuddle?

'I asked you to feed Beryl this morning, and you forgot,' he accused. 'Poor baby.' He stroked his face against the cat's. 'Poor hungry baby.'

With a cold, hard, little thump to her heart, Tara realized he'd been talking to the bloody cat all along. 'I'm sorry,' she said wearily, 'but I had other things on my mind.'

Thomas sighed. 'What do we think of girls who care more about their friends than feeding Beryl?' he asked Beryl. 'We're not impressed, are we? No.' He shook his head, and so, it seemed to Tara, did Beryl.

'Oh for God's sake,' Tara exploded. Thomas's insecurity had always been behind his unpleasantness to her friends, but this was going too far. 'Fintan's got cancer!'

'Oh, really?' Thomas asked, disbelievingly.

'Yes, really.'

'But think about it, Tara, his lymphatic system is part of his immune system. And he has a *deficiency* with his immune system. Maybe an *acquired* deficiency with his immune system . . .'

'Thomas, Fintan doesn't have Aids. He's HIV negative.'

Thomas huffed and puffed scathingly.

'He's got cancer,' Tara reiterated.

'Well, what does he expect?' Thomas demanded. 'It's bludeh unnatural what they get up to.'

'Thomas, you don't get cancer from having anal sex.'

Thomas winced and put his hands over Beryl's ears. 'Do you have to be so brutal?'

Tara eyed him for a long, silent, thoughtful time. 'Do *you* have to be so brutal?' she eventually heard herself reply.

33

While they waited for the result of the bone-marrow biopsy, and Fintan almost drowned in a sea of visitors and get-well cards, life took the liberty of going on.

Lorcan's so-called career was causing him great anxiety. The morning after Amy had set the filth on him he'd done an audition for understudy to Hamlet. And not just a church-hall production either, but a real play, with real actors, with a real audience paying – most importantly – real money.

As he waited a full week to hear if he'd got the part, Lorcan intoned repeatedly, 'If I don't get it, I'll *die*. I'll just *die*.'

But it looked like he could hold off on the dying for a while. On Monday evening his agent rang him and told him he'd been called back for a second audition, and there were only three other candidates.

Lorcan still hadn't spoken to Amy, even though she had now left well over a hundred messages on his machine, of varying tenor. On some she sounded jolly and upbeat, chirruping, 'Hi, there! Amy calling. Hoped to catch you in. Oh dear, never mind! Trust all is well with you, we must get together for a drink some-time.' Bye for now.' These usually came at the start of the evening.

Later on, at about nine o'clock, the mood changed to sombre. 'It's Amy here. I need to speak to you. There are some matters that we must discuss. We can't just leave things as they are. It's irresponsible. It's your duty to talk to me. Call me.'

Then, after midnight, she turned nasty. Her voice was usually drunk and tearful. ''S me,' she'd say thickly. 'Jusht calling to say I won't be calling you any more. I've got lotsh of offers from other men, and do you know something? I'm glad, *glad* I'm not going out with you any more. You made me completely bloody miserable the whole goddamn time. You're a total sadist and I've met a lovely man at work, and he thinksh I'm fantashtic and I jusht want you to know that you needn't worry about me because I'm fine. Just FINE. Got that? Fine. F. I. N. N. Never been happier, actual – BEEEEEP,' as she went over the message time.

Seconds later she always rang back. ''S me,' she'd say again. 'Look, I'm sorry, very sorry. You're not a total sadist and there isn't any lovely man at work. Just give me a call some time, because this is terrible.' Then she filled the rest of the message time sobbing. He never returned any of her calls.

On Tuesday morning, as Lorcan got the tube to the Angel he felt that everyone on the train must know how important his journey was. That the air around him was surely buzzing with momentousness. Look at them all, he thought, in pity. Off to their sad little jobs. In a way I almost envy them, it'd be great to have nothing to worry about. The burden of being an unacknowledged genius was a heavy one. But what can you do?

When he got off the train, he made a bargain with himself. If he could walk from the station to the King's Head without standing on a crack in the pavement, he'd get the part. And if he didn't get the part? 'Well, I'll die,' he whispered in horror. 'I'll have no choice but to die!'

Lorcan was the last of the four short-listed candidates and the moment he began watching the others auditioning, he almost expired from insecurity, racked with jealousy and terror because the others seemed variously, younger, taller, fitter, richer, better-trained, more experienced and better connected than him. He hated feeling this way. But, as always, Lorcan hid his sense of inadequacy under a veneer of arrogance.

And then it was his turn. He did Hamlet's soliloquy, standing alone on the stage, under one spotlight, his large, lean body contorted with indecision, confusion writhing across his beautiful face.

'He gives good tormented procrastinator,' Heidi, the stage manager, murmured.

'He does,' the director agreed.

When he finished, Lorcan had to clamp his jaw closed to stop himself pleading, 'Please tell me I was good. Please let me be in this production.'

He wasn't to know that the person they'd really wanted to understudy Hamlet had accepted the lead in *The Iceman Cometh* at the Almeida. So when Heidi told him he'd got the part, he had a moment of joyous disbelief, before the pendulum of his self-esteem swung violently in the opposite direction. Instantly he was thinking that this was nothing less than his due. *Of course they'd picked him. Why wouldn't they?* His recent terror melted like snow in the sun.

'Congratulations.' Heidi beamed.

Lorcan gave an Aw-shucks-it-was-nothing grin.

'I know it's only the understudy role to Frasier Tippett,' she said, 'but well done.'

'Yeah, well, maybe Frasier Tippett will have a terrible accident. You never know and here's hoping.' Lorcan elaborately crossed his fingers, flashed Heidi a devastating smile, and lounged away.

Heidi's beam wavered, wobbled, then disappeared. Frasier Tippett was her boyfriend.

The following day Lorcan was due to make a television commercial for butter. He'd had the audition six weeks before, and when he'd got the part he'd been unutterably grateful. Television ads paid phenomenally well. It was possible to earn enough to live on for a year. But now that he was about to be restored to his rightful home – in the spotlight of serious theatre – his mammoth ego was back in the driving seat. Why should he be grateful for the butter ad? So what if it paid thousands? They were lucky to get him, and he intended that they knew all about it.

At the appointed hour – well, only forty minutes after it – he showed up at a freezing cold, windowless converted warehouse in Chalk Farm to begin shooting. He was greeted by a mob of hysterical people – producers, directors, casting agents, best-boys, advertising executives, representatives of the Butter Board, make-up girls, stylists, hairdressers and the countless people who appeared on every shoot to stand around drinking tea, with keys and bleepers hanging from their belts.

I control all this, Lorcan thought, savouring the sensation of invincibility. *I'm back*. Wonderful stuff.

'Where've you been? We tried to ring you on your mobile, but your agent says you don't have one!' Ffyon, the producer, gasped. 'Surely there's some mistake?'

'No mistake,' Lorcan smiled, his low voice soothing Ffyon. 'I don't have a mobile.'

'But why ever not?'

'No peace with a mobile,' Lorcan lied. No money to buy one, more like.

After climbing over an ocean of orange cables to shake hands with the bigwigs from the advertising agency and the Butter Board, Lorcan was ferried off to Make-up. Next, a young girl approached him with a comb and a can of hair-spray, but Lorcan caught her arm tightly and arrested its progress. 'Don't touch the hair,' he said curtly.

'But . . .'

'No one touches the hair unless I say so.'

Lorcan treated his hair like a prize-winning pet. He indulged it, pampered it, gave it little titbits when it behaved itself and was very reluctant to entrust it to the care of strangers.

Then it was time for Wardrobe. After myriad changes, the two stylists had to admit that, despite the truckloads of garments they'd brought, Lorcan looked at his most devastating in his own clothes – faded jeans and a turquoise silk shirt which made his eyes look violet.

'OK, you can wear them,' Mandii conceded.

'But they have to be ironed,' Vanessa said quickly. She wanted to see him standing in his socks and underpants just one more time. She'd never seen a man so unspeakably beautiful. His legs long and muscled, his waist tiny, his back broad, his chest hard. And his skin a smooth, taut gold that just begged to be touched.

Finally, two hours after his arrival, Lorcan was almost ready. For the final touch, he swept his hair back off his beautiful forehead. The hand that held the hairdresser's comb twitched involuntarily.

'Worth Butter, take one,' the director shouted. The clapperboard went down and the cameraman sprang into action.

A sitting room had been mocked up and sat, like a carpeted, spotlit island, in the vastness of the concrete floor. The ad began with Lorcan draping his lean, powerful body on a purple velvet sofa, one foot on the other knee, a plate of toast on his lap.

The camera panned over him and the idea was that he'd look up, arch an eyebrow, smile and say, 'Real butter?' Then take a crunchy bite from the slice of toast, followed by a knowing, sexy pause. Before he continued, with a soul-intimate smile, 'Because I'm worth it.'

He'd been fantastic in the audition. Absolutely blinding. If there were Oscars for butter appreciation Lorcan would have got one. The people who cast him weren't to know that he hadn't eaten for over a day and that his genuine hunger had given great conviction to his performance.

But things were different now. He'd got a part in a proper play, he was a serious actor and he didn't want anyone to be in any doubt about it. So he overacted wildly, still in pompous, boomy, Shakespearean mode from his audition the day before.

'Action. And, Lorcan . . .'

Projecting from his diaphragm to the back rows, Lorcan bellowed out, 'REAL BUTTER?' like it was the start of Hamlet's soliloquy. People at the furthermost reaches of the room winced and the cameraman was almost deafened. No one would have been surprised if Lorcan had continued, 'Real butter? That is the question. Whether 'tis nobler in the mind to suffer the slings and arrows of outrageous Flora . . .'

'Cut, cut,' Mikhail, the director, shouted. 'OK, take two, let's make it a tad quieter this time, shall we?'

Just as the cameras began to roll for take two, Lorcan yelled, 'Just a minute. Is this *butter* on the toast?'

'Yes,' confirmed Melissa, who was in charge of toast-making.

'Yuk,' Lorcan declared dramatically, throwing the plate on to the couch. 'Yuk, yuk, yuk. Are you trying to kill me? That stuff clogs your arteries.'

Mr Jackson from the Butter Board looked stricken.

'Get me some low-fat spread,' Lorcan ordered. So while Melissa ran to the nearest grocery shop Jeremy, the casting agent, spoke in soothing tones to Mr Jackson, assuring him warmly that no one would know it wasn't butter on the toast and that Lorcan would do a great job even though he didn't believe in the product. But even with polyunsaturated spread, the Shakespeare continued unabated.

'Take ten. And, Lorcan . . .'

'REAL BUTTER?' he declaimed once more, this time sounding like he was ready to do Lady Macbeth's speech. Everyone expected him to continue, 'Is this REAL BUTTER which I see before me, the butter-knife toward my hand? Come, let me clutch thee. I have thee not and yet I see thee still.'

'Cut, cut, cut!' Mikhail called. 'Please, Lorcan . . .'

'Who is this clown?' Mr Jackson looked around for the young man from the advertising agency to sort things out. 'Have a word with him,' he urged. 'Mikhail and Jeremy are getting nowhere.'

Lorcan was having a whale of a time and was delighted to see Mr Expensive Suit from the ad agency approach him. Another opportunity for caprice.

'How about keeping it more conversational?' he suggested to Lorcan. 'More chatty?'

'What's your name?' Lorcan demanded imperiously, even though they'd been introduced when Lorcan first arrived.

'Joe. Joe Roth.'

'OK, Joe Joe Roth, let me tell you something. I've done more commercials than you've had hot women. Telling me what to do is like teaching your granny to suck cocks.'

Joe sighed to himself. He could have done without this. He had a lot on his mind, including an important presentation to a breakfast cereal company the following day. Playing nursemaid to spoilt-brat actors wasn't really his thing. Especially considering he hadn't even cast the commercial – it was something he'd inherited when his predecessor had been sacked from Breen Helmsford. But at the end of the day the responsibility was his.

Lorcan assumed a defiant and provocative glare, as he itched for a fight. Gleefully, he wondered if he'd be able to make Joe Joe Roth cry – it'd been a while since he'd had such an opportunity. But to his dismay, Joe just gently reiterated his suggestion that Lorcan say the lines in a friendly, unhammy way. Which shook Lorcan. Who was this prick with his fat salary and pretty-boy looks and unexpected self-possession?

Joe Roth was tougher than Lorcan had assumed. Stronger measures were called for. To even things up, Lorcan became even more over-the-top with each subsequent shot. Eventually on take twenty-two, out of pure badness, just because he knew he could, he whined, 'What's my motivation here?'

'A pay cheque?' Joe deadpanned, leaning against the wall, his arms folded. No more Mr Nice-guy.

'I am an artist,' Lorcan declared haughtily.

'Maybe that's what's wrong,' Joe said, drily. 'We asked for an actor.'

Lorcan narrowed his eyes.

Mandii and Vanessa nudged each other and looked at Joe. Sexy.

'OK. Here we go again,' the director called. 'More toast, Melissa! Take twenty-three, and, Lorcan . . .'

'Real butter?' Lorcan said, in just the right pitch.

At last, everyone thought, in a frantic exhalation of relief.

Lorcan took a bite from the slice of toast, smiled wolfishly at the camera, and in the same beautiful, mellow voice said, 'It gives you heart-attacks.'

34

'OK, Lorcan,' Joe strode forward, a pleasant smile on his face. 'It's clear you don't want to make this commercial. Let's put you out of your misery right now. You're officially off the job.'

Lorcan opened his mouth to say something scathing, but Joe continued briskly, 'Naturally you won't receive your fee and you may be obliged to compensate us for the costs incurred this morning.'

As Lorcan gaped, Joe turned to the room at large. 'Everyone, sorry about your wasted time. Please bear with us while we try to get another actor. Jeremy, what do you reckon? How about Frasier Tippett?' Joe turned back to Lorcan, who was in a pose of frozen languidness on the couch, his face a picture of surprise. 'Still here?' Joe asked. 'Would you mind leaving, please? Our insurance doesn't cover us for people on-site who aren't working.'

Lorcan was shocked. It seemed he'd greatly underestimated Joe Joe Roth. It did not do to call his bluff. 'Hey,' he said, with an awkward wave of his hand. His voice came out as a croak. 'Lighten up, would you, man?'

Joe ignored him, as Jeremy handed him a mobile saying, 'It's Alicia, Frasier Tippett's agent.'

Joe spoke quietly into the phone, before announcing with a big smile, 'Good news, everyone, Frasier Tippett will be here in an hour. Amuse yourselves until then. Go for a bite to eat, get some air.'

Then Joe turned his back and walked away. Lorcan was speechless with astonishment. No one had ever done this before to him. Of course Joe was joking about Frasier Tippett coming, but all the same it was a pretty elaborate hoax.

Lorcan continued to sit on the purple sofa, as he waited for Joe to return and the shooting to recommence. But, to his alarm, everyone appeared to be leaving. Picking up bags and jackets, drifting off in twos and threes, chattering about going to the pub for a quick pint or a sandwich. There went the cameraman with Mandii and Vanessa in tow, off went the best-boy with the hairdresser, there went Melissa and Ffyon. 'Let's go for a toasted sandwich,' Ffyon suggested.

Melissa paled. 'Not toast,' she said quietly.

Soon there was almost no one left. Of course, they hadn't *really* gone, Lorcan told himself. In a moment they'd rush back in the door and yell, 'Gotcha!'

But they didn't.

He remained sitting on the sofa, feeling foolish and ignored.

In horror, he was forced to contemplate the unthinkable – that maybe this was for real. Then, to his massive relief, he saw Joe emerging from the little office with Mr Jackson. At last this fiasco could be sorted out! But they strolled past without even looking at him, chatting about Mr Jackson's children.

Lorcan jumped off the sofa and, skidding and getting caught in cables, ran after them. 'What's going on?' he demanded.

Joe turned to Lorcan in what appeared to be genuine surprise. 'You're still here? What for?'

'You've made your point, man,' Lorcan said, his face hard.

He twisted his mouth into a smile. 'I'm ready to start work again. We've got an ad to make here!'

'You're off the job,' Joe said.

'So I was a naughty boy,' Lorcan sneered, holding out his hand and smacking his wrist. 'OK? Punished. Now, let's get back to work and stop wasting time.'

'We've got another actor.'

'What do you need another actor for?' Lorcan contrived a laugh.

'Lorcan, I understand that sometimes people – actors especially – need to be coaxed before they give their best, but your behaviour was so disdainful it's clear you don't want to be a part of this,' Joe said. 'I don't believe in forcing people to do things they don't want to do. It's much more productive for me – and you – if I deal with someone who's genuinely enthusiastic.'

Lorcan suddenly realized he couldn't sense any malice from Joe. The great gaping hole in the middle of Lorcan's psyche gave a squeeze as it met its polar opposite in Joe Roth: someone with a strong moral centre. With shocking clarity, Lorcan understood that the bastard wasn't ordering him off the job out of spite, he was doing it because he thought it was the right thing for both of them. How odd.

'I think you'd better leave,' Joe said.

Lorcan glared. Finally he was in no doubt that this was genuinely happening. 'You're making the worst mistake of your pathetic little career,' he sneered. 'I wouldn't work with an amateur like you if you paid me. I'm out of here.'

He picked his way through the cables and headed for the door, still holding out a slender hope that Joe would say, 'OK, all right, come back, you've learnt your lesson.' But nothing doing. Pausing only to shout over his shoulder, 'You'll never work in this town again,' Lorcan found himself on the street, wandering. Nothing like this had ever happened to him before. He was so shocked, he couldn't even get properly angry.

The butter commercial would have paid thousands. *Thousands*. Apart from the initial fee, there would have been residuals every time it was shown. And Joe Roth had denied them to him. Joe Roth had as good as stolen the money. Lorcan vowed revenge – Joe Roth's ass is grass and I am the lawnmower – but in a dazed, demoralized kind of way.

How could this happen to him? How could he have misread the situation so badly? Granted, he'd behaved atrociously, but people had always indulged him before. In Ireland in 1992 he'd done a commercial for washing-powder where he made them do sixty-nine takes before he decided to do it right. Not once had there been a hint of a suggestion that he be replaced. That's the way they *expected* a star to carry on. Hey, they loved him for it!

He'd thought the whole star machine was about to crank up for him again, that this was just the start of another phase in his career. So sure was he that his days in the doldrums were over that he'd already gone back to behaving like a star in anticipation of it. But this wasn't Dublin at the start of the nineties, it was London at the dawn of a new millennium. Another world, with different rules, but no one had warned him until it was too late.

That all the kudos and acclaim had been snatched from his grasp before he'd even tasted it was unthinkable. That he was the one responsible was unbearable. He had no choice but to go home and duck calls from his furious agent. When he got there, he was unable to do anything except take off his make-up and sit on his futon in a fug of depression. The long, dark afternoon of the soul.

He was thirty-eight. Of course, he looked far younger and his resumé didn't have him as a day over thirty-three, but he knew the truth. I'm nearly forty, he realized, and I've nothing to show for my life. A failed marriage. No money, no friends, no fame outside Ireland. No British or American glory. Not even a proper bed to my name. You'd think at my age I wouldn't have to sleep on a lousy futon.

Most of all, he had no money. He couldn't let himself think about all the loot he'd let slip through his hands today. Adrift and frightened, he racked his brain for an assertion of some kind, a reminder that he still mattered.

But he drew a blank. Time hung heavy on his hands. He'd nothing to do and no one to play with. When, out of nowhere, he thought of Amy. Alarmed, he realized that she hadn't rung him in – he counted back – four days. Four days without a cheery, sombre or drunken message from her on the answering-machine. He hadn't even noticed at the time. Bigger fish to fry. A career to worry about. But now that he had nothing else, it suddenly seemed extremely important.

God forbid that she'd given up on him, or started to get over him. That made him panic.

It was time to get her back.

Then be mean to her again.

He looked at his watch. If he left now he could be in Hammersmith to meet her as she left work. Adrenalined-up with purpose, he checked his hair – still gorgeous, some nice gloss 'n' shine for it later if it continued to behave itself – and hurried from his flat. On the way to the tube, he smiled at a woman and watched her pale. But was it his imagination? Did it not feel as good as it used to? Was it becoming harder and harder to get the rush?

It was eleven days since Amy had sent the police around to Lorcan's flat. Eleven of the longest days of her life. Utter hell. She'd gone completely crazy, and she knew her life was over. But amid the agony of separation was a consolation prize – a strange nugget of relief. Lorcan was just too high-maintenance. His game-playing had turned her into an unrecognizable, shrewish lunatic and at least now she could reclaim her soul.

Nevertheless, she had to make her sister, Cindy, come and stay with her to guard the phone. 'Promise me,' Amy begged Cindy, 'that even if I tell you my leg has fallen off and it's an emergency, do not, I repeat, do not let me have access to the phone!' And although they'd had a couple of late-night wrestling matches, Cindy had managed to keep her promise.

Amy was leaving work, gearing up for another action-packed evening of not ringing Lorcan, when she saw something in the lobby that made her stumble. Lorcan. Big and bold, using his elbow to lean against a wall, his arm over his head, his jacket swinging open to reveal his flat stomach, his big chest. Oh, the sweet rush of joy as she realized that all wasn't lost.

Lorcan held the pose for a count of five as, in his head, the camera panned in on him. Then, with perfect timing, while his face filled the imaginary screen, he smiled, and Amy was blinded. Jump to camera two, showing Amy's willowy back, following her dazed, hypnotized progress towards him. No doubt but that she was powerless to resist. Cut to Lorcan's eyes, full of love, as he looked at Amy's upturned face. Nearly time for his line – but, *wait for it, wait for it*, the non-existent director cautioned. And . . . now!

'Baby, did you miss me?' Lorcan asked, with precisely the correct degree of gentle amusement. Cue, mute expression from Amy, followed by an affectionate little chuckle from him. Pan back out again to see Lorcan roughly clasp her head with his big hands, and pull her to his chest. A shot of Amy's face, her eyes closed, her expression transported, as she smelt the suede of his jacket, felt the hardness of his thigh manoeuvring between her legs.

Next, Lorcan pulled back, to trace Amy's mouth with his finger, slowly, almost in wonderment. Beautiful, he thought. A beautiful *gesture*, that is. Then once more he bundled her tightly in his arms, as, in his head, a joyous, tear-jerking soundtrack began, and the credits started to roll.

Tara, hurrying past on her way to the hospital, was both touched and envious. It was one of the most exquisite scenes she'd ever witnessed. The huge, handsome man holding the fragile beauty in a pose of aching tenderness.

Later on, she exclaimed to the throng around Fintan's bed, 'It was just like something out of a film!'

35

Fintan was due to get the results of the bone-marrow biopsy, chest X-rays and CT scan on Friday afternoon. Until then, Tara, Katherine, Sandro, Liv and the O'Gradys were condemned to live in limbo, unable to think any further. As far as they were concerned, the world stopped on Friday afternoon. Nothing of importance would ever happen thereafter.

They'd somehow managed to convince themselves that the cancer in his lymph nodes was very little to worry about. That if the disease didn't show up in his chest, bone-marrow or internal organs, Fintan was as good as cured.

All their energy was poured into enduring the wait to find out exactly how ill he was. While angst and hope played tug-of-war back and forth, havoc was wreaked on sleep patterns, appetites, concentration facilities, patience levels and the ability to decide between cheese or chicken sandwiches. Meanwhile, they read whatever they could find on the subject of Hodgkin's disease and bought every book on alternative healing they could get their hands on.

So many of Fintan's colleagues and friends were showing up at visiting time that he was moved to say in a sour, low moment, 'They've only come to see if I've got Aids.' But even after it was clear that he *didn't* have Aids, a swarm of good-humoured visitors descended on him every evening. And the inner circle of Tara, Katherine, Liv, his family and boyfriend practically did a non-stop vigil at his bedside, JaneAnn and Sandro graciously letting each other take turns to hold Fintan's hand.

On Wednesday, the O'Gradys' first morning in London, Tara drove them and Katherine to the hospital where they met Sandro and Liv.

'Good morning,' Tara carolled to Fintan, determinedly cheerful.

'What's good about it?' Fintan asked sullenly, thrown resentfully in the bed.

The collective mood nose-dived, and everyone tiptoed nervously around Fintan, asking the standard hospital-visitor questions.

'Did you sleep well?' Katherine tentatively inquired.

'Was your breakfast nice?' Tara wanted to know.

'Would you like a grape?' Sandro offered.

'What's wrong with your man in the bed over there?' Milo asked.

Fintan answered bitterly, 'I didn't fucking sleep well, my breakfast made me puke, you can stick your grapes up your arse, and if you want to know what's wrong with your man, why don't you go and ask him yourself?'

Wobbly fake smiles all round, and a series of stilted questions to each other – how was Sandro today, did JaneAnn sleep well in the strange bed, wouldn't they mind Tara and Katherine not being in work, how early would Milo and Timothy get up at home, did they have cows in Sweden?

'Oh, here we go again,' Fintan complained loudly, as he saw a nurse approaching to take his first blood sample of the day. 'I'm like a fucking pincushion. Someone comes along and sticks a needle in me every five minutes.' He stuck his arm out for the syringe, and all present recoiled when they saw the elbow crook with its black, purple, green and yellow colouring. Bruises upon bruises, with another about to follow.

Tara's heart bled as she yearned to endure the pain for him, yet simultaneously she found herself thanking God with passionate, violent relief that it wasn't she who lay in the bed, a human pincushion. Almost before the thought was fully formed, she was awash with sickening shame. *What was wrong with her?*

'Let's see if we can find the vein in the first ten attempts, shall we?' Fintan said sarcastically to the nurse.

'Have manners!' JaneAnn hissed. It was forgivable for him to be rude to her, his poor aged mother, who had spent eighteen hours in labour with him back in the days when epidurals weren't even a twinkle in a scientist's eye, but this nurse was a stranger. Worse again, an *English* stranger.

'We're very sunny today,' the nurse sang cheerfully.

'Speak for yourself!'

'Is your hip giving you grief?'

'No. But the diagnosis of the sample that they took out of it is,' Fintan replied.

Tara leant over and squeezed his hand. No wonder he was waspish.

His humours throughout the day were unpredictable and fast-changing. Less than an hour after his surly, ungracious greeting, his mood had noticeably lightened, and so, by association, had everyone else's. To the point where the atmosphere around his bed became unexpectedly party-like. At one stage their chat and laughter was so loud that the nurse had to ask them to keep the noise down, that they were cheering the other patients up.

Regularly and separately the visitors realized how inappropriate their merriment was. Then they were seized with guilt for not being sorrowful. Until, bizarrely, in no time, the jollity started up again. But while individuals got momentary relief, the dread never left them as a unit. Katherine watched as horror circulated like a Mexican wave. All the while the animated talk was going on, one person would be sitting stock-still, with an expression that was almost perplexed. *What am I doing here? Because Fintan is sick? Because Fintan might die? But that's ridiculous!*

Then they were washed with the balm of hope – *everything will be fine* – and the terror moved smoothly on to the next person.

At eleven o'clock Fintan turned to the little television beside his bed. 'It's nearly time for the reruns of *Supermarket Sweep*. Does anyone mind?'

'Of course not,' they murmured, prepared to humour him. But within moments, with the weird way that reality kept mutating, it was just like sitting around in someone's front room, watching telly.

JaneAnn, in particular, managed to lose herself. ''Tis there, 'tis there,' she shouted, in clenched-fist frustration, as the lucky contestant ran past the Lenor for the third time. 'Are you blind? Look, it's *there*!' She was on her feet, prodding at the television before she suddenly remembered where she was and sheepishly sat down again. 'We don't get *Sweepermarket Supe* where I come from,' she muttered to the nurse, who was looking at her askance.

By lunchtime everyone had drifted off to work, Milo and Timothy went out for a smoke and JaneAnn was alone with the sleeping Fintan. She sat gazing at him, her youngest child, her baby, tears leaking down her tissue-paper cheeks. She ran her rosary beads through her hands and silently mouthed prayers and wondered what God's reason was for striking down a young man in his prime.

When Milo and Timothy returned, they tried to eat a ham sandwich from the stockpile JaneAnn had got up at six that morning to make, but no one had an appetite. 'Let's go out into the air for a while,' Milo suggested. 'Maybe there's some grass somewhere.' But it was cold and they couldn't find a park, so they traipsed up and down the Fulham Road and appalled the keepers of the chichi little shops they called into.

'Look,' JaneAnn exclaimed, holding up a tiny, intricately patterned enamel box. 'Fifteen pounds for a small yoke like this.'

'I think you'll find that's fifteen hundred pounds,' the sales-woman said contemptuously, smoothly retrieving the box from JaneAnn's hand.

But her disdain didn't have the required effect: Milo, Timothy and JaneAnn snorted with laughter. 'Fifteen hundred! For that little thing. You could nearly buy an acre of land for that!'

'This was a good idea,' JaneAnn said, when they were back out on the street. 'My heart isn't so heavy now.'

But the next bijou antique emporium they visited had its door locked, and even when they rang the bell and smiled ingratiatingly through the glass, it remained shut.

'Maybe the shop's closed,' Timothy suggested.

'No, there's someone in there,' JaneAnn said, then knocked on the glass and waved at the chic woman sitting behind a gold rococo desk within. 'Hello,' JaneAnn called. 'We'd like to come in.'

Yasmin Al-Shari stared in horror at the two huge wild-haired men and the tiny grey-haired woman who were trying to gain admittance into her lovely shop. 'Shoo!' she shouted, waving her arm ineffectually.

'God bless you,' Milo, Timothy and JaneAnn called automatically.

Yasmin looked distastefully at them, and suddenly Milo saw himself, his brother and mother through Yasmin's eyes. They weren't wanted. An instant of depression, of diminishment. They didn't belong in this city, but they needed to be here. 'I think she thinks we're undesirables.' Milo took care to sound cheerful.

'*Us*?' JaneAnn was appalled. She was one of the most respectable people she knew!

'We're eccentric millionaires,' Milo cupped his hands around his mouth and called through the glass. 'But you've insulted us, so we're taking our custom elsewhere.' Forcing a wide grin, he turned to the others. 'Off we go,' he said. 'Let's go over here and look at the flowers in the flower shop and pretend we're at home.'

Yasmin Al-Shari anxiously watched them shamble off. The old lady *did* look very like the grandmother in *The Beverly Hillbillies*. Had she just lost an enormous sale?

'Could we take Fintan home?' JaneAnn voiced what they were all thinking. 'Back to Clare?'

Late afternoon, when Tara and Katherine reappeared at the hospital, Fintan was once more in disagreeable humour. Desperately, Tara launched into her anecdote about Amy being reunited with her gorgeous-looking boyfriend in the reception area of work. 'It was beautiful,' she exclaimed, one eye on Fintan to gauge whether or not he was enjoying it. 'Like something out of a film.'

Katherine and Liv quickly weighed in with light-hearted stories of their own. They'd stored anything even remotely interesting or entertaining that had happened to them that day, in the event of Fintan being sour or depressed. But the only time Fintan perked up was when Sandro came in, waving a pile of holiday brochures. 'Long-haul,' Sandro announced. 'Just out. Fourteen new destinations in Asia and the Caribbean.'

That evening, when they all had to leave the hospital to give Fintan some space for his posse of new visitors, they were reluctant to part so everyone went back to Katherine's where they ordered pizzas and reassured themselves repeatedly, incessantly, that everything would be fine.

'How did he seem to you today?' JaneAnn inquired anxiously. 'You see, if we could escape with him just having it in his lymph glands, we'd be on the pig's back. I read that it's easy to treat and there's a great recovery rate. So how did you think he was?'

'A bit tired,' Sandro offered.

'A bit tired? Yes, he seemed tired to me, but we all get tired. It doesn't mean anything terrible. In fact, isn't it great that he keeps falling asleep? Sleep is very healing.'

'And he ate his lunch,' Timothy chipped out.

'And what harm that he didn't eat his dinner?' Milo said.

'Don't we all have days where we couldn't be bothered eating our dinner?' JaneAnn agreed.

'Besides, he'd had a Smartie at about six o'clock,' Liv valiantly offered.

'Two,' Sandro said triumphantly. 'A blue one and an orange one.'

'And he was in great form nearly all day,' Tara said.

'Apart from that time he was cross and told us to go away, using the F-word.' JaneAnn looked sorrowful.

'And he was cranky with that social worker,' Timothy said. 'Small wonder. She was asking highly inquisitive questions and she'd only just met him. How was he feeling? Was he angry? Was he frightened? If he hadn't told her to be on her way, I would have.'

This was the longest speech Timothy had ever made.

'It's good for Fintan to be bad-tempered,' Milo soothed. 'Wouldn't you worry if he was as sweet as sugar all the time? Sure, that isn't normal.'

'And maybe his other visitors will sweeten his humour.' JaneAnn had been moved to tears, as Frederick, Geraint, Javier, Butch, Harry, Didier, Neville and Geoff had shown up in dribs and drabs around seven o'clock, bearing four pounds of grapes, three books, twelve magazines, two Barbie lollipops, two bags of Hula Hoops, four little apricot tarts from Maison Bertaux, five litres of mineral water, a bottle of Marks and Spencer's Buck's fizz and one Kinder Surprise between them.

'It's right marvellous for him to have so many visitors. There's not many people lucky enough to have eight young men sitting around their sick bed,' JaneAnn said proudly. 'And all of them so well turned out.'

'*Very* well turned out,' Milo agreed.

'But terrible noisy,' JaneAnn sighed. 'My head was ruz. So did you think his lump looked like it had got a bit smaller?'

'Now that you mention it, it did,' Tara lied.

'He certainly didn't look like someone who was dying, now did he?' JaneAnn asked, jovially.

'Dying? Hardly!' went the scornful response. 'Would a dying person be so bad-humoured?'

Everything about Fintan – good, bad or indifferent – continued to be turned into something positive, to shore up their version of the cosmic plot, the one where he recovers.

But JaneAnn couldn't sustain it. In the midst of the positive thinking, she burst into tears and blurted, 'I wish it was me instead of him. To see him thrown in the bed, so sick and weak. He's too *young* for that but I've one foot in the grave and another on a banana-skin.

'You know what?' she said, angrily. 'It's my fault. I should never have let him come over here to England. The other four lads stayed at home and none of them got cancer.'

As people rushed to comfort her, the pizzas arrived. And when JaneAnn discovered she was just supposed to eat it as it was, without potatoes or vegetables, she became even more upset. 'Are you in earnest?' she asked. 'But that's no dinner at all. Small wonder Fintan got sick if that's all he'd eat of an evening. A mother's home cooking could have prevented all this.'

Later on, JaneAnn turned businesslike. 'Now, girls, I want to talk to you,' she said. 'You both have fine important jobs and I couldn't have it on my conscience if you lost them because of all the time you're spending looking after us. You don't have to drive us everywhere, we can get that tube yoke.'

Tara and Katherine both protested enthusiastically. But never so energetically as when Timothy said, 'Those lifts in the hospital are great, aren't they?'

'Um, yes,' Katherine said, tentatively.

'I was never in one until yesterday,' Timothy elaborated.

'Me either,' JaneAnn said. 'Great sport, wasn't it?'

'You could go up and down all day in it,' Milo agreed. 'It was like going on the merries in Kilkee.'

'We can't set them loose on the London Underground,'

Katherine hissed quietly to Tara. 'Not without lessons. They'll be going up the down escalators and breaking the ticket-machines and not minding the gap and getting stuck in the doors and whatnot. I can just see it! It'd probably get on the news.'

36

Somebody had slept with Angie.

Katherine hadn't been in the office much all week – just running in between hospital visits to do a couple of hours here and there, and her mind wasn't on the place when she *was* in – so it took her longer than it usually would to realize that a new nickname was doing the rounds. Gillette.

Despite all the horrors that were going on with Fintan, Katherine was surprised to find she still had emotion left over for Joe Roth. The few times she'd been to work that week she was highly sensitized around him and remained on full alert for any signs of sexual chemistry between him and Angie. She was very ashamed of this, but not ashamed enough to be able to stop. With her heart in her mouth, she listened anxiously to the men's conversations to see just who 'Gillette' was and when her worst fear was realized and it became clear they were talking about Angie, she got a dull, heavy pain in her stomach, as if she'd eaten raw bread.

Gillette – why Gillette? What elaborate sexual tricks had Angie done that merited her being rechristened as a razor-blade? Katherine's imagination went wild as she thought of the story she'd once heard from someone who'd been to a strip-show in Thailand and allegedly witnessed girls pulling strings of razor-blades out of their vaginas. But would Angie have done that? Where would she have learnt to do it? And would Joe like it? Katherine was a ball of emotion – jealousy, anxiety, but mostly self-loathing for being so boring in bed. She wouldn't know what to do with razor-blades – she'd be afraid of cutting herself. And, frankly, she couldn't see how it was sexy. What was wrong with suspender-belts, little knickers and the odd bit of bondage?

Or maybe they were calling Angie Gillette because she shaved her pubic hair. Could be. Then Katherine found herself wondering if Angie had done it on her own initiative. Or did Joe ask her to do it? Did Joe help her to do it? Did Joe tie her up and *insist* on doing it? Jealous and strangely turned on at the image, Katherine didn't notice in the expenses claim in front of her that Darren had included one restaurant bill three times.

As she continued earwigging, Katherine realized she hadn't thought of Fintan in about ten minutes and was shocked and ashamed. How could she be worried about Joe Roth and Angie at a time like this? What kind of friend was she?

But she couldn't help it. Again her ears pricked up as she overheard more talk of Gillette. She stopped banging away at her calculator, just in time to hear Myles singing, 'Gillette! The best a man can ge-eh-et!'

Aaaahhh. Katherine suddenly understood. Gillette had nothing to do with Angie shaving her pubes or playing jack-in-the-box with razors. It was because – in the words of the ad – she was the best a man can get. Unlike her male colleagues' usual rechristening of women, Gillette was a *nice* name, a complimentary name. The jealous pain in Katherine's stomach increased. Angie was the best a man could get. Which man was getting her, anyway? There was no proof that it was Joe. Despite Katherine's beady surveillance, she couldn't find any definite indication that something was going on between Angie and

Joe. And at no stage had he been overheard referring to Angie as Gillette. But Katherine wouldn't take that as any reason to stop worrying. She always liked to expect the worst, to meet disappointment half-way. She'd die rather than be caught on the hop.

On Thursday morning, Katherine went to work looking as if she'd slept in her clothes. It had been a rough few days, as they waited for the result of the biopsy, and she didn't have the energy or the concentration that she usually devoted to her appearance. Though the O'Gradys had only been staying with her since Tuesday night, it already felt as if they'd been there for ever. As the lads were used to rising at the crack of dawn to tend to their farms, Katherine was woken at half six each morning by them watching telly. Then when the time came to iron her shirt, she found that access to the ironing-board was blocked by the pair of them cooking scores of rashers in the kitchen.

Also she'd lost her black work shoes. They'd disappeared into the twilight zone created by all the extra people and possessions in the flat, so she had to go to the office wearing a grey suit and brown shoes. In a vague, exhausted way she was mortified.

As Katherine pushed open the office door she was hit by the atmosphere of tension and exhaustion. Cigarette fug swirled in the air, coffee cups and takeaway bags littered the 'creative' area, four or five of Joe's team were slumped around a storyboard, looking dishevelled, grey-faced and sleep-deprived. 'You look as if you've been here all night,' she said, in surprise. She wouldn't usually have commented, but her defences were down and normal services were suspended.

'That's because we have,' Darren replied wearily. 'Presentation to Multi-nut Muesli this morning. Bastards never told us they were adding chocolate chips to their recipe. Only found out five o'clock yesterday. Had to change everything.'

Katherine couldn't stop herself glancing at Joe – now that he no longer came near her, she was constantly aware of him. He was unshaven and bad-tempered-looking. For a cold moment he held her eyes, then stood up and stretched. Hypnotized, Katherine watched as his shirt pulled itself out of his trousers, revealing for a brief, breath-catching moment the pearly skin of his concave stomach, the line of hair that trailed like a frayed rope from his navel. Then he slumped his arms back down by his sides and the beautiful view disappeared. Katherine felt bereft.

'I'm going to have a shower,' he announced, and stalked out of the office.

There was a shower in the gents' at Breen Helmsford, ostensibly for occasions such as this – although company rumour had it that the real reason was that the head honcho, 'Call me Johnny' Denning, had insisted on it so that he could wash off traces of the sex he'd had with his employees before going home to his wife.

Katherine sat down and tried to make a list of things to delegate to Breda. But she couldn't concentrate on her work, hadn't been able to since Tara had made that life-altering phone call on Monday. For once, though, instead of agonizing about Fintan, Katherine was transported, imagining what would happen if – just *if* – she followed Joe into the shower. The steam, the slipperiness of the soap as she rubbed herself against his thighs, his stomach, his groin. His erection flipping stiffly, heavily, this way, then that, as she moved against it. The feel of his big hands on her waist, her buttocks, lathering the soap, using it to lubricate between her . . . Christ Almighty! She exhaled in a shudder and forced herself to stop. Work. She was here to *work*.

An awful thought hit her. Where the hell was Angie? Breathlessly she scanned the office and to her relief saw her at her desk. Good. If she couldn't have a shower with Joe Roth she was damned if Angie Hiller could.

Joe returned to the office in a cloud of sharp freshness. His dark hair was wet and slicked back and he was dressed in his suit. But his tie hung loosely around his neck and his shirt was open a few buttons down. Through the gap in his shirt, Katherine stared at the hair on his chest. She was shocked. Deeply affected by the incongruity of having such naked sex appeal in a place as inappropriate as an office. And alarmed by the intensity of her own response.

She couldn't stop herself watching as he buttoned up his shirt, then grasped both strands of his tie.

'I really need a mirror for this,' he realized, and, as he made to return to the gents', Angie was over to his desk waving a little compact.

'I've got one here. I'll hold it for you,' she offered.

Briefly, Joe looked discomfited, then smiled, 'Thanks,' and began deftly to knot his tie, folding it back and forth on itself, as he hunched over and stared into the mirror with great concentration.

Clammy dread flushed down Katherine's body. Angie holding the mirror was a gesture that was way too intimate for Katherine's liking. But weak with wanting, she kept watching, as Joe rubbernecked backwards and forwards, from side to side, tying a big, fat knot. Why did she find this such a turn-on?

Was it his single-mindedness as he tried to get it right? Because it was such a uniquely male thing? Echoes of masturbation?

Smoothly Joe glided the knot along the shaft of the tie, until it was in place. Katherine felt another wave of desire. Then he gave a final tug, his big hand clasped around the length of fabric and her mouth went dry. He looked great. His shirt collar snow-white against his shaven jaw, the tie knot fat and even. 'Thanks.' He smiled at Angie.

'No problem.' She smiled back, snapping her compact closed. She lingered in front of him, smiling goofily. Katherine tasted metal in her mouth. There was no mistaking the intimacy, the connection between the two of them. Joe Roth had to be the mystery man, Mr Gillette. Katherine felt terrible. But whom could she blame? Only herself. She'd messed it up. She could have had him and she'd sabotaged it.

Then she thought of Fintan lying in his hospital bed, not knowing whether he was going to live or die, and waited for things to assume their correct proportions. To her great shame, they didn't. Joe and Angie still seemed important.

37

A little hospital-visiting routine got going so that Thursday followed much the same pattern as Wednesday. Tara spent the morning at the hospital and Katherine did the afternoon shift.

When Tara and the O'Gradys arrived at nine a.m., Sandro was already there, his head next to Fintan's, both of them chatting intimately. They looked so close and united that everyone felt uncomfortable at disturbing them.

'Sorry to bother ye,' JaneAnn said, wondering why she wasn't jealous of Sandro.

'No problem,' Sandro smiled, 'I've been here for hours.'

'He couldn't sleep,' Fintan said.

'The bed's too big without him,' Sandro said, then horror zigzagged across his little face. Had he offended JaneAnn?

But although she was mildly shocked, she couldn't find it in her heart to hold it against him. Either of them. Somehow it didn't seem that important, no matter what the Church's view on the matter was . . .

Next to arrive was Liv, who stayed only a short time because she had to go to work in Hampshire.

'You'll miss *Supermarket Sweep*,' Milo teased.

'Watch it for me, then tell me what happens.' She smiled, shyly.

Supermarket Sweep had already become a fixture in the morning and *Fifteen-to-One* in the afternoon. Half an hour twice a day when reality was suspended. Something other than craven dread to unite them.

'We're normalizing the abnormal,' Liv, the behavioural expert, explained. 'It's a survival technique.'

'I just thought it was because I liked Dale Winton,' Sandro said.

'Don't be silly!' Liv admonished. 'You're simply responding to a terrible trauma.'

In contrast to the previous day Fintan lay in lethargic apathy.

Suddenly his caustic tongue seemed far more desirable. The only time he stirred was when a nurse walked into the ward, and automatically he began struggling to roll up his sleeve. Already he inhabited the strange world of the sick person, Tara thought, stricken with exclusion, seeing the huge gulf between them, they who'd always been so close. She could never share in what he was going through, or be part of the relationship he had with his nurse. He belonged to other people now.

At one thirty, when Katherine was sitting at her desk, completely unable to decide whether to have a cheese or a chicken sandwich for her lunch, her phone rang, breaking the deadlock. Cheese! Cheese, it would be. Cheese, without a doubt. Unless, of course, it was chicken . . .

Desmond the porter was on the line, saying there was a 'gentleman' in the lobby who wanted to see her. From the heavy irony with which he said 'gentleman' Katherine was led to believe her visitor was anything but. Confused, she got the lift down and found Milo, grinning his head off, an *A–Z* in his hip pocket. 'How did you get here?' she asked in astonishment.

'Piccadilly line to Piccadilly Circus,' he said, the words sounding incongruous in his soft Clare accent. 'Then Bakerloo line to Oxford Circus. Fintan's asleep, JaneAnn's doing some heavy-duty praying, Timothy is reading, so I thought I'd have an adventure.'

'Do you know this man?' Desmond asked, looking in disdain at Milo's mad hair, his work-worn dungarees, his big boots.

'Yes, Desmond, thank you.'

As Desmond disbelievingly shook his head, in a exaggerated version of *it's-always-the-quiet-ones*, Katherine turned back to Milo. 'And you didn't get lost or anything. Fair play.'

'Oh, I did get lost. I went the wrong way from South Kensington, but I got off at Earl's Court and asked a woman for directions.'

'And she helped you?' Katherine sighed in relief.

'No, she didn't. She said – I must see if I can remember the exact words. She said, "Do I look like a fucking talking map?"'

'Oh, Milo.' Katherine touched his arm protectively, and barely noticed Joe Roth and Bruce passing through the lobby. 'I'm sorry about that.'

'Not at all!' Milo declared. 'I thought it was the height of hilarity. I'm getting used to this London place now – it's all about people speaking their minds. It's refreshing.

'Do I look like a fucking talking map?' he chuckled to himself. 'A talking map? How do you like that? I never heard the beat of it. Right, now I'm off to Hammersmith to see Tara. Piccadilly or District line. And, er, I'd visit Liv if I knew where she worked.'

Katherine looked at him with indulgent amusement. 'She's down in Hampshire.'

'What line is that on?'

JaneAnn prayed incessantly. She had a set of rosary beads in her hands at all times and frequently visited the chapel in the hospital, often accompanied by Sandro. In an attempt to win her approval, he had told her many elaborate lies about his religious experiences and his visits to Catholic shrines. But it was when he'd hinted heavily that he'd actually had visions that he'd realized he'd bitten off more than he could chew.

'Child!' JaneAnn had gasped, clutching his collar fervently. 'You'll have to tell your parish priest. It's your duty. You can't keep this to yourself.'

Sandro had set about back-pedalling with great haste and managed to talk JaneAnn down by saying that the visions were probably just due to too much to drink. She was so disappointed that, to compensate, he upped the time spent in the hospital chapel with her.

'With all the praying the pair of you are doing for Fintan,' Katherine said, 'I'd say we're in with a fighting chance.'

'Not at all.' JaneAnn sniffed. 'I wouldn't say our prayers are having their normal impact because that chapel in the hospital is only a non-denominational one.'

'But isn't it all the one God?' Tara made the mistake of asking.

JaneAnn cast her a disgusted look and murmured, 'Learn your catechism, child. Tell her, Sandro.'

On Friday morning as they left Katherine's flat, JaneAnn dropped a bombshell. 'I'm dying for Sunday,' she said, greedily. 'A good oul' Mass. I might even go a couple of times.'

Katherine and Tara gave each other horrified looks. Mass? Neither of them had any idea where Katherine's local Catholic church was. For the first time in days they were worried about something other than the biopsy result. As soon as they could they went into a head-to-head outside Fintan's ward.

'Why don't I just tell her I don't know?' Katherine suggested.

'No.' Tara was adamant. 'The shock might kill her. She needs fixed points in her world right now. Finding out you're not a bumlick would be too much for her.'

Liv came striding up the corridor, her hair streaming behind her. She looked at the anxious huddle and faltered. 'The result of the biopsy already?'

'No, not that bad. But bad enough. JaneAnn needs a Catholic church for Sunday Mass.'

Liv looked puzzled, 'But what's wrong with St Dominic's? On Malden Road – just around the corner from you?'

Tara and Katherine were stunned. How did Liv know? 'You weirdo,' Tara complained. 'Next you'll be telling me you go sometimes.'

'I do.'

'But you're not a Catholic.'

'So what? In my search for happiness I also frequent synagogues, mosques, Quaker meeting houses, Hindu temples, the Samaritans' head office, psychiatrists' couches and Harvey Nichols. And I've always been given a warm welcome. Except maybe in Harvey Nichols,' she added.

'You wouldn't happen to know the names of any of the priests?' Katherine chanced her luck.

'Of course. Father Gilligan. Tell him I said hi. I must go to the ladies'. See you in a minute.'

When Liv arrived back, all the chairs around the bed were gone. Milo stood up. 'Have my seat.'

'No, I couldn't.'

While Milo demurred, JaneAnn suggested, 'Sit on Milo's knee, then.'

Liv went tomato-red with embarrassment. 'I'm too large.'

Milo seemed amused by this. 'I'm large too. Plenty of room here,' and slapped his bedungareed knee.

'Really, I couldn't.'

'Go on,' Fintan urged weakly.

'Do,' Tara and Katherine chorused. 'Do, Liv, do.'

So, with a scorching face, Liv gingerly placed herself on Milo's knee, while everyone nudged each other.

JaneAnn was later heard to mutter, 'When God closes one door he opens another. I'll see some good comes out of this visit if it's the last thing I do.'

Even the most hardened atheists among them – and there was stiff competition – found themselves praying on Friday as the deadline approached.

Fintan had been told to expect the results at about four o'clock. So from two onwards all eyes were trained on the door. Whenever a person in a white coat walked in, there was a tiny but perceptible collective jump. Conversation was poor.

Finally, at ten to four, as their endurance stretched to snapping point, Dr Singh approached the bed. He seemed to recoil slightly when he saw the white-faced throng. 'If I could have a word with my patient?'

'No, I want them to stay,' Fintan insisted weakly.

Dr Singh assented. 'I'm afraid I've bad news,' he said.

Katherine's heart thudded in her chest. She couldn't look at the others.

'We won't have the results today. The lab has been too busy,' Dr Singh continued. 'You're going to have to wait until Monday.'

38

'I reckon she's looking for another job,' Bruce said.

'Nah, mate,' Myles contradicted. 'I reckon she's ill.'

'She don't look ill,' Bruce pointed out.

'She don't look too chipper neither,' Jason replied.

Furious speculation abounded about Katherine's absences from work, because in her three years at Breen Helmsford she'd never even taken a day off sick before. Darren claimed to have seen her crying on the phone on Monday morning, but this information was discounted because it was so unlikely. Besides, it wouldn't have been the first time Darren had told an outrageous lie.

Then word filtered down via Fred Franklin that on Tuesday morning she'd told 'Call me Johnny' that she'd be taking some time off because of a 'personal matter'. When this news reached the rank and file, great mirth broke out. 'Do what? A personal matter? Leave it out.' Myles guffawed. 'The girl's a machine!'

'Maybe her dishwasher broke down,' Bruce suggested. 'That'd probably qualify as a tragedy for Icequeen.'

On Friday lunchtime in the Frog and Fawn, Joe's team batted possibilities back and forth.

'She might be getting married,' Bruce theorized. 'Girls take shedloads of time off to organize that.'

'Maybe she's had a breast enlargement,' Jason suggested, hopefully. 'You have to rest lots after one of them.'

'Could be she's getting divorced,' Myles said. 'She looks a bit creamed, like she's having a hard time.'

Bruce agreed. 'Normal times the girl looks like she lives in a bleeding dry-cleaner's, but this week her clobber's been wrinkled to fuck.'

'Hard to iron with new tits,' Jason reminded them. 'They'd sting for a while.'

'She looks like she's not getting much sleep,' Bruce said.

'That's 'cos she has to lie on her back until her new tits are better,' Jason said.

Myles rounded on him in wild irritation. 'What are you going on about? Do her tits look any bigger? Well?'

'Suppose not,' Jason admitted sulkily.

'What do you think is up with her?' Myles asked Joe, who'd sat in grim silence throughout the speculation.

He shrugged, and said shortly, 'No idea.'

Myles exchanged a what-the-hell's-up-with-him? look with Bruce and Jason. Joe Roth was off his usual sunny form.

'Me and Joe saw her with a bloke yesterday lunchtime,' Bruce surprised the others by saying. 'Some poncy pop-star.'

'You what! Now you tell us.' Myles and Jason were agog. 'This changes everything. Who is he?'

'Don't know his name,' Bruce admitted. 'But I think he might have been one of Dexy's Midnight Runners. Big bloke, wearing wanky dungarees, designer ones, natch. Looked like he'd been pulled through a hedge backwards.'

'Definitely a pop-star,' Myles conceded. 'What happened to the days when our singers took pride in their appearance?'

'Yeah. Well, Icequeen and Dexy were very cosy-looking,' Bruce said. 'Which backs up my theory that she's getting married.'

'Jesus!' Myles was astonished. 'Could be true. No accounting for taste.' He glanced nervously at Joe.

Darren burst into the Frog and Fawn, agitatedly waving a piece of paper about. 'Look at this,' he ordered. 'Icequeen's paid my expenses.'

'So what? It's her job.'

'But I included three copies of the bill from the Oxo Tower. Two of them were messy photocopies – I only put them in to wind her up. And she's done a cheque for the whole lot!'

'You lying toerag,' Myles scorned. 'I suppose she was crying again while she did it.'

'On Alan Shearer's life, she *was* crying Monday morning, and she *has* paid the photocopies.' Darren was wounded. 'I admit I never had a threesome with Martini and Flora, but I'm telling the truth this time.'

'But Icequeen's impossible to con,' Jason said.

'That's what I thought,' Darren said. 'But, stand on me, the girl is losing it. Take a look.'

The proof was passed before all the Doubting Thomas eyes. It was undeniable.

'Maybe she's having a nervous breakdown,' Myles said, awe-struck.

'It's the silicone,' Jason concluded. 'Turning her brain as soft as her new breasts. Mmmmm, my ideal bird!'

'Bloody good news for us!' Bruce pointed out.

Immediately there was a flurry of activity as everyone searched in their wallets for receipts to swizz Katherine with. Everyone except Joe.

39

'What do you mean you can't?' Thomas whined at Tara.

'I mean I can't,' she explained. 'They need looking after, and it's not fair to land Katherine with all the responsibility.'

'They've had you all week. It's Saturday night and you're coming out with me and Eddie and his new bird, and that's the end of the matter.'

'Thomas, I can't abandon the O'Gradys.'

'What about me?' Thomas stuck his bottom lip out in a sulky-little-boy pout. 'When do I get to see you?'

Tara wavered. She and Thomas had been getting on so badly lately that she was relieved by his insistence on being with her. 'I really feel I have a responsibility to look after the O'Gradys,' she tried again. But when Thomas's face darkened with the anger of rejection, Tara gave in. 'Oh, all right. But you're a disgrace,' she complained, indulgently.

He strutted, and gave her a swaggery smile. 'I am what I am. Tek me or leave me.' Instantly he was sure of himself again and, though she could never explain why, Tara found his bossy ways very sexy.

Thomas masterminded what Tara wore, hoping to hold his own against Eddie and his sexy new girlfriend – 'Wear your short black skirt, aye, the right short one, your highest shoes and that V-neck top. And hold in your stomach.'

Tara paid particular attention to her hair, make-up and accessories but a bucket of blue hair mascara wouldn't have diverted Thomas from noticing her size. As he surveyed the finished product with bitter dissatisfaction, he complained, 'You've got fatter since last weekend. This is what happens when you don't go to the gym.' She hadn't managed to do any exercise all week because her routine had been shot to hell with hospital visits. 'And I bet you haven't been sticking to your diet, either,' Thomas accused.

He was right. There was too much food around Fintan's bed for a woman with no willpower. Everyone brought him chocolate, buns, crisps, popcorn, sweets and grapes as they tried to fatten the sickness away. JaneAnn had more faith in a daily infusion of ham sandwiches than in a daily infusion of medication. But Fintan barely looked at the goodies that surrounded him, and no one else had any appetite either. Except for Tara who couldn't *stop* eating. Agitatedly, incessantly, her hand crammed food into her mouth, attempting to fill the hole burnt by her corrosive anxiety.

All the same, she'd hoped that Thomas would make allowances because of her ordeal, that he might issue a special dispensation to knock off her diet until life was back to normal. But fat – what other kind? – chance. 'It's been a difficult time, Thomas,' she tried.

'Where is all this going to end, Tara?' Thomas demanded, in exasperation. 'In Evans, that's where. I'm trying to help you and, to be honest, you're being very ungrateful.'

'I'm sorry and I am grateful.'

'Do you think I enjoy having to police you like this?' Thomas asked.

Yes, actually, Tara thought. And immediately regretted it. He was difficult – sometimes even brutal – but she had to keep reminding herself that *it was for her good*.

Beryl stalked into the room and Thomas turned to her. 'Who's a good girl?' he crooned. 'Oh, who's a pretty girl?'

If only he'd be as nice to me, Tara thought, wistfully. One day she'd pull it off. If she could just manage to stop eating. 'Will I ring a taxi?' she asked wearily.

'Aren't you going to drive us?'

'No, Thomas. What if I want to have a few drinks?'

'A few drinks? But what about this?' Thomas put his hand on Tara's belly and pinched lots more than an inch.

'Just for once, Thomas,' she wheedled, miserably. 'I've had such a horrible week . . .'

'Just this once, then,' he conceded, adding, 'seeing as your mate might be dying.'

Astonished by his savagery, Tara suddenly realized she was sick, sick, *sick* of Thomas and his crude, roughshod ways. Of his relentless, gratuitous cruelty. Of never winning arguments. Of being insulted and hurt. All in the name of the great absolver, honesty.

'Doesn't it upset you?' Her voice shook with rage and grief. 'A young man, the same age as you, being so ill, possibly going to die?'

With a surprised, slightly gormless face, Thomas said, 'No, it doesn't get to me.'

Tara looked at him steadily, hoping to shame him.

'I don't know him well enough,' he admitted, awkwardly, unsettled by her intensity. 'Maybe if he was me mate, I'd be different.'

She continued to look at him. Waiting.

'He's not me mate,' he protested. But without his customary crassness.

'But you understand what I'm going through?'

Something appeared in his eyes. Not exactly compassion, just a reluctant acknowledgement that it was hard for her. It was as close as they'd been in a long time and it would have to do. He shrugged, uncomfortably. 'I'm sorry I can't pretend to be choked up about him. I'm only being . . .'

'I know,' Tara finished, with a trace of contempt, 'honest.'

He flicked her an uncertain look. She was in a funny mood! Just because her mate was ill. She'd want to see what it was like when your mam abandoned you!

Before they left, Tara watched Thomas put his little brown change purse into his pocket, and she was shocked at how cringy it suddenly seemed to her.

'Lend us twenty quid, Tara,' he coaxed.

Eddie's new girlfriend Dawn was a skinny, sexy young thing with long, brown sinewy legs and dark, darting eyes. Tara felt like a fourteen-stone marshmallow by comparison. Anxiously she watched Thomas look from Dawn to herself and back again. Taking notes, making comparisons, finding Tara lacking. She found him staring at her bottom, spilled on either side of her like a cushion, and panic tightened her chest and sent her temperature soaring. Her earlier burst of contempt had disappeared and she was truly terrified of losing him.

She got plastered that night, so plastered that she felt better. At the club they ended up going to, she danced drunkenly with Dawn and had skittish, overblown fun. She decided she liked Dawn.

Later, as Tara and Thomas came home in the taxi, Thomas was drunk and affectionate, holding her hand and stroking her hair.

'Why do you love me?' Tara asked playfully.

'Who says I love you?' he challenged, but with a sidelong, crinkle-eyed smile that, in her drunken, hopeful state, Tara took to mean that of course he did.

'Well, why are you with me, then?'

'Cos you give me money, of course.'

He laughed, and she swallowed away the sting. This was nice – they were bantering, making gentle fun with each other, the way lovers did. 'OK,' she smiled, playing the game, 'you're with me because I give you money, so what does that make you?

'A kept man,' she elaborated, opening her eyes wide with mock horror. 'A prostitute, even! So I must be a pimp.'

But he didn't smile or reply with a light-hearted insult. His face went hard and thoughtful. No more repartee. Oh, God, she thought, why did it always go wrong, why did it always turn nasty? The warm, cosy mood of togetherness went into freefall.

I don't want to do this any more, Tara thought wearily. After the terrible week, she had no more coping skills left. She was fresh out of endurance, excuses and hope.

40

'What kind of Mass does this Father Gilligan do?' JaneAnn asked.

Katherine went very still. What was the right answer? 'A nice one,' she chanced.

'A long one?'

Was long desirable? Probably. 'Ages. Hours.'

'Good.' JaneAnn gave a firm nod of her little head.

The doorbell rang and it was Sandro, in his best suit.

'What are you doing here?' Katherine asked in surprise.

'I'm going to eleven o'clock Mass with JaneAnn.'

Katherine burst out laughing, then stopped abruptly when she saw JaneAnn behind her.

'I'm surprised at you, Katherine Casey, making fun of a young man's faith.'

'Sorry,' Katherine said, humbly.

Sandro recoiled when he saw that Katherine's normally pristine, tasteful flat had deteriorated even further since the previous evening. It was as if a bomb had exploded. Clothes, shoes, suitcases and bed-linen everywhere. Socks were draped on top of the television, a teacup was upended in a pot plant, the previous night's wine and whiskey bottles were thrown on the floor, and though the sofa-bed had been folded back into a couch, a huge corner of sheet lolled out of it like a tongue from a slack mouth. From the kitchen came clattering, sizzling and the smell of food being fried. 'It's as if twenty students live here,' he breathed, surveying the chaos, searching for an orange traffic cone.

'It is, isn't it?' Katherine laughed darkly.

'But you are always such a Miss Prissy-knickers,' he protested.

'What's the point?' She lifted her arms, then let them flop to her sides. 'If I tidy, it's a shambles again five minutes later.'

'You are feeling all right?' He watched her closely.

'Fine!' she declared, shrilly. 'Great. Except, you know,' she continued, her voice getting thinner and shriller, 'once in a while it'd be nice to be able to get into my bathroom. There's always someone in it. And I don't really mind that JaneAnn used my loofah-mitt to scrub the kitchen floor, or that Timothy cleaned my non-stick frying-pan by scraping off all the black so that it's not non-stick any more. But what kind of upset me this morning when I finally got into *my* bathroom was that someone – I think it was Milo – used all my Kerastase leave-in conditioner.'

'Why do you think it was him?'

'Just look at his hair,' Katherine screeched. 'See how bloody shiny it is!' Her face was a ball of red and she glared at Sandro, daring him to try and talk her down. 'I'm sorry,' she wailed, and burst out crying. 'I'm sorry, I'm sorry!' She shuddered with tears. 'I'm such a selfish brat. How can these things matter when Fintan's so sick?'

The bell rang again. This time it was Liv, soberly dressed.

'Don't tell me,' Katherine laughed through her tears, 'you're going to eleven o'clock Mass with JaneAnn?'

Katherine couldn't go to Mass, even though she knew it was expected of her. She was just too upset.

'But surely if you're upset,' JaneAnn fretted, 'Mass is the best place for you.'

Milo didn't go either, which caused JaneAnn to look sorrowful. But when they all arrived back two hours later, JaneAnn was in top form and even more enamoured of Liv because she knew Father Gilligan personally. 'You missed a great Mass,' JaneAnn sang. 'The sermon was particularly beautiful. About the Prodigal Son. It doesn't matter how long you've been away from the Lord, he'll always welcome you back, no questions asked.' She looked with heavy emphasis at Milo.

Then Tara arrived and it was time to visit Fintan.

As soon as Tara walked through the hospital doors, she was running on empty. She was wrecked, wrung dry from all the emotion, fed up of her clothes and hair reeking of the ferrousy hospital smell, worn out from sitting on the hard visitors' chairs and it was a real struggle to do without cigarettes for hours on end. She hadn't managed to knit any of Thomas's jumper or go to the gym all week, her work was suffering and she couldn't stop eating. She yearned for a night at home, alone, watching soaps and speaking to no one. She flicked a glance at Katherine and saw that she'd just hit an identical wall.

'It's queer,' JaneAnn articulated everyone's feelings. 'It's like it's only five minutes since we were last here. Last night's sleep might as well not have happened.'

'Groundhog day.' Tara laughed wearily.

'This is only our . . .' Liv counted on her fingers '. . . fifth day doing this.'

'I know,' Milo finished for her. 'It feels like the millionth.'

'But maybe he'll be coming home tomorrow,' JaneAnn suggested hopefully.

'Maybe,' the others agreed, and for once they weren't trying to fool themselves. If Fintan got the all-clear on his tests, he could have his lymph glands treated as an outpatient.

And, as luck would have it, he was better that day than he'd been in a while. Though the lump on his neck was still in evidence, he wasn't so listless or yellow-looking, and he was managing to eat and keep food down. The mood eddied and rose. Everything was going to be all right.

'When's Thomas coming to visit me?' he mischievously asked Tara.

'I don't know.' She blushed. 'He's very busy, you know, with his work and his football . . .'

'Tell him I'd like to see him.' Fintan grinned. 'I think it would help me get better.'

'I'll try.'

'Ask him to do it for you,' Fintan urged. 'The woman he loves.'

'OK,' Tara promised, embarrassed and confused. Of course she'd asked Thomas to come with her to the hospital, or even to meet the O'Gradys, but he'd stubbornly refused to. 'I'll not be a hypocrite,' he'd said, and that was that.

And what was Fintan up to? He hated Thomas.

Tara's thoughts were interrupted by a loud, 'Hi there!' and she looked up to see Fintan's friends Frederick, Claude and Geraint swoop excitedly into the room, weighed down with goodies. Everyone budged up to make room. But a short while later Harry and Didier arrived. And then Butch and Javier.

Fintan constantly had so many visitors that they often over-flowed into the corridor outside, where conversations were lively, spirits were high and networking was in operation. Already someone called Davy, a friend of Javier's, had slept with Harry's friend Jimbob, whom he'd met at the door of Fintan's ward.

'Ward seventeen,' Fintan was amused, 'where love stories begin.' He joked that some of his friends were coming to the hospital and not even bothering to visit him, so attractive was the party atmosphere in the corridor. In fact, he went so far as to suggest that some of the people coming didn't actually know him.

Eventually, to make a bit of room, Liv, Tara and Katherine repaired to the day room where Liv opened up a line of inquiry that she'd been keen to pursue for some time. 'Timothy is married, isn't he?' she asked, oh-so-casually.

'Yes.'

'And Ambrose is married? And Jerome?'

'Yes.'

'So why isn't Milo? Is he gay too?'

'No,' Tara said. 'But he was disappointed by a girl once.'

'Disappointed?' Liv exclaimed. 'What on earth do you mean? Is that another of your strange Irish euphemisms?'

'It means dumped,' Katherine explained. 'He was engaged to be married to Eleanor Devine, they had what we'd call an "understanding", and she did a runner.'

'Why?'

'She didn't want to be a farmer's wife. She went to San Francisco and became a conceptual artist.'

'What did she look like?' Liv sounded slightly choked. 'Ugly? Fat?'

'Good-looking, I suppose,' Katherine said.

'*How* good-looking?' Liv pounced. 'On a scale of one to ten?'

'Five.'

'Four, three even.' Tara nudged Katherine. 'Tell us, Liv, why are you so interested anyway?'

'He's six foot two,' Liv said, dreamily, 'built like a fridge-freezer, has long, black, shiny hair . . .'

Katherine stiffened at the mention of shiny hair.

'. . . navy-blue eyes and a beautiful smile.' Liv came out of her reverie. 'No reason, really . . .' and they all laughed.

'You're not serious, though?' Tara asked.

'Of course I am.'

'But,' Tara said, uncomfortably, 'but you're Swedish, you're stylish, you're an interior designer, he's . . . Well, he's Milo O'Grady.'

'He wears dungarees,' Katherine threw in her twopence-worth.

'He's never heard of Tricia Guild.'

'And you've never heard of liver fluke. How could it work?'

'He's a man of the land.' Liv had a glint in her eyes. 'Creating new life, with his hands, reaping and sowing. What could be more worthy than that?'

'A brain surgeon,' Katherine suggested.

'A social worker,' Tara said.

'An accountant.'

'A shoe designer.'

'He works with his hands. His big, strong, sexy hands. Can't you see how beautiful he is?'

'No,' Tara said bluntly.

'Liv, you're upset,' Katherine soothed. 'None of us are ourselves at the moment. And surely you haven't forgotten about your beloved Lars?'

'That prick,' Liv replied, vaguely. Then she caught sight of her behaviour, and it was her turn to moan in shame, 'How could I? How could I think about a man at a time like this? I hate myself.'

'Don't,' Tara comforted her. 'Please don't. It's a very weird time and if it's any consolation I've been worried about myself and Thomas and I've been *mortified*. It seems so unworthy!'

Katherine felt a burden roll away from her. 'Thank God you said that, Tara. This week I've found myself concerned about things besides Fintan too, and I thought there must be something wrong with me for being so selfish. I've hated myself.'

'Did you really? *I've* hated *my*self,' Tara exclaimed.

'I'm so glad you said that. I've hated myself also,' Liv threw in.

They smiled in sheepish relief at each other, their shameful secrets out in the open, the liberation making them feel weightless.

'Either we're a trio of evil bitches,' Tara announced, 'or else we're really normal.'

'Poor Fintan, though,' Katherine said. 'How must he *feel*? How *would* you feel if you thought you had only a short time to live? I keep trying to put myself in his head.'

'Me too,' said Tara.

'Me too,' said Liv.

'Just imagine that you only have six months left to live,' Tara challenged. 'That you'd be dead before next May.'

'Go on,' she urged, as both Katherine and Liv looked at her, slightly shocked.

Feeling foolish, Katherine closed her eyes. What *would* it be like? she forced herself to wonder. This would be her last Christmas. There wouldn't ever be another summer for her. One hundred and eighty days, instead of the thousands and thousands she'd always assumed were rolling out ahead of her, forming a chain of years, pulling her into old age.

To her surprise, something altered. A single day, unthrilling by virtue of its sheer availability, valueless because there were so many others, loomed at her in close-up and blossomed so that every nuance seemed sweet and precious. As priceless as a diamond, from waking up with morning expectation, to winding down in evening light. She had a frantic need to fill it, to use it wisely, to do all the desirable things, the truly important things.

Never mind being responsible, she wouldn't be around to reap the rewards. More importantly, never mind being *careful*, she wouldn't be around to deal with the consequences. She felt almost panicky as she thought of all the things she wanted to do in her six months – it'd have to be the miracle of the loaves and fishes if she was to fit everything in.

Her rules and barricades appeared stifling to her. Crazy, even. She wanted to immerse herself fully in life. Experience everything. Have fun. Lots and lots of fun. Have sex. With Joe Roth. Christ Almighty! Terrified, she snapped her eyes open. Tara and Liv were looking at her.

'Scary, isn't it?' Tara breathed out with a shudder. 'I'll tell you one thing. If I had six months left to live I wouldn't worry about trying to get Thomas to marry me so that I wouldn't be lonely in my old age. Because I wouldn't have an old age to be lonely in!'

'What would you do?' Katherine asked eagerly, keen to stop thinking about herself.

'I'd dump Lars and make my move on Milo,' Liv said.

'But you're going to do that anyway,' Tara said. 'You don't need to be dying. Now, me, I'd have a fling.'

'With who?'

'I don't know. Someone I think is gorgeous, someone who thinks *I'm* gorgeous! One of those mad, breathless, sexy affairs, where you never get out of bed, where you wake in the middle of the night because you fancy each other so much.' She shivered in pleasure.

'You mean it's not like that all the time with you and Thomas?' Katherine asked, drily.

'You know that once you're past the three-month mark you hardly ever have sex,' Tara said. 'And don't look at me like that. I love Thomas, this is just pretend.'

'You've as good as told us that you don't even fancy him.'

'I did not! I only said that if things were . . . Look, it's not real, it's only imaginary!'

'You're right,' Katherine reminded them. 'We don't have only six months to live, we're not going to die, this discussion is stupid and maudlin.'

'Glad to hear it,' Tara cried. 'I was just thinking, what if I left him, went off and had my mad fling with someone else, and then I didn't die? I'd feel like such an eejit!'

41

Just after ten o'clock on Monday morning, while the usual suspects were grouped around Fintan's bed, Dr Singh strode in. From his faint agitation, it looked as though he had information to impart. The air sparked with tension and everyone's already over-active nerves went on full alert. *Please, God, let it be good news.*

'I have the result of the bone-marrow biopsy,' he said, looking at Fintan.

Tell us, tell us.

'Would you prefer to hear it alone?'

'No,' Fintan said, trembling with calm. 'You might as well tell the lot of us. It'll save me having to repeat it.'

Dr Singh took a breath to speak, then paused. He didn't find this easy. 'I'm afraid it's bad news.'

No one spoke. Eight chalk-white faces beseeched him, willing him to be wrong.

'The disease is active in the bone-marrow,' he continued, nervously. *I'm only the messenger.*

'How active?' Katherine croaked.

'I'm afraid it's quite advanced.'

Katherine looked at Fintan. His eyes were huge and dark, like those of a terrified child.

'I also have the result of the CT scan,' Dr Singh added, apologetically.

Eight agonized faces turned upon him.

'That also shows activity of the disease in the pancreas. And,' Dr Singh was mortified, 'I also have the results of the chest X-rays.'

His face said it all.

'It's in his chest too?' Milo asked.

The doctor nodded. 'However, there's no sign of activity in any of the main organs, like the liver, kidneys or lungs,' he added. 'That would have been very serious *indeed*.'

Fintan spoke for the first time. 'Will I die?' he asked hoarsely.

'We'll start treatment immediately.' Dr Singh ignored the question. 'Now that we know what we're dealing with, we know what to treat you with.'

'About time,' Tara said, bitterly, shocking everyone. That wasn't how you spoke to doctors. 'He was getting worse and worse each day that passed,' she charged. 'And you did nothing. Just left him lying here while your bloody lab was too busy to tell him how sick he was. What if those days make all the difference between life and ... and ...' She began to cry, gasping, yelping sobs, which shook her whole body. She turned to Fintan. 'You must have had symptoms for ages,' she heaved, tears sluicing down her cheeks. 'Months.'

'I did.'

'Well, why didn't you go to the doctor about them?' She was breathless, panting with anger and grief. 'Why didn't Sandro make you?'

'Because we thought we knew what was wrong with me. Night sweats, so bad we sometimes had to change the sheets. Me losing weight steadily. My stomach constantly upset. You see, Sandro had been through it once before.'

A horrible picture of Sandro and Fintan in a conspiracy of

silence. Fintan getting sicker and sicker, and nothing being done to help him because they thought nothing *could* be done.

'You big pair of eejits.' Tara shuddered. 'You pair of thick gobshites.'

JaneAnn took Tara's arm in a painful grip and quick-marched her away from the bed. 'Stop that nonsense, Tara Butler,' she threatened. 'He's not dead yet.'

Fintan's treatment started that morning. He was to remain in hospital and have five days of concentrated chemotherapy. Everyone was told to leave.

'But I'm his mother.' JaneAnn's feisty resistance vanished. 'I shouldn't have to go.'

'Come on, Mam,' Milo urged, trying to shift her. 'You can see him tonight.'

They scattered apart – JaneAnn, Milo, Timothy, Liv, Tara, Katherine, and Sandro. They, who'd been inseparable during the waiting period, were blown away from each other by the explosive news.

The mood was one of strange embarrassment, a resentment of themselves and of each other. What good had all their buoyed-up, hopeful vigilance done? Why had they bothered shoring up themselves and Fintan, steadfastly willing the best? They were – and clearly always had been – utterly useless.

There was no point in sitting by his bed any more, human amulets, warding off disaster. His fate now lay with powerful drugs. Chemicals so toxic that the nurses administering them had to wear protective clothing. Medication with such savage side-effects that at times Fintan would rather die than endure the cure.

They each, separately, set about the enormous task of processing, bit by bit, such a huge bottleneck of emotion. JaneAnn took up almost permanent residence at St Dominic's, where she negotiated with God, offering to take Fintan's place if someone had to die. Timothy returned to Katherine's flat, where he watched daytime television, smoked heavily and left his boots lying about, obscuring the floor. Milo walked for miles, visiting Harvey Nichols, the Museum of Mankind, the V&A and various landmarks and tourist attractions. The others went to work. It had seemed imperative to neglect their jobs while they stood guard over Fintan. But the worst had happened. And instead of making their jobs even less important, it suddenly seemed vital to regain control.

It was a bright, blue, cold October morning, and as Katherine left the hospital and drove up the Fulham Road in a taxi, she passed a woman her own age, walking along, swinging a plastic shopping bag through which she could see a carton of orange juice and a pint of milk.

Katherine watched, fascinated, turning back to look at her. The woman wasn't particularly carefree-looking, she looked as if she wasn't thinking about much at all. Katherine yearned to be her. There had been times when she'd strolled, swinging a bag of groceries. She must have done it *hundreds* of times and never appreciated the bliss of it, the utter joy of a life free from the stench of nightmare.

When she walked into her office, she was astonished by everyone scurrying around. Busy, busy, busy. They looked like aliens, chasing their tails. She'd been catapulted to the edge of life, where everything seemed warped, skewed and peculiar. *What does any of it matter?*

315

People nodded hello at her as she moved across the floor in a dream. When she got to her desk, she had to pause to check that it really was hers. All her thoughts and reactions were wrapped in Styrofoam, making them muffled and fuzzy.

Before she'd even sat down, her eyes sought Joe Roth. She knew she should stop herself but she hadn't her usual strength of will to fight it.

He was on the phone, leaning back in the chair, playing a pen through his long, elegant fingers. The phone lay close to his face, up against the cheekbones that were like the long convex razor shells that littered the beach at Knockavoy.

She wanted him. That became the one crystal-clear thought in a blurred, unreachable world. Shining like a lighthouse through fog. She wanted Joe Roth passionately, violently. Inappropriately. Once again she wondered, in disbelief, *How could I?*

The reason for all the frantic activity, it turned out, was that news had just come in that the account for Multi-nut Muesli had gone to a rival advertising firm. It was Joe Roth's first failure at Breen Helmsford.

'You win some, you lose some.' Joe shrugged, with dignity, trying to keep the morale of his team up.

'Not in this business, son,' Fred Franklin said, brutally. 'You win some, you win some. You lose some, you lose your job.'

Katherine should have been glad because Joe could easily be sacked for losing the account, but she wanted to go and give him comfort – lay his beautiful head in her lap and stroke her fingers through his hair.

'Not your week, is it?' Fred cackled at Joe. 'What with your beloved Arsenal losing on Saturday.'

Better do some work, Katherine decided. She looked at the figures on her desk but they might as well have been written in Urdu. She turned her spreadsheet upside down to see if it made better sense and found Breda staring at her in alarm. 'I'll be with you shortly, Breda.' Katherine tried to sound like a woman in control, 'Just catching up here.' *Get it together*, Katherine admonished herself. Joe Roth wouldn't be the only one getting the boot if she didn't watch it.

'Is now a good time?' she heard, and looked up to find Joe Roth standing over her.

'For what?' she stammered, her heart pounding.

'Expenses.'

'Again?'

'Again.' He gave a wry smile. 'Best if I do. Just in case I'm told to clear out my desk before the end of today.'

'You're joking, aren't you?' she asked, aghast.

'Advertising. It's a dog-eat-dog world.' He smiled.

'But it's only your first offence,' she protested. 'That wouldn't be fair.'

He put his hand on her desk and leant over. 'Katherine,' he said, with quiet intensity, laughter in his eyes, 'calm down.'

She caught a whiff of him, the sharp, fresh smell of clean man. Soap and citrus and an undercurrent of something slightly more feral. He moved back, and she felt confused and abandoned. 'Pull up a pew,' she managed. She was glad she'd said 'pew'. It sounded relaxed and casual.

Joe sat in front of her in a crisp white shirt. Clean-shaven, lean-jawed, sallow-skinned. As she sorted through the small bundle of receipts, his presence played havoc with her fingers on her calculator. She kept hitting the percentage key or the square-root button instead of the plus sign. 'I'm sorry about your Multi-nut Muesli account.'

If he was surprised by her unprecedented forwardness he

didn't show it. He just shrugged. 'It's life, isn't it?' He did a good job of pretending it didn't matter, but she'd always sensed how important his job was to him. 'You can't always get what you want.' He held her eyes when he finished speaking. Was she imagining there was meaning in his expression? 'Or maybe *you* do,' he added.

Did she always get what she wanted?

And as Joe watched, transfixed, tears filled Katherine's eyes, then overflowed neatly, prettily, down her smooth face. Surprising them both. 'I'm so sorry,' she whispered, putting her head down and whisking the tears away with the back of her hand. 'I had some – some bad news this morning.'

'I'm sorry to hear that.' He sounded like he meant it.

That made her cry even more. She wanted to go to him, to feel the hardness of his arms around the small of her back, pulling her against him, to lay her cheek on the cashmere of his lapel, to turn her face into the crisp cotton of his shirt and *inhale* him.

'Would you like to . . . ?' He was about to ask if she'd like to go for a cup of coffee to talk, then stopped himself. Of course she wouldn't want to.

Katherine was distracted by Angie slowly walking by, twisting her head into an impossible angle. Katherine realized she was trying to get a look at Joe. Come to think of it, she'd vaguely noticed Angie passing at least twice already during the conversation. What did it mean?

'This is all fine.' She indicated the expenses claim with a watery smile. 'I'll do a cheque in a day or so.'

As Joe returned to his desk, he was met by an excited deputation headed by Myles.

'Was Icequeen *crying*?' he demanded eagerly.

'No,' Joe said shortly, and turned away.

318

42

Fintan had flipped. There was no other explanation for his behaviour. He'd summoned Tara and Katherine to his bedside because he had a request to make of each of them, and they decided that the cancer must have spread to his brain when they heard what he wanted them to do.

It was five days since his diagnosis and he'd been given a day off from chemo because it was so gruelling. The cocktail of drugs had made him sick, he'd developed monstrous mouth ulcers and already his hair had started to fall out.

'Jesus,' he'd mumbled, when he could find the energy to speak, 'I'd rather take my chances with the cancer.'

His reaction to conventional medicine sent everyone into a mad flurry of reading all the books on alternative cures they'd bought. 'I'd normally laugh at this kind of thing,' Katherine admitted, looking up from a page that suggested Fintan could be cured by imagining himself being bathed in yellow light, 'but maybe it's worth a try.'

Fintan responded to suggestions that he imagine breathing in pure, healing, silvery light or zapping his cancer cells as if he was playing Space Invaders by mumbling, 'Fuck off, I'm too fucking sick.'

But today, as only saline solution dripped into him, despite being weak as a kitten, X-ray thin and greyish-yellow, he was

better than he'd been in days. 'Gather around!' he croaked, in
a travesty of his erstwhile flamboyance. 'Now, you know the
way you all keep saying that if there's anything you can do for
me . . .'

Tara and Katherine nodded eagerly.

'Good. You promise?'

'We promise.'

'Promise, promise?'

They rolled their eyes – as if they wouldn't do exactly what
he wanted! 'Promise, promise.'

'Right, I'll start with you, Tara.'

She assumed an attentive expression.

'You're to leave Thomas.'

The smile remained on her face, but the light behind it had
gone, and her eyes were startled. 'Excuse me?' she managed.
She'd been expecting him to ask her to bring in new pyjamas
or – God forbid – visit an undertaker's for leaflets for him, or
even to extract a promise that she'd take care of Sandro if the
worst happened. But not this.

'I want you to leave Thomas,' he repeated.

She elbowed Katherine. 'Next he'll want me to climb Mount
Everest,' she laughed, uncertainly, 'and while I'm at it straighten
the Leaning Tower of Pisa and –'

'Not funny, Tara.' He silenced her. 'This is no joke.'

Startled by his intense tone, she looked into his skeletal face
for clues. Her heart banged in her chest, as she realized he was
serious. 'But why?' she faltered.

'Because I want you to be happy.' His voice was faint but
surprisingly firm.

'I am happy.' The erratic, inexplicable dissatisfaction she'd
been feeling with Thomas was instantly wiped out. 'I'd be very

*un*happy without him. Wouldn't I?' She turned to Katherine for support.

'No point asking her,' Fintan sang, hoarsely. 'She agrees with me.'

'What exactly does my relationship with Thomas have to do with you?' Tara attempted defiance.

Fintan took a breath to speak, then paused. He looked at his blanket, seemingly for inspiration, before saying, 'If I'm going to die, I'm damned if you're going to waste your life.'

Tara was shocked, shamed – and angry. How dare he play God with her life just because he might die?

'Yes, I am a bastard,' Fintan said cheerfully, speaking her mind and embarrassing her. 'Shamelessly manipulating my position. Might as well get what I can out of it. Christ knows, it hasn't much else going for it.'

'I'm sorry you don't like Thomas.'

'The only reason I don't like him is because he's bad to you.' Fintan's glittering eyes held hers. 'Look at how he hasn't even come to see me and I've been here nearly two weeks. Even Ravi's been in to visit.'

Tara suspected that Ravi went to the hospital for the same reason that people slow down, their eyes out on stalks, passing a road accident, but all she said was, 'That's Thomas being bad to *you*, not to me. If you want to see him that badly, Fintan, I'll organize it.'

'I don't want to see him at all. Jesus, the very sight of him would set me back months. But I'm making the point that he's not supporting *you*.'

'Fintan, I'll do anything else for you, anything at all,' she flapped, 'but there's no way I'm going to leave Thomas.'

'You *promised*.' He thrust his chapped-to-bits lower lip out in joke sulkiness. 'Look.' He stuck out his tongue. 'Do you want to see my mouth ulcers? They're amazing.'

'Fintan . . .'

'Look at the ones on my tongue. Aren't they huge? Look,' he ordered her. 'Look!'

'Huge,' she said, flatly. 'Fintan, please don't ask me to leave Thomas. He doesn't treat me badly *as such* . . .'

'No!' Fintan attempted to sit up, but couldn't summon the energy. 'Katherine and I don't want to hear about how it's for your own good when Thomas insults you, a sign of how much he cares. And we don't want to hear that it's not his fault that he's an obnoxious prick. If he treated his mother the way he treats you who'd blame the woman for scarpering? You said you'd do anything for me. So do it.'

'Anything other than this.'

'It's easy,' he urged, weakly, as his burst of defiance dissolved and he was flung once more against his pillows. 'Tell her, Katherine. Just throw all your things in the car and go!'

For the first time Tara visualized it and she contracted with fear. It was like being told to jump off a cliff.

Fintan moved his head along on the pillow and left a hank of thick, black hair behind. He didn't notice, which somehow made it worse.

'But what would become of me without Thomas?' Tara managed, sick from witnessing the hair loss. 'I'd never get anyone else and I hate not having a man.

'And it's not something I'm proud of,' she added quickly.

'I'm going to puke,' Fintan interrupted, urgently. 'Katherine, pass me that bowl.' He empty-retched, then, sweating and exhausted, flopped back on his pillows. Everyone remained silent, and Tara and Katherine were both trying to work up to leaving when Fintan spoke again. 'How do you know you hate being without a man, Tara? You've only been single for about a week since we moved to London twelve years ago! The minute it ends with one, you're off with another. Go on,' he urged weakly, 'break the fear barrier.'

Like a fish on a line, she struggled and fought to get free. 'No, Fintan. I'm thirty-one. You can't teach an old dog new tricks. I'm in the Last Chance Saloon and –'

'You and your Last Chance Saloon.' Fintan laughed, bitterly. 'If anyone's in the Last Chance Saloon it's me.'

Tara couldn't speak. Anger and guilt and fear tangled together. This was blackmail.

'Do you want to end up just like your mother?' Fintan asked. Tara's head shot up. 'Living with a cranky old bollocks?' he suggested archly. 'Doing everything bar standing on your head yet never pleasing him? Sure, that's what you're like already!'

Tara was inflamed. It was one thing for her to complain about her father, but it stung to hear another person, even someone as close as Fintan, speak that way about her family. And, anyway, she was nothing like her mother, who was a pet but undeniably a doormat. Even though Thomas was sometimes difficult, Tara wasn't a doormat. She was a modern, independent woman with choices and power. Wasn't she?

'You can't deny me anything I want. I've cancer.' Then he put the final boot in. 'If you don't leave Thomas,' he twinkled, 'I'll die, just to spite you.'

Tara wanted to kill him. She was as furious as she was grief-stricken. Over her throbbing head she heard him saying, 'All right, I'm prepared to compromise. Ask Thomas to marry you and if he says yes, then you have my blessing. But if he says no, then tell him to sling his hook. How about that?'

'Maybe,' Tara mumbled, thinking, *No way. Not in a hairy fit. Not in a million years.*

'Good!' In his exhausted, nauseous way, Fintan was pleased. Until it occurred to him that there was a small chance that Thomas might accept. Oh, no!

'Now, your turn, Katherine,' Fintan declared. 'You, missy, are to take yourself out of cold storage.'

Katherine assumed an expression of polite interest, as if she had no idea what Fintan was on about.

'Get yourself a man,' he elaborated.

Tara erupted angrily. 'Why does she get the nice task and I get the awful one?'

'I don't think Katherine sees it that way.' Instantly, Katherine forced a smile. It looked as if it had been stapled on. 'Haven't you noticed a pattern? Because I sure as hell have,' Fintan murmured. His eyes were closed again and he sounded almost like he was talking to himself. 'Every twelve months or so you show up with some insanely handsome man on your arm. He sticks around for a couple of weeks, then, bam! he's gone and you're telling us you don't want to talk about it. Can't you pick someone who's, like, *moderately* good-looking? Stop building failure into every relationship you embark on. And don't think I don't know why you do it.' His voice was so low they both had to lean in on him to hear him. 'You're just like your mother. One bad experience with a man and you turn chicken. *Bockbockbockbockbock.*' Still with his eyes closed, Fintan bent his arms at the elbow and weakly flapped them. 'Chicken,' he repeated meaningfully, and opened his eyes to stare directly at Katherine.

'I'm nothing like my mother.' Katherine swallowed.

'You're just like her! Ducking men like a big scaredy-cat.'

'My mother is bonkers.'

'So will you be, eventually, if you carry on the way you're going.'

'Fintan,' Katherine's voice was controlled, 'it's not imperative for every human being to have a partner to be happy.'

'Oh, God, puke bowl again, please.'

Wishing they could run away, they sat as, once more without success, Fintain tried to vomit. 'If I could only throw up I know I'd feel better,' he mumbled, when he'd given up on it again.

Katherine and Tara looked at their shoes and wished they were living someone else's life.

'So, Katherine,' Fintan broke the silence, 'I quite agree that some people are meant to be on their own. And you're not one of them. Tara tells me there's some fella at work.'

Katherine glared at Tara, redirecting all the rage she was forbidden to expel on to Fintan. 'Not any more,' it gave her sour pleasure to tell him.

'Has he left work?'

'No, he's just gone off me.'

'Why?'

Katherine didn't speak.

'You have to tell me,' he ordered. 'I have cancer. I might die!'

Resentfully Katherine elaborated, 'I think it's because I accused him of sexual harassment when he kept asking me out.'

'What did you do that for?'

'I didn't want to go out with him.'

'But why not? Is he a bad person?'

'No! He's so nice he'd get on your nerves.'

'Aha!' Fintan seemed to have perked up. 'So you'd have gone out with him if he was a tosser? Then he'd dump you and you'd be safe once more – single, with your low opinion of men reinforced. Katherine, you have it all worked out.'

She shrugged, hating this.

'Is he married?'

'Not to my knowledge.'

'How good-looking is he?'

'Very.'

'Dangerously? Insanely?'

'No, just very.'

'Does he do any part-time modelling?'

'No.'

'Good, I like him already. Do you fancy him?'

There was a pause, then Katherine nodded shakily.

'What's his name?'

'Joe Roth.'

'Your mission, Katherine Casey, should you choose to accept it – and believe me, you'd better, if you ever want to see Fintan O'Grady alive again – is to bag this Joe Roth.'

'I think he's got another girl,' Katherine protested.

'You love a challenge!'

She said nothing.

'Promise me,' Fintan urged, weakly. 'Promise me you'll try.'

'I'll think about it.'

'I know you both hate me,' Fintan flashed a grin at them, 'but if you could see what I see, you'd be downright disgusted by the way you're wasting your lives. You're enduring maintenance-level misery because you think that at some point in your future things will just click into being perfect.

'Go on, go home now, the pair of you have worn me out. And remember, Tara, get packing your bags and, Katherine, wear your best knickers to work on Monday! And most of all,' he urged, like a football coach, 'get out there and live, live, live!'

Stiffly they bade him goodbye. As they left his bedside, Neville and Geoff arrived. 'Sorry, girls,' Fintan groaned at them, 'I feel too shitty for visitors.'

Tara and Katherine didn't speak as they went down in the lift or left the hospital, except to wave wanly at Harry, Didier and Will who were noisily en route to Fintan, laden with flowers, magazines and beer. The flowers and magazines were for Fintan but the beer was for them.

As Tara steered the Beetle out of the car park, a car was coming in. Katherine twiddled her fingers at the people in it – Javier and Butch. 'I wonder if Didier is going to get off with Butch?' she mused idly.

'I wonder.'

Then they drove in silence for almost twenty minutes.

Finally Tara spoke. 'Fintan's a scream, isn't he?' She forced a laugh. 'An absolute madman.'

Katherine caught her breath. Had she been tying herself in knots for nothing? 'You think he was joking?'

Tara gave Katherine a wry look. 'Sure, what else? Who could take that seriously? Isn't he a hoot?'

Katherine looked anxiously at Tara. She wasn't at all sure that Fintan had been having them on. But it was such a relief if he had been . . .

'A hoot,' she agreed, wildly. 'He's out of his mind.'

Then the laughter gathered steam and became real.

'The mere thought . . .'

'As if . . .'

'He's *cracked*.'

'Him and his harebrained schemes!'

'And we're as bad – I took him seriously for a while,' Katherine admitted.

'I could see that,' Tara said. 'I didn't, of course.'

Then they howled once more at Fintan's endearingly off-the-wall carry-on.

43

Lorcan was in bed with an exemplification of heroin chic: a pale-haired twenty-three-year-old 'resting' actress called Adrienne, who was the far side of anorexic. She was a great believer in mind over matter – the only way she could deal with her omnipresent hunger. It was also how she'd run Lorcan to ground. She'd kept bumping into him at auditions and, despite knowing he had a girlfriend, had pursued him relentlessly. Telling herself over and over to keep visualizing herself with him – the way she visualized eating three imaginary square meals a day, with imaginary snacks at eleven and four o'clock – and it would eventually become a reality. All she had to do was want him badly enough and he would be hers.

And it had worked! Which came as a pleasant surprise because she'd been using the same technique to try and get an acting job and had been so spectacularly unsuccessful that she'd ended up having to moonlight as a beautician to keep the wolf from the door.

In post-coital repose, their long limbs tangled, they lay on her second-hand futon. Not a buttock between the pair of them.

Adrienne thrummed with well-being. Now that she'd bagged Lorcan she couldn't believe she ever doubted that she would. And she had no intention of standing for any nonsense from him. Start as you mean to continue.

She propped herself up on her bony elbow, the starved muscles in her arm trembling slightly as she leant her too-big-for-her-body head on her hand. 'I hope this isn't a one-night stand,' she warned teasingly, looking down on him, stretched out in all his naked magnificence.

Lorcan laced his fingers together behind his head, displaying silky tufts of golden underarm hair. 'A one-night stand?' he echoed, in high-pitched surprise. 'Are you kidding?'

Smugness bathed Adrienne in a warm glow. She'd been fairly certain she was on top of things with this man, but you never really knew . . .

'I wouldn't even *dream* of a one-night stand,' Lorcan went on. 'I don't believe in them.'

Her confidence burgeoned and swelled, and she had a surge of contempt for all the women who let men ride roughshod over them. You wouldn't catch that happening to her. No, sir.

'I mean,' Lorcan said, with a glinty smile, 'an *entire* night? Are you mad? Who wants that kind of commitment?'

Even before Adrienne's disproportionately large head had the chance to start reeling with confusion, Lorcan sprang gracefully from the futon.

'What are you doing?' She was panic-stricken.

'Getting dressed.'

'But why?' Adrienne tried to sit up, unable to believe her surprise defeat.

'I can hardly go home like this.' He chortled, indicating his big, naked body.

As he scouted on the floor for his abandoned underpants, Adrienne stammered, 'But it's one in the morning. You can't leave.'

She was too young and beautiful to be skilled at hiding

disappointment. Not enough practice. Never mind, all in the fullness of time.

'But I have to go,' Lorcan protested, with affected innocence. 'Why?'

'Because,' he bellowed, as if he'd never heard such a stupid question in all his life, 'because my girlfriend will be wondering where I am!'

'But you don't live with her.'

'I said I'd call to see her.'

Adrienne had retained a small pocket of hope that he might be joking, but as he pulled on his jeans and boots with head-spinning alacrity, she realized he was deadly serious and she'd been had. In more ways than one. Somewhere inside she began to weep. 'I feel sorry for you,' she threw at his back as, already fully dressed, he stood at her mirror.

'Why?' He sounded genuinely worried. 'Is it because of my hair?'

She goggled, sidetracked from the you-must-be-very-unhappy-if-you-have-to-be-so-cruel speech she'd been about to make.

'No,' she managed, 'not because of your hair. I pity you because you must be really badly messed up to behave –' She stopped. The curiosity was too much. 'What about your hair?'

'Well,' Lorcan chuckled indulgently and circled his hand in a halo around his head, 'look at the state of it. It's a mess!'

After the sexual shenanigans it was undeniably all over the place. A little curl stuck up on either side of the front of his head and in her humiliated, stunned state, they seemed to Adrienne like horns. Gleefully, Lorcan spotted a little jar of styling wax on her dressing table. Not what he'd usually apply, and certainly not a reputable brand – as far as he remembered it had only got two out of five stars in a survey he'd studied in *Hairdressing Now!* – but needs must. 'How do you find this?' He held the shiny magenta pot out to Adrienne. 'I hear it gives good hold but can leave the hair slightly sticky.'

'How can you talk about hair? I want to talk about our relationship!'

Lorcan's face creased with amusement. 'Our what?'

She didn't answer. That had been a mistake.

'You'll never be happy,' Adrienne declared thickly, parroting what some of Lorcan's other leavings had said.

Lorcan shrugged, briskly rubbing a penny-sized piece of pink wax between the palms of his hands, as instructed.

'Why are you doing this to me?' she demanded.

Why indeed? He began lovingly to stroke the wax through his hair. *There, my beauties, my pretties.*

'Speak to me,' she shouted in frustration. 'What do you want from life? What are you looking for? I mean, what do you WANT?'

Lorcan looked at her reflection in the mirror for a long, thoughtful moment. 'World peace.'

In fact, as Lorcan let himself out of Adrienne's flat he felt oddly bleak.

In the three weeks since the Real Butter fiasco he hadn't got any work. Nor had he been given the opportunity to leap from his understudy role and set the world ablaze as Hamlet. His numerous prayers that Frasier Tippett would break his neck or catch meningitis had come to nothing. What kind of God was there? Lorcan often raged. What kind of sick world was he running? Was there no justice?

To fill in the gaps in his self-confidence, he continually

reminded himself that he was irresistible to women, playing power games with them when no one else would play with him. But as he lounged up the road away from Adrienne's he didn't feel triumphant or restored. Instead he felt mild disgust. For Adrienne? Well, who else? But he realized his contempt for her had something to do with Amy.

Lorcan burrowed through unfamiliar feelings, trying to figure it out. Finally he came to rest: Adrienne should have shown more respect for Amy, he decided. It hadn't been very considerate of Amy's feelings when Adrienne had put her hand on his thigh and said meaningfully, 'I do a hundred pelvic-floor exercises a day.'

Yes, Lorcan tut-tutted sanctimoniously, it was no way for her to treat Amy.

44

On Saturday night Liv and Milo became officially boyfriend
and girlfriend. They launched their relationship by announcing
coyly that they were going to a late-night film, to which Timothy
responded joyously. 'Grand! Let's go to a horse opera. Is there
a Clint Eastwood one on?'

An awkward silence fell, then Liv blushed and muttered,
'You see, it's just Milo and I who are going.'

JaneAnn was thrilled. 'Every oul' stocking meets an oul' shoe,'
she opined. 'I knew he'd find someone in the heel of the hunt.
Milo's a fine man, but there's no one in Knockavoy for him to
make a match with. Isn't it true that travel broadens the mind?
He deserves a good woman. Especially after he was so badly,' she
paused and bit back tears, '*disappointed* by Eleanor Devine. I
warned him,' she went on. 'I said to him not to trust any of that
crowd out of Quinard. I know them seed, breed and generation.
They wouldn't be above stealing a cow on you and blaming the
poor tinkers. But we've to make our own mistakes, I suppose.'
She smiled dreamily. 'Liv will love it in Knockavoy.'

Tara and Katherine exchanged astonished looks. JaneAnn
already had Liv and Milo married off.

'It's the best ever that she's a good Catholic,' JaneAnn said.
Although Liv was also a good Buddhist, Hindu, Sikh, Christian
Scientist, Jew and atheist when it suited her. But no one disillu-
sioned JaneAnn.

'You don't think she'll find it hard in Knockavoy, so far from home?' Tara felt obliged to say.

'But she's so far from home anyway,' JaneAnn pointed out, with undeniable logic.

'Well, what about her job?'

'Milo has enough and more to take care of her. She won't go short of anything with him.'

'Maybe Milo will move to London,' Katherine suggested carefully.

JaneAnn exploded into peals of laughter. She laughed and laughed and laughed. 'Have sense, child,' she said, wiping her eyes. 'Have a bit of sense. And him with a fine farm of land. Live in London, how are you!'

'Why is he doing this to me, O Wise One?' Tara asked Liv. 'O Swedish Anna Raeburn, tell me why he wants to ruin my life? He's supposed to be my *friend*.'

It was Sunday afternoon and Tara, Katherine and Liv had escaped the hospital for a while and gone to a nearby pub.

The problem was that Fintan had done it again – reiterated his unorthodox requests. Then, to make matters worse, he'd told Sandro and his family about what he wanted.

JaneAnn had looked in shock from Tara to Katherine. 'Girls,' she stuttered, 'you'll have to do what he asks. How could you have that on your conscience?'

Tara and Katherine flicked around, searching for an ally, but all they saw was Milo, Timothy, Sandro, Liv and, of course, JaneAnn, looking at them as if they were murderers.

'Fintan's become aware of his own mortality,' Liv explained to Tara, quoting directly from *Good Grief*, her book of the moment. 'Because time might be in short supply, it suddenly seems very precious. Not just his own but everyone's.'

All three had a short burst of empathy, then it passed.

'The thing is,' Tara said hopefully, 'he hasn't a leg to stand on because he's not going to die. He's on very powerful treatment and Hodgkin's disease has a high rate of recovery.'

Liv couldn't let that pass. 'The lump on his neck hasn't become any smaller, and the spot tests don't show any response to the drugs. You're in denial, you can't cope with how bad things are.'

'All this might pass in a couple of days,' Katherine cheered. 'He's had a hard time of it. No wonder he's a bit mental.'

Liv's face darkened. 'He's not mental. I think he's right. You *should* leave Thomas,' she nodded at Tara, 'and you,' she headbutted in Katherine's direction and shouted, 'what you need is a good SEEING-TO!'

Most of the pub turned to look. Before the apoplectic Tara and horrorstruck Katherine got a chance to tell her to shag off and mind her own business, Liv stomped from the pub.

'What on earth's up with her?' Tara exclaimed.

'How the hell would I know?' Katherine replied hotly.

They sat in resentful silence, Tara smoking, Katherine fiddling with Tara's car keys.

'Do you fucking *mind*?' Tara exploded, slapping Katherine's hand away with force. 'You're driving me mad.'

Katherine set her face in a mutinous expression, but left the keys alone.

'We should go back to the hospital,' Tara eventually said.

'Not yet.'

'Good, I don't want to go, either. I'm terrified that they'll all start on at us again.'

'They can stick it.' Katherine snorted.

'How about if *you* leave Thomas,' Tara suggested, 'and *I* sleep with Joe Roth?'

They laughed nervously, shakily reunited.

'You don't think . . .' Tara paused. She had to say this delicately. 'You don't think Fintan's asked us to do these things because he's bitter that he's very sick and we're not? You don't think it's a kind of revenge? That our lives have to be destroyed like his?'

That was going too far for Katherine. 'I'd say this is simply a passing notion of his,' she said, sharply. 'He's just having a shocking time, and gone a bit off the wall.'

'I hope so,' Tara threatened, 'because if he doesn't knock it off I'm not coming to visit him any more.'

'That's a terrible thing to say!' exclaimed Katherine, who had entertained the very same idea herself.

'It's easy for you.' Tara was defensive. 'You get the best part of the bargain. You'll go to bed with a gorgeous bloke and in return I walk out on the man I love.'

'It's not like you think,' Katherine said irritably. 'I'm paralysed even thinking about it.'

'Yeah, right!'

'I am! You know I couldn't.'

'Couldn't what? Give the glad eye to some lovely man who fancies you anyway? Try contemplating leaving a two-year relationship and being on your own at thirty-goddamn-one. *That's* paralysing. Anyway, exactly *why* won't you approach this Joe?'

Before Katherine got a chance to refuse to answer, Tara exhaled with unexpected fury. Suddenly she knew exactly what needed to be said. 'I'll be frank, Katherine,' she heard herself saying, and fixed Katherine with a burning look. 'I didn't want to say it, but it needs to be said. Fintan is right about you. You'd want to get involved. With life, as well as with a man.' She couldn't stop herself now. Too much pent-up emotion slopped over as she took a big, risky, angry breath, 'The way you live is ridiculous, with your knickers and your control and your clean flat and your no boyfriends. Fintan's not off the wall at all, he's spot on with you! He loves you and wants you to be *happy*!'

As Katherine's face turned thunderous, Tara gathered speed and volume. 'Whatever happened that time in Limerick, you can't use that as an excuse for ever, not that I know what it was. I'm your best friend and I haven't a clue.'

Katherine finally found her voice. 'Me?' she hooted, in outrage. 'Spot on with *me*? You cow. I wasn't going to say anything, but I will now. Fintan has your best interests at heart. And you *know* you should leave Thomas, that's why you're so angry with Fintan –'

'That is *not* why I'm angry with him –'

'And you say the way *I* live is ridiculous! What about you?' Katherine demanded, her cheekbones liver-coloured. 'You'd rather be with someone as *awful* as Thomas than be without a man. I mean, that's so *pathetic*. And look at how *fat* you've got.'

Tara flinched, and so, fathoms deep, did Katherine, but she rushed on, unstoppable as a runaway train. 'You overeat because he makes you miserable. And then you have the nerve to say Fintan's trying to destroy your life when anyone can see he's trying to help you, because he *loves* you.'

'How could he love me?' Torrents of rage from the past difficult weeks rushed to the surface. 'When he's asking me to leave the man I love.'

'I can't think of anything nicer than walking out on Thomas.' Katherine radiated hot, sour bile. 'I'm telling you I'd pay to see the expression on his clob, I really would.'

'Why are you so mean about him?' Tara shrieked, through clenched teeth.

'Does he still have his little brown change purse?' Katherine asked in contempt.

'Why wouldn't he?'

'Well, that'll do for a start.'

'I'm going.' Tara snatched up her car keys. 'I'm not staying here to be called names and have my boyfriend insulted.'

'What names did I call you?'

'You called me a cow.' Then Tara's voice wobbled. 'And you called me fat.'

'You started it,' Katherine shouted after her. 'Going on about my knickers.'

But Tara was gone, swept from the pub on a tide of hatred for Katherine, while Katherine remained, shaking. What was happening? They should be pulling together at this awful time. Why were they all turning against each other? When they'd always been the best of friends?

45

Joe Roth thought he was hallucinating. On Thursday morning he'd come into work as usual and Katherine 'Sexual Harassment' Casey had smiled at him. *Smiled*. At *him*. And it didn't seem to be motivated by malice either. Not as a prelude to telling him she'd lost his expenses claim or that she'd had orders from on high to calculate his redundancy package. No, she just flashed her little pearly teeth, twinkled her normally solemn grey eyes, let the look linger a fraction too long, and said – pleasantly! – 'Good morning, Joe.'

What was going on? It was about ten days since she'd wept in front of him and told him she'd had bad news, but immediately afterwards she'd resumed her customary, distant, offhand manner. This morning's friendliness was a bolt from the blue.

And, as she undulated to her desk, he noticed something different about the way she was dressed. Shorter? Tighter? Whatever it was, he liked it. If he didn't know different – and he knew *very* different – he'd think she was flirting with him.

As Katherine reached her desk, she was shaking. What if this didn't work? What if the only thing he'd really liked about her was her inaccessibility? She'd be completely wasting her time by becoming sweet and approachable.

She hated having to do this but she'd no choice because she always had to do *everything*. She bristled with self-righteousness. No one else could be depended upon. She always had to pay the bills, lend people money, remember birthdays, drive when everyone else was drinking their heads off. Now she had to save Fintan's life. No point expecting that irresponsible, selfish coward Tara Butler to lift a finger to help.

At the thought of Tara, Katherine buzzed with high-voltage guilt: she'd broken the worst taboo and told Tara she was fat. Although she was only stating a fact, she bolstered herself. All that she'd said was true. God, she thought, I'm turning into Thomas. Speaking as I find. It was four days since Katherine and Tara had had their terrible row and, though they'd both mended their fences with Liv, they hadn't made it up with each other. But they were coldly civil for the sake of the O'Gradys.

Though Katherine knew it was patently ridiculous to suggest that how she lived her life could affect or arrest the progress of someone else's cancer, throw enough mud and it sticks. She was haunted by the idea that the O'Gradys, Sandro and Liv were looking at her accusingly. With each passing day her paranoia got worse, as she suspected the nurses were eyeing her with contempt, then the other patients, then their visitors, then strangers in the street . . .

What made it all so messy was that she was also squeezed with overpowering love for Fintan. She'd find herself remembering the way he was before he got sick – healthy and robust as an animal, with glowing skin, thick lustrous hair, shiny eyes. Then she'd look at the shrunken, dead-eyed, listless creature in the bed, with his patchy hair and swollen neck and be unable to avoid the realization that he might never recover. At those times of intestine-clenching terror and unbearable sorrow, she'd have done anything for him. Anything.

On other – rarer – occasions, she got the six-months-to-live feeling, when her vision of life was channelled through Fintan's and she genuinely agreed that it was *imperative* to make the most of every single day. She'd be swept along on a sparkling love of life, where it all seemed so beautifully, joyously simple. Of course she'd try her best with Joe Roth!

But then the moment would pass and Katherine always returned with a thud to mundanity. Lumbered with an impossibly burdensome task that five minutes earlier had seemed like the easiest thing in the world.

Until her mood would change again and she'd see Fintan's request from yet another angle. Fintan loved her. He'd want the best for her, so surely she should trust him.

Surely?

For short periods of time she managed to, then the conviction trickled away again.

All the voices in Katherine's head gathered steam and clamoured louder and louder. Everyone – including, at times, herself – was pushing her towards Joe Roth and she realized she'd get no peace until she'd, at least, tried.

Naturally, being a cautious kind of a girl, she spent days agonizing before she finally made her decision, her conviction morphing from out-of-the-question to manageable to downright desirable, then back to out-of-the-question again.

In the end it seemed easier for her to try than not to try, with so much guilt and pressure and fear and conscientiousness washing around. And there was one final factor. Buried under all the other feelings was one she wouldn't have admitted to under torture: she wanted Joe Roth. In an invisible, shameful way, Fintan's request was merely an excuse.

On Thursday morning, feeling like she was going into battle, she plucked up all her daring and forced herself to wear a short black Lycra 'pulling' – though Katherine had never thought of it like that before – skirt to work. She was as self-conscious as if she was naked and, even wrapped in an all-enveloping coat, could hardly shoehorn herself out of her flat. She was certain that every man in Breen Helmsford would notice and suspect what she was up to.

Of course she knew that her version of short and tight was lickbum chaste compared to the snug pelmets barely covering some of her colleague's bottoms, but all these things are relative.

On the way to work she prayed Joe wouldn't be there. On a shoot or sick or dead, maybe. But as she walked in the door he was the first person she saw. Lounging on his chair, with his skin and his cheekbones and his long, rangy frame. Paralysing terror engulfed her. How could she flirt with this man? She fancied him way too much. In an instant she'd scrapped her plans. She wouldn't do anything, she decided, she'd just behave as normal and completely ignore him.

Then she remembered Fintan, in his hospital bed, and felt like John Malkovich in *Dangerous Liaisons*. *It's beyond my control*, she intoned in her head. *It's beyond my control*. She had to do this.

Starting by revealing her saucy skirt to all and sundry. Oh, God! Wildly she considered doing her day's work still wearing her coat, but reluctantly realized that that would engender even more comment. It nearly killed her to peel it off, first one sleeve, then the other. Flicking paranoid glances left and right to see if all the men were nudging each other and commenting, she prepared for the walk across the office to her desk.

Dignity in the face of adversity, she urged herself. Think Padraig Pearse before the firing squad, think Joan of Arc being burned at the stake. Thus fortified, she squared her shoulders, lifted her head high, fought the urge to pull her skirt down and embarked towards him.

Establish eye-contact! she ordered herself, in a sergeant-major voice.

She did.

Prepare to smile!

She smiled.

With feeling!

With feeling.

Hold it . . .

She held it.

Now, speak to him! And make it good!

Feeling that her tongue had swollen to ten times its normal size, she managed, 'Good morning, Joe.'

Was that the best you could do? That's shocking! I've no choice but to tell you to wiggle your bum.

Stiffly, woodenly, she attempted an undulation of her hips as she walked away until, with frantic relief, she reached her chair and was allowed to stop.

Then, trembling, she sat at her desk and waited for the fruits of her labours. With her wanton behaviour she'd sent him an unmistakable invitation. Would he take her up on it by coming over and asking her out? Perhaps not, she acknowledged, if the only thing he'd liked about her in the past had been her unavailability.

And then there was the Angie factor. Katherine still had no definite proof that Joe and Angie were seeing each other, but if they were, it was bad news for Katherine. And Fintan.

She spent an uneasy morning, full of anxious anticipation, observing Joe discreetly. She eyed his long, sensitive fingers

344

swooping back his hair and yearned for them to touch her. She itched to put her arms around his narrow waist.

By lunchtime he hadn't been over, so she girded her loins, smiled at him once more and said, 'Have a nice lunch.' Let no one say that Katherine Casey shirked her duties!

All afternoon she was tensed for his arrival. Keeping a surreptitious lookout, watching him at his desk. She was unnerved by how handsome she found him. Leaning back in his chair, on the phone, laughing at something the other person had said. Or talking to one of his team, ideas flitting across his face. Or tapping a biro thoughtfully off his teeth, his eyes faraway and speculative. It gave her a warm, nervous, expectant hum in her stomach.

But still he didn't show. So around five o'clock she smiled at him *again*, to indicate that she was game for a drink after work. But he just returned her smile cautiously, showing some – but not all – of his white teeth, and said nothing, while Katherine began to feel mild resentment that she was the one doing all the work here. He wasn't what you might call pulling his weight, she thought huffily. Or meeting her half-way.

As the very long day came to an end, and Katherine packed up her stuff, she tried to exude with her body language, *I'm going now. I am, you know. Last chance for any Joe Roths who want to ask any Katherine Caseys out for a drink.* But nothing doing.

What more could she do? she asked herself. Short of physically attacking him? Flashing him a breast across the office?

So that was the end of that. She was disappointed, but also relieved – and not entirely surprised. Somewhere along the line she'd realized that Joe Roth was strong and stubborn. Once firmly rejected, he wouldn't try again.

But at least she'd given it a shot. Maybe, if she was truthful, she'd admit that it had been a little half-hearted. And, of course, it hadn't had the desired result. But she could go to Fintan in all honesty and say that she'd tried.

And hopefully he wouldn't withhold his recovery, like a lawyer's clients who withhold payment when they lose the case. No win, no fee. No shag, no recovery.

46

When Katherine showed up at the hospital, the phalanx of friends and relations were briefly absent and Sandro and Fintan were having a hard-to-come-by one-to-one. They sat, their heads close together, holding hands, with a comfortable unity about them that she was loath to disturb. Sandro was murmuring something, which caused Fintan to smile. When she got closer she heard what it was.

'. . . fresh-water pool, resident masseuse, award-winning chef, nightly entertainment and day-trips to the nearby jungle, where you have an opportunity to ride on an elephant.'

'Hi,' Katherine whispered, quietly pulling up a chair.

'Thailand.' Fintan's mouth curved happily. 'The Orchid Palace in Chiang Mai.'

'Sounds great.'

'We're travelling around Thailand,' Sandro explained.

'Going to Phuket next.'

'Staying in a five-star hotel.'

'Water-skiing, among other things.'

'When Fintan's better we'll do it for real.'

'After the safari in Kenya. And two weeks in La Source in Grenada. Show Katherine the brochure of La Source, Sandro.'

Sandro flicked through the pile of travel brochures on the floor beside him, eventually locating La Source, which Katherine politely admired. Then Sandro went to get drinks, leaving Katherine alone with Fintan. 'I've good news for you,' she announced. 'I came on strong to Joe Roth.'

Maybe 'came on strong' was a slight exaggeration for three smiles and seven words, but Fintan needn't know.

'Great!' In delight Fintan struggled to sit up and found he couldn't.

'Are you OK?' Katherine asked anxiously. 'Why are you so weak? It's three days since you've had any chemo.'

'My immune system is shagged, white blood cells completely flattened.' He threw his eyes to heaven. 'A side-effect of the chemo. Though they say everything is a side-effect of the chemo. If I fell off a ladder and broke my leg it'd be a side-effect of the chemo.'

'Oh dear, it just doesn't let up.'

'Ah, never mind.' He switched his focus to happier things. 'Tell me about Joe Roth. Are you going out or what? When? Where's he taking you?'

'Er, nowhere,' Katherine felt awful letting Fintan down. 'He didn't ask me out.'

'But you said you'd good news for me.'

'And I had.' Katherine forced a bright smile. 'I did as you asked. I tried my best by smiling and speaking to him, and I know I didn't get a result, but that's hardly my fault.'

Fintan sat in silence.

'I did what you asked,' she repeated, feebly.

'No, that won't do at all,' Fintan declared imperiously. 'It just won't.'

Katherine's heart sank and once again she contemplated not being friends with Fintan any more.

'Did you apologize for accusing him of sexual harassment?' Fintan asked.

'Well, no . . .'

'But how can you expect anything to happen when that's still hanging between you?' Fintan scolded. 'Cop on, Katherine Casey!'

'What can I do about it?' she said, stubbornly. 'What's said is said.'

'Apologize to him!'

'*I can't.*' The very thought of going to Joe, all humble and hangdog! She cringed and shuddered.

'You can't go around treating people that way,' Fintan said earnestly. 'What you did to him was very wrong.'

'You weren't there,' Katherine said, bad-temperedly. 'He was so pushy, wouldn't leave me alone . . .'

'Was it actual harassment?' Fintan asked. 'Was your job in danger if you didn't do what he wanted?'

'No, but . . .'

'Did he touch you? Or make sexual innuendo?'

'Yes!' Katherine said stoutly, remembering how he'd told her he loved her accent, and that she was fabulous.

'Compliments aren't the same thing.' Fintan could be very astute. 'And didn't he go away as soon as you told him to?'

'Yes, but until then he was pushy,' Katherine said stubbornly. 'He kept, he kept – *talking* to me.'

'Listen to yourself, you head case.'

'And he asked me out for lunch at least four times.'

'You're digging yourself in deeper. You're well on the way to being as loopy as your mother. Now, it's very simple – apologize, then ask him out for a drink. So what if he says no?

349

The word no never killed anyone. Go on, you know you want to.' He twinkled at her roguishly.

'I do not,' she insisted, stoutly.

'Yes, you do. I know you, you're very stubborn. You wouldn't have even *smiled* at him if you really hadn't wanted to. Sure, I'm only a catalyst. For all the complaining you're doing about me, it's very handy for you that I got sick, Katherine Casey.'

Deeply uncomfortable, Katherine tried to figure out whether he was joking or not.

'Isn't it a godsend for you and your love life!' Fintan laughed.

'How can you say such a thing?' Katherine protested frantically. 'You couldn't be more wrong. I only smiled at Joe Roth to get you off my back.'

'All right,' Fintan said cheerfully. 'If that's the way you want to play it, consider me still on your back.'

Was there no way out of this? Katherine struggled, trying to get free.

'Please, Katherine,' Fintan urged, 'you're my only hope. There's no chance that soft-hearted, yellow-bellied Butler will leave the dread Thomas. If you want something done, ask Katherine "Dependable" Casey – she won't let you down.'

Katherine had a swell of pride before she realized he'd just tightened the trap. 'You've changed.' She sighed. 'You've become very manipulative.'

'But you'll try?'

What else could she say? 'I'll try.'

'Now feast your eyes on me, Katherine,' Fintan declared. 'You're looking at a man of leisure!'

'Man of leisure' conjured up suave and urbane pictures: David Niven moustaches, cigarette holders, martini glasses, speedboats, coupés. She took in Fintan's bony skull-face, his veiny eyes, his meagre, and becoming more meagre by the hour, hair. Christ. 'How come?'

'I've been sacked!'

'By who?'

'By my boss, who d'you think? Dr Singh? Dale Winton? Richard and Judy? Rikki Lake? God,' he was sidetracked by wonder, 'my world has become very small.'

'But I mean . . .'

'It was Carmella. Herself. In sharply tailored, coke-crazed person.'

'You mean she came into the hospital and sacked you in bed? But why? Can you be sacked for being sick?'

'She was concerned – get this – that I'd give the wrong image of the company.'

Suddenly Katherine understood. 'She thinks you're HIV positive.'

Fintan nodded.

'But that's so unjust,' Katherine protested. 'And I thought the fashion industry was very accommodating to people with HIV.'

'Well, maybe she sacked me because I'm *not* HIV,' Fintan said tartly. 'I don't know.' He set his mouth in a hard line. Then his mutinous face dissolved as his bottom lip started to spasm and tears filled his red-veined eyes. 'What's going to happen to me?' he choked. 'What's going to happen? It's not just the money.' Katherine was dumbfounded by helplessness. 'I've worked for her for eight years,' Fintan said miserably. 'I thought she was my friend. She said she depended on me, and now I've been thrown away, human detritus. I never asked to get this horrible illness, and I love my job. I feel so alone. At least if I had Aids, there'd be others in the same boat and we could talk about T-cells and do all that huggy, touchy-feely stuff and . . . and . . . make a quilt!'

'There are support groups for people with Hodgkin's disease,' Katherine said. Since Fintan had first been diagnosed Liv had been saying that he should seek out others with the same condition. In fact she'd been suggesting loudly that they should *all* go to support groups – Mothers of People with Cancer, Partners of People with Cancer. Siblings of People with Cancer, Friends of People with Cancer.

'Katherine, I know I'm supposed to be strong and nobody likes to see self-pity, but I have to say something,' Fintan said.

'What is it?'

'I'm afraid of the pain. I'm terrified that I'll die in terrible pain and that they won't give me enough morphine.'

'It'll never come to that,' Katherine said weakly. 'Oh, here's Sandro back.'

Sandro took one look at Fintan, put down the drinks, snatched up a brochure and quickly began to read, 'Sans Souci Lido in Jamaica. All-inclusive luxury hotel, with private beach, extensive range of water-sports, reflexology, aromatherapy, Caribbean and European restaurants . . .'

47

'Thomas, will you marry me?'

Thomas turned to Tara with shining eyes. 'Tara,' his voice was thick with emotion, 'I hardly know what to say.'

'Just say yes,' she said, huskily.

'In that case, yes! I'd be delighted. Honoured.'

Relief swirled around Tara in great gusts, and Beryl gave her a congratulatory smile as she stacked her Whiskas bowl in the dishwasher. But wait a minute – they didn't have a dishwasher. And Beryl never smiled at her, she hated her. Just as Thomas exclaimed, 'I beg your pardon, will I *marry* you? I thought you asked if I'd like all your money. An easy mistake to make.' Tara woke up, her heart pounding.

Tara had been having nightmares, often while she was still awake. Centring around proposing to Thomas.

She blamed Fintan. And Katherine 'Swinging Brick For A Heart' Casey. But mostly she blamed the people she worked with. Especially Ravi. On Wednesday lunchtime, in the almost-deserted office, he brayed, 'Cheer up. Care to lick my chocolate-mousse lid?'

'Thanks.' Wearily, Tara accepted the round of tinfoil, and licked it half-heartedly, while Ravi tipped his head back and shook the entire carton into his mouth, expertly guiding in any wayward lumps that strayed to his chin.

Next he tore open a honey-roast-ham bloomer sandwich. 'Fancy smelling the paper?' he offered deferentially.

Silently, she accepted.

Having made short work of his sandwich, he whipped out a Crunchie and declared, 'Crunchies! Full of health-giving nutrition!'

Enviously Tara watched, as he scoffed it in two bites.

'How's Fintan?' he mumbled, through a mouthful of honey-comb and milk chocolate.

Tara paused. Good question. How *was* Fintan? The knobbly swelling on his neck hadn't reduced one bit. Nor had the nodes on his pancreas, which anyone could feel – not that they wanted to – simply by pressing hard on his left side. Should she mention how upset he'd got when he'd found out that the chemo was going to make him sterile? How the oncologist had implied that because he was gay it didn't matter?

'He's getting out of hospital on Saturday,' Tara opted for. It sounded positive.

'So he's on the mend. Bloody good.'

'He's not on the mend!' Vinnie looked up from his work to glare managerially at Ravi. 'It's not like he's broken his arm or had an ingrowing toenail removed. The chap has cancer, you don't shake that after a few weeks in hospital. It takes months!' He rubbed his balding scalp anxiously and returned to his screen.

They continued in quieter tones, their heads close to-gether.

'The MenChel pressure's getting to Vinnie,' Ravi observed. 'His cock is finally on the block and he can't handle it.'

'Don't mind him,' Tara said softly. 'And there's always a chance Fintan *might* be on the mend. We just don't know yet.

It could take up to nine months of treatment before we know if it's worked.'

'So why is he getting out of hospital?'

'No real need for him to be there. From now on he'll have chemo twice a month as an outpatient.'

'Twice a month?' Ravi sounded doubtful. 'That can't be enough. Jack it up. Double it. That should do the trick.'

Tara had a heavy weight in her stomach. Would that it were that simple. There was only so much chemo they could give him before they killed him.

'Are his mother and brothers going to be here for the entire nine months?'

'No, they're going home on Sunday. Or at least JaneAnn and Timothy are.'

Ravi grasped Tara's shoulders in excitement. 'You mean . . . ? You mean the Milo chap is staying?'

'Not just staying,' Tara nodded meaningfully, 'but staying with whom?'

Ravi could barely speak. 'Not Liv?' he squeaked. 'That's superb.'

'Just for a few extra weeks,' Tara elaborated.

'And what about Lars? Has she kicked him into touch yet?'

'Oh, yes. Last night.'

'Oooh, I wish I could have heard.'

'You could have, actually. She put him on the speakerphone for me while she delivered the news.'

Ravi was almost speechless with disappointment. 'Why didn't you tell me? I would have liked to be there.'

'Sorry, sorry, sorry! But I've had a lot on my mind. You may have noticed. Anyway, it wasn't as much fun as it sounds because they both spoke in Swedish.'

'Boo.'

'I'm sorry, Ravi, I truly am.'

'Did he cry?'

Tara hesitated, then nodded.

'Aw, boo. Did he offer to leave his wife and did she tell him it was too late?'

Tara shrank from Ravi's accusing eyes. 'I don't speak Swedish but I believe so,' she admitted.

'Did he say he'd do anything and did she say there was nothing he could do?'

Tara hung her head in shame.

'And it's not even as if I can watch the omnibus edition on Sunday,' Ravi said bitterly.

They sat in silence.

'Have you had a falling-out with Katherine?' Ravi asked suddenly.

'Why do you ask?'

'Because your average number of phone calls a day has gone down by seventeen point four per cent since last Friday. Teddy did a program to calculate it. What's going on?'

'Nothing.'

'Tell me. I won't understand.'

The relief of being with someone uncomplicated like Ravi! The need to talk was suddenly imperative. Tara opened her mouth and it all gushed out like water from a burst dam. In hushed, but entertaining, you'll-never-believe-what-happened-next mode she told him about Fintan's outrageous promise that if she didn't leave Thomas or ask him to marry her, he'd die to spite her. About the terrible row with Katherine – though she made no mention of Katherine using the F-word. About the O'Gradys looking at her like she'd gone for Fintan with a meat cleaver. About her own robust superstition. 'I believe him,' she admitted, 'when he says he'll die and haunt me if I don't do what he wants.' She finished by saying, gaily, 'Isn't Fintan mental?'

Ravi didn't speak. Thought after thought passed over the landscape of his face, like scudding clouds creating light and dark on mountains.

'All you have to do is nod, Ravi,' Tara said anxiously.

Ravi's smooth, boyish face was a twist of perplexity. 'But Fintan's your chum,' he struggled. 'He's not likely to stitch you up. You've known him since you were fourteen, right?'

Tara nodded reluctantly.

'And you're now, what, twenty-eight?'

'Thirty-one, you big thick.'

'Golly, are you? That old?'

'Yes, that old.'

'OK. So when you're friends with someone that long they're in your corner.' Ravi delivered a winning smile. He'd sorted things out for Tara. Funny that she still looked miserable.

'Ravi, I don't think you're listening to me,' she begged. 'He wants me to leave Thomas. He's sick, he doesn't know what he's talking about.'

'I'm not so sure,' Ravi said thoughtfully. 'Once saw a documentary about a man caught in a storm, stuck on a boat for seven weeks, got frostbite on his ears, had to eat pieces of his boat, nearly bloody died! Rescued by a trawler, saw the light, changed his life. Nice to everyone, sold his business, lived life to the full. Said everyone should. Sounds like you've got the same problem with Fintan. Another bloke on a hijacked plane –'

'No, Ravi, no!' Tara was bitterly disappointed. 'I rely on you to be a boy. Emotionally illiterate. I don't want you having bursts of enlightenment. You were my one dark spot in an irritatingly bright, carey-sharey world.'

'Sorr-ee!'

'You were supposed to tell me that Fintan was bonkers and to ignore him.'

'Righty-ho, Tara. Fintan is bonkers. Ignore him.'

'It's too late.'

'I know.' Ravi had a moment of inspiration. 'You could lie to Fintan. Tell him you've left Thomas, when you haven't.'

'I've thought of it. But so has he. He said he'll know if I'm lying. He said he'll do spot-checks and call on Thomas's flat unexpectedly like the TV-licensing people. He said he'll even get a van with surveillance equipment.'

'Bugger.' Ravi sucked his teeth thoughtfully. 'I know! How about if you leave Thomas, tell Fintan, wait for him to get better, then go back to Thomas?'

'But what if Thomas didn't wait for me?'

'Then it wasn't much of a love affair to begin with,' Ravi said cheerfully. Christ, even he could see that!

Tara had a dull, ominous ache in her stomach. Ravi was saying all the wrong things. Was there no one to back her up?

'If this was a film,' she said wearily, 'of course I'd leave Thomas. It'd be so clear. But it's not clear at all. I love Fintan and I badly, *badly* want him to get well, and if he doesn't . . . But, you see, I love Thomas too.'

'Maybe you don't have to leave Thomas.' Ravi began another suggestion.

'You're right,' Tara said, aggressively. 'I don't have to.'

'I mean, there's another way. Why don't you ask him to marry you, as Fintan suggested? If Thomas says yes, then you're home and dry.'

Tara shrugged noncommittally.

'Just ask Thomas what his intentions are.'

But she didn't want to. She suspected she knew what his intentions were. She had a feeling he had *no* intentions. Since the night after her birthday she'd had little doubt that that was the case. But until she knew for sure, then it wasn't true.

Yet she couldn't help feeling that a crisis was moving inexorably closer to her. That she was holding on to this relationship like someone holding on with their fingernails to the side of a cliff. It would be so easy to let go, to lose her grip, to fall. In despair she put her face in her hands. 'I can't leave him, Ravi,' she whispered. 'This has got to work.'

'But why?' Ravi panicked. Girlies crying alarmed him unutterably. Desperately he sought to perk her up. 'So what if it doesn't work?' he consoled. 'He makes you bloody miserable, Tara.'

As Tara peeped out an aghast face, Ravi suddenly knew the perfect thing to say. 'Remember,' he coaxed, 'how happy you were with Alasdair.'

Alasdair! *Alasdair.* As Ravi swelled with pride at his quick-thinking, out-of-nowhere memories zoomed at Tara. She and Alasdair. Jesus Christ.

'Alasdair was a bloody nice bloke,' Ravi said warmly.

'Then he did a runner and married some tart.' Tara's jaw was clenched.

'He told you you were a top girl. He told *me* you were a top girl. I had to start avoiding him whenever he came to our work dos.'

'Then he did a runner and married some tart,' Tara repeated, tonelessly.

'At least he came to our work dos. Unlike some.'

'Then he did a runner and married some tart.'

'You never bothered with all that diet stuff when you were going out with Alasdair.'

'Yes, I did.'

'You didn't. You ate out all the time. Don't you remember? Every Monday morning you tried to make me cry by telling me which famous restaurant you'd gone to with Alasdair for Sunday lunch?'

'Then he did a runner and married some tart,' Tara intoned.

But she was catapulted into the past. A shimmering, golden past. Her time with Alasdair seemed like a faraway field drenched in glorious sunshine, while where she stood now was shrouded in iron cloud. OK, so he did a runner and married some tart, but hadn't they had a blast? Compared to the battlefield of living with Thomas? Alasdair would have given her anything she wanted, anything. Before he did a runner and married some tart. But that was then and this is now. A bird in the hand is worth two birds who do a runner and marry some tart. Alasdair was long gone and Thomas was still present.

'Ravi, if you were trying to help, I'm afraid you haven't.'

'I'm a boy,' he said miserably. 'It was never going to work.'

'Look, it's obvious what you should do,' an irate voice interrupted.

Tara and Ravi looked up in surprise. It was Vinnie, who leapt to his feet, rolled up the sleeves of his unpressed suit and began pacing. 'The way I see it is,' Vinnie bounced a biro on his palm, in major brainstorming mode, 'the first thing you have to do is ask Thomas to marry you.'

'Is nothing sacred? That was a private conversation.'

'MenChel are paying a hundred pounds an hour for my expertise,' Vinnie replied. 'You're lucky you're getting it for nothing. Now, where were we? Let's think this project through.'

He rushed over to the office whiteboard and began scribbling a diagram with a squeaky marker. 'The starting point is here.' He indicated a wobbly red oblong, then drew an arrow out of it. 'Until Thomas turns you down – and he may not – there's no problem. So you must propose to him.'

'Why? Will you sack me if I don't?'

Vinnie looked startled.

'Why not?' Tara asked herself. 'My friend has threatened to die on me if I don't. Why should I be surprised to be threatened with the boot?'

'I'm sorry.' Vinnie suddenly realized the inappropriateness of his behaviour. 'I got carried away. I shouldn't have earwigged. But it was so interesting ... such a challenge ... You see, I haven't been getting much sleep, my fourteen-month-old is teething ...'

'He's right,' Ravi muttered, when Vinnie had slunk back to his desk, pawing at the crown of his head. 'I hate to say it but he has a point. Ask Thomas to marry you. You know it makes sense!'

'But ...' How could she put words on the terrible fear that if she began to interfere, the whole house of cards would come tumbling down?

'Time to start work again,' Ravi announced, looking at his watch. 'I must wash my hands.'

As soon as Ravi left the room, Tara snatched up the phone and dialled a number. 'Hello,' she said. 'I wonder if you can help me. I'm afraid my purse was stolen, with my Visa card in it. I'd like to order a replacement.'

48

Amongst the cocktail of emotions that washed around in Katherine was the feeling that she had nothing left to lose. The terrible events of recent weeks had cut her adrift and the fixed points in her world were left long behind.

Liv, Sandro and the O'Gradys were pissed off with her. Tara wasn't talking to her. *She* wasn't talking to Tara. And, in a way, she'd already let go of Fintan. She had nobody now. What harm could it do to apologize to Joe Roth? Even if he was horrible, what did one more person matter?

A strange recklessness took hold of her. The adventurous spirit that she'd always denied, suppressed, quashed. At the end of the day she was her mother's daughter, and it was bound to catch up with her sooner or later.

All the same, that didn't stop her quaking with nerves on her way to work on Friday morning. She thought she'd been worried the day before? She hadn't known she was born! With her wishy-washy smiles and handful of words, she'd delivered nothing more than a highly unconvincing dress rehearsal. But this was the genuine article. Real bullets in the guns, this time. People could get hurt.

Her fear made her dizzy.

Today Joe wore a narrow-cut suit in darkest aubergine, with a dazzlingly white shirt. He glowed with attractiveness.

Despite her nerves, Katherine wanted to get it over with as

soon as possible. Waiting was even worse than doing it. So from the moment she – finally – took off her coat, she tried to get Joe on his own so that half of Breen Helmsford wouldn't hear what she had to say. However, that proved impossible. Joe was a busy, popular man, who went to plenty of meetings, got and made hundreds of phone calls and had lots of people dropping by his desk for a chat. Every time one person left him, Katherine made a monumental, bootstrap effort and propelled herself up out of her chair. But before she'd even straightened her legs fully, either his phone rang or a new person joined him, and all her teeth-gritted force would come to nothing and she'd have to sit down again. She spent a work-free morning on the verge of screaming with frustration, her adrenaline amped to the max.

At lunchtime he went out to meet clients, so she endured a couple of nerve-stretching hours, working hard to keep her resolve pumped. But when he came back at three o'clock, his dizzying round of visitors and calls started again.

She thought she might cry. She was fast running out of any resolve to do what Fintan wanted. All that unused adrenaline was turning on her, making her feel hopeless and depressed.

But at twenty to four, as she came back from the ladies' she saw him standing in the little glass room that housed the binding machine. And he was *alone*. Now! Now! Breathlessly, she hurried down the corridor, which seemed as vast as the Serengeti plain, willing no one to join him. She forced all her energy on keeping him isolated. So far, so good. No one – only him. But no! She could hear a person behind her. A woman, from the sounds of her shoes. Also in a hurry. Just as Katherine reached the door to the room, she looked to see who it was. Bloody Angie, of all people, a sheaf of papers in her arms.

Joe looked at Katherine without interest. 'Just finished.' He indicated the machine. 'It's all yours.'

At the exact moment that Katherine realized that she had no sheets of paper in her hands that justified her needing to use the binder, so did Joe and Angie. And there was nothing else to do in the binding room, only bind.

They both looked at her empty hands. Their eyes seemed to loom in and she could feel her hands grow and expand, becoming bigger and bigger, the size of plates.

'Forgot . . .' Katherine said, her voice thin, '. . . forgot my report.'

Angie nodded, looking with hard suspicion at Katherine. 'Sure.'

'You go ahead,' Katherine said to Angie, making for the door.

'Don't worry,' she said, with heavy emphasis. 'I will. Joe, can you show me how to use this?'

When Joe returned to his desk he was miraculously undisturbed by visitors or phone calls. But Katherine didn't bother. What's the point? she asked herself. I'll go to that awful effort of plucking up my courage, then someone will come along and it'll all be wasted.

But she sneaked another look at him a few minutes later, and he was still alone, moodily flicking through papers.

And before she could stop herself, she was on her feet and, feeling like she was having a bad dream, moving across the floor in her weeny skirt. Then she was beside his desk. Quaking and shaking, she opened her mouth and heard herself say, 'May I speak to you?'

With a graceful wave of his hand, Joe indicated a chair. His face was curious. Suspicious, almost. Dazed, she sat down, leant her elbows on his desk, then realized the moment of reckoning had arrived. Oh, Christ!

'You may remember,' she began haltingly, 'some time ago, I, um . . .'

His face was unfriendly. No helpful, white-toothed smile, no encouraging nods, no warmth in his eyes.

She changed tack. 'A few weeks ago,' she started, 'you came over to my desk and I, er, said something. Something that may have given you to think that I –' She stopped abruptly. She was getting on her own nerves. 'I accused you of sexual harassment,' she said baldly.

'Less of an accusation and more of an implication.' Joe inclined his head. 'But, yes, I remember.'

He didn't laugh or make a joke and she realized she'd been hoping he would. He looked grim and serious and suddenly she saw it from his point of view. People lost their jobs for less.

'I'd like to apologize,' she said, feeling for the first time genuinely ashamed of it. 'I'm sorry. It wasn't true, and I should never have said it.'

His face was expressionless. 'Apology accepted.

'And,' he continued, his brown eyes cool, 'I owe you an apology. I came on too strong. I should just have taken no for an answer.'

That was the last thing she wanted to hear! 'No, no!' she protested. At his question-mark face, she almost lost her nerve and bottled out. Her voice emerged as a squeak, and she rushed into saying, 'If that offer to go for a drink is still on the cards, I'd be delighted to accept.'

She squirmed in mortification. *I hate you, Fintan O'Grady.*

Joe looked at her, assessing her ruddy little face. She stared back, trying to read what was going on in his hard eyes, utterly despising her vulnerability as she waited. She abhorred being at someone's mercy. Particularly a man's. Worse still, a man that she fancied.

Finally he spoke. He said, his watchful eyes never leaving her face, 'I'll think about it.'

She thought she was going to kill someone. Nodding, flushed, forcing a smile, she got up, her knees trembling. Clumsy with rage and shock, she stumbled en route to her own desk.

She had to go out. She walked around Hanover Square and up to Oxford Street, mimicking, over and over again in a namby-pamby voice, 'I'll think about it. I'll think about it.'

As emotion invaded her like a virus, she swore that Fintan O'Grady would pay for this.

She went back to the office, picked up her tap-dancing gear, which hadn't been used since Fintan got sick, and went to the gym. She never usually had any truck with the gym, but she felt the need to pound the stuffing out of a punch-bag, seeing as it was illegal to do it to Joe Roth. Or Fintan O'Grady, for that matter.

The instructor tried to tell her that she hadn't got the right shoes, but her rage was somehow very persuasive. And when she began, her forearms were a blur, as she belted the punch-bag again and again and again. With a furiously red face, she stood in little flared shorts and patent dance-shoes with a big bow across the instep and pounded out her terrible anger at Joe and Fintan and Tara and the person who'd made her this way in the first place.

People, mostly men, came to look. Such a slight girl, with such great strength! 'She could box for England,' one huge, muscle-bound jock commented, in admiration. Katherine stopped for a moment. Normally a grade three (deep contempt

366

cut with savage antagonism) or grade four (deeper contempt cut with even more savage antagonism, often delivered with a silent snarl) would suffice, but, hell, this was no ordinary day. So she flashed him one of her grade five looks (an entrail-freezing promise of actual bodily harm), and permitted herself a smirk as he stumbled back in dazed shock. Then she started up again, pummelling away her vulnerability, the hot flush of exposure. Shunted it out of her, in the hope that she might feel like herself again.

Abruptly she stopped boxing, to the disappointment of the small crowd who'd gathered. She'd suddenly realized what she had to do. She had to leave and find someone. Someone who'd make her feel better. Someone who would make everything all right. Someone who always made everything OK, one way or another. Tara.

49

When Tara opened the door, Katherine nearly keeled over at the dreadful stench, but couldn't let herself be distracted from her main purpose.

'I'm sorry,' Katherine said quickly, before Tara could slam the door in her face. 'I'm sorry for the fight. I'm sorry for the terrible things I said to you. I'm really, really sorry.' She swallowed the aching lump in her throat. 'I got you these.' She thrust a bunch of twenty-four-hour-shop flowers at Tara. Tara's face crumpled. 'I'm sorry they're so cheap and nasty,' Katherine's voice quaked, 'but all the other flower shops were closed.'

'They're lovely.' Tara's eyes swam with tears. 'I'm sorry too, for the things I said to you, Katherine. I had no right.'

'You had every right,' Katherine exclaimed.

In a floodtide of sentiment, they body-slammed each other and hugged tightly, both of them sobbing, 'I'm sorry, I'm so sorry.'

'Oh, Tara, be nice to me!' Katherine begged into Tara's neck.

'Of course I will. What's wrong?'

'Joe Roth was horrible. I'm so humiliated! How can I ever go to work again?'

'Oh, my God, you mean you did it . . . Oh, poor Katherine.' Tara squeezed and rocked her in her arms until Katherine simply couldn't bear any more.

'Tara?' she asked, in a little voice. 'What's the terrible smell?'

Tara sighed heavily, and her eyes were far away. 'Come in and I'll tell you all about it.'

Katherine followed her into the brown cavern.

'I've done something that I shouldn't have,' Tara admitted. 'But I was desperate.'

'You haven't . . . ?' Katherine was frightened. 'You haven't . . . ?'

'Haven't what?'

'You haven't murdered Thomas?'

Tara laughed. 'Not yet. No, it was my old trouble. Looking for a magic solution to my great girth.'

Katherine burned with shame. 'I'm so, so sorry for what I said about you being . . . er . . . not thin.'

'But it's the truth,' Tara admitted, ruefully.

She'd put on so much weight during the three weeks that Fintan was sick that on Friday morning, as Tara looked at herself in the mirror, the familiar panic took hold. She had to do *something*. She was constantly uncomfortable, everything was too tight, shirts stuck to her, jackets were so inhibiting she couldn't lift her arms, waistbands cut into her so much that they hurt, she was always sweating. Clothes were her enemy.

Lots of people lost tons of weight, she consoled herself. Look at Oprah Winfrey. It can be done, but she needed it to be achieved *quickly*. After the toning-tables shambles, she'd been off snake-oil salesmen for a while. But desperate measures were called for. Again. 'If there was such a thing as a back-street liposuctionist I'd have gone,' she admitted.

Instead, she suddenly remembered a beautician's near her work, which had a sandwich board outside, urging, 'Perspire away those unwanted inches with a mud wrap.' She almost wept with relief. She knew about mud wraps, and she liked what she'd heard. Being coated neck-to-toe in a warm, luxurious, chocolate-type substance, so that she became a human Bounty, all her fatness sweating away effortlessly, jumping ship from her lardy body into the thick, creamy mud sounded like heaven. Weight-loss and pampering all in one. What could be nicer?

She rang the beauty salon as soon as she got into work and they said they guaranteed a minimum loss of eight inches. *Eight inches*! Starry-eyed, thinking of losing four inches from her stomach and two from each of her thighs, she made an appointment for that lunchtime. And if it all worked out, she could go again on Monday and lose another eight inches and again the day after. And keep on going until she was as thin as her new friend Amy.

'The old Chinese proverb springs to mind,' Ravi said gravely, when she hung up the phone. 'No pain, no gain.'

'Mind your own business. This office is like a goldfish bowl.'

'I was going to ask if you'd like to smell my Yorkie paper, but I won't bother now. Have you got down on bended knee and proposed to Thomas yet?'

'I was kind of hoping that if I de-larded myself enough *he* might propose to *me*.' Then she laughed so Ravi wouldn't think she was pathetic.

At twelve thirty, Tara bounded along to Poppy's with a spring in her step. There she met a racehorse-thin white-coated beautician called Adrienne, who was so heavily made-up that if someone had hit her on the back of her head, her foundation would have fallen off like a papier-mâché mask.

'What do you work at?' Adrienne asked, brusquely, when she'd marched Tara into a bare, chilly room.

'Computer analyst,' Tara answered.

'You know, this isn't my real job.' Adrienne quivered with displacement. 'I'm an actress, really. If there was any justice – but take it from me, there isn't – I wouldn't have to do this beautician stuff.' At her bitterness, Tara's mood dipped. It dipped even further when Adrienne ordered her to undress to her bra and knickers. The shame. 'A bit like being strip-searched,' Tara observed with a weak, nervous laugh, trying to deflect attention from her great wibbly-wobbly belly. Adrienne ignored her and pulled hard on both ends of her tape-measure, with barely suppressed resentment. Three years in RADA to end up doing this!

Then the measuring began.

'Is this necessary?' Tara asked anxiously. The disgrace of someone knowing her vital statistics.

'How else will we know how many inches you've lost?' Adrienne asked. Stupid!

'OK, but don't tell me how many inches my bum is. Or my stomach,' Tara said, frantically. 'Or my thighs. Or the tops of my arms. Or my –'

'I won't tell you anything,' Adrienne cut in, wondering if the tape-measure would be long enough to do Tara's hips. What was wrong with these fat girls? All they needed was a little willpower. A week's starvation never hurt anyone.

In uncomfortable silence Tara was measured about forty different times – each arm alone was done no less than four times. With creeping dread she realized that if she lost a fifth of an inch from each measuring place, the promised eight inches wouldn't be too hard to accumulate, but wouldn't make much difference to her overall appearance. Oh dear.

When all the measurements were written down – this took some time – Adrienne approached Tara with a plastic bottle, the type that people like Katherine sprayed plants with, and squirted her with water. Tara jumped and yelped. She continued to wobble long after she'd stopped moving.

'The hot water's broken,' Adrienne said, with bad grace, watching Tara shiver. My God, she thought in disgust, even when a *goose-pimple* popped on to the surface of this woman's skin, it caused her flesh to sway like Stevie Wonder's head!

'Now for the mud.'

In every fantasy she'd ever had about mud wraps, Tara thought she'd be smothered in an unctuous, glistening cream and left to wallow in it like a happy hippo. Instead, as she stood shivering, Adrienne approached her with a mixing-bowl and a wooden spoon.

'Making a cake?' Tara joked.

Adrienne gave her a look of contemptuous pity, and scooped some warm, foul-smelling mix out of the bowl, then splatted it on to Tara's thigh and used the wooden spoon to even it out. Daubing randomly, a stripe of smelly muck here, a stripe of smelly muck there, she emptied the bowl.

Tara looked down at herself, her white body criss-crossed with occasional brown stripes. I look like I'm on a dirty protest, she thought.

'Now for the wrap,' Adrienne said.

'But I'm not all covered with the mud,' Tara squeaked.

'You don't need to be.'

The 'wrap' turned out to be six tatty old salmon-pink bandages, the type that Tara's mother used to practise her Order of Malta routine with. They were wound around Tara's midriff, thighs and arms, then each one was secured with a big nappy-pin. Tara couldn't bear to visualize what she looked like.

'Next,' Adrienne declared, 'we put you into the special rubber suit, which heats up the mud, increasing toxin loss.' Tara's heart leapt with a fierce hope because this sounded scientific and viable. A lot more so than plastic plant-spraying bottles and Order of Malta bandages. But, to her great disappointment, the special rubber suit wasn't a special rubber suit at all. It was just a cheap plastic tracksuit that a twelve-year-old girl might wear on a shoplifting expedition into town. She could have wept.

According to Adrienne, the de-larding process took about an hour to kick in. She left, leaving Tara lying on a table in the bleak little room, listening through the cardboard walls to the rhythmic rip of other people having their legs waxed, without even a copy of *OK* to take her mind off her ignominy. At one stage she dozed off, only to wake herself up with her own terrible stench.

Things got worse. After a while the bandages cooled and felt damp and cold under the tracksuit. The horrible feeling of soaked, clammy underclothes reminded her of days at school as a four-year-old when she'd wet her knickers and woollen tights but was carrying on as if everything was normal.

After an hour Adrienne came back, reclaimed the tracksuit, unpeeled the bandages and measured Tara again, this time pulling the tape-measure tourniquet-tight. 'Oh, yes,' she kept saying, as she squeezed Tara's circulation to a standstill. 'Much smaller.' After she'd added it all up, she announced, 'Eleven inches, you've lost eleven inches.'

'Sure,' Tara whispered. She might be fat, but she wasn't stupid. 'Where are the showers?'

'No shower,' Adrienne said quickly.

'But I'm filthy!' The gloopy mixture had dried and hardened on her skin and was flaking away with every movement.

'Er . . . the mud will continue to detoxify you for another twenty-four hours,' Adrienne insisted.

Oh, yeah? Tara's face said. *And this has nothing to do with the hot water being broken?*

But after paying forty quid for the experience, she wanted to get every possible benefit from it. So the mud stayed on and she got dressed. Naturally she left a hefty tip, due to feeling inferior for being so much fatter than Adrienne. Then she left, her morale and hopes at rock bottom.

As soon as she returned to work, people began sniffing in alarm.

'What's that awful stink?' Ravi demanded.

Tara sat very still at her desk, trying not to move, because she was shedding dried muck with every gesture.

'Someone must have trod in dog do,' Vinnie announced. 'Everybody check your shoes.'

There was a flurry of people pushing themselves from their desks and examining the soles of their shoes.

'You too, Tara.' Ravi frowned.

Cautiously, slowly, Tara lifted her foot, but it wasn't cautious or slow enough because a cloud of dust rose, obscuring everyone's view of her.

'What's going on?' Ravi demanded. 'Have you just been *exhumed?*' He came and stood beside her. 'Eeee-oooo,' he declared, dramatically pinching his nose. 'Call off the search, everyone,' he announced. 'It's Tara's liposuction thingy.'

'It wasn't liposuction!' Tara sat up and defended herself angrily, causing more dried muck to billow forth. 'It was only a mud wrap. For my skin!'

God forbid that people would know to what desperate measures she'd gone to to lose weight.

Ravi made a big show of moving his desk. 'I have to. I can't concentrate due to the pong,' he claimed.

In the end, by popular demand, Tara left work early, a trail of brown dust following her, as if she was rotting. 'Don't come back until you've had a good scrub,' Vinnie ordered, wearily. It was bad enough to have four children of his own . . .

Tara went home. She should have gone to Katherine's to pick up the O'Gradys and take them to the hospital. But she was too depressed – not to mention smelly. Alone and honking she sat in Thomas's gloomy flat and tried to read Louise L. Hay's *You Can Heal Your Body*, one of the many books on alternative healing they'd bought. But she couldn't concentrate on it. Instead of visualizing Fintan's cancer cells fading away to nothing, she found herself visualizing leaving Thomas. Too many thoughts had been planted by too many people for her to be able to continue completely immersing her head in the sand.

She loved Fintan. She really did. Now he was sick, possibly dying, and he wanted her to leave Thomas.

Reluctantly Tara admitted she could see how it looked to him. Compared to the time she'd spent with Alasdair, her relationship with Thomas might seem a bit of an emotional route march. *At least to the outsider.*

She looked around the front room, imagining packing up her pictures and books and (four) CDs, pulling the front door behind her for the last time and going out alone into the big, bad world. It made her flinch and the fear welled up again. There was no way she could do it. Clutching at straws she remembered that Thomas might marry her. All she had to do was ask. But not just yet . . .

She longed for Katherine. She missed her and, for some reason, the anger she had felt for her had gone. Then the doorbell rang, and, as if her thoughts had conjured her up, there was Katherine, holding a tatty bunch of flowers and looking more distraught than Tara had seen her in a long time.

50

On Saturday afternoon Tara and Sandro brought Fintan home. He had spent nearly three weeks in hospital.

He looked atrocious and was so weak he had to lean on a male nurse and Sandro to get to the car park. Strictly speaking, at five foot four, Sandro was more of a hindrance than a help, but he insisted on supporting. And emotions were running too high to deny that kind of request.

Seeing Fintan framed by the outside world staggered Tara. She realized that you can get away with looking like you're dying in a hospital bed: you kind of blend in. But it's a different kettle of fish outside where people are, for the most part, healthy.

Tara noticed one good thing. Fintan was wearing the pistachio-green sheepskin coat he'd 'borrowed' from the stock-room at work. 'Don't suppose this'll be going back now.' Tara twinkled.

'My redundancy package,' he said, grimly.

Tara and Sandro exchanged an oh-yikes! look.

They arrived at the empty flat in Notting Hill to find that while they'd been out JaneAnn had gone on a Jif frenzy in honour of Fintan's homecoming. Afternoon tea could have been taken on the rubber-tiled kitchen floor. JaneAnn had nearly worn holes in the Purves and Purves rugs with her enthusiastic Hoovering, and almost shone away the protective laminate from the polished concrete floors. The alabaster-framed mirrors were lucky not to have cracked from her energetic buffing.

A big, pink, crackly 'Welcome Home' sign looped across the top of the stainless-steel living-room door. Balloons and paper streamers were Sellotaped to original paintings, Japanese lamps and the industrial-style tallboy. Get well cards lined the Philippe Starck shelves. There were fresh flowers in every room.

Dazed, Fintan sat on the tan leather sofa they'd had specially made and imported from New York, while Sandro fussed around like an old woman, fiddling with the flowers, plumping leather cushions, straightening the original seventies Formica coffee table. He approached with a tartan rug, which he attempted to tuck in around Fintan's knees. 'I bought this specially. Your mother told me tartan rugs are good for sick people.'

'Get it off me.' Petulantly Fintan tore the rug from him and flung it away.

'Oh. But JaneAnn said you would like it.'

'I'm thirty-two. Not eighty-two. And never likely to be,' he added bitterly.

'Er, I will listen to the answering-machine.' Sandro backed from the room.

'Isn't it great that you're home?' Tara asked nervously.

'Is it? What goddamn difference does it make? And can we lose the bloody flowers? It feels like a hospital in here.'

'Um, Katherine has some hot news for you.' It was up to Katherine to tell Fintan about Joe Roth and the apology but Tara was desperate to lighten the atmosphere. 'Yesterday, she apologized to the Joe Roth bloke!'

A dismissive pout.

Sandro returned and listed proudly, 'You have had telephone

calls from Ethan, Frederick, Claude, Didier, Neville, Julia and Stephanie. Everyone wants to come and visit, but I say, no, they must wait. Fintan will call when he is ready and good.'

'No call from Carmella Garcia offering me my job back?' Sandro looked stricken.

'That's the only phone call I'm interested in. Do you know what I want?'

'What?' Already Sandro had his feet on the starter's blocks.

'I want to get twisted drunk.'

'You can't do that!' Tara was dumbfounded. 'You're sick. You need to get better.'

'I'm not going to get better.'

'Of course you are. You've got to think positive.' Tara insisted. That was the message the nurses repeatedly pressed home. People with a good attitude stood a better chance of recovery.

'Think positive?' Fintan barked with joyless laughter. 'I haven't the energy.'

'I have things for you to eat,' Sandro tempted. 'All your favourites. Strawberries? Pork pies? Petit Filous? Sugar Puffs? Toffee Pops?'

'I don't want anything.'

'But, *bambino*, you have to eat.'

'I don't want *anything*,' Fintan suddenly roared. 'I keep telling you, everything tastes horrible. And you know I'm only supposed to eat raw, unprocessed food in any case!'

Letting a sob burst forth, Sandro rushed dramatically into the kitchen. Torn, Tara followed, and found him bent over the Icelandic lava-stone worktop, crying his eyes out next to an (unused) pale-green Alessi juicer.

'Everything I do is wrong.'

379

'He's not well. He can't help it. If you hadn't done anything, that would annoy him too.'

'He's a different person, so angry and nasty. Not my Fintan.'

'It's so hard for him,' Tara consoled.

'But it's hard for me too.'

'Come on.' Tara led him back to the front room, where they sat in uncomfortable silence waiting for Katherine to return from shopping with JaneAnn and Timothy.

'I'm going to have a shower. I haven't had one in weeks.' Fintan announced.

'But you can barely stand.'

'I'll manage.' He glared.

Sandro and Tara sat with knots in their stomachs wondering how all the triumph of Fintan's homecoming had managed to trickle away.

Suddenly they became aware of a strange, high-pitched yelping noise coming from the bathroom. They looked in confusion at each other for a split second, then they were on their feet and through the door.

Fintan was out of the shower, crouching on the tiles, water sluicing off his naked, Belsen-thin body. He was gibbering, his expression a rictus of revulsion.

Something was different about him, Tara thought. He didn't look quite like Fintan.

Then she realized what it was.

He was bald.

There were locks of hair draped on his shoulders and chest. But almost none on his head.

They looked where he was jabbing his finger. At the floor of the shower. They followed three frothy, frilly tidemarks of shower gel as far as the plug-hole. Which was blocked.

With hair.

So *much* of it. Black, heavy and wet-shiny. Rainbow iridescence twinkling from shampoo he hadn't managed to rinse before the hair was swept from his scalp.

'My hair,' he managed.

Tara wanted to weep. 'Your hair,' she confirmed.

'I'm bald.'

'It will grow back when you're better.' Sandro's voice trembled with shock.

'They told you this would probably happen, didn't they?' Tara asked gently.

'Yes, but I didn't think it would happen to me . . . I mean, I didn't think it would be like this . . . all my hair,' he stuttered. 'Look at it. It's like a horror film.'

'Come away.' Sandro pulled a big towel from the rack and began to tenderly dry Fintan, as a mother would a child. His hands, his arms, his underarms, his chest.

'Lift your foot.' Sandro crouched on the floor, drying between Fintan's toes, as Fintan wobbled and held on to the wall. 'Other one.'

Her heart breaking, Tara gathered up the sopping hair into her hands. This was the worst. Truly the worst.

Fintan wrapped a towel in a turban around his head, then went to the bedroom, threw himself on the bed and began to cry. For half an hour he bawled like a baby, while Tara and Sandro imploded with helplessness.

'I'm grisly looking,' he wept, gasping between syllables. 'I'm. Griz. Lee. Look. Ing.'

'You're not, you're not.'

'I am, I am.' A fresh wave of sorrow overtook him. 'I'm. Griz. Lee. Look. Ing. I'm. Griz. Lee. Look. Ing.'

'It'll grow back when you're better.'

'I'll never be better.'

After some time he sat up and went to the mirror. Slowly, painfully, he peeled off the towel and forced himself to check out his new appearance, initially only looking at his profile.

'Jesus Christ.' He winced when he finally did the full frontal. 'I'd take the night's sleep off myself.' He ran his hand over his smooth pate in bitter, irremediable regret. 'My crowning glory. All gone. All gone. I'm dog-ugly without it.'

'You're not, you're not!'

'Holy Jesus.' Fintan noticed something, then buried his face in his hands. 'One of my ears is higher than the other.'

'It's not.'

'It is. Have a look.'

It was.

'I never knew my head was so lumpy. Oh, God, the ugliness! And this is just the beginning, you know. My eyelashes are next. And eyebrows. And my you-know-where.'

'You can get a wig.' Tara was weighed with depression. 'Perhaps not for your you-know-where, but you can for your head.

'Hey,' she forced herself to sound jolly, 'you're a gay man. For shame if you don't already have several!'

'Actually,' Fintan rallied, 'now that you mention it, I have my Pamela Anderson one.'

'Perhaps you shouldn't have taken a shower.' Sandro lamented. 'Maybe you could have kept your hair.'

'It was just hanging on by the skin of its teeth,' Fintan admitted. 'Though it looked like I still had hair, it was already gone. It was simply a matter of time before it was all over. I just didn't want to face it.'

Now, what did that remind Tara of?

Meanwhile Katherine was having a rough afternoon of her own. The consensus had been that it mightn't be good to overwhelm Fintan the minute he returned home, so she had been elected to keep JaneAnn and Timothy out of the way for a while. Milo would have loved to help but unfortunately he was tied up.

Literally.

Liv was a terrible woman.

Because JaneAnn and Timothy were going home the following day and wanted to buy presents for Ambrose and Jerome and all the neighbours who'd helped run the farms while they were away, Katherine took them shopping. She decided on Harrods because that was what tourists usually seemed to want, but it was a mistake.

JaneAnn went on and on about how expensive everything was and how immoral it was to charge those kinds of prices, and Katherine was hard put to humour her because her head was full of the enormity of having to go to work on Monday and face Joe Roth – oh, the shame! As JaneAnn wondered loudly how they could ask twenty-five pounds for a bread-knife when she knew for a fact that you could get a fine one in Tully's Hardware, Main Street, Knockavoy for four pounds fifty, Katherine was facing into the nightmare of what if, once Joe had 'thought about it', he decided he *didn't* want to go for a drink with her?

'And if it goes blunt on you, Curly Tully will sharpen it again at no extra cost.' JaneAnn got her attention once more. 'I can't see them doing that here, Katherine. I've a good mind to tell her,' JaneAnn indicated a young girl on the pay desk, 'and maybe she could mention it to her father.'

'No, don't,' Katherine said wearily. 'She only works here. I don't think she's actually part of the Harrods family.'

Timothy was keen to buy his wife Esther a present. 'Keep JaneAnn talking,' he muttered to Katherine, 'and point me towards the linger-ee.'

Fifteen minutes later Timothy returned, trying to hide a bagful of red and black underwear that Esther would wear once to humour him, then pretend had been stolen.

They left Harrods and JaneAnn went to a street stall and purchased two 'My mother went to London and all I got was this lousy T-shirt' T-shirts, three 'My mother-in-law went to London and all I got was this lousy T-shirt' T-shirts and seven 'My neighbour went to London and all I got was this lousy T-shirt' T-shirts, bargaining the trader down from seven pounds fifty per shirt to sixty pounds for the twelve. Leaving him reeling and not at all sure that he hadn't actually sold at a loss, they got a taxi to Sandro and Fintan's flat.

To be greeted by a strange creature that had Fintan's face, but waist-length blond hair.

On Sunday afternoon they went in convoy to Heathrow to put JaneAnn and Timothy on the plane home. JaneAnn had only agreed to leave Fintan behind because of the high quality of medical care he was getting.

There was a time when she would have scorned drugs and trusted solely in the power of prayer, especially when it was someone else's relation who was sick. Countless times she'd stood on Main Street, Knockavoy mouthing sanctimoniously,

'The doctors can only do so much, but the true healer is the power of prayer. The power of prayer can work miracles!'

Now it was a belt-and-braces-type scenario. She wanted to talk to Sandro about taking Fintan to Lourdes (or Knock, if funds didn't run to France), but she was also keen that Fintan get every drug available. JaneAnn thanked Katherine effusively for having them. 'I got you a little something.' Discreetly she handed over a small, heavy bundle. 'It's a statue of the Child of Prague. Don't worry if the head falls off. It's good luck.' She thrust her face into Katherine's. 'You'll mind Fintan, won't you? You'll ring me regularly, won't you? And we'll see ye all at Christmas.' She lunged even closer to Katherine. 'And you'll do your best to get off with the boy from your work?' she urged. 'Love makes the world go round, you know. Sure, look how happy Milo and Liv are together.'

'I'm trying my best,' Katherine muttered.

JaneAnn moved on to Tara, extracting a promise that Tara would guard Fintan with her life. 'And you'll tell your young man we're sorry we didn't get to meet him?'

Sharp, sudden rage stabbed Tara. She was deeply ashamed of Thomas's rudeness. 'He was very busy, you know.'

'Sure I do, of course, and him a schoolmaster. It's a highly responsible job. Well, maybe he'll come home with you at Christmas? Unless,' she added, mildly, 'you do that thing that Fintan wants. I don't suppose we'd meet him then.'

Tara shifted unhappily. She didn't think JaneAnn would meet him either way.

51

Katherine slunk into work on Monday morning, nervy with anxiety and braced for shame. How could she face Joe Roth? Worse still, what if he didn't respond to her blatant come-on? She'd die.

She'd actually contemplated not coming in at all. Having to decide between wearing lots of make-up, to give a mask of brazen indifference, or wearing none at all, in the hope that her pale little face would disappear into invisibility, had nearly been too much for her. She tried to be positive. After she'd returned from the airport, she'd had an emotional reunion with her remote control. And Fintan was home from hospital. This was good news, was it not? Even if he was sour and bad-tempered – when she'd told him the whole sorry story of her mortifying apology to Joe Roth, he'd barely grunted in response.

Despite her best intentions to not look directly at Joe, as she took off her coat there was a flicker of eye-contact with him. She nearly slipped a disc in her neck with the speed that she ducked her head. She couldn't avoid noticing that he'd been smiling at her. Smiling? her paranoid head asked. *Or laughing?*

She'd prayed over the weekend and she prayed now that he'd erase her humiliation in one fell swoop by asking her out. She yearned for him to lounge over to her with his easy grace, perch himself on the edge of her desk and say, with an emphasis that only the two of them would understand, 'That project you mentioned to me on Friday? Why don't we discuss it over lunch?'

But he didn't. He stayed resolutely at his desk, and as the morning passed, she downgraded her hopes. It didn't have to be lunch. A drink would be fine. Then she decided it needn't be a drink. Just a walk with no offer of any refreshments would do. And he didn't have to ask her personally. A phone call was acceptable. Or an e-mail. Or an internal memo. By one o'clock she'd have been delighted with anything. A paper plane emblazoned with 'Fancy a shag?' would have done nicely.

But nothing. Nor did he approach her in the afternoon, while she went into a loop trying to justify it. Perhaps he was going out with Angie – although she'd nearly discounted that. Wouldn't Joe have just said, 'I have a girlfriend,' instead of 'I'll think about it'? But if Angie wasn't the obstacle, that meant he simply didn't want Katherine, which was far too unpleasant to contemplate. So, quick as a flash, she wondered if it was because of Angie. But wouldn't Joe have just said, 'I have a girlfriend'? Round and round she went, like a rat on a wheel, until going-home time. Trying to exude, *I have a life, I always had one*, she left and went to Fintan's.

On Tuesday she got up and did it all over again while Tara rang almost hourly to monitor the non-existent progress. 'Is he being unpleasant?' she asked.

'No. He seems friendly enough whenever I catch his eye. Which isn't often,' Katherine admitted. 'My eyes are glued to the floor.'

'It's nice that he's friendly,' Tara consoled.

'It's not friendship I want from him. I have enough friends!'

On Wednesday, Katherine finally admitted it wasn't going

to happen. She'd given Joe long enough, extending and stretching the appropriate time span to its furthest reach. The last piece of hope evaporated. He had rejected her – it was official. He'd 'thought about it' and decided he wasn't interested.

She waited for the slump. A disappointment with a man usually moved her one step closer to death. Doused her joy in living a tiny bit more. But oddly enough, the plummet didn't happen. Why? she wondered. Because she had other things on her mind, namely Fintan? But her worry about Fintan hadn't stopped her getting her knickers in a twist about Joe Roth in the first place.

Whatever the reason, she had a strange faith that life would go on and she would survive. With untimely hope, she knew she had some sort of future. Joe Roth didn't want her, but while she was alive anything could happen.

That evening she went tap-dancing for the first time in six weeks, then to All Bar One with Tara, Liv and Milo – Sandro had requested an evening alone with Fintan.

In the bar they gathered around a table and Katherine was surprised by the thrill of well-being that lunged at her. She was excited to be out, looking forward to some fun. Not only had the nervy anxiety about Joe Roth lifted but so had the worry for Fintan that she'd been dragging like a bag of rocks.

Milo was unrecognizable from the rough-hewn eejit who'd arrived in London less than a month before. His hair had been shaped and tidied so that it no longer looked like he'd trimmed it with a chain-saw, and he was decked out in shiny-new gear, the trendy, design-conscious hand of Liv apparent in every thread. He was astonishingly handsome, all bulk and black curls and navy-blue eyes. 'Look at them.' He laughed, pointing at the pair of peculiar, asymmetrical shoes he was wearing. 'Aren't they the gassest things you ever clapped eyes on? They're from some mad place. Reds under the Bed, or something.' He looked at Liv for guidance.

'Red or Dead,' she murmured. It made a change being the person who corrected rather than the one who was corrected. She *loved* it.

Milo and Liv were still in the first, antisocial flush of love and while they made half-hearted efforts to speak to Tara and Katherine, they kept whispering and giggling to each other, touching fingertips, brushing kisses. Milo muttered something into Liv's ear, and Liv lowered her eyes, smiled broadly, nudged Milo in his Diesel-clad ribs and murmured with put-on reluctance, 'Stop.'

Milo muttered something else. Obviously even more suggestive, because Liv's smile widened further and again she whispered, with a little giggle and an elbow, 'Staw-hop.'

Milo leant his mouth against Liv's ear once more, Liv squeezed his Carhartt knee and Tara and Katherine swivelled to look at each other, with deadpan expressions.

'For God's sake,' Tara complained.

'What do you want to drink?' Katherine asked Milo. He ignored her and continued with his whish-whish-whishing into Liv's hair.

'What do you want to drink?' she asked again, louder.

On her fourth go, Milo gave her a dazed look and said, 'Oh, um, sorry, did you say something?'

Tara said to Katherine, 'Looks like we'll have to make our own entertainment tonight.'

When they had glasses of wine in front of them, Tara began her cross-examination. 'Are you devastated about Joe?'

'I don't actually feel that bad,' Katherine said.

'But you wouldn't say if you did,' Tara said sorrowfully. 'You never do.'

'No, honestly.' Katherine was earnest. 'I don't. It really stings that he didn't want me, but I did something good. I was brave and I took a risk.'

'You're only saying that so I'll leave Thomas.' Tara drew on her cigarette as though she was sucking poison from a wound. 'A blatant case of bumlickery. Doing what Fintan asked and showing me up for the scaredy-cat I am.'

'I'm not. I'm not.' Katherine flapped her hand. 'Hold on and I'll try and explain it. Do you remember when we tried to imagine that we only had six months left to live?'

At that Tara winced.

'That feeling that life is for living?' Katherine reminded her. 'That you only get one shot at it. Remember?'

'Life isn't a dress rehearsal. You'll be dead long enough. You only go around the once.' Tara's sarcasm was almost palpable.

'Exactly! That's —'

'Didn't you notice my irony?' Tara asked anxiously.

'Oh, were you being sarcastic? Each to their own. Well, anyway, I feel like I'm alive. And I'm glad,' Katherine said, simply.

'But you're always so cynical,' Tara said, helplessly, 'and a lovely man has rejected you. Any normal woman would want to die.'

'You never know.' Katherine gave her a sly look. 'I might meet another man.'

'But . . .' Tara was confused. Katherine never said things like that.

'Like him.' Katherine nudged Tara and directed her attention to a good-looking blond bloke leaning against the bar.

As Tara watched, he began to smile, and the smile was directed at Katherine. Tara whirled around to look at Katherine who, instead of giving the man a grade one (icy disdain) or a grade two (icy disdain with an undercurrent of steely hostility), was smiling back at him. Not a huge big ear-to-ear beam, but a smile nevertheless.

And then the really baffling truth dawned on Tara. Katherine wasn't returning the blond bloke's smile. She'd smiled at him first.

What was going on? There was an unusual slightly loose-cannonish air about Katherine tonight. She looked different, reminding Tara of someone. Who was it? A person familiar yet not. Ah! Something turned and settled into place. How unexpected. It was her mother, Delia.

On Thursday Katherine went to work with a mild hangover and soldiered on with her Joe Roth-free life. Low with disappointment, yet still oddly convinced she'd be OK.

Work was a great distraction. But in the midst of inputting a fixed assets schedule, the longing to look at Joe hurtled at her out of nowhere. She kept her head turned to the screen and resisted. And resisted. But the yearning tugged at her, until she couldn't fight it any more. Shifting her head infinitesimally, she allowed herself the merest sliver of a glance out of the tiniest corner of her eye.

And her skin flamed when she saw him watching her. Sideways, furtively, but with great intensity. Then, his eyes locked on to hers, he smiled. Wide, intimate, meaningful.

What was he grinning at?

She turned back to her screen. In the top left-hand corner a little envelope was flashing. *You have mail*. She clicked her mouse and opened it. It was an e-mail.

From Joe.

52

The day of the apology Joe Roth had told Katherine he'd think about it. And Joe Roth was a man of his word. So he thought about it.

A pragmatic man, when Katherine had rejected him with her hints of sexual harassment, he'd doused his feelings for her. But he hadn't poured the acid of bitterness on them, corroding them into something ugly and twisted. So, though considerably faded, they were perfectly preserved and ready to be regenerated at a moment's notice.

Not only did Joe want to go out with Katherine, but he wanted to take her somewhere totally, mindblowingly special.

Somewhere magical. Somewhere meaningful. Somewhere that showed how interested in her he was. But where? Out for a spectacular dinner? Hot-air ballooning? Away for the weekend? To a country hotel? To Reykjavík? Or Barcelona?

Nothing but the very best would suffice.

He racked his brains over the weekend to no avail. Monday and Tuesday were an agony of no inspiration.

And suddenly on Wednesday he knew. In an instant it was so very clear. It was the obvious thing to do for a woman of Katherine's calibre.

But how would he pull it off? By next Saturday? That kind of thing normally took months – even for members the waiting list was eight weeks.

He realized he needed his mate Rob's co-operation, there was no other way around it. He just couldn't do it on his own. That evening he called to Rob's flat because such an onerous request merited a personal visit.

'I've met a girl,' Joe prefaced.

'I know.'

'No, a different one.'

'Blimey!'

'Her name is Katherine and she's really special.'

'Good for you, mate.'

'And I need you to make the ultimate sacrifice.'

Rob's eyes flickered uncertainly. 'What are you on about?'

'Saturday . . .'

'Saturday!' Rob exclaimed. Surely he couldn't mean . . . ?

'Saturday,' Joe repeated meaningfully.

'No, mate,' Rob beseeched, backing away from him. 'No way, mate. It's out of order, don't ask me to do that. A refusal often offends.'

'So does a smack in the mouth.'

'So it's like that.'

'Only because I'm desperate.'

'We've been mates for a long time. I never thought you'd do something like this to me.'

'Yeah, well, I'm sorry. I am. But I've no choice.'

'Who is this woman? Pamela Anderson?'

'Better. So what do you say? Yes? Or yes?'

'Can't you take her somewhere else?'

'No. Nothing but the best for Katherine. Go on, Rob. I'll make it up to you. I'll pay you whatever you want.'

'Money is meaningless, you know that. I'm insulted.'

'Do I have a yes?'

'I'll think about it.'

'No, I need to know *now*.'

Rob looked in astonishment at Joe. 'Blimey, you have it bad.'

'Perhaps I do.'

'Well, so do I.' Rob trembled aggressively at Joe.

'Too right. But please. Two hundred quid?'

Rob sighed. He wasn't going to win this. 'Go on, then. Two fifty and you've a deal.'

On Thursday afternoon Tara's phone at work rang. It was Katherine and she sounded low.

'What's up?' Tara gasped, ever poised for bad news of Fintan.

'I've had an e-mail from our subject.'

'And?'

'He's invited me out on Saturday.'

Tara almost had a heart-attack. 'I don't believe you! I thought you said he was horrible and ignored you all week. And now you tell me you're going out with him on Saturday night! Fair play to you.'

'Not Saturday night. *Saturday*.'

'Paris on the Eurostar?'

A laugh from Katherine that sounded oddly bitter.

'Oh. Lunch? Somewhere fabulous?'

'No.'

'What, then? Not the bloody zoo? Not in November?'

'No, er . . .' Katherine could hardly say it, she was so embarrassed.

'Where? What?'

'He's um . . . he's, er . . . he's . . .'

'He's what?'

'He's taking me to a football match,' she finally blurted, queasy with shame. She knew a public humiliation when she saw one.

'Football is the new rock 'n' roll,' Tara said, carefully.

'You don't have to be nice.'

'Who's playing?' A lot hinged on this. Would Katherine be spending Saturday afternoon standing with three others on a muddy field in outer suburbia watching two non-league teams boring everyone to death? Or in a big, sexy stadium with seats and burgers and programmes and souvenir knickers, at a Premier match, where tickets cost more than those of a West End theatre?

'Oh, I don't know. Arsenal versus someone or other.'

'Arsenal!'

'I know. God, Tara, I wish I'd never got involved in this. I could die with shame. The outrageous cheek of him. If it wasn't for Fintan –'

'But Arsenal tickets are like gold dust.'

'*Are* they?' Suddenly things had started to look up.

'It's harder to get a ticket to an Arsenal game than it is for me to fit into size eight jeans.'

'How do you know?'

'Ravi supports the Gunners.'

'What are they?'

'The Gunners are Arsenal. Christ, you've a lot to learn. We'll have to send you on a crash course to Ravi.'

Ravi made throat-cutting motions and rolled his eyes in alarm. He was terrified of Katherine. Her enigmatic mystique didn't work for him, he just thought she was spooky.

'How do you know so much about football?' Katherine asked.

'Because Ravi runs a league for us. Tell me what Joe says in the e-mail.' Tara hugged the phone in excitement. 'Read out *exactly* what he says.'

Katherine looked furtively around her office and dropped her voice even more. 'It says, "Saturday afternoon, Highbury. A pint of beer, Arsenal v Everton, and thou? How about it? I pledge to explain the offside rule to you and feed you afterwards."'

Tara couldn't speak because she was so close to tears. 'That's beautiful,' she squeaked. 'And he's taking you for dinner afterwards. You never said that.'

'We-elll . . .' Warm pride was creeping up on Katherine. 'Well, indeed!'

'So, um,' Katherine said archly, 'would you mind waiting until after Saturday before leaving Thomas? I might need my flat to myself.'

'Darn,' Tara lamented. 'And I'd so wanted to leave him this evening.'

'If only!'

'So what are you going to wear?' Tara demanded gleefully. 'Wear jeans! I wish I could wear jeans. I treble dare you to wear jeans. Go on. Zipped hipsters. I quadruple dare you. I *five*tuple dare you.'

'But what if . . . ?'

'If what?'

'Well, just say, we . . . you know, er, get it together?'

'Katherine Casey. On a first date. I'm shocked.'

'I might have the marks of my jeans on my legs and stomach. And that's not very sexy. And what about my underwear?' she asked tentatively.

Tara was astonished at such openness. 'Do you mean suspender belts and all that gear?'

'Mmmm.'

'Well, I'm delighted. It's about time a man got a look at them. But you're right, you couldn't really wear them with jeans. Why don't you wear knickers that say, "I scored at Highbury"? He's bound to like that. Or alternatively no knickers at all. So long as you have your pubes shaved, won't he be delighted! Hahahaha.'

Katherine was sorry she'd ever told Tara her thoughts on the Gillette incident.

'Fintan is going to be thrilled.' Tara sang, absolutely delighted herself. The more Katherine and Joe became a reality the better the chance that Fintan would take the pressure off Tara. Although it had been a few days since he'd brought up the subject of Tara leaving Thomas, once she thought about it. In fact, it was nearly a week since he'd mentioned it. Not that she was taking that as any reason to relax.

53

'Well!' Ravi declared, when Tara hung up.

'Well, indeed,' Tara agreed.

'So she bagged a date with the chap from her work.'

'Certainly did.'

'And he's an Arsenal supporter. Sounds like a nice bloke to me. Don't think much of his taste in women, though.'

'Ravi!' Tara paused from her scolding and clutched her stomach. 'Oh, Ravi . . .'

'What is it this time?'

'Almonds. Bakewell tarts.'

Tara was once more back on starvation rations. Not only did everything she see and hear remind her of food, but now even smells were tormenting her.

It began that morning when the strawberry air freshener in her car put her in mind of the fake sugary smell of jelly babies. The urge to screech to a halt outside a newsagent's and buy up their entire stock possessed her like a demon. As soon as she got on the Westway, the focus changed and she had an almost irresistible desire to lick herself. She smelt of delicious, sweet Bounty bars or coconut ice-cream. Which drove her mad until she remembered that the body lotion she'd slapped on after her morning shower was coconut-flavoured. Then when she arrived at her office she was hit by a profound urge for lemon cheesecake. The entire building seemed to be fragranced by it.

She wondered if she was finally cracking up, until Ravi pointed out that the agent used by the contract cleaners to wash the corridors was lemon-scented.

'Where are the Bakewell tarts coming from?' Ravi asked.

Tara pointed towards Evelyn and Teddy, and Ravi got up and began sniffing around them.

'What are you doing?' Teddy demanded.

'Checking for Tara. Do either of you have almond perfume? Or almond soap?'

'Actually,' Evelyn sounded amazed, 'I washed my hair with almond shampoo this morning.'

'Perhaps you could use another flavour until Tara falls off the wagon again,' Ravi asked. 'Something inedible.'

'Sure.' Evelyn eyed Tara with compassion. 'Eucalyptus do you?'

'Sorry,' Tara mumbled, mortified. 'Pay him no heed . . .'

Tara remained haunted by food. When she and Ravi went for their aimless lunchtime ramble to Hammersmith, she was briefly distracted by the new long-last lipstick from Clinique. Distracted enough to buy two colours. But when they came back out on to the street the round green, orange and red traffic lights looked so like giant fruit gums that Ravi almost had to restrain Tara from shinning up the pole and licking them. 'I'll buy you a tube,' he offered.

Tara shook her head. 'I used up my week's calories last night. I blame Milo O'Grady. He made us all go for a Vietnamese meal after the pub. He's mad keen to try everything London has to offer.'

'You should eat.' Ravi displayed some rare common sense. 'With Fintan being ill, it's a rotten time for you.'

'Life's got to go on.'

'You're being rather tough.'

'I am not. I'm a mess. Between Thomas and Fintan I'm a complete state.'

'Um, so how are things with Thomas?'

'Dreadful! I don't understand why but we're barely civil to each other. I have this continual terrible feeling that something awful's about to happen.'

'Maybe it's actually Fintan you're thinking about.'

'Not really,' she admitted. 'At least, not only. Which makes me feel even worse. How can I be worried about my boyfriend when one of my oldest friends is really sick? But the thing is,' she justified quickly, 'even though Fintan looks terrible, he still has eight months of treatment to go, so there's plenty of time for him to get better. And because he's not getting obviously worse, things feel . . . well, not exactly *normal*,' Tara mumbled, 'but I've got used to it. Katherine feels the same. Liv says it's a survival technique, that you can't sustain being in a continual state of shock or terror. You've got to normalize the abnormal.'

'You girlies. Why is everything so complicated?'

'Oh, God, I just got a rush of it!' Tara stopped still in the street, early Christmas shoppers banging into her, ready to berate her with seasonal ire, until they saw the appalled rictus on her face. 'The thought that he mightn't get better. It's like looking into hell. It seems . . . evil.'

'You need a drink.' Ravi took her elbow and steered her into the nearest pub, sat her down and bought her a gin and tonic. 'Has he cheered up any since he came home from hospital?'

'Oh, no.' Tara took a sip of her drink, and shuddered with relief. 'Thanks, Ravi, this is saving my life. No, he's awful. You know there are stories about people whose lives blossom in the face of death? Well, it hasn't been like that for Fintan. Almost from the second he came home he turned into a real brat – spiteful, demanding, bad-tempered. Not that you could blame him, he nearly died when his hair fell out.' She winced. 'Wrong choice of words. He feels lousy,' she continued, 'because his white blood count is in bits after the high dose of chemo they gave him. And he's angry and scared. But it's hard to be nice to him all the time.'

Tara turned to Ravi, tears in her eyes. 'Sometimes I want to smack him because I'm angry and scared too. And I feel so guilty!'

Ravi awkwardly pawed Tara's hand. 'I'm sure what you feel is normal.' Actually, he hadn't a clue, but he so badly wanted to help. 'Another drink?' he asked hopefully, though she'd barely started on her first. 'And I'm sure Katherine bagging the bloke from her work will cheer him up.'

'It'll have to. I'll never be able to do what he wants, and that's part of the reason that I'm angry and scared.'

'You never know what you can do till you try.'

'I do know. I've never been more sure of anything. I can't leave Thomas and that's that.'

'But you said things aren't good with him.'

'Yeah, but . . . it's only temporary. He's jealous of Fintan and the pressure is making me overeat and . . . Don't worry, it'll all be fine. Soon.'

'Whatever,' Ravi said heartily. 'You've enough on your plate.'

'Plate,' Tara said wistfully. 'Food. I'm obsessed.'

'Give yourself a break.'

'You're so sweet.' Tara gratefully leant her head into Ravi's neck and nervously he put his arm around her shoulder.

'Mmmm.' Tara snuggled. 'You smell lov –' She pulled away

in torment. 'Crème brûlée! You smell of crème brûlée. Vanilla pods, burnt sugar. What aftershave are you wearing?'

'JPG. Danielle bought it for me. And, now that you mention it, I do remember her saying something about vanilla top notes, whatever they are.'

After work Tara visited Fintan, bringing a magazine article about Chinese herbalists that Vinnie had given her.

Sandro intercepted her at the door. 'Fintan's gone bananas on the shopping channel,' he whispered. 'He's bought an abdominizer, a country-and-Western album that you can't buy in the shops, a horrible gold chain and bracelet set and a cross-country skiing machine. He is constantly on the phone telling them our credit-card details!'

Fintan was enthroned on the sofa, wearing a Diana Vreeland turban, and a sourpuss face. Since he'd got out of hospital he'd been rancid and nasty, like milk that had turned. He glanced at Vinnie's article, then spun it aside. 'Tara, every time I see you you've found some new form of mumbo-jumbo for me to try. Homeopathy, acupuncture, raw diets, massage, colour therapy, meditation and now Chinese herbs.'

'But, Fintan,' Tara said, desperately, 'they're all worth a try. They can't do any harm.'

'Turn on the box,' he interrupted, rudely. 'Let's have some entertaining nonsense. As opposed to the non-entertaining variety.'

'Fintan,' Sandro wrung his hands, tearfully, 'please, you mustn't. You will have no friends left, you've been so rude to everyone . . .'

'I've no worries about Tara,' Fintan said, archly. 'The worse men treat her, the more devoted she becomes.'

Tara flinched as if she'd been slapped, but Fintan, unresponsive to her hurt, pressed the remote. As the lights of the television played over them, Tara sat in silence, her face burning with shame. She hated being an object of pity and derision. But what was she to do?

Katherine arrived – strangely enough, not until about nine o'clock – with her calculator, allegedly about to help Fintan and Sandro work out a financial plan until Fintan got redundancy money or disability benefit.

'You must stop spending money,' Sandro pleaded and Fintan rewarded him with a glare.

'Oh, by the way,' Katherine reached into her bag and pulled out a page torn from a newspaper, 'there was something in today's *Independent* about chakra healing. It might be worth a try . . .'

Fintan had the grace to smile – albeit bitterly.

Hoping that Katherine's great news about Joe's e-mail would lift Fintan from the pit of bile he was mired in, Tara made her escape home to Thomas.

When she reached the Holloway Road and circled the block looking for a parking space, she was not prepared for the thought that spun idly into her head. *If I didn't live on this road any more, I'd choose somewhere that had residents' parking.*

She caught herself in amazement. When Fintan had first suggested she leave Thomas, her denial had been automatic. But something had obviously filtered through.

Then she thought of what it would be like being on her own and her innards froze.

She let herself in. The first thing she did every time she came home was wonder what kind of mood Thomas was in. Tonight he was hunched over a bundle of essays, his vicious red pen turning each page into a bloodbath.

'Where've you been?'

'With Fintan.'

'Hhhhumph.'

'How's Fintan, Tara?' Tara surprised herself by saying, ladling on the sarcasm. 'He's not too good, Thomas, but thanks for asking.'

'And what about me?' Thomas asked. 'When do I get to see you?'

Thomas's resentment of the time and attention that Tara lavished on Fintan was worsening. Because he was insecure. But Tara was weary of making excuses for him – and that's what they were, she realized in sudden shock, excuses.

'I thought we might go out tonight,' Thomas said. 'Go round the corner for a curreh.'

'I'm not eating.'

Thomas was on the horns of a dilemma. 'Bludeh good for you, Tara.' But he didn't want to go on his own to the curry-house. 'But I don't mind if you have a night off.'

She shook her head firmly.

'You ate plenty, all the times you were in the hospital with bludeh Fintan!'

I'd have to get a van, she thought. *All my stuff won't fit in the car.* Then the aperture shut again, as she considered a life on her own.

She flicked on the television and, interestingly, what came on was a documentary about women who flip one day and murder their partners after years of abuse.

'That'll be me.' Tara laughed, watching Thomas for a response.

'It'll be me, more like,' he countered, confidently.

As she watched him scoring lines through teenage essays, Tara realized, with unprecedented clarity, how much she'd grown to dislike Thomas since Fintan got sick. Her habitual trepidation mysteriously lifted, making her reckless and daring. Reckless and daring enough that – ironically – she thought now might be the time to ask him *that* question.

She opened her mouth and instantly her heart began to beat like the Kodo drummers.

She wondered exactly how she should frame it.

'Thomas?' she asked. She could hear nervousness in her voice and she didn't like it.

'What?' He didn't even look up from the pile of essays.

'Nothing.'

They eddied back into silence. Then the feelings propelled her forward once more.

'Thomas?'

'What?'

'Why don't we get married?'

Eyes still down, he chuckled. 'Don't talk daft.'

'Oh. OK.'

'That's a good one.' He laughed quietly to himself. 'Us getting wed!'

Silence resumed in the brown basement sitting-room, the air heavy and gloomy. Tara felt a peculiar absence of emotion – no loss, no disappointment, no surprise – nothing. She had expected to feel heartbroken.

'Why?' Thomas asked, after a while. 'Are you up the duff?'

'Hardly.' They hadn't had sex since her birthday, more than a month before.

Another ten minutes of silence elapsed.

'You *look* like you're up the duff,' he said.

'You're not exactly Kate fucking Moss yourself,' Tara countered.

He looked up from correcting, his eyes stunned and childlike. 'That was mean.' He was surprised.

'Now you know how I feel.'

'But I say it for your own good.'

'I'm saying it for your own good, too.'

Thomas looked at her and, in one of his quick, about-turn changes of mood, grinned suggestively. 'It takes a big hammer to drive a big nail.' His crotch was angled towards her, and the leer on his face said it all.

She looked at him, bewildered, her forehead furrowed like she was trying to read tiny writing. Why did he look like a gnome?

She didn't want to sleep with him. That was the only thing she was certain of.

'You laugh at the idea of us getting married then you expect me to go to bed with you. What's wrong with this picture?'

Thomas looked genuinely confused. 'Aw, Tara, come on,' he whined. 'You've got me all horny. Don't be such a tease.'

'Make your own arrangements.' Then she stood up and walked from the room.

She wasn't upset. She didn't know what she was. Other than hungry.

But the thought of food made her queasy.

In the past when she'd been too hungry to sleep she took two Nytols to knock herself out. It worked for her then and it worked for her now. But her last thought before she descended into drugged sleep was not – unusually – *I'd love a bacon sandwich*. Instead it was, *I wonder how Alasdair is*?

54

On Friday Tara woke to foreboding, her jaw aching from grinding her teeth in her sleep.

She was humiliated by Thomas's amusement. What was so funny about wanting to get married? They'd been together for two years. People sometimes got married, it wasn't that bloody hilarious. She smarted with rejection, even if he hadn't known that's what his careless words had done.

Though she insisted unconvincingly that she wasn't even sure *she* wanted to get married – after all, she'd spent her teenage years shouting about what a bourgeois institution marriage was – she wanted some indication that Thomas took their relationship seriously.

On the drive to work, she was tortured with anxiety about what was going to happen next. Surely things couldn't just stay as they were? Or could they? She had a horrible feeling that she was obliged, for her own self-respect, to do *something*, make some stand. As she should have done a month before.

But she didn't want to. She'd rather tiptoe through her life, as though through a condemned building. Afraid that the whole edifice could come toppling down if she put a foot wrong, stood on one rotten floorboard, leant against one shaky beam.

It used to be nice with Thomas, she thought. It used to be lovely. Perhaps she didn't need to be worried, she bolstered herself in a burst of wild hope. The entire relationship hadn't blown up in her face. Essentially nothing had changed and the structure still seemed sound.

Perhaps *sound* wasn't quite the word, she admitted. But it looked the same as before. Whatever that was.

'How's the new lippy?' Ravi yelled as soon as she walked into the office. 'Kiss resistant?'

'I wouldn't know.'

'Care to discover if it's doughnut resistant?' He waved a sugary ring in front of her. 'Sorry,' he said, when she winced and looked away. 'How about a coffee?'

Ravi fetched her a cup of coffee, and Vinnie, Teddy, Evelyn, Slim Cheryl and Sleepy Steve couldn't help downing tools in order to see what happened when Tara's mouth came into contact with the side of her mug. She lifted the coffee to her lips, took a tiny sip, then held out the mug for all to see. Everyone exhaled a big 'Oh' of disappointment at the sight of a taupe, lip-shaped curve on the yellow enamel. 'It said it was *long-last*,' Ravi consoled. 'It never said it was *indelible*.'

Tara sighed and said, 'I think I'll just give up. This is not something I'm going to win.'

After work she went for a couple of drinks with Ravi and some of the others, and didn't mention Thomas or Fintan or anything unpleasant. But her head wasn't her own and she couldn't manage to shake the elusive but omnipresent dread.

So she went home and the minute she saw Thomas her stung humiliation increased. Forcing a conversational tone, she said, 'Guess what? Katherine's going on a date tomorrow.'

He snorted. 'Will she be taking the padlock off her knickers?'

She clamped her mouth shut. Losing her temper was a luxury she couldn't afford. But she couldn't help watching them both from a faraway place and thinking what an odd way for two people who were supposed to love each other to behave.

What a bizarre way to live. What a *waste*.

Though she couldn't say when they'd crossed the line, it hadn't always been this way.

She was so tired. She'd lived with enough weirdness for the moment.

'Get me a drink,' she said. 'A glass of white wine.'

Startled he obeyed.

Something fundamental was in the process of shifting for Tara. She just didn't know what it was yet. And she wasn't sure she could bear to find out.

55

Tara had learnt a long time ago to compartmentalize her life –
Thomas hadn't ever wanted any involvement with her friends.
So on Saturday morning, when she drove to Katherine's to help
her get ready for the date with Joe Roth, it was easy to leave
her humiliation and dread about Thomas behind. Easier than
easy, actually. Her life had become an uncomfortable place
where she didn't know what to think or what to do. It was a
pleasure to leave it for a short time.

Almost combusting with excitement, she arrived at
Katherine's.

Katherine was wearing a bra and a pair of tight jeans, the
zipped front emphasizing her flat stomach and visible hipbones.

'It's because you know how much I wish I could wear them,
isn't it?' Tara said, gleefully. 'It's because you're very fond of
me.'

'It's because there's not much call for short black dresses at
a football match,' Katherine replied.

'Not at all, you're just being kind to your fat chum, letting
me wear jeans vicariously. How I wish I was you,' Tara said
wistfully, 'with your no-bum and your skinny legs. Just as well
you're my friend, else I'd have to murder you.'

Tara looked around the flat. Something was wrong. The
place was still a shambles, though it was nearly a week since
the O'Gradys had left. The living-room carpet could have done

with a good Hoover, everything looked dusty and askew and through the open kitchen door the sink was piled higgledy-piggledy with dirty plates.

'Oh.' Katherine twirled her hand vaguely. 'Yeah, I know. I'd planned to do a big clean when they left, but, ah . . .' Her voice trailed away. 'It doesn't seem so bad. It's fine. Messy, but at least it's clean.'

It wasn't, actually, but Tara swallowed anxiously and said nothing.

'Do you know, I miss them,' Katherine admitted. 'I'd got used to them.'

'But they were driving you bonkers,' Tara exclaimed. 'Milo using your Coco Chanel body-lotion that time.'

'We have no actual proof it was Milo,' Katherine defended. 'It could have been JaneAnn or Timothy.'

'It *smelt* like Milo. You know, I think he's got a real taste for nice things.'

'He's taken to Liv's lifestyle like a duck to water,' Katherine agreed.

Tara began sniffing the air. 'What's the pooey smell?' She inhaled again. 'Singed hair?'

Katherine looked uncomfortable. 'I might have overdone it with the hair straightener.'

'God, it really is all systems go on Project Joe Roth. So what happens if you get off with him? Aren't you worried that your flat's a bit . . .' she faltered '. . . untidy?'

'I've bought expensive new underwear,' Katherine confessed. 'I've tempted fate enough.'

'*More* underwear?' Tara choked. 'If you wore a different pair of your knickers every day between now and when you die, you'd still have a pair or two left over!'

'There we go again, assuming we're going to live for ever,' Katherine said lightly.

Immediately Tara went pale. 'Every time I think of it, it's as bad as the first time. He'll be OK, won't he?'

'Maybe. Hopefully.'

Death hung in the air until Katherine interrupted, 'Come on, do what you came here to do and help me get dressed.'

Despite everything, Tara couldn't help filling with excitement.

'What should I wear on top?' Katherine wondered.

Tara flicked through Katherine's immaculate hangers. 'You and your capsule wardrobe,' she muttered, in a schoolmarm voice. 'Buy in neutral colours, make sure the item fits in with the rest of your wardrobe, at the beginning of each season choose a few staple items – a grey trouser suit, a navy skirt suit, narrow-legged black pants and a black skirt – and build on them.' She'd come to the end of the hangers. 'Sorry, Katherine, I see no tops here that are sexy, and you can hardly wear a work blouse with those jeans.' She put her hands on her hips in a wit's-end way. 'I don't suppose you'd just go in your bra?'

Katherine surprised her by saying, uneasily, 'Well, actually, I went shopping . . .' she pulled a bag from under the bed '. . . and I bought this. But it's not really me,' she added apologetically. 'It's a boomerang.'

Tara looked perplexed.

'I mean, it's going back,' Katherine explained.

'Let me see.' Tara pulled a raspberry-coloured little sweater from the bag. 'On!' she ordered. 'This minute.'

'But –'

'On!'

Katherine stood awkwardly before Tara. She looked beautiful. The dark-pink colour made her face glow as if it had uplighters within it. The silky fabric clung to her arms and breasts and was just short enough to give a tantalizing glimpse of her concave stomach. Tara wished they'd thought in time of getting Katherine's belly-button pierced – something she'd love to get done herself except she feared they'd need the equipment that excavated the Channel Tunnel to burrow through the fat to pierce the hole, then the ring would have to be the circumference of a dinner-plate.

'You've got to wear it!' Tara was passionate.

'I can't,' Katherine protested. 'I look so obvious. And it's too young for me.'

'Please,' Tara begged. 'You look sexy and waif-like. And he's so used to seeing you all buttoned up in your bumlick suits that he won't know what's hit him.'

'But it's November. I'll get a cold.'

'Colds are caused by viruses. And you'll have a coat. Which were you thinking of wearing?'

There was an unexpected pause and Katherine's face was an agony of guilt. 'Well, when I was shopping I saw this,' she confessed, pulling another bag from under the bed. 'But I shouldn't have bought it. I'm going to bring it back on Monday. It's just here for a little holiday in Gospel Oak. I don't know what I was thinking of . . .'

Tara grabbed the bag from her and pulled out a three-quarter-length petrol-blue jacket, in liquid-soft leather, still in its tissue paper. 'Jesus Christ! What else is under there?' Tara hit the floor like a hostage in a bank raid.

'Nothing,' Katherine said, hastily. 'Only a pair of boots. And some jewellery and make-up. Oh, and a few pieces of underwear. But they're not me, *at all*, whatever about the other stuff, these were a big, big mistake.'

'Baabaa 'oots!' Tara was under the bed, her voice muffled, but ecstatic.

Katherine took it to understand that Tara had found the Prada boots. 'Please come out.'

Tara re-emerged. 'So that's why you didn't get to Fintan's until nine o'clock on Thursday night. You were shopping!'

Reverentially she began to unfold the jacket. 'Oh, God, I don't believe it,' she exclaimed, when she saw the label. 'Dolce and Gab –'

'We won't talk about it,' Katherine interrupted smoothly. 'The unbearable guilt, you understand.'

Tara felt relieved. Katherine had behaved wildly out of character by splurging on impractical, expensive clothes, but at least she had the decency to feel horribly guilty about it.

Finally Katherine was ready, wearing the new top, jacket, boots, choker, earrings, thong knickers, lacy bra, lipstick, eyeliner and a squirt of Boudoir on her neck, wrists and modest cleavage. She even let Tara put her hair in bunches.

'You look about fourteen,' Tara said. 'Go forth in sin, my child.'

'You can depend upon it.'

'Not really? Not on a first date?'

'Life is for living,' Katherine quipped. 'We could be dead tomorrow.'

She really seemed to believe that and Tara's anxiety started up again. She could have done without Katherine going weird on her.

As they left the house, Tara glanced furtively up and down the road.

'Who are you looking for?'

'Ravi. I wouldn't put it past him to cosh you on the head, steal your clothes and impersonate you to get your ticket.'

'It's that big a deal, is it?' Katherine was pleased.

Fintan had been invited to Katherine's for the great preparations, but had unpleasantly declined to come. So, hoping it would cheer him up, they decided to show him the fruits of their labours before Katherine met Joe.

Sandro answered the door, white and worried, swathed in a miasma of oppression. Silently, tight-lipped, he nodded towards the front room.

Fintan was thrown on the couch wearing a Diana Ross and the Supremes beehive wig. The first sight of him and his wasted grey appearance was always a jolt. Even though it could be put down to the after-effects of the chemo and the drop in his white blood cell count, it was impossible to avoid the impact that they were staring death in the face. But the shock receded quickly – they'd been told he had to get worse before he got better.

'How are you?' Tara asked him.

'Shite!' he declared.

'But no worse?' Katherine asked.

'No,' he conceded, grumpily.

Even a couple of weeks before, they'd have devoted half an hour to discussing his health but, reassured that there were no new tumours, or swellings, or inexplicable pains, things seemed almost normal.

'Are you sitting comfortably?' Tara asked, building dramatic tension.

'No. My arse has all but disappeared.'

'Listen to him showing off. Are you ready, Katherine?'

At her nod, Tara declared, 'Da-dah! I give you Katherine Casey, *über*babe, sex-kitten and Joe Roth fancier. This girl is on a promise, and no mistake.'

Katherine rushed into the middle of the floor and did a dance, modelling her new clothes, opening her jacket and sticking her pointy little hips this way and that.

'You were always a crap dancer,' Fintan said, startling Katherine into stunned, hurt immobility.

Just then Tara noticed the open can of Sapporo on the table in front of him, and fear lunged at her, dropping her temperature. Her eyes met Katherine's. She'd noticed too.

'Katherine's off on her date with Joe Roth today.' Tara couldn't avoid using the slow, patronizing way that people speak to the mad or afflicted.

'Don't bother on my account, dear,' Fintan said, bitchily.

'But aren't you glad?' Tara faltered, while Katherine became very still. 'Aren't you excited? I mean, you made it happen. In a way, sort of . . .'

'I think you're confusing me with the cancer patient who gives a shit.'

'But she's done it for you.' Tara was suddenly dying for a fag.

'No, she hasn't,' Fintan retorted. 'She's done it for herself.'

'I *did* do it for you,' Katherine insisted, croakily.

'Well, you can stop now.'

'It's a bit late.'

'Not at all. Better late than never. You're off the hook. In fact, I don't want you to meet him, I'm asking you not to,' Fintan threw like a dagger at Katherine.

'You can't do that.' Tara yelped. 'She's bought a Dolce and

417

Gabbana jacket. And Agent Provocateur underwear. And boots from Prada – show him the boots, Katherine, pull up your jeans, look at those *heels*, Fintan. And though the jumper only came from French Connection . . .'

As Katherine obediently pulled up her jeans her face was a plea of horrified beseechment. The thought of not going on the date with Joe was unbearably disappointing.

'You see,' Fintan said, his mouth twisted in a bitter smile, 'you want to meet him. This has nothing to do with me. I was just a catalyst.'

Conflict raged in Katherine. She hadn't wanted to have anything to do with Joe. Well, she *had*, but she'd never have done anything about it. And she had been genuinely afraid that Fintan would deteriorate if she didn't do what he asked. But she was forced to admit that there was a part of her which had welcomed the excuse to come on to Joe. And she didn't want to stop now. She felt it no longer had anything to do with Fintan.

Perhaps, other than his illness being a trigger, it never had.

This made her horribly uncomfortable, and she suddenly understood how Tara had felt, being told to leave Thomas.

'But why did you ask me to, if you were only going to change your mind?' she mumbled.

'I've cancer, dear. I can do whatever I like.' Fintan's tone changed to weariness. 'It seemed like a good idea at the time, Katherine. It really did. I thought that if you and Tara lived life to the full, I'd be OK. Liv tells me I was going through the third phase of response to bad news – bargaining.'

'What's the first and second?' Tara asked.

'Denial and depression.'

'And where are you now?'

418

'Mired in phase four.'

'Which is?'

'Self-pity. Isn't it obvious?'

'It's not self-pity, actually.' Katherine, too, had been informed by Liv. 'It's anger.'

'Whatever.'

'Is there a phase five?' Tara asked, warily. What could they expect next?

'Yup. Acceptance, apparently. But I'll be dead by then.'

Tara opened her mouth to begin an automatic clamour of denial, but Fintan stopped her. 'Please don't. Being patronized is so supremely irritating. Just look at me, still with my kiwi-neck despite superhuman, baldy-bastard doses of chemo. I'm a walking tumour, so what am I to think?' He turned to Katherine, and said, half apologetically, 'Oh, go on. Go out with him, have fun, enjoy yourself.'

She wavered, reluctant to admit openly that she was seeing Joe Roth because she actually wanted to. Desperate to still involve Fintan, she said, 'If it all works out with Joe I'll bring him to see you.'

'Don't bother.'

'Well, er, I'd better go,' Katherine said. 'If not I'll be late.'

She made for the tube station, power-walking in her four-and-a-half-inch heels, trying to go fast enough to shake off the anger and confusion that clung to her.

Tara was left alone with Fintan. She was horribly uncomfortable with him, and so was Sandro, judging from the way he avoided coming into the front room. Once Fintan's life had been a vessel that overflowed with sweet joy. Now it had become a small, sour, worthless thing. She was dreading him mentioning Thomas. Though he'd absolved Katherine – even if the nasty way he'd done it hadn't seemed like absolution – Tara didn't know whether she, too, was off the hook. Instead, perhaps everything was riding on her now and she couldn't bring herself to ask. 'Should you be drinking that?' She nodded at the beer can on the table.

'Why? Do you want it? Isn't it a bit early in the day for you?'

'I might ask you the same question.'

'Ah, but I've cancer.'

Tara sighed inwardly. 'All the more reason.' She plucked up her courage to ask him, 'Would you like us to do a visualization together?'

'A what?'

'A visualization. From the book. You know where we visualize you being filled with,' at his savagely amused expression, she faltered, 'goodness and purity and light and, ah, all that.'

'How's Thomas?' he threw at her. The question she'd been dreading.

'Um, I had a chat with him, and I suspect it's no-go on the marriage front and I haven't forgotten what you said about leaving him and, er, it's on my mind, I'm thinking about what you said, you know –'

To her surprise he interrupted, repeating what he'd said to Katherine earlier. 'Don't bother on my account, dear.'

'What do you mean?'

'I couldn't give a flying fuck what you do. Spend the rest of your life with him, if you want.'

'You don't want me to leave him?'

'No, Tara. I couldn't give a fiddler's. Marry him or don't marry him. Stay with him, be a doormat, just like you are now.

It's your life, not mine, so do what you like with it. Waste it –
that's what everyone else does.'

'Oh, right.'

'Life,' Fintan said, heavily, 'is wasted on the living.'

'So I'm in the clear?' Tara asked, tentatively.

'Free to go now and all that.'

'Well, er, that's good, then.' She managed a smile. 'I didn't
know whether it was just Katherine that you'd changed your
mind about. But, well . . . thanks, you know.'

She waited for the burden to roll away from her, she waited
to feel free, soaring, liberated. Everything was all right. She
could stay with Thomas. Fintan had given her his blessing and
she could stay with Thomas as long as she liked.

Yippee, she yelled in her head. She could stay with Thomas
for ever. She could stay with Thomas *for ever*!

Why did that suddenly sound more like a threat than a dream
come true?

56

Joe was waiting in the ticket hall of Finsbury Park tube station as arranged. There were so many people milling around, wearing Arsenal shirts, that for a moment she didn't see him. Then she spotted him leaning against the wall, his hands in his jacket pockets. He wore a pair of faded jeans, tough workman's boots and a big square leather jacket. A lick of dark hair hung on to his forehead and his brown eyes were distant. As she nervously walked towards him his face remained shut, stony almost. She began to regret she'd come.

She was almost nose-to-nose with him before the closed face altered.

'Katherine!' He pushed himself away from the wall, and stood up straight, making him much taller than her. 'I didn't recognize you.

'I didn't recognize you,' he repeated, as, shamelessly, he checked out her hair, her jacket, her jeans, her boots. Shaking his head in disbelief, he exhaled long and hard, lifting the lick of hair from his forehead. 'Wow!'

She squirmed self-consciously. 'I don't look that different.'

'No, but . . .' His grin spread and grew as he didn't even attempt to hide his appreciation.

She flicked a smile at him, then had to look away again, embarrassed, happy. 'Sorry I'm late,' she said.

He looked at his watch and sucked his teeth. 'Three and a

half minutes, Katherine. You really had me worried there.' She had actually. 'But at least you came. This way.' He steered her out into the street. As they walked to the ground, he didn't touch her. No hand-holding or even elbow-guiding. But he stayed close, providing a safe force-field around her. He was as pleasant as he'd been at the height of his niceness to her, but she no longer took it as a reason to be cruel or dismissive of him.

The stadium seemed enormous. After they'd shown their tickets, they had a quick drink in the bar. Then it took nearly ten minutes, jostling with hundreds of others along walkways and up steps, before they emerged into the cold open air, to the sound of chanting, near and far away.

The tickets were numbered and there was a huge canopy to protect against bad weather. All very civilized. A far cry from elbowing on the terraces in the rain, trying to see over other people's heads, as Katherine had initially visualized.

And there were women there – lots of them. She wasn't the only one! Through rows and rows of plastic seats they made their way down and along. When they found their places, they sat side by side, their thighs almost but not quite touching, their arms wedged together, Joe's big black shoulder towering over Katherine's dainty blue one. She was amazed by the number of people there. *Thousands*. Below her, rows and rows of people's heads led down to the pitch. She twisted around for a look behind her and saw acres of torsos forming an almost vertical pattern up to the metal roof. Then she leant forward and watched yards of knees stretching out from her in both directions. The three other stands were packed too, the people so far away that moving en masse they looked like red seaweed in the tide. It was awesome.

The clapping and drumming of feet echoing against the metal roof of the stadium was deafening and somehow primal. Powerful and very macho. Her blood pounded in time to the thundering stamping. She could feel it in her stomach.

Joe turned and murmured, 'OK?'

'OK.' She nodded up at him, with the teeniest of smiles.

'Are you warm enough?'

She nodded again.

'Can you see?'

Another nod.

'Not that there's anything to see yet, of course,' he added.

After a short pause. 'Would you like a hamburger?' he asked. 'Or a look at the programme?'

Joe had gone into a mild panic that maybe Katherine wasn't as thrilled with this date as he was.

Reassured by his anxiety she found herself saying, 'I didn't think it would feel this . . .'

He watched her anxiously. 'This what?'

'Exciting,' she admitted.

Gratitude and gratification rushed through him, filling every corner. He was right, he'd always been right about her! There was untold fire and passion going on beneath her cool exterior. 'You think this is exciting,' he grinned, 'wait till later!'

Startled, she opened her eyes wide. How presumptuous of him!

'After kick-off, I mean,' he stuttered.

The singing started all around her.

'My old man
Said, "Be an Everton fan,"
I said, "Fuck off, bollocks, you're a . . ."'

Luckily Joe didn't sing. She just wasn't sure how she would

have felt about. But the tribal energy was highly potent, very male and sexy. Though the day was cold, it didn't seem to matter.

'Have you been a football fan for a long time?' she asked, shyly.

'Oh, yeah. Long before Nick Hornby made it fashionable for the middle classes. I've been a devoted follower of Torquay United since I was four.'

Katherine thought of Joe as a four-year-old boy and briefly her heart twisted with yearning. 'And are Torquay United good?'

'Christ, no.' He shook his head vehemently and grinned. 'They're . . . How shall I put it? Success-challenged. Or maybe it's talently challenged. They're only in the third division.'

'So why do you support them? Sticking up for the underdog?'

Again he shook his head. 'Nah. It's a question of where you're born and brought up. I'm from Torquay so I don't get any choice in the matter.'

'Kismet.' She understood.

'That's right.' What a woman! 'Destiny. Fate.' Every other woman he knew, no matter where they were from, supported Manchester United and wanted him to also. He gave her a sidelong smile. Every time they made eye-contact, her stomach squeezed with nervy pleasure.

'So why are we at an Arsenal match?' she asked.

'Because when I first moved to London, traipsing down to Devon every other weekend just wasn't on. And I happened to be living a hundred yards from the Arsenal ground and seeing some football was better than nothing . . .'

'I see,' Katherine said, sternly. 'So it's not because you love Arsenal as such?'

'I do now.' He hurried to reassure her. 'But, back then, I was anybody's.' He crinkled his eyes at her. 'But, hey, I was young, merely a boy. I knew nothing about loyalty.'

'And you're mature now?' Katherine smiled back at him.

'Oh, very.'

'Glad to hear it,' she said solemnly.

'And though it was a slow burner, eventually I fell in love.' He swallowed and added hastily, 'With Arsenal, I mean.'

The pitch stretched ahead of them, enormous, emerald green, stripy and, as yet, empty.

'We should be about to start,' Joe said. And he turned, casually picked up her arm and looked at her watch. It was a nothing gesture, what anyone would do to anyone. But it was the closest, most intimate thing Joe had ever done to her. Her breath caught in her chest, as his chilled fingers closed around and held her wrist. But then he said, 'Thanks,' gently let her go and it was over. It took a while for her breathing to return to normal.

Suddenly a charge seemed to run through the air. 'Here we go,' Joe said quietly to her while, as one, the entire stand stood up, clapping, whistling and cheering. Apparently the Arsenal team had run on to the pitch, but all Katherine could see was the backs and heads of people in front of her. Then, from the booing and catcalls, she concluded that the Everton boys had arrived.

They sat down again and from the moment the game started the atmosphere in the entire stand tightened up, becoming electric with expectation and tension. The dormant aggression became overt and the thrill beneath Katherine's skin was pleasantly just the right side of fear.

'The team in the red and white are our boys,' Joe murmured to her.

'I know!' Tara had conveyed the basics.

'Nice one,' Joe praised. This got better and better.

The man on Katherine's other side was a diehard who seemed to have a personal grudge against Everton. Repeatedly he leapt to his feet and roared, '*Come and have a go if you think you're hard enough!*'

When Everton missed an open goal he burst into lusty and triumphant song. '*Score in a brothel,*' he roared. '*You couldn't score in a brothel. Score in a bro-oth-el. You couldn't score in a brothel.*'

Then to Katherine's alarm, he elbowed her and said, 'Come on, gewl, sing along. Everton bastards, *Score, in a brothel . . .*'

'Sore throat,' she murmured. 'Can't.'

Joe didn't sing, but he was very focused and genuinely interested in what was going on. Katherine felt she should resent this – after all, why had he taken her if he'd planned to ignore her? – but she couldn't get cross. His eyes were narrowed, flicking around, following the ball. Joe watched the match and Katherine watched Joe, his knife-handle cheekbones, his touch-me skin, his messier-than-at-work hair. Repeatedly he checked that she was all right. He was worried that she might be chilly but, though her cheeks had pinkened from the cold, it didn't seem to matter.

Twenty minutes into the match, he shifted to her, bulky in his leather jacket. 'You OK?' he asked for the umpteenth time.

'Yes.' She flashed her little teeth prettily.

'I can't hear you,' he said, quietly, angling his face towards hers. 'Come closer.'

Thinking it was because of all the singing around them, she leant nearer and repeated, 'I said, yes.'

'I still can't hear you,' he echoed softly, his eyes dark. 'Closer.'

Embarrassed at invading his personal space, she moved slightly more towards him, and said, 'Yes, I'm OK.'

She was so close that she could see beneath his skin to where his stubble was growing in a mask around his jaw and mouth.

'Still can't hear you,' he said again. By now his voice was nearly soundless, so that she was almost lip-reading.

Baffled, she pushed herself an inch or so further, so that they were breathing each other's air, and reiterated, 'I'm OK.'

'Still can't hear you,' he mouthed.

There was about four inches between them, his warm apple-sweet breath surprising her chilled face. She couldn't move any closer. Utterly still, their eyes locked, intensity in his, confusion in hers. And then she understood . . .

Somewhere, in another dimension, Everton missed another open goal and as her ears filled with the sound of thirty thousand Arsenal fans singing tunelessly, *You're shi-i-i-it and you know you are,* Joe Roth moved a short, short distance, darkening her vision. And kissed her.

57

Rob would have wept if he'd thought that his precious ticket had been frittered away by the occupant of his seat spending the entire match snogging. Luckily for him, they kissed only once.

But, as Katherine thought, what a kiss!

Her eyes were closed, her hands were on Joe's face, pinpricks of stubble dragging on the pads of her fingers. A special, lime-sharp, clean-man smell reached her, and she noticed, from some remote place, how firm and dry his lips were. He clasped her nearer, his hand cradling the back of her silky head, and the kiss hardened and deepened, the heat of their fevered mouths contrasting with the coldness of their faces, making it all the more secret and delicious.

But, too soon, it stopped. Reluctantly they opened their eyes, and pulled away from each other, teetering on the edge of too much want. Reality came back into focus.

'Sorry, I shouldn't have . . . This isn't the right place,' Joe mumbled, his eyes opaque and stunned.

'You're right,' she agreed, stupefied. Baffled at finding that they weren't the only two people in the world.

They watched the rest of the match in a twilight agony of waiting. Apparently Arsenal won.

Then they got a taxi back to her place.

As soon as they were there, Katherine felt panicky. It was

only five thirty, way too early for shenanigans. This was a mistake.

His presence filled her flat, and she wanted him to go. She hated feeling that she had a tiger by the tail, that she'd bitten off more than she could chew.

'That's the living-room,' she fluttered, her nerves getting the better of her, 'Sit down and I'll put the kettle –'

She stopped abruptly as Joe put his fingers into the belt-loop of her jeans. 'Come here,' he said softly, pulling her towards him. She felt the tug, felt her feet moving across to him, felt her body arrive next to his. Silently, she watched the intimate, meaningful look as he lowered his face. Her skin was warmed by the heat of his sweet breath, then his mouth was on hers.

As she closed her eyes, she felt her body blossom like a flower. *It's too soon*, she told herself, trying to want to stop. *It's too soon and I'll stop in a minute.*

But it was Joe who severed them. Trying to get his heart-rate back to normal, he smiled ruefully. 'I'll have you know I never sleep with someone on the first date.'

'Neither do I,' she said, haughtily.

'Lucky we're going on our second one later today, then, isn't it?' Joe grinned.

'Don't presume for one moment –'

'I'm not,' he said quickly, contritely. 'Believe it or not, I was joking.'

'Oh. So you *do* sleep with people on the first date?'

'No, I . . . Oh, I see, another joke.' And they smiled at each other.

'So about this second date?' she asked, smoothly.

'Well, I said I'd feed you.'

'And?'

'I thought we'd go out. Up for that?'

'Out where?'

'Er . . . the Ivy,' he said, embarrassed by his lavishness.

But she just said, 'Fine. But would it be OK if I see you there?'

The thought of him waiting while she got ready was an intimacy that she just wasn't ready for yet.

He looked disappointed, but said, 'The table's booked for eight. See you, then.'

He kissed her cheek, and as soon as the door had closed behind him, she did a most unKatherine-like dance in the hallway. She knew how hard it was to get a table at the Ivy.

Then she ran into her bedroom and pulled yet another bag from under the bed and unfolded a black, tight-sleeved, tailored dress. You wouldn't exactly call it short, but it was short for *her*. After all, he was taking her to the Ivy, fair was fair.

In trembling anticipation she put her nail through the first pair of 7-denier black stockings. Luckily she was the kind of woman who always had several new pairs in her drawer. Then, in a fit of indecisiveness, she spent several seconds dithering between high-heeled black satin ankle boots and a pair of black patent sandals and finally decided on the boots because the sandals made her feel too vulnerable. Then the most excellent Jil Sander coat that she'd got in the January sales and she was ready.

She couldn't resist ringing Tara. She knew she'd be mad keen to know how everything was going. But when the phone was answered Katherine thought she must have dialled the wrong number. She didn't recognize the hoarse, incoherent voice that gasped, 'Hello.'

'Tara?' she asked hesitantly.

'Oh, Katherine.' The voice collapsed.

Then Katherine realized that it *was* Tara, and that she was crying so hard she could hardly speak. 'What's wrong? Is it Fintan?'

'No, it's nothing, really.'

'It can't be nothing.'

'It's just Thomas. He's such a prick.'

'What's he done?' Katherine was horrified. She wouldn't put it past Thomas to do something like have an affair.

'He's just a complete prick.'

'Yes, but . . .' Katherine didn't know what to say. Of *course* Thomas was a prick. Nothing new there. Something else must have happened. 'He's not having an affair, is he?'

'Why? Do you think there's another woman in the world as stupid as me? Oh, I've just remembered,' Tara interrupted, tearfully. 'You're on the date. Please tell me this is a happy phone call. Is it going well?'

'Never mind that. Tell me what's happened.'

'Tomorrow. Please, Katherine, I honestly want to know if it's going well.'

'He's kissed me twice and he's taking me to the Ivy for dinner.'

'The Ivy! I'm so glad, he obviously means business.' Tara made a big effort to sound cheerful. 'When you're having the double chocolate mousse spare a thought for me.'

'You don't want me to come over to you?' Katherine crossed her fingers, her arms, her legs and tried to do her toes, then clenched her eyes in fervent prayer.

Even Tara managed a little laugh. 'As if.'

'But will you be OK?'

'Certainly I will. I'm sorry if I've messed with your buzz.

Have a wonderful, wonderful time tonight and insist on your conjugals.'

'If you're sure . . .'

'I swear on my granny's life, I'm sure.'

When the taxi dropped Katherine outside the Ivy, it was just gone eight and she made herself go for a walk. It was OK waiting in a restaurant on her own when she was meeting the likes of Tara, but this was different. With great effort of will she managed to be a full ten minutes late. Not exactly super-model-petulance, but groundbreaking for her all the same.

'I'm meeting a Mr Roth,' she told the maître d'.

He checked the list, then he checked it again. 'I'm sorry, there's no table in the name of Roth.'

Katherine's stomach yawned with fear. Panicking she looked around the room and, with frantic relief, saw Joe sitting at a table behind a partition. He'd just seen her too and had hastily got up.

'Oh, there he is, it's OK.' She smiled, indicating Joe.

'That's Mr Stallone,' said the maître d', his face unreadable.

'Is it . . . ?'

Joe had reached them.

'Your guest has arrived, Mr Stallone,' the maître d' said politely.

'Er, yes, thank you. This way, Katherine.'

'Mr Stallone?' Katherine whispered, as Joe held her chair for her.

'It was the only way I could get a table at such short notice,' he muttered.

There was a tiny, stunned pause, then a heave of mirth burst up through her. 'Mr Stallone,' she exploded, and began to laugh and couldn't stop, doubled on to the table, crying tears of hilarity. Patiently, indulgently, he watched her. 'Oh, God,' she wheezed, wiping under her eyes. 'I haven't laughed so much in years.'

'I'd hoped you wouldn't find out. I was keeping an eye out for you but that bloody great partition blocked the view.'

'I'm *delighted* I found out.' She leant across the table towards him, her face radiant with sincerity. 'I swear to God.'

The menus came and they ordered their food and wine.

Though there was so much that they didn't know about each other, they mostly talked about their food. He described his deep-fried Brie to her and she told him all she could about the warm bacon salad she'd ordered. *Almost like a conversation I'd have with Tara or Fintan*, Katherine thought in surprise. *Especially Tara.*

This didn't seem like a bad thing.

When the main course arrived, Katherine asked, genuinely interested, 'Is your sole nice?'

'Yes,' said Joe. 'Would you like some?' He was already proffering his fork at her.

'Er . . . no.' She squirmed, heat in her cheeks.

'Go on,' he urged, in a low voice. 'It's delicious.'

'That's one of the corniest lines I've heard in a long time,' she said, embarrassment making her want to deflate him. But it didn't.

'Go on,' he repeated.

And aroused by his voice and the intimacy of the gesture, Katherine leant forward and let Joe put his fork in her mouth.

'Nice?' Joe asked her, meaningfully.

'Nice,' she agreed, shyly.

He watched every mouthful that she ate, focused on her

434

mouth as she put food into it, his eyes warm on her lips as she chewed. She was embarrassed and aroused, and after the main course had to escape to the ladies' for a breather from the sexual tension at the table.

At pudding time, in honour of Tara, she had the double chocolate mousse. As she was sliding a spoonful of white and dark chocolate into her mouth, she looked up and found Joe watching her intensely. The combination of the chocolate exploding on her tongue and the promise in his look, made her tingle like she'd just had a mini-orgasm.

Her body prickled with such anticipation she was almost afraid. It might happen tonight. It really might.

58

Afterwards they stood outside in the cold night.

What now?

'We could have coffee at my place?' Joe suggested.

'In Battersea?' she replied, her tone implying that it was a ridiculous notion. Reclaiming her right to be a schoolmarm.

'Why not?' he asked, seemingly unfazed by her derision.

Make him wait, she begged herself. *Make him wait. Don't give it away too easily.*

'No,' she said.

Watching his anticipatory smile fade away gave her a moment of fierce pleasure before she said, 'We'll go to my place instead.'

In the taxi they held hands in silence. Without speaking she let them into her flat, then carefully shut the door. And prepared to embark on the first carnal knowledge she'd had of a man in over two years.

It was as if they'd been catapulted at each other. Immediately, still in their coats, standing right beside the front door, they were in each other's arms, kissing frantically, desperately. She was barely aware of Joe deftly removing her coat, which fell in an abandoned crumple on the hall floor, before he steered her into the living-room and to the couch. Still kissing her, he put gentle pressure on her shoulders and forced her down, so that she was lying on her back. Then he kissed her for what seemed like several hours. Every time she tried to sit up or speak to him he'd force her back on to the couch and start again. He devoted himself to it, to her. *Kissing is an art form in itself*, she thought, in a daze. *Not just a precursor to the main event.*

She had her eyes closed and felt as if she'd gone into a trance. Deep inside her head she was flying, over fields of colour, over landscapes of stars. Who needs drugs? she thought.

It was a long time since she'd been kissed like that. Well, it was a long time since she'd been kissed *at all*. How could she have lived without it?

She barely knew where she was and when she opened her eyes she was surprised by the mundanity of her living-room.

All the time he was kissing her he touched and stroked her, slowly, maddeningly. Feathery circles with his long, sensitive fingers on her skin, her face, her neck, her arms. Then he was caressing her stomach through her dress, and then slowly moved higher to her ribcage. And then higher still until he was almost at her breasts. Beneath her lacy bra her nipples made two tents. They were shrieking for his touch, but instead he stroked underneath her breast and then the softness of the side, then around to the hollow of her cleavage. In slowly decreasing circles, he began to move inwards until he was touching the mound of her right breast. Slowly, too slowly, he kept moving inwards, inching across the tight fabric. When, after what seemed like hours, he reached her nipple and gently flicked it with his forefinger, she felt as if she'd come.

He lay half on half off her and his erection dug into her hipbone. It was excruciatingly pleasurable.

When he put his hand on her leg and moved it up under her skirt and when he found that she was – as he'd hoped – wearing stockings instead of tights, his mastery nearly deserted him.

He started circling her thighs. First the front, then the outside, then dipping into the soft virgin skin of her inner thighs, before moving back to the front again.

'No,' he chided, as she began to buck her hips, and he forced them back on to the couch, with the palm of his hand pressed against her pubic bone. Again, sweet pleasure rippled through her.

She itched to touch him, to splay her fingers between his ribs, to stroke his stomach with her thumb, to feel the muscles in his thighs. With fumbling fingers she undid his shirt buttons, then shifted, sat up and placed her hands flat against the crispness of his chest hair. To his surprise she pushed him so that he was lying flat on the couch and she was looking down on him.

They smiled silently, dazedly, at each other.

His shirt was all undone and there was something about the way his hollowed-out belly created a gap between the waistband of his jeans that made Katherine slip her hand in. Laying the palm of her hand against the frayed-rope line of hair on his stomach, and then with a little swivel, moving her fingers slightly lower. And lower still. And then into contact with his pubic hair.

He groaned and murmured, 'Katherine . . .'

Looking into her eyes he barely recognized her as the buttoned-up girl he worked with. She was a predatory woman.

Again he began to kiss her and turned her around so that once more she was the one underneath. But she couldn't wait any longer.

'Please,' she begged, tugging at her dress and trying to shuffle it up around her waist. He stood up and quickly undid his belt and buttons and stepped out of his jeans, underpants and socks.

His skin was moonstone translucent, so pale that the darkness of his pubic hair came as a shock against it. His waist was tiny, his stomach concave and tugged-looking, as if there wasn't enough skin to stretch all the way down to his groin. His thighs were long and lean, his hips as narrow as hers, his erection taut and quivery. He was beautiful.

He helped her out of her dress but, with silent, mutual consent, they left her underwear on. Joe knelt with one leg between both of hers as he snapped on a condom, then he pulled her lace panties to one side. As he slid into her and lowered his heavy weight down on top of her, Katherine thought she'd died and gone to heaven.

Afterwards he was full of wonder. 'I never thought this would happen,' he declared, looking down at her.

'Didn't you?' she asked neutrally.

'I was crazy about you for so long and I can't actually believe . . .'

In silence they lay in each other's arms, until Katherine began to feel his hands moving over her again. Gently he snapped open her bra, unhooked her stockings, took off her suspender belt and panties then, leaving their clothing strewn all around the already shambolic living-room, they went to the bedroom where they made love for a second time.

Afterwards Joe showed no sign of wanting to go to sleep, which suited Katherine.

'Come on.' She poked him.

'Come on where?'

'The bathroom, we'll have a shower.'

'Why? Do you have to go home to your wife?'

'Come on.'

Giggling, they tumbled into the bathroom, where they

climbed into the bath and Katherine handed him a sponge and a tube of shower gel. 'Wash me.'

'OK,' he said, eyeing her slender body, then the sponge. 'But we'll have to get you wet first.'

He turned on the jet of hot water and pulled Katherine under it. The silent, speculative way he looked at her body, at the shower water sluicing down the curve of her breasts and over the peak of her nipples and the appraising way he squeezed the shower gel on to the sponge, was charged with eroticism.

'You're filthy,' he said, sternly.

'I know.' She could hardly speak.

Slowly, he began to apply the sponge to her shiny-wet body, to circle it over her stomach, her arms, her legs. Then her breasts, soaping them until her skin was slippery. 'Particularly grubby here,' he said.

'I know,' she gasped.

He moved the sponge to between her legs and she squirmed with desire. 'Stand still,' he ordered.

She tried, but the firm, relentless massage was irresistible. The warm water, his wet body, her slick skin became too much for them both.

With her back against the cold wall tiles, her legs around his waist, Joe entered her again. For a few blissful moments they clung together, teeth gritted from desire, while he rhythmically stroked himself into her. Until he lost his footing on the wet bath and they both tumbled to the floor where, sprawled and tangled, still clinging to each other, they laughed their heads off.

The morning after, Katherine woke early. She turned to the pillow next to her and there he was. Joe. Joe Roth. Joe Roth from work. Without his suits. In her bed. Asleep and beautiful, his eyelashes thick, the beginnings of stubble poking through his jaw, the room filled with the smell of his *otherness*.

The thrill was like waking up on Christmas morning to find that Santa has been.

I won't mess this up, I won't mess this up, I won't . . . she repeated over and over again in her head.

She knew this was the trickiest moment. Tara assured her it was difficult no matter who you were. But Katherine felt it was especially hard for someone like her, whose most alluring feature to men was her aloofness. Which disappeared as soon as she'd slept with them – it was kind of hard to have sex with someone and remain untouchable and icy. Not if you want to enjoy it, in any case. But, very often, men who'd chased Katherine for weeks and even months, maddened by her unattainability, found that after they'd screwed her, they lost interest. Her mystique dissolved and she was suddenly just an ordinary woman. Toppled from her pedestal and fighting for her man on the same terms as everyone else.

Worse still, the contact would have rekindled old fires in Katherine. No doubt about it, it was a delicate time.

Joe opened his eyes, his eyelids languid, his look meaningful. 'Hi,' he said, groggily.

'Hi,' she whispered.

'What a lovely sight first thing in the morning.' He reached out his hand and pulled her to him under the crumple of duvet. Her heart swelled as she felt the heat of his body. Chest against chest, the smooth skin of her leg rubbing against the hairs on his. She closed her eyes to savour the softness of his morning-languourous caresses and when they made love it was slower, more lazy and sensuous than it had been the previous night.

Afterwards Joe went to the bathroom while Katherine frantically raked her hands through her hair, then swept her fingers under her eyes to remove any rogue bits of mascara. When Joe returned, he looked uncertain. Thoughtfully he rubbed his hand across his mouth, stretching and pulling his skin out of shape, then letting it spring back.

'I suppose I should be off,' he said, questioningly.

'I suppose you should,' Katherine said, with an enigmatic smile. But she was bitterly disappointed. What about the croissants, the freshly squeezed orange juice and the white linen napkins on the gilt tray, like the ads promised? Shouldn't she be wearing a pyjama top and Joe the bottoms? Shouldn't she be sinking back into goose-down pillows, Joe bending over, feeding her spoonfuls of yoghurt? Then putting a blob of it on the tip of her nose, both of them laughing with crinkle-eyed joy?

Then shouldn't they go for a walk, holding hands, feeding the ducks, their lovers' laughter ringing across the park? Shouldn't Katherine dip her toe into the water, and wear a stupid hat which only stayed on by her holding her hand on the crown of her head?

Joe left the bedroom and when he returned he was dressed. This made her feel horribly empty.

'I'll call you,' he promised.

'Will you?' Katherine smirked sagely. So that if he had no intention, she was letting him know, and thereby keeping her dignity intact. And if he genuinely meant to call her, then she was giving him some of the mysterious Katherine he was so keen on. Christ, it was exhausting!

'And of course I'll see you at work,' he said.

'I've no doubt you will,' she agreed, lightly.

'And thank you for a wonderful evening. And day,' he added.

She inclined her head graciously. 'Don't mention it.'

The slamming of the door behind him was echoed by a thunderclap of bleakness deep within her. Was that it?

But at least she'd kept the floodtide of need at bay. Better. Better than the last time. Maybe she'd finally grown out of it. If she had, she acknowledged ruefully, it had taken twelve long years.

59

First cut is the deepest. And Katherine's was deeper than most. She'd been nineteen the first time her heart was broken – quite old; maybe that had been part of the trouble. Then, not even a full month later, she wrote to her father and found out he had died. Thus crystallizing her pain.

So, the following week, when Tara said, 'Fintan and I have enough money saved to leave Knockavoy. We think you should come with us,' Katherine felt she'd been thrown a lifeline. On the one hand her life was over, so technically it didn't matter where she eked out her days. But the idea of escape was a wildly inviting one.

'Where are you going?' she'd demanded.

'To a faraway city,' Tara had tempted.

'Not Limerick?' Katherine's voice had quaked.

'Jesus, no. Further afield.'

'Dublin?'

'Further afield again,' Tara had swaggered.

'Not . . . not New York?' Katherine could hardly contain her excitement.

'Er . . . no . . . not New York.' Tara had been slightly shame-faced. 'But how would London suit you?'

Katherine would have preferred it if it was further. Like Los Angeles. Or Wellington. Or the moon. But London would do.

Early on the morning of 3 October 1986 the three of them

arrived at Euston station, bought an *Evening Standard* and landed a flat in Willesden Green.

During the following week Tara got a job with a computer company, Fintan found employment on the shop-floor of an expensive menswear emporium, Katherine got a placement as a trainee accountant and their new life began.

There were lots of men in London. Lots and lots of men. Tara and Fintan had rolled up their sleeves and set about working their way through them, but Katherine had kept her distance. It was no hardship for her. But her lack of interest wasn't always reciprocated. Though she wasn't exactly fighting them off with sticks, she was occasionally asked out. Without it costing her a thought she always said no, as unpleasantly as she could. No one asked a second time.

Until one Friday night, fourteen months after her arrival in London, Katherine went to the pub with Tara's workmates. Among the people she was introduced to was a man called Simon Armstrong, the official office heart-throb. Confident, charming, well-built, good-looking and blond, he enjoyed great success with women. But Katherine barely noticed him. It was as if she had a blind spot. With his acute antennae, Simon picked up on her *genuine* lack of interest in him – you can't fake these things. He could have had any of the women present, but contrarily he wanted Katherine, intrigued and maddened by her unavailability, his ego telling him he'd be the man to get behind her mask – that he *had* to be.

Katherine wasn't as sleek and beautiful as the women he usually dated but, somehow, that made it even more important to win her. He found himself going after her, blocking her way, and grinning. 'Resistance is futile.'

The other girls there looked on in disbelief, scorning

Katherine's neat hair and her ordered, unremarkable appearance. 'Maybe she reminds him of his mother,' they concluded.

Simon got her work number from Tara and rang and asked her out. She said no. So he rang again. Again she said no. He told her he didn't take no for an answer.

Katherine was initially alarmed by his attention. And then she was flattered. And then she was excited. The bombardment of Simon's attentions managed to break through her protective walls and old, buried desires came bobbing to the surface. She wanted to be loved. And if she could make things work with this Simon Armstrong, her life would get back on the right track. All's well that ends well.

So she went on a date with him. Then another. Then another. After three weeks she slept with him. As she left his bed he said he'd call her that evening, but he didn't. So she called him early – too early – the following day. And, trying to keep the tremor from her voice, suggested that they go out that night. When Simon gave an evasive answer, she begged, her eyes clenched shut, 'Please don't do this to me.' Which, of course, had Simon running for the hills.

He'd lost interest, anyway. She was too young and inexperienced, not tough enough, and he'd hung on merely for the notch-on-the-bedpost bonk. All he'd really liked about her was her unavailability and once he'd slept with her that had disappeared immediately. Though slim and pretty, she was no stunna and Simon Armstrong liked stunnas. Not to mention that he was picking up very needy signals from her, which made him itchy and uncomfortable.

He knew an obsessive when he facilitated one.

In the weeks and months that followed, Katherine was like a shell-shock victim. She couldn't believe she'd been dumped again. It seemed that her ability to handle men had worsened, if anything, and she felt more out of control than ever.

That was the last time she'd ever go out with a man, she swore to herself. She'd really learnt her lesson this time.

Over the next couple of years her life came together for her. She worked hard, passed accountancy exams, lived with Fintan and Tara, watched their romantic exploits with a wry smile, but steered well clear of any liaisons herself. Not that you'd know she'd opted out of love: she still bought trendy – though not too trendy – clothes, spent a lot of money on her hair, talked to men in a light-hearted, distant way and went partying every time her flatmates did. The only difference was that she always went home alone.

Until she met Alex Holst.

It was almost four years since she'd moved to London. Fintan had just started work for Carmella Garcia, and Alex was one of the models. He had a stubbly jaw, perfectly capped teeth, raven's-wing hair, and a dancing, mischievous smile. But to his alarm, when he was introduced to Katherine, her eyes didn't light up with a lascivious gleam. She was polite but not really present, and this completely unnerved him. His ravenous ego needed her adoration.

He was incredibly insecure, having spent his childhood as an overweight blimp. Via the twin tools of weightlifting and bulimia he was now lean and beautiful, but he hadn't made the emotional shift. In his own head, he was still a mountain of lard, ostracized and ridiculed. As Katherine moved away from him, the chant of, 'You're nothing but a fat bastard,' started internally.

He was gentler than Simon had been, but just as persistent. He kept up a steady flow of phone calls, sent her flowers at work and wrote her a poem, telling her that she was the most interesting and intriguing woman he'd ever met.

And Katherine resisted a lot harder than she had with Simon. When Alex told her that he never usually pursued women so relentlessly, she sneered, 'I bet you say that to all the girls.'

When he swore to her that he wasn't a womanizer, she laughed nastily and said, 'You must take me for a fool.'

When he decided to surprise her one night by waiting outside her office, she told him coldly that stalking was a criminal offence.

But he didn't give up and she began to soften. She couldn't help herself. His attention was so seductive and she started to believe his protestations of devotion. Because she so desperately wanted to. Then one night he told her about the shame of his tubby past, and the last of her barriers was washed away in a tide of compassion.

As with Simon, Alex became an opportunity to fix where she'd gone wrong. And in the end, begging herself, steeling herself, gritting her teeth and swearing to God that she wouldn't act needy in any way, she went out with Alex.

It lasted slightly longer than the Simon encounter, but sooner rather than later, she sensed a slipping away of his interest. When she questioned him on it, he denied that he was any less ardent than he'd been all along, but she didn't believe him. She watched herself mutate from a breezy, self-contained young woman to a desperate, paranoid, insecure obsessive. And she could do nothing to stop herself. She accused Alex of looking at other girls and of not really caring about her. He protested, not very convincingly, that he did care about her, but then he didn't ring for three days. And when he finally did, it was to tell her that he was seeing someone else.

All her old wounds were torn open. The mortifying feeling that she wasn't good enough and the huge gaping ache of loss reappeared. Back she went into the pit of self-hatred. The pain was unbearable. She felt like a fool and a terrible failure.

Eventually, she righted herself. And though she swore she'd never, ever again, for as long as she lived, have anything to do with a man, she wasn't convinced. She'd sabotaged herself twice now. She lived in terror of doing it again.

When she was between men, her life was nice and ordered. She became a fully qualified accountant, she bought her beloved car; eventually she bought her own flat. As she became more confident in her professional life she transformed herself from fresh-faced girl to sleek child-woman.

But the desire for love was relentless. It kept coming back at her like a boomerang. Reappearing every so often, usually when she was being wooed by a good-looking man.

'Maybe you shouldn't go out with such hunks,' Tara had suggested gently. 'Usually they're so in love with themselves they've none left over for anyone else.'

'I don't want to talk about it,' Katherine snapped.

'I know.' Tara sighed.

Katherine couldn't go out with ordinary blokes. She just couldn't. They held no interest for her.

She had slept with six men before Joe. The longest 'romance' lasted seven weeks, and all six of the men dumped her. Not once did she get what she so desired – the upper hand.

In the end the fear of being left made her desperate to pre-empt it. She couldn't bear waiting for the man to gradually go off her as soon as he realized she was just an ordinary woman and not the mysterious enigma he'd expected. So she precipitated it. Began behaving like a psycho bitch from hell.

All the better to hasten the inevitable. She lurched through life, long tracts of celibacy intercut with short-lived romance, followed by lengthy periods of wound-licking. Every time a man lost interest in her, and implied that she wasn't good enough, it triggered an avalanche of old pain.

In saner moments she knew she was stuck in the past and that she wasn't normal. It had taken her until four years ago, aged twenty-seven, to wonder if perhaps it was the discovery of her father's death so soon after her first heartbreak that had knocked her so far off course. After all, everyone gets ditched at some stage. Only the truly weird don't get over it. But the double wound had the effect of bricking her in, of keeping her stuck. Somehow twelve years had passed, and when she thought about it, she really couldn't figure out where the time had gone.

Then came that day, two months ago, when she'd been introduced to the new account director, Joe Roth, and he'd begun to rain attention down on top of her in a way that was frighteningly familiar.

60

But this time I behaved myself, Katherine thought, with pride, looking around at her rumpled bed. The emptiness left by Joe's departure had evaporated and she was skittish and overexcited after her night with him.

She picked up a pillow, pressed it to her face, and caught a faint whiff of him. A thrill of memory charged her and she wriggled with glee. She was *dying* to talk about it. It was nearly midday – too early to ring Tara?

Oh, Jesus – Tara! Whatever had happened to her yesterday? Katherine grabbed the phone, but just got Tara's answering-machine. So she tried her mobile and got her voicemail. Next she rang Liv and got *her* answering-machine. She left a message and then rang Fintan.

'Hello,' he barked.

'It's me. Will I come over?'

'Not now. This evening.'

'Oh. OK. I'll have my mobile if you change your mind.'

She felt at an unexpectedly loose end. This was the first Sunday in what seemed like months that the O'Gradys weren't staying with her. She wasn't used to having free time. Especially when the best part of the day had already happened.

She could have scrubbed her flat from top to bottom, but felt too buzzed up to do anything boring. Or she could have spent the day sprawled in front of the telly on an omnibus binge. But she fancied that her remote control was looking accusingly at her. Worse still, she had an urge to apologize and to reassure it that she still loved it. So she drove into town and went to Selfridges but instead of making for the clothes, found herself wandering around the men's toiletries department. Idly she picked up an aftershave, sniffed it, then put it down again. Then another. Then another. Vaguely, she worked her way from counter to counter until she picked one bottle up, sniffed it and nearly fainted. All the lust and longing of the previous night returned in a rush. She inhaled it again, deeper this time, her eyes closed in remembrance. Gorgeous! And again. She could feel his skin, the excitement that had thrashed about in her like a caged bird, the way he'd made her feel adored and cherished. She opened her eyes and looked at it. Davidoff For Men, so that was what Joe Roth wore. She half played with buying a bottle of it, but managed not to. That kind of behaviour was for mad people. Smelling it was OK, but buying a bottle was just too sad.

'You're looking at a fallen woman,' Katherine declared, swaddled in a loved-up glow.

'I don't want to hear,' Fintan said haughtily.

'Well, I do,' Tara insisted, pale and exhausted-looking.

'And we do,' Liv and Milo chorused.

'And so do I,' poor oppressed Sandro admitted.

It was later the same day, they were gathered in Fintan's and the pizzas were on their way.

Despite her lack of sleep and the worry that Joe mightn't ring again, Katherine was buzzing with super-alert glee. Bursting with desire to relive the entire fabulous experience.

As she related the whole story – the football match, the kiss, dinner at the Ivy, the Mr Stallone drama – everyone interrupted with detailed questions.

'What did he smell like?' Tara asked.

'And how did you feel?' Milo interjected.

'Who made the first move?' Sandro quizzed.

'Did you know he was going to kiss you?' Liv interrogated.

'Did you have the chocolate mousse?' Tara wanted to know.

'And he paid the bill while you were at the ladies'?' Liv said.

'Were you nervous?' Sandro wondered.

'Did he admire your knickers?' Tara asked.

'Do you have the address of Agent Provocateur?' Milo inquired.

At every detail they gasped and wriggled with relish while Katherine screamed with delight.

'This is as good as sex,' Tara yelped, then slumped into a brief, silent sadness. She had refused to tell Katherine what had upset her the previous day. 'I really don't want to talk about it. God,' she'd added, in wonder, 'I'm turning into you.'

Throughout Katherine's story Fintan lay on the couch in a Mary Quant wig, his expression curdled and sulkily uninterested. But as the story hotted up, he cocked his ear (the lower one) with reluctant attention. Then he sat up, then leant forward, then made involuntary whistles and 'oohs', then he just couldn't help demanding, 'And you left your lovely black Jil Sander coat flung on the hall floor all night?'

Katherine nodded, proud and embarrassed.

'*All* night?'

Another smirky nod.

'You didn't sneak out between bonks to hang it up on its special hanger?'

A triumphant shake of Katherine's head.

'Well, it was last season's, I suppose,' Fintan said. 'But all the *same.*'

No one could believe how much Katherine told. When she got to the part where Joe stood in the middle of the floor and took off all his clothes, everyone clutched each other and shrieked, 'Oh, my GOD!'

'Shagtastic!' Tara screeched.

'Babelicious!' Liv roared.

The bell rang. The pizzas had arrived. Sandro nearly exploded with frustration. 'What a time they pick,' he complained. 'You mustn't say anything, not a single word, until I return,' he ordered Katherine, then ran, fussing and puffing, to the door. When he returned, his face almost obscured by the tower of pizza boxes, he demanded, muffled but anxious, 'Did I miss anything?'

'No, but it's time for *Ballykissangel*,' Liv felt she had better point out.

There was a vocal chorus of, 'Bollocks to that! This is far more interesting. Carry on, Katherine. So there he was larging it, buck-naked, in your living-room . . .'

'Larging it is right.' She laughed, in shivery elation.

'Oooooohhhhh, Missus!'

She even spilt the beans about the middle-of-the-night shower. 'A shower! Oh, Matron!' they gasped.

Milo and Liv exchanged a searing look.

'I shouldn't really be saying all this,' Katherine admitted. 'He might never ring me again. It's happened before.'

'Well, if he doesn't ring, then you ring him,' Tara urged.

'No, I don't think . . .'

With almost indecent haste, Milo and Liv were gathering up

their things. In a flurry of hurried thanks and 'byes, they were gone.

'But we got a good hour out of them before they had to leave and have sex,' Tara remarked.

'A whole hour?' Fintan grinned. 'I'd say it's already peaked and they're on the wane.'

Everyone noticed, but tried not to let it show: Fintan had smiled!

'They're just staying together for the sake of the children.' Katherine laughed.

'For the sake of their bedclothes, in any case,' Tara said. 'They bought a new duvet cover yesterday. I believe they're devoted to it.'

'Now, aren't you glad I was a big, bossy bastard?' Fintan slyly asked Katherine. 'Isn't your night of passion down to me, really?'

'I thought you didn't care any more what I do?'

'I don't. Well, I didn't, but seeing as it's been such a success consider me back on the case.'

'Who's to say it's a success? It might just be a one-night stand, made all the worse because I've to work with him.'

'There might be a message on your machine when you get home tonight,' Fintan exclaimed. 'He might be trying to ring this very minute. Does he have your mobile number?'

She shook her head, but she was excited. He *might* ring her tonight. But to her disappointment when she got home, the number of messages on her machine was a big fat zero.

61

'Ravi,' Tara said, 'where would I get a van?'

'A van? Do you mean like a removal van?'

'A smallish one, but that's what I mean.'

'Dunno, we could ask the grown-ups.' He nodded at Vinnie, Teddy and Evelyn.

Suddenly he realized the import of her question and his head jerked up in shock. 'Why? What's happened?'

'First I'll need a fag.'

'To the smoking room!'

Tara sat in the tiny yellow-walled room and sucked hard on a cigarette, watched by Ravi who was vehemently anti-smoking, except when it was Tara who was doing it.

'Are you going to leave Thomas?' Ravi couldn't believe it.

'I think I am.'

'But why?'

Tara managed a wry half-smile. 'Oh, Ravi. Even *you've* tried to tell me that things with Thomas are as dodgy as anything, and you're a boy!'

'Yes, but you've always been able to give a reason for his dodginess.'

Tara winced. 'God, the excuses I've made . . .'

'Are you leaving him only because Fintan wants you to?'

'No, it's because Fintan *doesn't* want me to. He's changed his mind and doesn't give a damn. And I thought I'd be delighted. Well, I should have been, but I wasn't. I felt depressed, and trapped.'

Ravi sighed silently. Women were so bloody complicated.

'Then the minute I got home on Saturday afternoon it all just blew up.'

Tara dragged deep on her cigarette as she remembered the scene. As soon as she'd walked in the door, Thomas had yelled, 'Just because that bludeh pouf has picked up some antisocial disease is no excuse for you to not stick to your diet, Tara.'

He was waving a Turkish Delight wrapper that he'd just found in her gym-bag and a huge, hot bubble of rage had burst in Tara. *What was she doing with this awful man?*

'Excuse me?' she hissed.

'I said,' Thomas repeated, 'just because that bludeh pouf . . .' He'd been pushing and pushing it, becoming more and more unpleasant and controlling, and this time he'd gone too far.

'Don't you dare talk like that about my friend!' Tara said, with low menace.

'But I –'

'Just don't, right!'

'I'm entitled to my opinion,' he demanded, belligerently. 'Aren't I?'

'No! It's cruel and, anyway, it's not an antisocial disease, you make it sound like it's his *fault*.'

'Am I or am I not entitled to my opinion?'

'But –'

'AM I,' he shouted, 'OR AM I NOT entitled to my opinion? Yes or no?'

'It's not a question of opinion.' She raised her voice in response to his.

'Listen to me. He is a bludeh pouf. All I'm talking is the truth.'

'You're a disgusting bigot,' she said, in a deceptively calm voice. 'A caveman with your throwback, time-warp machismo.'

He surprised her by laughing warmly. 'Aye, I am. I like that, say it again, the bit about the machismo.'

Tara swallowed, stunned into silence. A brief window opened: with boyfriends like him, who needed enemies?

'Go on,' he urged, playfully. 'Say it again.'

'It's not a compliment.' Her jaw was clenched.

'Isn't it? Sounds like one. I'm a caveman with my throwback machismo.' He laughed again, genuinely entertained and said. 'But you love me for it.'

This is what you're stuck with.

Each time she'd had a tiny revelation that all wasn't well with herself and Thomas, she'd worked hard to obscure it, to cover her tracks. But every bit of obfuscation had now been washed away by the floodtide of her rage and she had no choice but to see. And what she saw made her despise not only Thomas but herself. She'd always detested homophobics, and here she was living with one! Where were her principles? Sidelined because her desire for a boyfriend was more important.

The dominoes began to fall and suddenly Tara saw, naked and clear, how unforgivable his refusal to meet the O'Gradys had been. His insistence on not visiting Fintan, his filthy innuendo about Fintan's illness, his casual contempt for his future with her, the constant monitoring of her weight, the corrosive criticism of her appearance, the non-stop erosion of her confidence, the relentless borrowing of money, the playing off of Beryl against her. And worst of all were the excuses she had made for him.

She'd always tried to defend Fintan when Thomas started on him. She'd never defended herself. Just tried to tell herself it was for her good. But she'd been wrong, and she was crawling with self-loathing as well as anger.

She found she was crying. Tears of shame and rage and sorrow.

'Why are you boohoohooing?' Thomas demanded. 'Have you the decorators in?'

'What?'

'Is it your monthlies?'

'No.' She sobbed as if her heart were breaking.

'Aw, Tara, don't bludeh cry. Do you want a cup of tea?'

'No. Just leave me alone.'

He glared at her. How dare she? Didn't she know how sensitive he was? 'Fine then,' he swaggered, 'I *will* leave you alone.'

He slammed from the flat and she cried and cried and cried. For the wasted years, for the loss of hope, for the cruelty to Fintan, for her shameful self-delusion, for the happy life she didn't have, for the empty one stretching ahead of her.

At some point Katherine rang but, gasping and choking, Tara could hardly speak.

Lighting a cigarette, she sat staring into space, wondering why nothing ever worked for her. *Why me? Why can't I have a successful relationship? Why do I always end up alone?*

She'd managed to keep one step ahead of the knowledge that had been accreting slowly, especially since Fintan had got sick. But it had become too big and she couldn't outrun it any more.

Had Thomas always been like this? Had he got worse? Or had she just not seen? Refused to see?

She was in shock. Couldn't take it all in. It was her body

trying to protect itself, breaking the news to her gently. She kept trying to tell herself there was nothing to worry about. After all, he'd offered her a cup of tea, maybe he wasn't so bad. But she couldn't unsee what she'd seen, much as she'd like to. The knowledge was a huge burden and she'd have to act on it even though it meant her life was over.

A few hours later Thomas returned and, behaving as if everything was fine, wanted them to go out.

'No,' she said, white-faced and implacable. 'You go.'

She sat in the flat on Saturday night and prepared herself to leave. Trying to bridge the huge gap between knowing she should and actually being able to.

She spent Sunday with Fintan and made no mention of the turmoil she was in. It wasn't that she didn't want to, it was because she wasn't able to. Couldn't put words on the enormousness of the task hanging over her, like an axe waiting to fall.

Instead she watched Milo and Liv, listened to Katherine's glowing tale, and thought, *That's the way it's supposed to be.*

'So, Ravi,' Tara forced a smile, 'now you know why I asked about the van.'

'I'll look up the *Yellow Pages* immediately,' he promised.

'You think I should leave him, don't you?' She buttonholed him anxiously.

'But you've just said . . .'

'I was hoping you'd tell me that I was overreacting wildly.'

'You're not,' he said, sadly.

'I'm so scared.' She thrust a cigarette in her mouth and he lit it for her. 'Of being on my own. Of being old and on the shelf. I'll never get anyone else.'

'Of course you will –'

'How do you know? A fat cow like me. Oh, Ravi, you should have seen Katherine on Saturday. The excitement, and the looking-forwardness. It was wonderful, like being a teenager again, even I could feel it.'

'Yeah, but that mad buzz doesn't last long,' he said anxiously. 'Even Danielle and I –'

'But all the same,' she interrupted, 'if two people are going out with each other, shouldn't they at least like each other?'

'And you don't like Thomas?'

'No. And he doesn't like me. If he did he wouldn't spend so much time telling me I'm a fat cow. Isn't there something wrong with him constantly trying to change me?'

'Yes. Bloody right. I've tried to tell you.'

Tara's face was thoughtful. 'I knew it, but I didn't know it, do you know what I mean?'

'You knew it, but you didn't *want* to know.'

The silent, black and white slow motion of her life suddenly clicked into noisy, normal-speed colour.

The shock was fading, the grief had receded, and all Tara was left with was anger.

Lots of it.

62

When Katherine arrived at work on Monday morning, Joe was already there, but he didn't even look up. So that's how it's going to be, she thought, with unutterable misery. I got it wrong. Again.

Wearily, she hung up her coat and traipsed to her desk. In the centre of which a parcel was placed. Wrapped in blue and gold Designers Guild wrapping paper, it clearly wasn't a batch of new tax tables from the government printing office.

'What's this?' she asked Charmaine.

'Dunno, it was there when I got in.'

Katherine picked it up and felt it. Whatever was inside was soft and bendable.

'Open it,' Charmaine said.

'OK . . .' she said slowly, wondering whether she should be getting excited. Who would send something to her, other than Joe?

Careful not to tear the good paper, Katherine tried to undo the Sellotape.

'Rip it off!' Charmaine urged. 'Go on, girl. Go crazy.'

So she did, and something white and plastic unfolded itself and flopped out.

'Whut the . . . ?' Charmaine demanded.

Katherine looked at it and a broad smile slapped itself on her face.

'*What is it*?' Charmaine was going mental.

'It's a mat to put on the floor of your bath.' Katherine grinned. 'To stop you slipping.'

Under her eyelashes she looked over at Joe, but he was very, very, very focused on whatever was on his screen. Very focused indeed. Katherine could almost see his neck muscles trembling with the exertion of not looking up at her.

'Who's it from?' Charmaine asked suspiciously.

'No idea.'

'No note?'

'No.'

'Weirdos.'

But when Katherine switched on her computer she'd been sent an e-mail. Saying, 'Just so we won't slip next time.'

Quick as a flash she typed in, 'When would you like to not slip?' pressed Send and waited. Then wondered if she'd been too brazen. *Go on*, she silently urged Joe. *Reply to me.*

After about three minutes, she saw him clicking his mouse. Oh, yikes, he was opening the message, he was reading it! Then, his expression remaining resolutely deadpan and smooth, he typed something at high speed.

Katherine impatiently drummed her fingers, desperate for a new message to start flashing. When it did, her heart was pounding. 'Would like to not slip asap. Let me know what suits you,' it said.

She did some frantic calculations and sent back, 'Wednesday night?' She thought that was nice and casual.

Seconds later a new message appeared. 'Am concerned I may slip. Wednesday night very far away.'

'Understand concern. Tomorrow night?' she replied.

'Am concerned I may slip. Tomorrow night very far away,' came the reply.

With fingers shaking with delight Katherine keyed in, 'Understand concern. Tonight may be the safest option.'

Not once had they made eye-contact.

All day they were ultra polite whenever they had any dealings with each other. At one stage Joe was coming into the office while Katherine was going out. He stood back to let her pass and they took great care not to touch each other.

'Excuse me,' Katherine murmured.

'By all means.'

'Thank you.'

'Don't mention it.'

At times Katherine felt she could barely contain the thrill of it all, like her skin was going to split open from too much excitement. She had to rub her legs together under her desk to disperse the overflow of joy. Sometimes, looking at Joe, tall and professional in his suit, she had a mad urge to stand up and shout out to the office, 'I've seen Joe Roth in the noddy. I could describe every inch of him to you. And he's bloody gorgeous!'

Katherine's phone rang in the afternoon.

It was Tara. 'I may have to ask you a favour.'

'Ask away,' Katherine said breezily. Nothing could faze her.

'Can I move in with you?'

'Oh. Oh, God.'

'I'm so, so, so sorry,' Tara said, abjectly. 'I really pick my times, I know. There's you with a new fella and you'll be wanting to do it all over the place, and you've been celibate for two years and I could have left Thomas in any of that time, and I wait until now.'

'Have you ... *left*... Thomas?'

'Not as such. But I'm going to after work. I'll just move a carload of stuff tonight and Ravi's organizing a van for the rest of my things later in the week.'

'Well, I can hardly believe it. I'm delighted,' Katherine blustered. Of *course* she was delighted, but of all the bloody times . . .

An hour later Joe sent Katherine an e-mail saying, 'Further to our not slipping tonight, would you like to go to a restaurant, a bar, a cinema, a theatre, a chippy, a video shop, a night-club, a bowling alley, a Jacuzzi or my flat? Tick as preferred.'

And Katherine had to reply, 'I'm afraid there's been a slight change of plan. You see my friend Tara's having a bit of a drama . . .'

Katherine was adamant that no one at work should know about them, so Joe arrived at her flat half an hour after she did. When she opened the door his huge, intimate smile was in extreme contrast to the cool detachment they'd shown each other all day.

Bundling her into his coat, he kissed her with violent relief.

'I hope you weren't followed,' she said sternly.

'I was, but I ran through a Chinese laundry and out the back.'

'Into an alley filled with cardboard boxes?'

'And hens. Then I legged it up a fire-escape and climbed through a window.'

'Into a room where a man and woman were in bed together?'

'Actually, I think it was a man and a man. So I doffed my hat politely and said, "Pardon me."'

'And one of them said, "Did you see that?" and the other said, "See what?"'

'But I was gone!'

They laughed, giddy with the connection.

'Thank you for the bathmat,' she said, shyly.

'When can we try it?'

She shook her head. 'We'll have to behave ourselves tonight because Tara could arrive with some of her worldly goods at any minute. Sorry. Definitely not what you were expecting.'

'We can still go to the chippy and the video shop,' he said gamely. 'All isn't lost.'

'Yes, but . . .' It was far too early for nights in with videos and takeaways. You had to be going out with each other for at least three weeks before that was acceptable. 'I could try and cook something,' she said, doubtfully.

'I'd prefer if you didn't.'

'Oi!'

'Don't forget, Katherine, you told me ages ago that you can't cook.'

'Well, would you chance a cup of tea made by me?'

'We can go one better than that.' He fished a bottle of wine from his coat pocket. 'Da-dah! Oddbins' finest.'

'Nice day yesterday?' she called from the kitchen, as she fetched the corkscrew.

'It began well.' He sounded thoughtful. 'But at about eleven it started to go downhill. And after that the only highlight was a trip to Homebase to buy a bathmat.'

'You should have stayed here with me,' she teased.

'Should I?' He sounded surprised. 'I was well up for it, but I didn't want to overstay my welcome.'

As she came back in, she hoped the relief didn't show in her face. They walked up to the local chip shop. It had started to rain. 'From the Ivy to this in two short days,' she observed, wryly, pushing open the door.

'What will you have?' Joe tempted, looking up at the plastic sign. 'Sausage in batter? Chicken wings? Cheeseburger?'

'Depends on what you're having.'

'Two saveloys and chips. And perhaps we could share a portion of onion rings?'

'If I give you some of my smoked cod,' she calculated, 'can I have a bite of your saveloy?'

'You can have as much as you want of my saveloy,' he said, softly.

And suddenly the chip shop disappeared and there was just the two of them. Stock-still and gazing at each other, mute with magic union. Erno, behind the Formica and glass counter, paused from his banging and clattering, and contemplated crying. Young love. There was nothing like it.

They bought two cans of Tizer to go with the food and Erno threw in four free sachets of ketchup and a pickled egg. His way of toasting their happiness and wishing them well.

Then to the video shop where Joe immediately picked out *Roman Holiday*. 'Do you remember? The day we had lunch?' He stopped and squirmed. 'The day I *bullied* you into having lunch.'

It was her turn to squirm. 'You didn't bully me.'

'Anyway, we were talking about a rainy night in, watching a black and white film on the telly, and we both said *Roman Holiday*. Remember?'

Of course she remembered, but she just said, 'Did we? Oh, OK.'

At nine thirty they'd finished watching the video, Tara still hadn't arrived and it was getting harder and harder to keep their hands off each other.

'We can't.' Katherine reluctantly broke off a passionate kiss. 'Tara's bound to arrive at a vital moment!'

'OK,' Joe squeaked, his heart pounding. When his voice returned to normal he asked, 'So why's she leaving her boyfriend?'

Leaking little bits of information, Katherine ended up telling him the whole lot about Thomas and what a creep he was. Then Joe told Katherine about Lindsay, the girl he'd gone out with for three years.

'Who ended it?' Katherine tried to sound casual.

'Saatchi and Saatchi.' Joe laughed. 'She got a great job in New York,' he explained. 'But we were kind of on the way out anyway.'

'Were you . . .' she hesitated '. . . *wounded*?'

'Yes. But you know what they say.'

'What *do* they say?'

'Time wounds all heals.'

Then Katherine told Joe about Fintan and his cancer.

'One day at work you had a little weep,' Joe asked awkwardly. 'You were doing my expenses and you said you'd had bad news. Was it the news about Fintan?'

Vaguely she said, 'I suppose it must have been.' No point letting him know that she'd catalogued every contact they'd ever had.

Next she found herself telling him about Milo, JaneAnn and Timothy, how funny they were about London. And how Milo and Liv had fallen for each other, even though Liv was a style goddess and Milo had lived in a pair of worn dungarees until recently.

'Dungarees!' Joe exclaimed. Perhaps the bloke he'd seen Katherine with one day was just Fintan's brother.

'Yes, dungarees.' Katherine was puzzled. 'I didn't think they were only an Irish thing. They're kind of blue overalls with a bib front –'

'I know,' Joe grinned. 'And what does this Milo do for a living?'

'He's a farmer.' What an odd question.

'He's not in a band or anything?'

'Who, Milo? You must be joking.'

At eleven o'clock the phone rang. To Katherine's surprise it was Tara.

'Where are you?'

'Still at home. Lost my nerve,' Tara said miserably. 'I'm sorry I've ruined your evening.'

'You haven't, Tara. I've had a lovely time. Don't worry.'

'I might get the nerve to do it tomorrow night.'

'Whenever.'

Katherine slammed down the phone. It was an ill wind. 'She's not coming. So it's all systems go on the bath mat!'

63

At seven o'clock on Tuesday evening, Tara was standing in her living room, boxes and bags at her feet.

She'd left work early. She wanted everything packed and ready to go, so that she could say her piece, then leave.

She'd fallen at the final hurdle the night before, still unable to come to terms with the hugeness of leaving her boyfriend and home and condemning herself to a life of lonely spinsterhood. It seemed so much easier to put up and shut up. What's a little self-respect between lovers?

And naturally enough Thomas had been very nice to her, as if he'd suspected that something was afoot. Telling her she looked like she'd lost a bit of weight. Offering to cook her dinner. So every time she opened her mouth to tell him she was leaving, her head swam with disbelief and the whole idea seemed like lunacy.

But in relentless two-steps-forward-and-one-step-back fashion, Tara was finally ready. She'd been sweeping things under the carpet for a very long time, and it was no longer an option. Arming herself with images of all the times he'd made her feel like dirt, she was ready to do battle. Every now and then a new memory would pop up, filling her with fresh, furious resolve. She wanted to hurt him, to humiliate him as he'd humiliated her. As she'd *let* him humiliate her.

She heard the crackle of his key in the door and her mouth went dry. Worn out from a hard day's berating teenagers, he barely looked at her as he flung his (brown) satchel on the (brown) couch.

Then he became aware that something funny was going on. An unusual atmosphere. And why was Tara standing in the middle of the room? Why wasn't she sitting down? And where had the books gone? Had they been burgled?

'Thomas?'

'What?'

'I've something to tell you.'

'Go on, then.'

'I'm leaving you.'

He groaned. 'Aw, Tara, what's bludeh up with you lately? I've had a hard day and I don't want to get into some premenstrual girly discussion with you.'

'I think you misunderstand. There's nothing to discuss. I'm leaving you. Now.'

He did his goldfish face. He goggled. 'Why?' was all he could manage.

'Let's see,' she said, thoughtfully. 'Could it be because you're needlessly cruel? Or pathologically stingy? Or a mad control freak? Or just because you're a horrible person, and I really dislike you? It's hard to know for sure, Thomas. All I know is, I must have been out of my mind to have stayed with you for the past two years.'

His face went whiter and whiter with each sentence. 'But . . .' he protested, shaking from this unprovoked attack. 'It's just my way. I speak as I find, but I love you and anything I said was for your own good.'

'You know,' she realized, 'I really think you need some sort of counselling or therapy. Your attitude to women is messed up.'

'Crap.' Thomas's tone was scornful. Oddly enough, it wasn't the first time something like this had been suggested by a girlfriend . . .

'You don't even like me,' Tara said.

'Course I do.'

'You don't. You'd have been a lot nicer if you did.'

Then, for the first time, Thomas noticed the bags and boxes at Tara's feet and made the connection between them and the empty shelves. Books, videos, CDs, all gone. He was jolted to the core. 'Are they –' He pointed. 'Have they your things in them?'

'Some of them. I'll be back for the rest during the week.'

'I don't believe it.'

Tara had to admit he looked gratifyingly dazed.

'Where would you go?'

'I *am* going,' she emphasized, 'to Katherine's.'

'Katherine's?'

'For a while anyway,' she said, breezily. 'Then I'll see about buying my own place.'

'Own place?'

'Is there an echo in here?' She looked around.

'We can talk about this,' he tried valiantly. Now that she actually seemed to be leaving, he suddenly desperately wanted her. He was that seven-year-old boy again.

'We've already talked.'

'When?'

'The night of my birthday, for example. When you said you'd ditch me if I got pregnant.'

'Oh, that.'

'And last Friday night, when I suggested we get married.'

'I didn't think you were serious,' he muttered.

'Exactly!'

'Tara, don't go.' He paused. 'Love,' he tried tentatively.

Her resolution wobbled. He'd never called her 'love' before.

'I'll admit that I've not always been good to you,' he beseeched.

'Could you say that again, please?'

'I'll admit I've not always been good to you,' he repeated, a little sullenly.

'That's a good one.' She laughed darkly. 'You've not always been good to me. That's one way of putting it.'

'Hey. No one forced you to stay with me.'

'I know.' She grinned. 'Mortifying, isn't it? Believe it or not, I'm far angrier with myself than I am with you.'

'How could you do this to me?' His face had caved in.

'How many times do I have to tell you? Because you're *awful*.'

'But you know why. I *told* you why. Cos of me mam leaving I find it hard to trust a woman. This is just like that Sunday morning. Coming in and finding the bags packed, it were awful, Tara.'

'Oh, change the record!'

Thomas just couldn't believe it. His wound, which he'd nurtured and protected, watered and nourished, was being disregarded in such a disrespectful fashion. It was his most precious commodity, enabling him to get people to behave the way he wanted them to. How dare this fat cow . . . !

'Oh, now I get it,' he said furiously. 'You've met some other bloke. That's what this is all about.'

'I have not. It's nothing to do with anyone else. It's to do with you. And me, unfortunately.'

'That Ravi. I bet you're shagging him.'

'I'm not shagging anyone.'

He looked at her bitterly. 'No. I suppose you're not. Who'd have you?'

'That's my Thomas. Well, goodbye.' She put on her coat. 'It's been real. Real horrible, that is.'

Stunned, he watched her heft up the bags and boxes and carry them to her car. As she came back for a second load his eyes widened in shock. 'Hey. Leave my bludeh coffee table alone!'

'*Whose* coffee table?'

'Mine.'

'Who paid for it?'

He didn't answer.

'I did. So, Thomas,' she said triumphantly, 'it's *my* bludeh coffee table.'

64

'Yippee!' Fintan snatched off his Marilyn Monroe wig and twirled it like a lasso above his head. 'I still can't believe she did it. Can you believe it, Katherine?'

Katherine thought of Tara, who'd been crying solidly for the past forty-eight hours and murmured, 'Mmmmm, I can, actually.'

'Tell me what you've found out. Was he devastated?'

'Quite upset, I believe.'

'Oooohhhh.' Fintan clenched his fists. 'To have been a fly on the wall. Isn't it a shame she didn't video it? How is she?'

'Broken-hearted, to be honest.'

'Roy Orbison?'

'No.' Katherine smiled mysteriously. Roy Orbison was currently languishing in a shoe-box, beneath four photo-albums on the top of her wardrobe. It was one of the first things she'd done when Tara had arrived with her stuff, because there was no way she could cope with another two months of 'It's oooooooohhhhhh-ver!'

'Is she going on about having to become a lesbian because she'll never meet another man?'

'Yes, just like old times.'

'Evening classes?'

'Talk of mosaic-making, learning Portuguese and banjo-playing so far. I'll give you fair warning, she's talking of roping you in.'

'Holy God – *banjo*-playing! Isn't it a stroke of luck that I've to go in for my next bout of chemo tomorrow and I'll be too sick to even look at a banjo?'

'There's lucky.'

'Listen, you don't think she'll get back with Thomas, do you?'

'Well, he's already rung to ask if they could still be friends.'

'I see. He wanted a shag. And what happened?'

'She said – actually it was great, Fintan. She said, "Still? How can we still be friends when we were never friends in the first place?"'

'Oh, lovely. She'll get over this yet. But what we mustn't do under any circumstances is suggest that she gets back on the horse. Look at what happened after Alasdair.'

'Quite. What's that box in the corner?'

'My abdominizer. Don't worry, it's going back. So how are things with you?'

'Very well.' Katherine smiled like a Cheshire cat. 'Very well, indeed.'

'Still averaging three hours of sleep a night?'

'If that.'

'And look at you! Positively thriving. When can I meet him?'

'When would you like?'

'Best to wait till the chemo is out of the way. I don't want to puke all over your new fella on our first encounter. It'd be very poor.' The phone rang and Fintan asked, 'Will you answer it? You're nearer. Who could it be? Oh, the mad social whirl, my dear!'

'Hello,' Katherine said. 'Oh, hello, Mrs O'Grady. Really? Are you sure? No, I knew nothing about it. No, really I didn't. I swear to God I didn't. I understand, ye – I underst – of course,

I understa – But wait a minute. Maybe you'd better find out if it's true before you start threatening to kill people.'

Katherine handed the phone to Fintan. 'It's your mother. Do you know anything about Milo selling his farm and moving to London for good?'

Tara climbed out of bed and the first thing she did was tick the calendar that Katherine had given her. Ten. The tenth night in a row that she'd managed to stay away from Thomas. Ten never-ending, sleep-free nights, her circadian rhythms shot to hell by displacement, the large quantities of alcohol she was ingesting to anaesthetize the pain and fear of her yawningly empty future.

Her initial bravado when she'd marched out on Thomas had dissolved before she'd even arrived at Katherine's. She'd almost turned the car around and driven back. But she knew that because of the extensive way she'd humiliated him, she'd burnt her bridges good and proper. Everyone told her that she'd get over him, but she knew her life was finished. She thought back to those heady, carefree days during her late twenties when she still had time. Of course, when Alasdair had dumped her, she'd thought it was all over for her. But this time, more than two years down the line, it really *was* all over.

She didn't have the same bounce-back resilience that she used to have. She'd had her last chance and blown it.

The thought of going back to Thomas was dangerously seductive. Now that they were sundered, he didn't seem so bad. His tetchiness didn't look like a high price to pay for companionship. Though they'd had their squabbles, they knew each other very well. There was a huge comfort in that bickery intimacy. Better someone to disagree with than no one at all.

Also, when she could bear to be honest, she admitted that though she missed Thomas, she also missed the validation of being one half of a couple. Alone, she felt naked and failed.

Yet, despite her loneliness, she had flashes of a deep-down conviction that to go back to Thomas would be wrong. Not unless he'd changed fundamentally. And she was desperate to avoid a repeat of the way she'd humiliated herself with Alasdair. *Please, God, don't let me ring Thomas*, she prayed, a thousand times a day. *Please, God, give me strength. Please, God, make him ring me. Make him tell me he's a changed man.*

Katherine was in the kitchen making coffee for herself and Joe. 'Hi,' she twinkled. She'd been getting almost no sleep but was wide, wide awake. Super-alert, apart from the odd lapse into languid dreaminess.

She looked different. Everyone noticed it. The other day at work, when a tight little bottom had wriggled past his glass office, Fred Franklin had nudged Myles and said, 'Nice arse. If you can get it.'

Then Fred had frozen. '*Whose* arse is it? Don't tell me it's Icequeen's? Oh, bloody hell, it is! How could I be polite about *that*?'

Back in the kitchen Tara managed a tight smile at Katherine.

'Tara,' Katherine said, slowly.

'What?'

'This.' Katherine put her finger inside Tara's waistband and pulled. A big gap appeared.

'Oh.' Tara gazed down in amazement.

'Are you eating *anything*?'

'This always happens. You split up with your fella, you can't eat a thing, you get lovely and skinny and you meet another man. It's Mother Nature's consolation prize.' Tara smiled faintly.

'But, Tara, you must eat.'

'I couldn't be bothered.'

'Don't give in to it,' Katherine said stoutly. 'He wasn't worth it.'

'He wasn't all bad,' Tara said. 'He was nice *sometimes*.'

'Give me one example.'

Tara thought for a second. 'He always filled out my forms for me. Like my car insurance and tax. He knew how much I hated doing it.'

'It was the least he could do, seeing as you drove him everywhere. Give me another.'

'He was gentlemanly. Opened doors for me, pulled out chairs.'

'Old-fashioned sexist.'

Tara sighed heavily. 'OK, he's great with his hands. When my silver chain got all tangled up he spent hours unknotting it without breaking it. I'd never have had the patience.'

Katherine harrumphed, not quite sure how to sneer at Thomas for his handymanism.

'And we smoked together, we tried to give up together, we failed together.' Tara sighed wistfully. 'He used to light my cigarettes, I used to light his. It was very companionable, and I never ran out of fags because he had some when I didn't.'

'You mean he let you have them for free?'

'*Obviously* I had to pay.' Tara attempted a wan smile. 'But it still meant that I wasn't ever deprived of them.'

'Cheer up, you're well shot of him. Let's face it, it was hardly the world's greatest love affair,' Katherine scorned.

She was right, Tara considered. It was neither tragic nor romantic enough. But it had been *her* love affair. 'Look,' Tara bowed her head, 'I *know* he was a bully and I *know* he was a meanie and I agree with you that I'm probably better off without him. But when people get a gangrenous limb amputated, it still itches, you know.'

Katherine was pleased that Tara had compared Thomas to a gangrenous limb. Obviously it was a terrible slight on a gangrenous limb, but it was progress.

'Thanks for last night, by the way,' Tara muttered.

'It's OK. Er, sorry I ripped the jumper.'

'You were right to. I was only fooling myself.'

The previous evening, to Katherine's horror, Tara had taken out the jumper that she'd been knitting for Thomas and said, 'I might as well finish it and give it to him. It's a shame to waste it.'

'No!' Katherine had jumped up, grabbed the needles, yanked the half-knitted sleeve from them and torn frantically at the wool, unravelling line after line of stitches. 'It's only an excuse to see him. Like the money he owes you, and the shower curtain you left behind and the fact that you forgot to kick Beryl before you left. No, Tara, no!'

Tara's face was luminous with amazement. 'OK,' she whispered.

Katherine stomped back to sit beside Joe and muttered, 'Sorry you had to witness that.'

'I'm scared!' He quailed, and everyone laughed, dispersing the tension.

God, Tara thought, he was lovely! And so obliging. Tara suspected that the reason Katherine and Joe were spending so much time at Katherine's instead of being holed up *à deux* in Joe's flat was to keep an eye on Tara. Katherine had even moved the phone from the front room to the bedroom and confiscated Tara's mobile. 'I can't stop you ringing him during the day,' she'd said, 'but at least you won't be able to when you come home plastered.'

And Joe and Katherine had blocked Tara's progress one night when she tried to leave for a drunken midnight drive. 'I don't want to call *in* to Thomas,' Tara explained angrily. 'I just want to drive *by*.'

'The only circumstance that I'll let you drive by Thomas's is if it's a drive-by *shooting*,' Katherine replied. 'Now, back to bed!'

Tara dragged herself out of bed and ticked the calendar. Twenty days. Nearly three weeks. And after three weeks it would be almost a month.

So far she'd managed not to ring him. But it was a super-human achievement, brought about by Herculean struggle. Every day seemed like a thousand-mile march, potholed with constant opportunities to pick up the phone. At times she literally sweated from the effort of not ringing him.

At weekends, without the distraction of work, the torment was magnified a hundredfold.

As the initial agonizing wrench receded she'd come to see that it wasn't just Thomas she missed, it was everything he'd represented: acceptance, endorsement, someone to consult on plans, a person to report to. She was deeply grateful for her friends, but without the unquestioned alliance of routine that existed between lovers, she ricocheted about like a free radical.

There had never been any great thrill in telling Thomas that she'd be home late. It was only now that there was no one to give a damn if she didn't come home at all that it had taken on desirability. And even though she and Thomas had never really gone on a proper holiday, all she could hope for now was that some couple – perhaps Milo and Liv or Katherine and Joe – would take pity on her and let her tag along. Knowing how unworthy such feelings were didn't lessen them. She just ended up feeling guilty as well as lonely.

So nostalgic was she for her old life that she even missed the awful, brown, burrow-like flat. Despite it being in Thomas's name, it had been her home. And now she was squashed like a refugee into a small bedroom in someone else's flat, afraid of being a nuisance and unable to relax. Worrying about spending too much time in the bathroom, thinking she had no right to say what she wanted to watch on telly, feeling guilty for using too much electricity and edgily aware that any mess had to be cleared up immediately.

Constant fantasies of Thomas arriving and pleading passion-ately with her to return buffered her. But apart from the one phone call where he'd asked if they could still be friends there had been no contact from him. In her more honest moments, Tara knew there wouldn't ever be. He had a macho closed-offness where it was shameful to admit to weakness or need. Even if he was dying without her, he wouldn't act on it.

Parallel to the teeth-gritted endurance of a life without Thomas was life-sapping worry about Fintan. He'd had three bouts of chemo now and still hadn't responded. His blood tests showed nothing had changed and you only had to look at him to see that his kiwi-neck was still as large as life.

The oncologists insisted that these things took time, that he had to get worse before he got better, but Tara remained on edge and retained an inordinate interest in *any* alternative remedy she heard about.

'Twenty days today!' Katherine and Joe burst into wild applause when Tara walked into the kitchen.

Tara flinched. 'It's Monday morning. How can you be so cheerful?'

'Time for your morning whinge,' Katherine glowed at her.

'Thank you. Today's grievance is that I hate having no one to go and see *The Horse Whisperer* with.'

'But Thomas wouldn't have gone with you, anyway.'

'Permit me my rose-tinted view of my past, please,' Tara asked, with dignity.

'We don't want to see *The Horse Whisperer*,' Katherine said.

'What night are we not going to see it on?' Joe dazzled Katherine with an abundant smile.

There was a time lapse where they beamed goofily at each other, before she managed to reply, 'Next Tuesday.'

'You don't need to see it,' Tara pointed out. 'You've got enough romance in your lives. Right, I'm off to work.'

'Enjoy your twenty-first Thomas-free day!'

'I'll be home late.' She paused in the hope that someone might insist they wanted her to come home early but when they didn't she continued, 'I'm going to the gym, then I'm going out.'

'Who with?'

'Anyone I can find – Ravi, a *Big Issue* seller, whoever. Textbook, I know, all this pubbing and clubbing and drinking my head off.'

'But at least you've broken with tradition by not having had at least one one-night stand,' Katherine sympathized.

'With a person you wouldn't have touched with a ten-foot pole if you hadn't just broken up with someone,' Joe added, with an I've-been-there smile.

'Give it time. I haven't sung yet.'

When Tara shut the front door behind her she was struck –

it happened a lot – by how wrong it all was. Why was she opening and closing someone else's front door when she had a perfectly good front door of her own only a few miles away?

It was out there somewhere. She stood in the street, aware of all the houses and flats and shops and offices that stretched between her and her real home, her real life.

I want to go home.

Well, you can't, she told herself. Miserably, she girded her loins and trudged to her car.

'Morning, Tara,' Ravi brayed, when she walked into the office. 'Great news. I read in *ES* there's a new lipstick out by Max Factor. It doesn't claim to be indelible, but it says it's *self-renewing*, which – I don't know about you but I think that's as good as. I feel a trip to Boots coming on!'

'Really?' Tara was pleased. 'Tell me what it said, Ravi.'

'Apparently you put it on and whenever you're worried that it's faded or whatever the word is, you simply press your lips together . . .' Ravi demonstrated by mashing his against each other '. . . and bosh! Fresh as the moment you put it on.'

Tara's phone rang. It was Liv on the line. 'What's wrong?' Tara demanded. 'Is it JaneAnn?'

Liv sighed. 'That woman is like a revenging angel. But it's not her. Have you any drugs?'

'Pardon?'

'Hash.'

'Not immediately to hand. What's going on?'

'It's for Fintan. He still feels dreadful from the chemo two days ago and someone told him that hash takes away the nausea. But I've no idea how to get some – I work in interiors! Cocaine is the only narcotic I am ever offered.'

65

'Got you some great red Leb, man,' Tara waved a tiny brown slab and drawled her dealer-spiel for Fintan. 'Or it might be Moroccan black, actually. I wouldn't know the difference. The *drama* myself and Ravi had trying to track it down. A friend of a friend of a friend of his has a sister who has a boyfriend who has a colleague who met us in a pool hall in Hammersmith and sold us the gear. Man,' she added. 'Hey, what's the lovely smell? Cake?'

Fintan ushered her into the kitchen, where a baking tray with one remaining bun on it sat on the worktop.

'Hash brownies,' Fintan explained. 'Sorry, Tara. Sandro managed to score a twenty-spot of blem this afternoon. Could have saved you and Ravi the bother. Man,' he also added.

'Oh, don't worry about us, it was great fun, I haven't done anything like that in ages. So have the brownies helped with the pukiness?'

'I've only just scoffed them. But I hope to Christ they do the trick. It's so *boring* constantly feeling like throwing up.'

'Fingers crossed! So what'll we do tonight?' Tara asked. 'It'd be so tempting to get stoned out of our minds, then stagger up to the twenty-four-hour garage and try to buy their entire stock of Maltesers —'

'— but not be able to speak because we're in hysterics at nothing.'

'Of course we must remember the gear is purely medicinal, we mustn't abuse it. It'd be nice to get a little bit stoned, though. It's been years.'

'Only problem is,' Fintan said, 'I'm going out.'

'*Going out*? Where?'

'Sandro's Christmas party.'

'Already? On the first of December?'

'The only night they could get a table at Nobu. Would you believe it's fully booked until the fourth of January?'

'But are you strong enough to go?'

'Where there's a willy there's a way.' He laughed. 'I want to have fun. Eat, drink and be merry.'

'Are you sure? After all, you're not well . . .'

'Oh, there's the bell, my taxi must be here.' Fintan began to gather himself up, and Tara noticed something that tightened her throat.

'Is it a fancy-dress Christmas party?'

'No.'

'So why have you a walking stick?'

'Oh, that. In all the excitement over the drugs and the sick stomach, I forgot to tell you.'

'Forgot to tell me *what*?'

'The last lot of chemo played havoc with the nerve endings in my feet.'

'What kind of havoc?' she asked, fear yawning inside her. This got worse and worse.

'They feel kind of tingly and it hurts to put too much weight on them, so a stick helps.' He laughed at her face. 'Oh, don't look so upset, it's only temporary, Tara. When I'm finished the chemo, it'll eventually get better. Now, is my wig on straight?'

She watched him, a skinny creature in a Tina Turner wig

486

doing a knock-kneed hobble to the door and thought, *He's only a year older than me.* 'Will I visit tomorrow night?' she asked, following in his wake as he switched off the lights.

'No. I'm going clubbing with twenty-seven of my closest friends, but you're welcome to join us.'

'You're going *clubbing*?'

'That's right, Tara. Clubbing,' Fintan's voice had a tight little edge. 'Rage, rage against the dying of the light, and all that. So I'm doing like the man said and I'm raging.'

Tara's heart thumped into the back of her throat as she realized that Fintan wasn't quite as Zen as she'd thought. 'You're angry?'

'Not exactly angry. At least, not at this precise moment. But if I'm stuck in the Last Chance Saloon I'm going to make the most of it.'

She couldn't say anything, muzzled by an odd mixture of shame and admiration.

'I'll go out fighting,' he promised. 'Or at least dancing. While there's breath in my body and Sister Sledge on the turntable, life goes on.'

66

'Work.' Tara sighed, as she staggered in, reeking of smoke and alcohol. 'I'm wrecked from it.'

'Busy time of year?' Katherine asked, sympathetically.

'Don't talk to me!' Tara declared. 'We had the project dinner last night, the team lunch yesterday, the office lunch the day before, our floor's drinks today, the department lunch tomorrow, Marketing's mulled wine do tomorrow afternoon and then the entire company party the night after. Bloody Christmas, I'm destroyed from it! My liver is begging for mercy.'

'I know what you mean,' Katherine agreed.

However, in Breen Helmsford, the difference between the crazed partying of the festive season and the crazed partying of the rest of the year was hardly visible to the naked eye.

The Christmas-party season couldn't have come at a better time for Tara. All the alcohol and high spirits kept her one step ahead of her demons. 'Though I have to admit I'm a human Third World country from it all,' Tara said. 'I'm skint!'

'You're always skint,' Katherine reminded her.

'I'm worse than usual. Drink and taxis and . . . drink and taxis. And clothes, of course. I might have to cut my credit cards up again.' Tara couldn't stop buying clothes. Though it was cold comfort, she was able to fit into things that wouldn't have gone near her six weeks previously. 'A couple more weeks of this agony,' she winced, then forced a smile, 'and I'll be able to wear jeans. Look at the lovely skirt I bought for our department lunch tomorrow.'

'Fabulous,' Katherine admired. 'Where's it being held? Somewhere nice?'

'Actually, no.'

It had been decided to hold their department lunch in-house because it had been impossible to secure a booking at any of the local restaurants. Either they were already booked out or else word had reached them of the performance GK Software's development department had put on last year, when the lunch had spilled over to the evening bookings and a hard-core of eight or nine rowdies had still refused to leave.

Even now, nearly a year later, one of the local Polish restaurateurs blessed himself and crossed the road rather than walk past the offices of GK Software and its savage staff.

This year's lunch began sedately enough. Every woman left her desk at ten thirty to get ready even though kick-off wasn't until one o'clock. No work was done all morning, on the pretext that everyone was so excited. Of course no one *was* excited, but they recognized a chance to swing the lead when they saw one.

'What d'you think, Ravi?' Tara asked, modelling her new skirt.

'What am I looking at? Clothes or lipstick?'

'Lipstick, shlipstick! I'm afraid that self-renewing one wasn't exactly the final solution. Suckered once more.'

'Oh, Tara, I've something for you.' Ravi rummaged around in his desk drawer. 'This could be the answer to all your problems. Here it is.' He brandished something torn from a magazine. 'Tattooing! On your lips. There's a place in California that can colour your lips in permanently. Sounds bloody grim, but at least you'd never have to worry about your lipstick coming off again.'

'Thanks, Ravi, but no.' Tara was deeply touched. 'It's very sweet of you to bother, but what, for example, if I wanted to try a different colour –?'

'Sorry. I just thought it was worth a try.'

'Oh, but it was!'

At one o'clock, thirty people piled into the boardroom for sherry, reheated turkey and shoddy crackers. Everyone drank enthusiastically. As usual Tara and Ravi sat next to each other and batted funny comments back and forth.

'Look at Vinnie.' Tara laughed, her face flushed. 'He's twisted. Even his scalp has gone red.'

'He doesn't get out much so he's lost the skill of drinking.'

'Pour us another sweet sherry there, Ravi, good man.'

'Just the one,' he said in his mincing 'lady's' voice and they clinked glasses coyly.

At some stage, responsible people like Vinnie went back to work, but several more stayed where they were, Ravi and Tara in the thick of them, spirits high.

However, at about half past four a combination of not having eaten for several weeks and having more alcohol than blood in her circulatory system meant things suddenly turned ropy for Tara. She started to cry about Fintan, then about Thomas, then about Fintan again. ''Sawful,' she wept. ''Sunbearable. Whaf he dies? Doan say he woan cos he's prolly goan to. 'Slike a knife through my heart. Worse than losing Thoms, miles worse.' Then she looked at Ravi beseechingly and said, 'Ravi, 'mgoing to puke.'

'Gangway!' Ravi bellowed, as he half dragged, half carried Tara to the ladies'. 'Excuse me,' he said, to the startled trio of girls from the payroll department who were preparing in front of the mirror for their department dinner. 'It's an emergency.'

'We can see that,' they said, jumping nimbly out of Tara's way.

'That'll be us in a couple of hours,' one of them said hopefully, watching Ravi as he held Tara's hair back from her face while, into the sink, she parted company with her sherry.

'C'ngo home, pliz, Ravi?' Tara begged him when she'd finished. 'Will you take me?'

'Course. Stay here and I'll order a taxi. Keep an eye on her,' he told the payroll girls.

The moment Ravi was gone, one of the payroll girls whipped a tube of toothpaste from her bag and insisted that Tara rinse her mouth out with it. 'Off!' Tara flailed weakly with her hand.

'He's cute,' the girl insisted.

''S not cute. 'S Ravi.'

But the mouth-washing was a pointless exercise because no sooner was it done than Tara threw up again. And again.

When the taxi arrived, Sleepy Steve knocked on the door of the ladies' toilet.

'Before we go, do you need to ... again, you know ...?' Ravi asked discreetly. But no, Tara was all puked out, for the time being anyway. She was in floods of tears again, however.

The door opened and in swept Amy, willowy and gorgeous. 'Tara,' she gasped, 'what's wrong? Why are you crying?'

Though she hadn't seen her in ages she hadn't forgotten how nice Tara had been after she'd set the police on Lorcan.

'M' friend's dyin' an' 'sall over with m' fella.'

Amy seized on the worst piece of news. 'Oh, no. That's

491

terrible. It's all over with your boyfriend. Oh, you poor, poor thing.' Then she had a wondrous, joyous idea. 'I know! My boyfriend has a lovely friend. You'd be just right for each other. His name is Benjy, we'll all go out in a foursome in January.'

'Sounds nice,' Tara said, through her tears. 'Does't it, Ravi?'

'Great.'

'So long as you don't fall in love with Lorcan.' Amy giggled nervously.

''Slong's I doan.'

Ravi assisted Tara, weeping and shambolic, through the reception area, where a cluster of smartly dressed men from the payroll department was about to depart for their dinner. They looked open-mouthed at the bleary-faced state of Tara.

'Something she ate,' Ravi said stoutly.

But as Ravi helped Tara down the short flight of stairs that led from the reception area to the exit, Tara began to heave again.

'Just a minute . . .' Ravi gasped, looking around in panic for something for Tara to vomit into. 'Try not to –'

But it was too late, Tara was unable to stop herself from puking the last of her sherry on to the small metal handrail that ran beside the steps. 'Sorry, Ravi,' she said, thickly. 'I'm 'sgusting.'

'You're OK, sweetheart,' Ravi soothed, hoping to Christ that the taxi-driver wouldn't refuse to take them. 'Could someone clean that up, please,' he called over his shoulder. But, of course, no one did. The staff from the payroll department had no intention of running the risk of splashing someone else's puke on to their good going-out clothes. If anyone's puke was going to be splashed on to them it would be their own.

Seconds later Alvin Honeycomb, the managing director of

492

GK Software, rushed out of the lift and into the reception area. Tall, distinguished of temple (grey, in other words) and handsome, he swept through in a navy cashmere overcoat, carrying a clunky briefcase and an I'm-a-busy-and-important-man air. He, too, was on his way to a function. 'Night all,' he called, in his deep, mellifluous tones as he galloped towards the exit. He prided himself on being pleasant to his staff and waited to hear the chorus of 'Goodnight, Mr Honeycomb.' He always ran down the short flight of stairs to the exit, as though doing a dance. A flurry of perfect little steps executed in his soft, slip-on Italian shoes, that led him on to the street, invariably just in time to hail the empty taxi that would be approaching. But this night, as he placed his hand on the railing to begin his little tap-dance into the street below, he connected with some of Tara's recently regurgitated sherry. To Mr Honeycomb's great alarm, his arm whooshed straight to the bottom of the rail, carried on a tide of vomit, the rest of him following rapidly, as though he'd just dived into a swimming-pool. His feet tried and failed to regain contact with the steps, and before he knew it he had tumbled down the entire seven steps and rolled into the street below, sustaining a bruised shoulder and a nasty crack to his chin. His briefcase skittered across the icy pavement, and for a few moments he remained sprawled, balanced on his chin, his arse in the air, too stunned to get up. A well-dressed couple en route to a work do sighed as they stepped over him and said, 'Honestly, some people take this Christmas thing too far. They shouldn't drink if they can't handle it.'

The following morning when Tara woke up she didn't feel too bad. There was a faint buzzing in her head and she couldn't really feel her feet on the floor but she was able to get up, shower, get dressed and organize her new slinky black dress and black wedge sandals for that evening's party.

Then she drove to work, strangely disconnected from what she was doing. When she got in, she passed Mr Honeycomb on the stairs. How did he get that big cut on his chin? she wondered vaguely. Probably out on the piss and fell flat on his face. A fine example to be setting his staff.

With shrugs and smiles she deflected the torrent of concerned inquiries from everyone in her section. 'Thanks,' she mouthed at Ravi, grateful that for some reason guilt and shame didn't seem to be a problem. She was mercifully numb.

Until she found that someone – probably Vinnie – had booked her in for a ten o'clock appointment with two irate punters. In fact, they were already there, hanging around and looking indeed irate, as advertised. Just as well she'd managed to come in, instead of spending the day lying in bed roaring for a basin, as one might have expected.

But just as Tara was welcoming them into the meeting room, it suddenly dawned on her that she was still very, very drunk. Not only that but she was actually slurring her words. 'Mishter Forde, Mishter Ransome, pleashe take a seat.'

Her tongue had swollen up to mammoth proportions and she could hardly unpeel it from the roof of her mouth. She began to sweat with fear. 'Yesh, I quite undershtand your complaints about the servish we've been providing,' she said desperately.

Was this a dream? she wondered.

She couldn't defend herself. She couldn't think of the right things to say. Her central nervous system was broken, the signals that normally zinged from one nerve-ending in her brain to another were bogged down in some treacle-like substance.

The little room was way too hot.

And then she smelt it. An odour that wasn't ever appropriate in the meeting room, and certainly not at ten fifteen in the morning.

Alcohol. She could smell alcohol. Warm and rank. Exuding from her fear-enlarged pores.

Enough, she decided, there and then. *That's enough.* She'd had her mandatory, post-split-up, drinking and partying, self-destructive spree. But now it was time to try to stop.

67

The first thing Frank Butler always said to Tara when he collected her from Shannon airport was 'When are you going back?' But in a momentous break with tradition, when he picked up Tara and Katherine on the Wednesday before Christmas, it was actually the second thing. The first thing was, 'I believe Fintan O'Grady has Aids.'

'No, Dad, he hasn't. He has cancer.'

'Heh! Cancer me foot. They must take us for a right crowd of goms. Come on, the car is this way.' Weaving through the throngs of people in the arrivals concourse, he demanded, 'Do they think we never pick up a newspaper or turn on the telly?'

'No, really, Mr Butler,' Katherine interjected, with just the right combination of meekness and authority. 'He hasn't got Aids.'

This threw Frank. Katherine Casey wouldn't lie. She was a good girl. Although he'd half noticed a different air about her. In fact, if he didn't think it was so unlikely, *brazen* would be the word he'd use.

'When are you going back?' he barked at Tara.

'New Year's day.'

'I suppose you'll want a lift.'

'You suppose correctly.'

Then Frank thought of something and cheered up immediately. He was a lot more sure of his facts on this one. 'Well,' he blustered, 'I hear Milo O'Grady's as thick as thieves with some Swiss divorcee, who's making him sell the farm.'

'She's not Swiss!'

'And she's not divorced, Mr Butler.'

'And she's not *making* him sell the farm. He's doing it of his own free will.'

'But they are as thick as thieves, Mr Butler, if that's any consolation.'

Frank marched on in dejected silence. Gloomily he threw their cases into the boot of the Cortina, then looked appraisingly at Tara. 'You're terrible scrawny.'

'Thanks, Dad!'

'Mind you, you were a right platterpuss before. A face like a full moon in a fog, heh, heh, heh!'

Déjà vu, Tara thought, in astonishment. *This is exactly the kind of conversation I used to have with Thomas. I must have been mad to put up with it.* And for the first time ever she knew this to be true: she'd rather be lonely for the rest of her life than live like that again.

Katherine and Tara were home for ten days. Because flights from London to Ireland were so oversubscribed at Christmas time, they'd booked theirs the previous March. At the time Katherine had congratulated herself for her in-like-Flynn behaviour. Now she was bitterly sorry. The idea of being away from Joe for ten days was awful.

Fintan had stayed in London because he was having another blast of chemo. He'd insisted that Tara and Katherine go to Ireland. 'I'll be swamped with people,' he complained. 'Sandro, Milo and Liv are staying in London. Harry, Didier, Neville, Geoff, Will, Andrew, Claude, Geraint and Stephanie have insisted on coming over on Christmas Day. And JaneAnn and Ambrose are coming from Ireland.'

'Yikes,' Tara gurned. 'JaneAnn and Liv! Has JaneAnn forgiven Liv for stealing Milo away from Knockavoy?'

'Not really. But she'll have to behave herself.'

'Where's Mam?' Tara asked her father when they got home.

'Here!' Fidelma rushed in, beaming with delight. She was covered in feathers and wearing a 'My neighbour went to London and all I got was this lousy T-shirt' T-shirt. 'I can't stay,' she explained. 'I only came up to say hello. I'm up to me oxters plucking turkeys below in the shed. There's so many feathers floating around the place I can nearly fly!

'Oh, Lord, you've turned into a right skinnymalinks,' she noticed. 'Is that because of the boyfriend?'

Tara nodded, her face trembling violently with the onset of tears. But it was fine to cry. She was with her mother.

'And because of poor Fintan, too, I'm sure.' Fidelma felt like bursting into tears herself, but now wasn't the time. 'Put all your worry behind you,' she assured Tara, taking her in her arms. 'We'll mind you. You won't know yourself going back.'

Tara snuggled into the squashy warmth of her mother, exhaling with relief at the healing power of maternal love. She could stop soldiering because her mammy was going to carry the burden for a while. For the first time in a very long time she felt safe.

Tara had a lovely Christmas. Delighted to be home and delighted to see her three younger brothers, Michael, Gerard and Kieran, who prided themselves on still behaving like surly adolescents even though they were variously twenty-three, twenty-four and twenty-eight. Katherine, on the other hand, was counting the days until they returned to London. She spent hours and hours on the phone to Joe in Devon, both of them unable to ever hang up.

'You go first.'

'No, you go.'

'No, you go.'

'OK, we'll count to three, then we'll both hang up.'

'OK.'

'Right, one . . .'

'. . . two . . .'

'. . . three!'

'Joe?'

'Yes?'

'You didn't hang up.'

'I know. I'm sorry. But neither did you.'

On Christmas morning, Agnes asked her, 'Did he give you a Christmas present, this young man of yours?'

'Yes, Granny,' Katherine purred. 'He gave me a star.'

'What do you mean he gave you a star?'

'He got a new star named after me. Somewhere up there,' she tilted her head ceilingwards, 'is a star called the Katherine Casey star. He said *I* was a star, do you see?' she confided, shyly. 'So having a star named after me seemed appropriate.'

'In my day we were glad of a charm for our charm bracelet,' Agnes muttered. Young Katherine was showing late but worrying signs of turning into another Delia.

Frank Butler and Agnes weren't the only ones who'd noticed that Katherine had changed. 'I don't know what it is, but she's gone very like her mother,' they puzzled in the shops and pubs of Knockavoy.

'Not that she's wearing the oul' tents or anything.'

'No, indeed! She has some very handsome costumes. Look at her now!'

All the men gathered at the counter in Forman's swivelled to look at Katherine, who was wearing a sleek black leather skirt and a short, tight cardigan.

'Everyone in Alco's Corner is looking at you,' Tara muttered.

Katherine glanced up and saw a selection of bulbous-nosed faces checking her out. Tara waited for the glare to flash across the bar and scare the living daylights out of them. But Katherine smiled prettily and Tara sighed. She kept forgetting about the new, improved Katherine Casey.

Back at the bar, the men muttered in agreement. 'It's the twinkle in her eye that does it.'

'. . . seven, six, five, four, three, two, one. HAPPY NEW YEAR!'

Tara looked at the half-smoked cigarette that she held in her hand. 'I've started so I'll finish,' she murmured. Then amid great ceremony she crumbled and broke her last sixteen cigarettes into an ashtray in Forman's.

'Ouch.' Timothy O'Grady winced. 'I bet that hurt.'

'No,' Tara lied, airily. 'My own personal Ramadan starts here. No eating, drinking and, most definitely, no smoking!'

Fourteen hours later, Katherine and Tara were sitting in the non-smoking part of Shannon airport, awaiting their flight back to Heathrow.

'It's fourteen hours since I had a cigarette,' Tara announced proudly. '*Fourteen* hours.'

'You've been asleep for eleven of them,' Katherine said drily.

'Look at your man over there.' Tara indicated a man in the

smoking section, sucking on a cigarette as though his life depended on it. 'Isn't it disgusting? How could he do that to himself? Putting that revolting gear into his body?'

Ten minutes later Tara broke open a packet of Nicorette. 'This is the business,' she said, chewing frantically. 'Who needs fags?' Twenty minutes later Tara was sitting in the smoking section, still chewing the piece of Nicorette and inhaling deeply on a cigarette she'd bummed from the man.

'I'm a smoker,' she sadly told him. 'I suppose I'd better just come to terms with it.'

68

Tara started evening classes. Now that she wasn't going on mad benders every night of the week – it was down to every second night and sometimes only every third night – she had to fill the time somehow and going to the gym and visiting Fintan weren't adequate distraction. But the banjo lessons lasted only a night. 'It was too hard,' she complained, 'and have you any *idea* how much a banjo costs? You'd be bankrupted.'

The mosaic-making didn't fare much better. 'Miles too fiddly. All those little tiles, they'd drive you mad.'

And as for the Portuguese lessons, 'Full of weirdoes. But never mind,' she said cheerfully, 'they still have vacancies in meditation, batik-making and canoeing. One of them is bound to be nice.'

They weren't.

'Meditation. God, the tedium! And my nerves were in shreds from the silence, it was like a particularly awkward dinner party.'

After the batik-making she demanded, 'Do I *look* like a hippie?'

She didn't say much about the canoeing. Just limped in dejectedly, her hair streely and straggly.

'How was it?' Joe asked.

'Not very nice. They turned me upside down into the water and I thought I was going to drown. I bumped my knee and my hair is ruined.'

She was very low that night and horribly aware of her single status. She craved comfort and affection, someone to put their arms around her and squeeze away the shock of being unexpectedly immersed in cold water, someone to kiss her poor bruised knee better.

No more evening classes, she decided. She'd loved the infusion of hope at the start of each class, the excitement as she waited for the activity to fix her. But it didn't work. There was no point trying to escape her loneliness through a new interest.

Now her only hobby was Not Ringing Thomas, which was still a teeth-grittingly difficult exercise. Not a day passed that he wasn't the first thing she thought of when she woke up. But Katherine made her remember how much more excruciating it had been in the beginning, ten weeks previously. 'Remember,' she said, 'you barely slept and you never ate. I know you still feel horrendous but you've made progress. I haven't had to stop you driving round to him late at night since before Christmas.'

'I suppose,' Tara said slowly, 'I've done well not to ring him. Because I'm very weak, you know. I've the willpower of a gnat.'

'You've been marvellous. And you'll get over him all the quicker because of the lack of contact. Making the break slowly only prolongs the agony. It's like pulling off a plaster. If you're brutal, it's more painful initially, but better in the long run.'

Katherine's words both comforted and unnerved Tara. She wanted to get over Thomas, but in a mad, paradoxical way the thought of him being consigned to her past made her sad.

She trudged on through her life. Sometimes she'd catch a glimpse of herself. A thirty-something woman with a good job – even if she was as poor as a church mouse it wasn't the fault of her job – who worked hard, went to the gym daily, bought nice clothes, hadn't a hint of a man on the horizon, and who filled in the gaps with good friends and white wine. She felt like a cliché and a failure.

She yearned for the days when she was so porky she had to stop buying *Vogue* because looking at all the beautiful clothes she couldn't fit into broke her heart – at least back then she'd had a boyfriend.

For Tara, Katherine, Milo and Liv, visiting Fintan was something that had become automatically built into their routine, as reflex as brushing their teeth in the morning. Daily visits were so much the norm that they felt odd if they didn't see him.

The extremes of emotion they'd felt in the early days of his diagnosis had evened out. Despite living with terrible, ongoing anticipation where any twinge or ache of Fintan's triggered wild anxiety, the horror wasn't as accessible as it used to be. The acute shock had receded and the aberrant had been assimilated. There was no other way, Liv explained. 'When you're carrying a burden, you eventually get used to it. It's still a drain and a strain, but the immediate shock of finding it weighing down your arms goes away.'

Nor did anyone have the same *hope* that they used to have – after four doses of chemo he'd made no visible progress.

Even Fintan's rage, despair and hope didn't reach the outer limits of the pendulum swing. In a way it all felt very ordinary.

Only now and then did the bizarre awfulness of the situation break through. Like the night that Katherine, Joe and Fintan went to a play, and Fintan couldn't get a taxi home afterwards.

'What a bummer I can't give you a lift,' Katherine lamented, as they stood on the street, taxi after taxi passing with their lights off. 'That's the problem with two-seater cars.'

'I could sit on Joe's lap,' Fintan offered.

Laughing, Katherine began to berate him for his constant flirting with Joe, then saw he was serious. The shock deepened when she realized that it was possible. Fintan was shrunken and wasted enough.

She couldn't speak as she drove them home, the once strong, healthy Fintan perched like a ventriloquist's dummy on Joe's knee, Joe's arms cradling him protectively.

Milo put his farm up for sale and announced he was going to become a landscape gardener. 'I love London, but I miss the land,' he said. 'I like the feel of earth between my fingers. We all have our own way of living.'

Liv looked like she was going to swoon from admiration.

'Are you happy, Liv?' Tara asked softly.

'Happy?' she said doubtfully. 'I don't really do happy. But I'm off my Prozac, St John's wort, evening-primrose oil, vitamin B supplements and my light-box and I haven't had a suicidal thought in ages.'

'But are you happy with *Milo*?'

Liv lit up. 'Oh, he's wonderful. I can't believe my luck. He's changed the way I see the world. When it starts to rain instead of worrying that his hair might go frizzy, he doesn't even notice it, or else he says things like "It's a lovely, growthy rain, good for the crops." Although,' Liv added hurriedly: never let it be said that everything in her garden was rosy, 'you must remember that we met because of Fintan's illness. It's made us closer in one way, but in another . . . It means we have worry and guilt. And, of course, JaneAnn is cross with me. Nothing is ever perfect.'

'No, indeed it isn't.' Tara tried not to smile.

'But,' Liv had the decency to admit, 'I think this is as good as it gets.'

Around mid-February news reached them that Thomas had a new girlfriend. She was Marcy, the woman who'd told Tara at Eddie's birthday party that she was trying to get pregnant from a sperm bank.

'It figures,' Tara said, bravely. 'She must be really desperate.' Though everyone rallied round it was a major setback for her. 'The jealousy is killing me,' she admitted, taut and pale. 'All I can think of is how nice he used to be to me.'

'He was never nice to you.' Katherine attempted to cheer her up.

'Yes, he was, Katherine. He was lovely in the beginning. He was mad about me and he acted like I was gorgeous. Why else would I have got off with him? And why else did I stay with him for so long?'

'You tell me.'

'Because I was trying to get back to the way it was in the beginning. I know I'm well out of it, but I still feel he's mine. And now he's being lovely to her instead of me.'

'He'll make her life a misery.'

'That's no comfort. It should be *my* life he's making a misery.' Tara put her head in her hands and moaned, 'I'm just so tired of feeling this way. And what makes it twenty times worse is that she's so bloody skinny.'

'Have you looked in a mirror lately?' Katherine eyed Tara's starved and Stairmastered body.

'She's permanently skinny,' Tara whispered. 'She's a real skinny person. I'm only an impostor and I'll be fat again soon.' Then she rallied, courageously. 'This is just another hurdle.

Once I'm over this I'll be much better. It just means,' she added sadly, 'that now there really is no going back.'

'But you weren't going to go back.' Sandro was shocked.

'No, but . . . It's a new level of "over" when your ex meets someone new.' She smiled weakly. 'It's a shock. And it's not pleasant to think of him getting on with his life without me.'

'But you're getting on with your life without him,' Liv consoled.

'Ah, I'm not really. I haven't met someone else. It really pisses me off that it always takes men no time whatsoever to hook up with someone new. Three months is all it took him. It's very unfair.'

'You could hook up with someone if you were really desperate,' Fintan pointed out. 'You've managed to sleep with two men in the last month.'

Tara shuddered. 'Blind-drunk one-night stands with two of the most hideous men in the northern hemisphere. Elephant Man and Elephant Man's ugly brother. I only slept with them to get some affection.'

'Them's the rules.' Fintan was jolly. 'Women have sex with men for affection, men are affectionate to women to have sex with them.'

'One-night stands make me feel even worse. They're really not worth it,' Tara insisted.

'How's that sweetheart Ravi?' Fintan asked, innocently.

'Ravi? The Ravi who I work with? The Ravi who's three years younger than me? The Ravi who stays up all night playing Nintendo? The Ravi who thought *Die Hard* was a documentary? *That* Ravi? He's fine, Fintan, why do you ask?'

'Only being polite.' He smirked. 'Is he still going out with Danielle?'

'No, they split up at Christmas.'

'Is that right?' Fintan and Sandro nudged each other in delight. 'Is – that – right? So he's on the loose. You could do worse than consider him.'

Tara looked darkly at Fintan. 'If I ever even think about it, somebody shoot me.'

The next day, Tara bumped into Amy in the entrance hall at work.

'Hi.' Amy beamed. 'How are you? I haven't seen you in ages. Not since before Christmas.'

'Oh, cripes.' Tara put her face in her hands. 'I've just remembered. I met you that awful day when I was plastered and throwing up. Oh, the shame.'

'Don't worry. I got alcohol poisoning that night, and had to get an injection in my bum to stop me vomiting.'

Tara laughed in relief. She was in awe of Amy's pre-Raphaelite beauty and it was nice to know she was human.

'We really must go out one night,' Amy went on. 'Unless you've got back with your bloke?'

Tara shook her head heavily.

'I don't know if you remember, but I told you that my boyfriend has a lovely friend called Benjy, and I bet you two would really like each other. So why don't we all go out?'

'OK,' Tara said, a slow burn of excitement beginning. Maybe he'd be half decent. 'When?'

'Saturday night?'

'Can't. The Saturday after?'

'Done.'

'And he's nice, this Barney?'

'Benjy. He's lovely.'

508

'Well, if he's anything like your boyfriend he's bound to be gorgeous,' Tara praised. She turned away too soon to see alarm zigzag across Amy's porcelain face.

69

'For the thirty-first year running, the award for Best Collection of Molecules goes to Katherine Casey.' Joe smiled down at Katherine, who was sprawled naked and languid on his bed. 'And that's not just on planet Earth, you know,' he added, knowledgeably. 'That's universe-wide.'

'We have to get up for work,' she said, without much conviction.

'You're going nowhere, young lady.' Joe was stern. 'Not until the doctor has examined you.'

Katherine giggled, but her heart squeezed a slow thump of excitement. This game was even better if you were wearing clothes to start with, but what harm?

'Now what appears to be the problem?' Joe's expression was severe.

'It hurts.'

'Where?'

She wavered, then pointed to her abdomen. 'Here.'

'Show me,' he ordered, strictly. 'I'm a busy man, show me exactly where.'

'Here.' She touched herself lightly and squirmed with embarrassment and arousal.

Joe placed a cool, doctorly hand on her pubic bone and, with his thumb, began to stroke in an idle fashion. 'Here?'

'Lower down.'

'Ms Casey, you must show me exactly where!'

Her eyes closed, she took his hand and moved it.

'Here?' he demanded.

'In more,' she gasped.

'Here?'

'Yes.'

Some time later Katherine's muffled voice emerged from under Joe. 'We really have to get up for work now.'

On the way for her shower she almost tripped on the collection of free weights that were gathering dust by the door. Then went into the bathroom where there was a long-dead plant on the windowsill, the only shampoo was Head 'n' Shoulders and there wasn't any conditioner at all.

Joe's flat was reassuringly that of a single man. But not for much longer. Katherine had every intention of changing it.

She darted back into the bedroom wrapped in a beige, threadbare towel. 'I'm late. I must iron my shirt.'

Joe tried to pull the towel off her and she scolded him, 'No. Leave me alone and have your shower or you'll be late too.'

'Yes, ma'am.'

Dejected, he trudged to the bathroom.

She was dressed when he returned and he checked her out in her slim pale-blue suit. 'Possibly the best girlfriend in the world,' he said softly.

'I bet you drink Carling Black Label,' she replied, her gaze focused on his groin. 'Now get dressed.'

'OK.' He sighed.

She dried her hair, put on her make-up and rummaged in her purse.

'Oh, Joe, I need change for my tube fare.'

'Help yourself.' He swept aside the jacket of his suit and angled his hip at her.

'No,' she giggled, 'I'm not putting my hand into your trouser pocket.'

'If you want your tube fare,' he grinned, wickedly, 'you'll have to.'

She hesitated for an awkward moment, then slid her palm into the secret cave of his pocket, over the slippery cool lining and the jut of his hipbone and into the recess weighed down by coins. But she'd lost interest in the money because under the pocket she could feel something else. A luscious, squeezy swelling. Expanding and moving, unfurling and hardening, coming to life beneath her. Her hand began to seek and stroke, moving and . . .

'No!' she exclaimed. 'We'll never get to work at this rate!'

She pulled out a pile of coins, selected what she needed and returned the rest, letting them fall and jangle back in.

'Sorry.' She was sheepish. 'I'll get you later.'

'Too right.' He smiled. 'How about a session in the gents' at work?'

'No.'

'Aw.'

'I was saving that for your birthday. Now you've ruined the surprise.'

'Were you really?' he asked, curiously. He never really knew with Katherine, she was such a funny mix of the prudish and the raunchy.

'You'll have to wait until July to find out, won't you?' She gathered up her things. 'Gosh, this phone weighs a ton.'

Katherine had unplugged the phone from the wall of her flat and taken it to Joe's, just in case Tara had any ideas about ringing Thomas in her absence. 'See you at work.' She kissed him. 'Give me a ten-minute head start.'

'You don't have to tell me every morning, Katherine,' he said, gently. 'I know. But I wish we didn't have to be a secret from everyone we work with. Are you ashamed of me?' He laughed, but she realized there was real hurt in the question.

'No,' she blustered. 'Of course I'm not ashamed of you. I just don't like people knowing my business. I have to maintain an air of authority at work and if they know I'm boffing you they'll think I'm *human*. Next thing they'll be trying to pull fast ones with their expenses and overspend the accounts . . .' She thought about it for a moment. Perhaps she was being too uptight. What the hell? 'OK, so long as we don't actually walk in together.'

They'd been seeing each other for almost five months now and, as far as Katherine was concerned, every day was another miracle. If only she'd known last November that they'd still be an item come April! A lesser man would have run screaming from all the drama in Katherine's life, but Joe had just rolled up his sleeves and got on with it. He'd witnessed first hand Tara's post-Thomas shenanigans, hadn't balked at listening to her tales of woe and had refereed the occasional, late-night tussle where Tara tried to wrest the phone from Katherine.

More importantly he was very supportive to Katherine in her dealings with Fintan. He never complained about the amount of time she spent with him and seemed happy to devote plenty of his own time too. He didn't even object when Fintan flirted outrageously the first time they met.

'Thank you,' Katherine had said, as they drove away.

'For what?'

'For not getting uncomfortable when he gave you the come-on.'

'What's to thank?' Joe had asked. 'A good-looking man flirts with me? I'm flattered.'

'Well, you'd better get used to it. I think he likes you.'

The intensity of emotion and events acted like a pressure-cooker, so that Katherine and Joe had become very close very quickly. She'd never had a relationship that had lasted as long as this one. And it was a long time since she'd trusted a man as much as she trusted Joe. Not that she trusted him *much*. 'But I trust you enough to tell you I don't trust you.' She laughed.

'Thank you.' He was utterly serious. 'And take your time. I'm not in a hurry, plenty of people trust me.'

Though she guarded her past as though it was a precious jewel, eventually she felt that she had to stop being so cagy about her family set-up. She knew all about his, and her dead silence whenever parents were mentioned began to feel like overreaction. So one day she sat him down and spilled the beans about her mad mother and her lack of a father. 'I thought you were going to tell me you'd murdered someone,' he exclaimed, when, after a dramatic build-up, she finally managed to blurt it out. 'Why do you act like it's something to be ashamed of?'

'You mean it isn't?'

'Of course not.'

'But I'm illegitimate.'

'You're Katherine Casey,' he replied.

Even though she had to go to bed for a couple of hours from the exhaustion of the revelation, Katherine began to inch her way into a fear-free life. While Joe reached a new understanding of what she was all about.

70

'Something weird's after happening,' Tara said to Katherine.

'What?'

'I think I'm over Thomas.'

'Great. Well, it was bound to ease off. As Joe says, "Time wounds all heals."'

'No, I don't just mean it's got easier,' Tara insisted with intensity. 'I mean when I woke up today it was all gone.'

It wasn't like those mornings when she woke up and had a few confused seconds during which the pain was absent, but then quickly rushed into focus, like a photograph developing, until the agony had returned in all its sharp definition.

'It's gone, like a puff of wind,' Tara said. 'My life with him seems like it belongs to someone else, and it seems so *sensible* to be over him because he just didn't deserve me.'

'You're preaching to the converted.'

'All I feel now is sorry for him.'

'Go easy.'

'But, Katherine, he'll never be happy.'

'Excellent. It couldn't happen to a nicer guy.'

'No matter what I did it wouldn't have pleased him. If I went down to five stone he'd have complained about some other aspect of me. Because I wasn't the problem. He is.'

'You're not just saying this?' Katherine asked suspiciously.

'No! Isn't it great? I've wanted to parade in front of him to

515

show him how skinny I've become, and now I don't care if he never finds out. And I don't give a damn about Marcy. You were absolutely right, he will make her life utter hell. And I'm sure he's told her I was always upset, like he told me about his previous girlfriends, so that she'll feel she can't ever show any negative emotion, the way I did. But what do I care? Because my life isn't a misery any more and that's the way I like it!'

They held hands and did a little dance of delight.

'And I'm not saying that I actually *want* to have children, but at least now I have a choice, unlike poor old Marcy. She'd have been better off with the turkey-baster,' Tara mused. 'Thank you, Katherine, for everything. For housing me – I'm going to start looking for my own place this very weekend – and putting up with me. But most of all thank you for not letting me ring him or visit him.'

'It was far better for you to have no contact with him,' Katherine agreed. 'The other way only prolongs the agony and keeps you hoping.'

'All the same, I can't believe it,' Tara said, in wonder. 'It's only five months since I've left him and I always thought that heartbreak was something that went on for years and years, basically until you met another man. That's how it's always worked for me before,' she added.

'I know.' Katherine had witnessed Tara's almost unbroken ten-year chain of boyfriends. 'This is nothing short of a miracle. It was always like a relay race before. You'd hardly be finished with one fella before you'd started on the next.'

'Was I that bad?'

'Oh, *yes*.'

'I've *wanted* a boyfriend since I left him,' Tara admitted. 'The loneliness has been unspeakable. And, in fairness, I had a couple of one-night stands.' She recoiled at the memory.

'But at least you left them as one-night stands. You didn't start going out with either of the men.'

'That's because they were eejits and I've wasted enough of my life on eejits. I don't want to do it any more.'

'But don't you see?' Katherine demanded in excitement. 'You were never like that before. You'd have gone out with an eejit rather than have nobody. You've changed.'

'So have you.'

'So have we all. Liv's different. You're different. I suppose even I'm different. Why?'

'It's because of Fintan, isn't it?'

Katherine tried to find the words. 'It's something to do with him being sick. And I know all that stuff about seizing the day and making the most of every second is hard to sustain constantly,' she admitted guiltily. 'It's so easy at times to forget and to take it all for granted.'

'But there are other times when I look at him,' Tara interrupted, 'so young and so much nearer to death than me. Then I think, That could be me, and I feel . . . it makes me . . .' She faltered, then smiled with enlightenment. 'It makes me want to live a better life.'

'That's exactly it.' Katherine was luminous and repeated, 'It makes me want to live a better life.'

'And going back to Thomas wasn't living a better life,' Tara said. 'And neither is going out with a gobshite. And falling in love with Joe Roth is.'

'Excu —'

'Sorry, that's none of my business. You haven't changed

completely,' Tara said ruefully. 'Do you want to know something else?'

'What?'

'I'm not sure I ever loved Thomas.'

'Makes sense to me.'

'And do you know why I didn't love him?'

'Why?'

'Because I don't think I ever got over Alasdair. So I've been thinking and do you know what?'

'What?'

'I'm going to give Alasdair a ring.'

Katherine's heart sank. She'd known it was too good to be true. She'd been just about to return Tara's mobile to her and all. Good job she hadn't. 'But he's married,' she tried. 'It's years since you've had any contact.'

'Oh, I don't think we'll get back together,' Tara said breezily. 'I just want to lay it to rest. And what better time than when I'm a size ten?'

Katherine looked very anxious.

'Don't worry,' Tara soothed. 'Even if I was desperate for a man – which I'm not – I'm going on a date on Saturday night. That girl at work I was telling you about, her boyfriend has a friend.'

'Weren't you supposed to do that ages ago?'

'Yes, but she got the flu, then she was away, then I was busy, but we're *definitely* going out this Saturday.'

Katherine prayed that Tara would forget about the Alasdair idea, or that she wouldn't be able to track him down. But, to her alarm, Tara announced that she'd spoken to him, that he was still in the same job, and that she was meeting him for a drink after work on Thursday.

At nine thirty on Thursday night Joe and Katherine were watching telly and sharing a bottle of wine when Tara stomped in.

'Well?'

'He was fat, balding and blissfully happy. They have a little boy and his wife is expecting another baby in August.'

'I see.'

'I'd be lying to you, Katherine, if I didn't say that a small part of me had been holding out some sort of hope.'

'No kidding.'

'I didn't even realize it until I saw him.'

'Well, there we are.'

'Also, I wanted some answers. How could he go out with me for so long and then turn around and marry someone else so quickly. He said that he couldn't explain. He just said that when he met what's-her-name it felt completely right. He just *knew*.'

Katherine and Joe avoided looking at each other.

'But you'd want to see him,' Tara exclaimed. 'I barely recognized him. He looks like someone's dad. Alasdair, plump! Remember how wiry he used to be? Sorry, Joe, I forgot you don't know him, but take it from me, he used to be as thin as a rake. Now he's got love handles. I suppose that's happiness for you. In fact, you've both put on a bit of weight yourselves.'

They shifted uncomfortably.

'He said I was looking great.'

'You are.'

'But I could tell he didn't really give a damn.'

'Ah, well.'

'So, this is one of me moving on with my life.'

'Excellent.'

71

'As a last resort, pretend that you're gay,' Lorcan harangued, 'or that you're having doubts about your sexuality.'

'Why?' Benjy asked. Surely that was the last thing you should do if you wanted to get a woman into bed?

'Because,' Lorcan sighed at Benjy's stupidity, 'a woman likes nothing better than to think that she was the one who cured a man of his homosexuality. It's a challenge and an ego trip. She'll hustle you into bed, asking, "Is this nice, is that nice?" and if you bonk her, instead of feeling besmirched she'll think it's a victory.'

'If you're sure.' Benjy was doubtful. Lorcan's advice never worked for him. Ever. He was still smarting from the memory of a party the previous weekend, where Lorcan had lent him his special, non-working lighter. Instead of the girl being charmed by Benjy's eager vulnerability and his elaborate mortification when the lighter didn't spark, she'd just sniffed, 'Loser,' and turned away.

Lorcan leant into the hall and yelled into Amy's bedroom, 'Tell us more about this Tara. She's kind of, er, cuddly, you say?'

'Yes. Although not as cuddly as she used to be. In fact, now that I think about it, not very much at all. And she's really pretty . . .'

'Yeah, whatever,' Lorcan said, impatiently, and pushed the

living-room door closed again. He did *not* want Amy to hear any of this. 'Right, so she's a fat girl.'

'But Amy just said she wasn't.'

'She was being nice, trying to sell her to you. Anyway, you're in luck, Benjy, my man.'

'Am I?' Benjy couldn't see anything lucky about being matched with a fatty.

'Yeah, I've a great technique for you, straight from the master's lips. Listen up, Benjy, this is what you do. No need to say to this Tara, "Hey, you're a fat girl! I'll do you a pity shag." Because she knows she's fat, *you* know she's fat, right? But without letting on that you think she could do with dropping a couple of stone, you complain about women always wanting to be skinny. Got that?'

Benjy nodded carefully.

'You say to her, like you're just making conversation, and that it's got nothing to do with her busting out of her clothes, you say that it's a myth that men like thin women. Tell her that you never hear men saying to each other, "She was gorgeous, so skinny, all her ribs were sticking out, like a skeleton or like a famine victim, I nearly sliced meself open on her hipbones, I'd a hard-on just looking at her." *Compris*?'

Benjy assented.

'Next – like you're just making idle chit-chat – you start complaining about models. Say that no red-blooded male wants a woman who looks like an anorexic teenager. Mention Jody Kidd. Of course, *you* know and *I* know that a night with Jody Kidd would be up there with the greats, but don't tell that to Fat Tara. Because, before you know it, Fat Tara thinks she's died and gone to heaven and is ready to deliver the goods.'

'Jesus, you're unbelievable. You've no morals whatsoever.'

'Thanks.' Lorcan shrugged and said shyly, 'Listen, man, no need to lay it on with a trowel. What are friends for?'

'There's only one problem,' Benjy admitted awkwardly. 'I don't know if I'd like a fat girl.'

'Fat girls have good points. What am I always telling you?'

'To ask women what shampoo they use.'

'Apart from that?'

Benjy didn't know and Lorcan exploded, 'Amn't I worn out telling you that fat girls try harder?'

'Oh, right, of course.'

'I feel like I'm just wasting my time here, Benjy.'

'Sorry.'

'Do you listen to anything I tell you?'

'I do. I do. Sorry.'

'Ah, you're OK. You're doing your best. Now another little gem I'm going to pass on to you – and not a lot of people know this – is that fat girls *feel* very nice.'

'Would you sleep with a fat girl?' Benjy asked hopefully. If Lorcan, his hero and mentor, would, then maybe it was all right.

'Sure I would,' he declared, magnanimously. 'Sure I would. Mind you,' he added, 'I wouldn't be seen in public with one of them. But in the privacy of their own home I'd have no problem playing hide the salami.'

'Right. But perhaps Tara will be nice.' Benjy was infused with wild hope.

'Yeah.' Lorcan's eyes were narrowed, thoughtfully. 'Perhaps she might be.'

Lorcan went to the bathroom to get ready. He felt strangely depressed. What was wrong with him? He'd had new and worrying feelings in the last six months or so and helping Benjy didn't thrill him the way it used to. He had neither the energy nor the stomach that he once had. He still went through his bad-boy motions with Amy, driving her insane with misery by neglecting her or flirting with other women when she was present. But it didn't feel as nice as it used to. He'd always roared with laughter at the thought of settling down again and, even worse, having children, but lately he'd had strange, endearing flashes of the thought of a little Lorcan. And perhaps a little girl, too. Who knew?

He was nearly forty. He sighed. Midlife-crisis time.

With a flourish, he swept Amy's brush through his vivacious, silky hair and his heart lifted. His hair never failed to cheer him. He played one of his favourite games for a while, which consisted of running the brush right down to the ends of his hair, stretching as far as it could go, then whisking the brush out and watching his hair bounce and spring with joyous elasticity back to its original position. He could never grow tired of it.

He entertained himself for a while longer by fluffing and fiddling, stroking and patting, twiddling and rearranging, then picked up the brush again – and saw something that made his blood curdle in his veins. There was hair caught in the bristles of the brush. Lots of hair. Red hair. *His* hair.

The brush fell from his lifeless hands as he instigated a frantic investigation of his crowning glory. Everyone moulted hair, but did the hair in the brush imply something more sinister? With minute detail he fingered his way through his scalp and to his horror his hair seemed to be thinner on top than it used to be. He was losing his hair! Black patches scudded before his panic-stricken eyes. He couldn't be going – he choked at the word – *bald*. He needed his hair. Especially for his career. But everything felt like it was coming to an end – over before it had even begun.

Moving to a deeper level of fear, he remembered his father. He'd lost his hair early, which was no problem when you were a postman. But Lorcan was an international actor. His appearance was his income. What would he do? he projected wildly. When the crown of his head was smooth and bare, would he keep the rest of it long, *à la* Michael Bolton? Or would he cut and shave the remaining hair, so that he was entirely bald, just like Grant Mitchell?

Diminished, almost in tears at the thought, he caught sight of himself in the mirror. And wondered what he was worrying about. He still had *loads* of hair. Tons of it. Long and luscious, lustrous and luminous. Volumizing shampoo. That's all he needed. A bit of lift over his forehead. And there was Wella's liquid hair, he'd only been waiting for an excuse to use it. Here was his chance.

He pointed a finger at the mirror, winked, clicked his tongue and, with a warm appreciative grin, ordered, 'Don't go changin'.'

'How do I look?' Tara, sleek and sexy in a black catsuit, paraded before Katherine and Joe.

'Great. Tara –'

'What if your man Benjy is nice?' Tara wondered.

'Tara, something's happened. While you were in the shower Sandro rang about Fintan.'

'Oh, God,' Tara breathed and sank into a chair.

'No, it's good news.'

Tara's pale face looked up hopefully from between her fingers.

'Really good news. He said that in the last day there's been a dramatic reduction in the size of the tumours.'

Tara was frozen, her fingers still half over her face.

'The one on his neck has halved, he says, and you can hardly feel the ones on his pancreas.'

'Oh, thank God.' Tara laughed tearfully. 'About bloody time too, after six months of chemo. What about his bone-marrow and chest?'

'More tests will have to be done, but if the lymph glands have improved we can only presume there's a high chance that the other sites have too.'

'I can't believe it,' Tara breathed tearfully. 'I can't believe it. I just can't believe it. It's been so long since anything positive has happened, I was fairly sure that, you know, there wasn't much, um, you know, hope.'

'I know.'

'I'd kind of come to terms – well, not come to terms,' she said hurriedly, 'but if he didn't ever get better, it wasn't going to be a massive shock, do you know what I mean?'

Katherine nodded.

'But this is brilliant!' Tara's eyes were shiny with tears.

'I suppose we shouldn't get too excited.' Katherine struck a note of caution. 'It's such an unpredictable illness.'

'Oh, come on, let's get a *little* bit excited. Will we go over there now to see him?'

'No.' Katherine could hardly hide her impatience. 'We'll see him tomorrow. Go out on your date and have fun.'

She was keen to get rid of Tara because there was something she'd been dying to discuss with Joe since the previous day.

'OK. See you later.'

'Have a nice time. 'Bye.'

The door slammed.

72

'Joe?'

'Mmmm.'

'Did anything ever happen with you and Angie? Angie at work.'

Katherine felt him go very still, as though his blood had stopped flowing, then he moved and sat up properly on the couch. He looked at her and his face was sad.

'You don't have to tell me,' she lied, quickly. 'It's none of my business, really, but she saw us when we came in together yesterday morning and asked me if I was seeing you. And I said I wasn't but she seemed upset. So . . . I wondered if anything happened with the two of you. Did it?'

He looked at her with infinite tenderness, then frowned as though in pain. He opened his mouth to speak and she watched, willing him to say no. 'Yes,' he said, and she felt a heavy stone plummet through her. Don't overreact, she begged herself. Please don't turn into a bunny-boiler.

'How long?' Her heart was pounding. 'I mean, what happ – I mean, did you go out with each other for a long time? Were you in love?'

'No.' He said kind of wearily. 'Nothing like that. It was just one night.'

One night was bad enough, she thought, her soul corroding with jealous agony. She thought of Angie's lovely figure and wanted to kill Joe. And she had a horrible inkling she knew

526

which night it was too. That's what made it so bad. The day after she'd accused him of sexual harassment he'd gone for a drink with Angie and shown up at the office the next day wearing the same clothes. She'd had a bad feeling then and she had a worse one now. On and off during the last five months she'd thought about asking Joe what had happened, but she hadn't dared in case the answer wasn't what she wanted to hear. But after seeing how upset Angie had been, she had no choice.

'I shouldn't have,' Joe said, miserably. 'It's not the kind of thing I'd normally do. But I'm a human being and I make mistakes.'

'I'm sure Angie Hiller wouldn't like to hear of herself being referred to as a mistake,' Katherine said haughtily.

'No, I didn't mean that. But getting involved with her was.'

'Involved? I thought it was only one night.'

'It was.'

'Must have been pretty intense if you're talking about being –' she took a deep breath before spitting contemptuously '– *involved*.'

'It's just a word. Obviously the wrong one.'

Katherine held her breath, waiting for him to tell her that all he'd done was kiss her or that he'd slept on the couch or that he'd been too drunk to perform. But he didn't, so she asked, 'So you slept with her?'

'Yes.'

'What I mean is, you had sex with her?' She felt she was going to throw up.

He nodded. Yes.

Her seasick stomach churned faster. 'And then you went around and told everyone to call her Gillette. That's very mature, Joe.'

'I didn't.' He looked alarmed and disgusted. 'I don't know who started that – Myles, probably – but it was nothing to do with me.'

'Well, you obviously went around telling everyone you fucked her. Very nice, Joe!'

'I didn't tell anyone. Angie told Myles, if you must know.'

'So did you see her again?'

'Not in that way. The following morning we talked about it, I explained that I was sorry it happened and that it wouldn't happen again.'

'And how do you think she felt?' A sharp, vicious little upsurge of rage maddened her. 'You get her into bed, screw her, then tell her once is enough. How gentlemanly.'

'I'm sorry,' he said.

'For what?' she said, coldly. 'You're a free agent.'

'Please don't be like this,' he said, softly.

'Like what?'

'Why are you so angry? We weren't seeing each other then. In fact, it was just after you implied I was sexually harassing you –'

I know, she wanted to scream.

'– and I thought you didn't give a toss about me. And, to be honest, Katherine, I was really cut up –'

'And what other way to deal with it than sleep with another woman. Oh, how like a man.'

'It shouldn't have happened,' he repeated. 'I was sorry it did. It's no excuse but I was drunk and cut up. I was out of order, I was wrong, I made a mistake. People do.'

She clamped her mouth in a hard, cold line.

'Everyone has a past, you know,' he said, gently. 'No one comes to a relationship with a clean slate.'

528

Still she wouldn't speak. Then rent the silence by snarling, 'Why didn't you tell me?'

'I *tried*. But you told me that you didn't want to discuss our past romances, remember?'

'Yes, but . . . I only meant that I didn't want to tell you about mine. I wanted to hear about yours.'

He sighed. 'That's not really fair, is it, Katherine?'

'You told me about Lindsay,' she accused, changing tack. 'If you told me about Lindsay, why didn't you tell me about Angie?'

'I tried,' he exclaimed. 'But you told me you needed time and that you found it hard to trust. So I respected that. I tried not to push anything or move things too fast for you –'

'How do you think I feel?' she interrupted. 'I've been going in to work day in, day out, and now I find out that Angie Hiller was having a good laugh at me all along because she slept with my boyfriend.'

'But she didn't know about us. And why would she laugh? You're the one who's my girlfriend, not Angie.'

'Oh, so I'm the lucky one, am I?' she sneered.

She knew she was out of control, that she was in danger of ruining everything, but she couldn't stop herself. She heard the sour, spiky words spilling from her, felt them relieve and burn, but couldn't stem the flow.

'Katherine,' he crooned, in a low voice, 'if you're worried that it would ever happen again or that I would ever be unfaithful to you, you are way, way wrong. I'm not just saying this now because you're angry with me, but the way I feel about you is –' Joe stopped. He'd thought he'd heard the sound of a key jiggling in the lock. Seconds later Tara burst into the room, with what seemed like an army of people. His heart sank. The sooner Tara got her own place the better.

As Joe tried to paste on a happy face for the visitors, Tara chattered enthusiastically, gesturing to the three people standing behind her. 'We were just passing and I thought it might be nice for you to meet, because you've all heard about each other. This is Amy from my work and this is Benjy . . .' She paused and mouthed exaggeratedly, 'My fella,' at Katherine and Joe, then discreetly clutched her stomach and rolled her eyes, indicating the desire to puke. And continued, 'And this is . . .'

Then Joe got a shock. He recognized the third person. It was impossible not to. He almost filled the room with his huge shoulders and great height and long red hair. It was that spoilt-brat actor from the butter commercial, Lorcan something-or-other.

Lorcan had obviously recognized Joe also, because he interrupted the introductions by exclaiming, in loud surprise, 'Hey, I know you.'

Joe sighed and braced himself for unpleasantness. Until something filled him with inexplicable fear. He'd followed the line of Lorcan's gaze and saw that Lorcan wasn't talking to him. He was talking to Katherine.

73

Katherine was death-white. 'Hello,' she said faintly.

'Hi.' Lorcan grinned, clicking his fingers as he tried to remember her name. He just couldn't place where he knew her from but he suspected that at some point in the past he'd had sex with her. What a guy!

Tara's excited introductions stopped abruptly as she picked up that another dynamic had taken over, that she was no longer in charge. 'Do you two *know* each other?' she hooted, in surprise, looking from Katherine to Lorcan and back again.

'Seems to me we do.' Lorcan gave Katherine an intimate smile. 'Do we?'

She nodded.

At that, for no obvious reason, the mood in the room turned. Joe sat frozen and fearful on the couch. Mid-floor, Benjy, Amy and Tara stood silent and unsmiling. Viscous, impenetrable emotion radiated from Katherine.

'I didn't recognize you with your clothes on,' Tara said gaily, desperate to dispel the heavy, ominous confusion. But it seemed to make everyone even more tense. Behind her Tara could sense Amy's fear. *Smell* it, in fact.

'You're ... ah ... um ...' Lorcan tried to remember the girl's name. Jessica? Inez? Mary? Christ, it could be anything. The catch-all 'Babe' had saved Lorcan's life on many occasions, especially those mornings when he woke up and couldn't remember the name of the woman lying beside him, but it wasn't going to work here. And where the hell did he know her from exactly? 'I'm hopeless with names,' Lorcan smiled his please-forgive-me smile as he looked down on Katherine slumped in a daze. She was a cute little thing, actually, he wouldn't mind refreshing his memory!

Despite her shock, Katherine was raging with herself. How many times had she prayed for this moment when she finally met him again and pretended that she hadn't a clue who he was? How many years had she practised reducing grown men to frightened children with one arch of her perfectly shaped eyebrow, just so that when the time came she'd be able to use it on him? And now she couldn't even raise her head from the back of the couch.

More shaming than her physical debilitation was that she wanted him to remember her. Trembling, she watched, willing him at least to know her name. But it *had* been a long time ago . . .

'It's Katherine,' she whispered.

With a dazzling smile Lorcan smacked the palm of his hand against his forehead. 'Of course it is. Katherine, *now* I remember you.'

'That's Katherine with a K,' Katherine emphasized slowly.

Lorcan repeated, with an indulgent grin, 'That's right, Katherine with a . . .' Abruptly, he paused, the blood draining from his face. He'd just remembered who she was. Christ! Instantly he regretted having ever opened his mouth about semi-recognizing her. 'You look different,' he blurted.

'It was a long time ago.'

'Yeah, it was, wasn't it? It must be, at least, let me see, seven years.'

'Twelve and a half,' she said, before she could stop herself.

Then she really, *really* hated herself. How could she have been so transparent?

'You've been keeping track.' Lorcan laughed nervously. He was now very, very keen to leave, but as he started moving towards the door, he noticed the man sitting beside Katherine with a K. Holy Jesus, what was going on here? It was the pretty-boy exec who'd had him thrown off the butter ad. With sudden, heart-clenching paranoia, Lorcan wondered if this was a set-up. A type of court, or a roll-call of his life? His past finally running him to ground? Were there several more pissed-off women and disgruntled ex-colleagues lurking in the bedroom, ready to make an appearance? Then he told himself to stop being stupid. Coincidence. That's all it was. 'Hey,' he tried to hide his anxiety with raucous, belittling laughter, 'it's Joe, Joe Roth.'

'Lockery Liggery.' Joe nodded with hostile politeness. 'What a surprise.'

'The name's Lorcan.'

'Isn't that what I said?' Joe's innocent tone fooled no one.

A gleam appeared in Lorcan's eye. He hadn't forgotten the humiliation he'd suffered on the day of the ad, or the poverty he'd lived in since, or the career that had remained in the doldrums.

'Are you two . . . ?' Lorcan slowly moved his finger between Katherine and Joe.

'Are we two *what*?' Joe asked.

'Going out with each other?'

'What's it to you?' Joe asked politely.

'No, don't tell me, you're *married*.' Lorcan laughed.

'We're not married,' Katherine said, her voice small and faraway.

'Great!' Lorcan said heartily. Then, to general alarm, he sat down on the other side of Katherine and, with slow deliberation, kissed her cheek. 'Still hope for me, so.'

Amy made a tiny, anguished noise and Joe started angrily. 'Just a –'

But, as everyone watched, stricken with disbelief, Katherine gave her shoulder to Joe and turned, like a flower reaching for the sun, towards Lorcan.

74

She'd never been able to resist him and she wasn't about to start now.

She'd been almost nineteen, standing at a bar in Limerick, earnestly chatting to a lady she worked with, when Lorcan had first spotted her. He'd been feeling bored and irritable, like a cat without a bird, and suddenly the ennui lifted. 'Look at that cute little girl there.' He elbowed his friend, Jack.

'She doesn't look like your usual type,' Jack said, in surprise.

'She's a girl,' Lorcan pointed out. 'That makes her my usual type. Cover me, I'm going in.'

When Delores, the woman she was with, went to get cigarettes, Katherine was surprised to hear a mellow, chocolatey voice behind her asking intimately, 'Did it hurt?'

Startled, she turned. And found herself looking into the face of the most handsome man she'd ever seen in her – admittedly sheltered – life. He was lounging, elbow on the bar, smiling down at her, burning her face with his naked admiration. 'Did what hurt?'

He paused and fixed his sherry-dark eyes on her intently. 'When you fell from Heaven.'

She flushed, as she wondered if she was being 'chatted-up'. If she was, it was a first. 'I'm not from Heaven. I'm from Knockavoy.' She'd always known she wasn't very witty but, nevertheless, she was still bitterly disappointed with her answer.

But Lorcan laughed. 'I love that. "I'm not from Heaven, I'm from Knockavoy." That's a good one.'

Some sort of nameless good feeling started to warm Katherine.

'What's your name?' Lorcan asked, softly.

'Katherine. That's Katherine with a K,' she added, with a solemnity that enchanted him.

'And I'm Lorcan. Lorcan with an L.'

She giggled, entertained at the thought. 'It's hardly likely to be Lorcan with a K. Unless,' she said thoughtfully, 'unless the "K" was silent.'

Then she giggled again and Lorcan looked at her small white teeth, her dewy, make-up-free skin, her straight, shining hair, her little-girl self-possession, and felt the old rush. He knew he'd have to handle this one delicately because there was a purity about her, a *cleanness*. Not just with her appearance but with her behaviour: no coquettish lowering of her eyelids, no double-entendres, no flirty pouts. He was powerfully attracted to her air of virtue. Because he wanted to sully it.

'So tell me, Katherine with a K, what brings you to Limerick?'

'I'm training to be an accountant,' she said, proudly.

He managed to give the appearance of acute interest as he asked all about her, and got the full nine yards. How she'd got great results in her Leaving Cert, had been living in Limerick for nine months, how lucky she'd been to get her placement in Good and Elder, how she lived in a nice bedsit with her own kettle, how she missed her two best friends in Knockavoy, Tara and Fintan, but that she sometimes managed to ring them from her office and she went home every second weekend.

'Why don't they come and work in Limerick?' Lorcan asked, all concern.

'They've got jobs in the hotel at home. They're saving to go abroad.'

'Well, I hope they at least come and visit you.'

'Not really,' she explained awkwardly. 'You see, they've to work most Saturday nights and I've to work during the week, and study at night, so there wouldn't be much point . . .'

'And the people you work with? Are they nice?'

'Well, yes.' Katherine flicked a glance around her and lowered her voice conspiratorially. 'It's just that they're all a bit old.'

'So you don't have many friends here?'

'Not many, I suppose.'

That didn't stop Katherine introducing Lorcan to the bunch of dusty old fogies she was with, and he was forced to make conversation with them for ages. When he could take no more he leant close to her ear. 'Why don't you and I escape,' he whispered, 'and go somewhere we can have a proper conversation?' Once out on the street, Lorcan suggested casually, 'Let's go to your place.'

Katherine paused. Did he take her for some thick little girl just up from the country? 'No,' she said, firmly. 'We'll go to another bar.'

Lorcan burst out laughing. 'There's no flies on you, Katherine with a K. Quite right to be careful, but you can trust me.'

'But you would say that!'

'Do I look like a rapist?' he asked, in wounded innocence, spreading his arms wide beseechingly.

'How would I know what a rapist looks like?' she asked, tartly.

Lorcan stopped, put his big hands on her tiny shoulders and moved himself close to her. 'I wouldn't hurt you,' he promised intently, in his low, melodic voice. 'I mean it.'

Katherine was so moved by his sincerity that she was struck dumb. She believed him. Being in the presence of his potent masculinity felt powerfully right, as if she should always have been there. The final piece of the jigsaw of her life slotted into place. 'OK,' she squeaked. 'You can come to my room for a cup of tea, but no funny business, mind.' Sternly, she waggled her finger, which, snapping and growling playfully, Lorcan tried to bite. Katherine collapsed into peals of giggles.

'Come on.' Lorcan put his arm around her waist and half hurried, half carried her along the pavement.

'I mean it.' She looked into his face as he whisked her along. 'No funny business.'

'None,' Lorcan agreed affectionately.

But funny business there was.

At her bedsit, no sooner had she handed him a cup of tea than he put it down on top of a pile of accountancy textbooks. Then firmly he took her cup and put it down also.

'What are you doing?' Her voice was croaky.

'I don't want you to spill your tea.'

'But I won't.'

'You might. It's very hard to drink tea and be kissed at the same time'

She was terrified. He was a rapist after all! She opened her mouth to protest, but he'd pulled her to him, his arm huge and hard around her back. Then he lowered his handsome face, placed his beautiful mouth on hers, and kissed her.

She felt a half-second of revulsion, but just before she shoved him away, the magic arrived. She'd been kissed before, but never like this, and by the time he stopped she didn't want him to. When she reluctantly opened her eyes, her entire body was leaning forward, angling into him.

'Meet me tomorrow, Katherine with a K?'

'OK,' she said breathlessly.

When the nuns had told them to never wear black patent shoes with a skirt for fear that a man might see the reflection of their knickers, even Katherine had scoffed. But, all the same, some of the teachings of the Catholic Church had their hooks deep into her. She didn't mind how Tara or Fintan lived their lives, but she'd always intended she'd be a virgin when she got married. She was adamant that she'd never go all the way with Lorcan, never more certain of anything in her life. But she was happy for him to kiss her. And kiss her he did.

They spent every evening together, sometimes going to his flat but mostly going to hers. Where they'd lie on her single bed and, while her accountancy books gathered dust on her tiny desk, kiss each other for hours. Long, hot, probing kisses, him half on top of her, the weight of his body both frightening and delicious, his leg thrown over her, his hand caressing the curve of her waist, her body turned into his.

The smoky, grown-up, masculine smell of his jacket, the silkiness of his hair beneath her hands, the way he groaned when she tantalized the nape of his neck, the hot, sweet pressure of his mouth on hers. But when he began to fiddle with her bra-clasp she was horrified: with him for his audacity and with herself because she'd wanted him to. She made them stop, pushed him off, sat up, told him that she wasn't that kind of girl and that he needn't try a repeat of his behaviour. He apologized profusely.

But the next time they were together he tried it again and Katherine was like an avenging angel. 'Go home now,' she ordered.

He was devastated. He actually wept, and swore that he'd never do it again. But she just repeated, 'I want you to go.'

So he went and she bawled crying and thought that it was all over. Though she'd only been going out with him for two weeks, never had she felt so abandoned or alone.

But at seven o'clock the following morning, there was a pounding on her door and when she opened it, white-faced and nauseous from her sleepless night, Lorcan was standing there, a picture of contrite anguish. Wordlessly, they flung themselves into each other's arms, then she led him in to lie down on her bed. And when he unbuttoned the front of her nightdress and touched her breasts and used his teeth to coax her pink nipples into hot, hard peaks, she made no protest.

Though she knew it was wrong she loved it. Shame mingled with dirty, horny desire and every time they were together she wanted to, but couldn't, tell Lorcan to stop touching her. Eventually she made peace with herself and her jumpy conscience by deciding that above the waist was allowable. After all, everyone did it – Tara had been letting boys feel her breasts since she was fourteen. And so long as Katherine and Lorcan weren't doing anything 'down there' she'd be all right. Besides he was mad about her. Couldn't be nicer. Loved everything about her.

During one of the intimate conversations they had between bouts of burning kisses, she was reassured that this was something special. Lorcan had looked at her meaningfully, his eyes half closed and said, 'I bet you've had millions of boyfriends.'

'No.' She was too inexperienced to lie. 'Not a lot. Just two.'

'Now you're making me jealous,' he said, huffily. And he wasn't acting.

'No, no, no, don't be!' she cried. 'They were just boys who

came to Knockavoy for their summer holidays. Neither of them was anything like . . . this.'

'Well, wasn't I worth waiting for?' He chuckled.

'Yes.' That was exactly what she thought – Lorcan was her reward for being a good girl. All things come to those who wait. 'And,' she asked, shyly, 'and have you had many girlfriends before me?' She steeled herself because she knew he was bound to have had. Especially considering that he was seven years older than she was. And so good-looking.

'One or two,' he said idly. 'No one special.'

In whispered phone calls from her office, Katherine told Tara and Fintan she had a boyfriend. Over the weeks she confided that he was 'gorgeous', that she was 'mad about him', and that he was 'mad about her'. How soon could they get down to Limerick so that she could show him off?

But neither of them could come for at least a month because they were working nights.

'Oh.' Katherine was disappointed.

'Sorry. We'd love to,' Tara said. 'We're dying to see him. Tell us again how good-looking he is. Is he as nice as Danny Hartigan?'

Katherine gave a bark of scornful laughter. Danny Hartigan had been Tara's for two weeks the summer before last, and was the yardstick by which every other boy was measured. But compared to Lorcan he was a *squirt*. 'Much better than Danny Hartigan. He's like a film star and he's actually an actor, you know.'

'Janey Mackers.' Tara could hardly contain her envy. An actor! 'Now you tell us.'

'He's an *actor*,' Katherine faintly heard Tara shout to Fintan. Her voice came back on the line at normal pitch. 'Would we know him?' she begged, in excitement. 'Have we seen him in anything?'

'Maybe.' Katherine overflowed with pride. 'You know the ad for fabric softener? When they're all playing football and . . . ?'

'I – don't – believe – it,' Tara intoned. 'Not the ref who tells them to take off their jerseys for the wash? He is FABULOUS!'

'Fabulous!' Katherine heard Fintan's echoey shriek. 'No, not the ref, actually,' Katherine admitted. 'He's one of the players, in the right-hand corner at the far end of the field.'

'Settle down.' Tara turned from the phone to Fintan. 'It's not the ref.'

'You can't miss him,' Katherine said. 'He's running away so there's a great shot of his back . . . Do you know him?'

'Maybe,' Tara said doubtfully.

'He has red hair and is really tall.'

'Red hair! You never mentioned that before. And really tall? Are you *sure* he's good-looking? He sounds more like Beaker from *The Muppet Show*!'

'Well, he's not,' Katherine said huffily.

'Sorry, I didn't mean to rain on your parade. So tell me, is it serious?'

'Oh, yes, I think so,' she said, confidently.

'Holy Maloney! Well, try and get a photo of him and come and see us at the hotel the very minute you get off the bus on Friday night.'

'Oh, I can't.' Katherine explained, hurriedly, 'I thought I'd stay down this weekend. To be with him, you see?'

'Again?'

The way Lorcan made her feel was irresistible. When he kissed her, she felt hot and frantic, when he took her nipple in his

542

mouth, she thought she'd explode. Sometimes when she was alone she'd touch herself through her panties and wonder at the hot, tingly sensations she felt. Though she hadn't been to confession for quite a while, she wondered how she'd ever go again.

The day came when they were lying on her bed as usual, kissing passionately, when she heard the whiz of a zip and felt Lorcan fumbling with himself. Then she heard the crumple of denim and crisp cotton and realized Lorcan was shucking down his jeans. 'What are you doing?' she asked in alarm.

'You don't have to do anything,' he said hoarsely, stroking himself. 'Just touch it. Just once.'

'No!'

'Please. You'll like it.'

'It's wrong.'

'How can it be wrong? We love each other.'

It was the first she'd heard of it, but she was delighted. Though it wasn't going to shake her resolve. 'We really shouldn't . . .'

'We should. We love each other.'

And so, trembling, she let him take her hand and guide it to his erect penis. Her eyes clenched shut, she yelped as soon as her fingertips touched the surprisingly silky skin, not allowing herself to register the hardness or the size. 'There,' she said, wrenching her hand away. 'I hope you're happy and I'm not doing it again.'

She truly meant it, but the next time they were together, he unzipped himself again. Instead of just brushing her hand against it, he clamped her palm along the shaft and wrapped her fingers tightly around it, his hand around hers. Then began to move her hand, up and down, up and down.

'No,' she begged.

'Tighter,' he groaned. 'Faster. I love you. Faster.'

The little bed was jiggling. His breath was harsh in her ear and his contorted, red-faced desire made him a stranger to her. She felt sullied and insulted, and as something hot gushed over her hand she was downright disgusted.

But when he was gone and she was alone, she found herself remembering it, and it filled the pit of her stomach – and lower – with excitement. To think she could make him feel like that. She felt powerful and sexy, dangerous and adult, and she wanted to do it again. With a lurch of fear she wondered if she was officially in a state of mortal sin. If she died now would she be condemned to spend all eternity burning in the flames? Though her logical side insisted that hellfire was just a load of super-stitious nonsense, her emotional response was one of anxiety and fear. You never *knew*. What if it *was* true?

She could have gone to confession and got absolution and been in the clear if she did drop dead unexpectedly. But she knew the priest would tell her to stop doing those things with Lorcan, maybe even to stop seeing him altogether.

And she couldn't do that. She was utterly addicted to what they did on her bed and it was inconceivable not to see him. So, trying not to see how far her standards had slipped, she decided that because they loved each other, it neutralized the question of mortal sin. She'd always told herself that no matter what else she did with him, she'd never Go All The Way. After all, even Tara hadn't Gone All The Way! But over the weeks Lorcan eroded Katherine's resistance to the stage where every time they lay on the bed, he had his jeans around his knees, her panties were mid-thigh, and he was allowed to place the tip of his erection against her entrance.

'We'll never go further than this, will we?' she whispered.

'Never,' he whispered back.

But sometimes he'd jab against her and it flooded them both with such powerfully sweet sensations that he'd jab it a bit more.

'But you won't put it in,' she'd whisper.

'I won't put it in,' he whispered. 'I'll just kind of move it like . . . that. Is that nice?'

She nodded. It was the most beautiful feeling she'd ever had. And, so long as they didn't actually go any further, she was all right.

'Is it OK if I just move it a bit?' Lorcan murmured.

'Well, all right, so long as you don't put it in.'

'I won't put it in.'

After a while Katherine said, in low alarm, 'I think you might be putting it in.'

'I'm not,' he said hoarsely, his hips making small, frantic movements. 'It's on the outside, and I'm just kind of moving . . .'

But his hip movements became bigger and tougher and faster, and to Katherine's horror just as a full, packed-tight sensation plunged into her, she heard Lorcan say triumphantly, '*Now* it's in!'

She cried afterwards and he held her in his arms, stroking her hair, saying over and over, 'It'll be all right, baby, it'll be all right.'

She turned a tear-stained face to him. 'We're never doing it again,' she said sullenly. 'Don't think you'll convince me because you won't. This is the wrongest thing I've ever done. If I died now I'd go straight to Hell.'

But they did it again. Another one-off. Then they did it again. But when Lorcan made noises about getting her 'sorted out', she snapped that there was no need because they'd never be doing it again.

Of course they did. Not because Lorcan threatened to break it off with her if she wouldn't play. He didn't have to. Her own treacherous body was the most persuasive factor – she just couldn't resist him.

And what consoled her, in her hours of shame and self-disgust, was the thought that he loved her. Once they were married it would make everything all right, retrospectively validate it, as it were.

Not that marriage had actually been mentioned, but it was implied. By the look in his eyes every time he saw her, by the warmth in his voice when he told her he loved her.

75

It was Benjy who spoke, shattering the horrified silence in Katherine's living-room.

'Er,' he said awkwardly, wondering why he was always the one who cleared up Lorcan's messes, 'it just goes to show that there's only thirteen people in the world and they do the rest with mirrors. But I suppose we should be off. Amy? Tara? Lorcan?'

'Yes, we should.' Amy's voice was choked.

Lorcan made no sign of having heard anything.

'Lorcan?' Benjy repeated, meaningfully.

'But it's nice here,' Lorcan said softly, cruelly. Then he smiled at Katherine, who was lifelessly wedged between him and Joe. And the smile said, *I'll be back*.

With lazy grace, Lorcan kept everyone waiting while he slowly unfolded himself from beside Katherine. ''Bye,' he drawled, swinging himself towards the door.

''Bye,' Tara and Benjy squeaked, unable to get out fast enough.

Amy opened her mouth to say goodbye but all that came out was 'Aaarrr.'

The door slammed, the silence hummed and the room was almost empty of people yet full of malevolence.

'How do you know Lorcan?' Katherine asked Joe, in a death-knell voice. She didn't turn to look at him.

'I worked with him on an ad. Or, rather, didn't work with him.'

'What do you mean?'

'He was such a handful we had to get another actor.'

'Figures. That's Lorcan. The big star.' He didn't know whether or not she was serious.

'How do you know him?'

'I lost my virginity – and a whole lot more – to him,' she said hollowly.

The way she said it chilled him with real fear. He tried to put his arm around her and she writhed away. 'No.'

'No?'

'I want you to leave,' she told him coldly.

'Don't do this,' he begged.

'I want you to leave.'

Joe didn't understand. He just knew something had shifted ineluctably; that he'd lost Katherine. Was it because she was angry about Angie? Or was it to do with Lorcan? He suspected it was more Lorcan than Angie. While Lorcan had been in the room, Joe had felt like he didn't exist.

'Go now,' she ordered.

In despair, he tried again, but she was unreachable.

'I'll call you tomorrow,' he promised, then reluctantly left.

Tara was mortified when she returned an hour later. 'Katherine, I am so, so sorry. What a terrible coincidence. If I'd had any idea, any sort of inkling, that you knew Lorcan I wouldn't have brought him *near* the place.'

'You're home early,' Katherine said heavily.

'Yeah, well . . .' The evening had gone off-the-chart downhill after they'd left because the tension between Lorcan and Amy was so toxic. 'So have I got this right?' Tara asked. 'Lorcan is

Beaker from *The Muppet Show*? The one who was your boyfriend when you lived in Limerick?'

Katherine tipped her head slowly.

'And he ditched you?'

'Yeah. He ditched me.'

'Fintan and I suspected at the time that your heart had been mashed.'

'But I didn't want to talk about it.'

'We noticed,' Tara said drily.

'Sorry.'

'He's very good-looking,' Tara said. 'No wonder you were so upset when you came back to Knockavoy. But he's a right prick at the same time. Thinks he's God's gift. Look at the way he flirted with you in front of his girlfriend.'

'Yeah, that's Lorcan.'

The weary way she near-groaned instead of speaking alerted Tara. Alarmed, she took in Katherine's demeanour. She looked drugged. 'Have you been smoking spliff?'

'No.'

'Are you drunk?'

'No.'

'Are you all right?'

'Fine.'

'You seem . . . not very with it. Are you upset? Was it a big shock to see Lorcan?'

'Why would it be a shock?'

'You tell me.' Tara watched her carefully, then realized something. 'Where's Joe?'

'Fuck Joe.'

Tara gasped. 'What do you mean?'

'Joe slept with a girl from work.'

'Oh, no. Oh, no. Please tell me you're joking.'

'I'm not joking.'

'He just didn't seem the type. And he seemed to be crazy about you. Men, they're all bastards, every single last one of them. And has it been going on all the time you've been seeing him?'

Katherine opened her mouth, but didn't speak. Ah, feck it, there was no getting around it, she had to tell the truth. 'Well, it actually happened before I got off with him. But all the same. He never told me, and I've been working in the same office –'

'No, just one moment. Can we have a reality check here? Katherine, have you gone mental? You're annoyed because he slept with someone *before* you got off with him? Did you expect him to be a virgin? Saving himself for you?'

'No, but –'

'You've slept with other people, Beaker from *The Muppet Show*, to take one example. You've no right to complain if Joe did too. Oh, come on! Show me a person who doesn't have a past and I'll show you a boring bastard.'

Katherine hitched and carelessly let fall her shoulders.

'This isn't anything to do with meeting Lorcan?' Alarm mushroomed in Tara. 'You're not hoping to, um, start up with him again? Because that would be pure lunacy, Katherine.'

'I know.'

'It was twelve and a half years ago. A lifetime. He's got a girlfriend, you've got Joe.'

'If Joe rings,' Katherine said, with cold finality, 'I won't speak to him, got that?'

'Until when?'

'I'll decide when.'

'But –'

'It's my flat.'

And that was the end of it.

Joe rang several times the following morning and left messages on the answering-machine. 'Please talk to me, Katherine,' he asked, his politeness not hiding his desperation.

Tara found it excruciating to listen to. 'Come on,' she said at two o'clock. 'We've to go to Fintan's.'

'Go out?' Katherine looked startled. 'I'm not going out.'

'But . . . Why not? Don't you want to see his lumps? Or, rather, the lack of them?'

'Not today.'

'But, Katherine, we've been waiting six months for him to improve. It's finally happened. Don't you care?'

'Yes, but I don't want to go today. Sorry.

'I am sorry,' she added, with seeming sincerity.

'Katherine, please let me help,' Tara begged. 'You're being so weird. Just talk to me, would you?'

'Go on your own. Give Fintan a kiss from me. I'll see him soon.'

Her heart heavy with foreboding, Tara finally left, and Katherine exhaled with relief.

She was glad of the solitude. Though she knew she was behaving oddly, it was as if she was observing herself from afar and was powerless to intervene, like watching a wind-up doll which whirs about randomly, banging into doors and walls, mindless of its safety. She'd spent so long fantasizing about Lorcan that she couldn't believe he'd been delivered into her lap. The shock was disconnecting. Though more than a decade had passed, she'd never really felt it was over. He was unfinished business and because the past had shaped the present, it was more important than the present.

Over the years she'd acted out many, many scenarios in her

head. In most of them Lorcan prostrated himself with apologies, she made him suffer for a while, then forgave him. In the other version he cockily assumed he could take up where he left off and, with a selection of well-practised glares and pithy put-downs, she annihilated him.

She intended that when Lorcan came back – and she was convinced he *would* be back in the next day or so – she'd be the person in control. The ending would be rewritten, this time to suit her. Even if she wasn't sure if it was the one where she rejected him scathingly or rode off into the sunset with him. Possibly both.

The one thing she was sure of was that the current ending wouldn't do. Images of that last terrible scene with him assailed her and even now she winced at the very memory.

'We have to get married.' Katherine's eyes were fixed on Lorcan's face.

'Why?'

She paused and flicked a glance around the pub. She'd thought a public place would be better to tell him her news in, but now she wasn't so sure. 'Because,' she swallowed, and could hardly continue, 'because I'm going to have a baby.' Though she knew Lorcan wouldn't do a runner on her, she couldn't help being nervous because mythology held that men were likely to make for the hills around this delicate time. But she calmed herself with the thought that runners only happened to stupid, careless girls and no one was as careful as she. 'Say something,' she urged, anxiously. 'Are you angry? If you are, you've no right to be, it takes two to tango . . .'

But he didn't look angry, just weary. 'I can't marry you,' he said, in pity and exasperation.

'*Why not?*' Her voice was high and her eyes were sunk like wells into the white landscape of her terrified face.

'Because,' he sighed, getting irritated, 'I'm already married.'

She almost passed out. With a roaring in her ears, the pub receded, transformed into a vision of Hell. As she watched Lorcan, his face changed from something familiar and desirable into a picture of the devil. His handsome mouth thinned into a cruel line, his exquisite nose became a pointy hatchet, his purple-brown eyes turned into red coals. 'I don't understand,' she said, because she didn't.

'I'm already married,' he snapped, guilt making him bad-tempered. 'I can't marry you because I'm already married.'

'You can't be married,' she insisted, trying to wade out of the nightmare. 'You never said.'

'Oh, come on. You must have known.'

'I didn't. I'd never have gone to ... done the ...'

'Oh, I see, you were trying to trap me into marrying you by getting pregnant,' Lorcan accused, desperate to turn the tables.

'No, I wasn't,' she defended herself, her breath coming in squeaky, shallow gasps, 'but I thought if we went, um, if we went,' she forced herself to go on, 'if we went to bed that you were going to marry me.'

'Well, I wasn't and I'm not. I can't, you see,' he added, in gentler tones.

'I can't believe it, I can't believe it,' Katherine muttered over and over, her face in her hands. Katherine Casey did not get impregnated by a man who wouldn't marry her. It simply wasn't part of her plan.

She peeked her face out at him. 'We'll have to live to-gether. Starting from now.' It was far from ideal, eminently unrespectable, but it would have to do. 'I mean,' she blustered, 'I *presume* you're separated from your wife.'

He exhaled heavily. 'You presume wrong.'

Again she thought she was going to black out.

'I don't necessarily mean a legal separation.' She was grasping at straws. 'But you're not *together*-together, are you?'

'We live together, if that's what you mean.' Lorcan was looking at the door and wondering how soon he could escape.

'What do you mean?' she shrieked. 'I've been in your flat. There was no wife there.'

'She was away.'

'Away?' Katherine asked, dazedly. She remembered the plants, the spice rack, the bowls of pot-pourri dotted around the place. She'd thought Lorcan had put them there.

'Yes, she was away those times you came over,' Lorcan confirmed, worn out.

Katherine couldn't speak, she could hardly breathe as the enormity of the information began to trickle through. *You're a mistress. A* mistress! *How on earth did that happen?*

It was at times like this that Lorcan wished he'd kept his willy to himself. He'd enjoyed his time with Katherine, she was sweet. And he'd marvelled at his master-craftmanship as he'd wooed her at just the right rate, but right now he wasn't sure if all this fall-out was worth it. And for her to be pregnant – Jesus, what a mess! One he wanted to get as far away from as possible.

Through the murk of sweaty terror Katherine saw a solution of sorts. 'You'll just have to leave your wife immediately. Come on,' she said crisply, gathering confidence, 'I'll come with you to tell her. We'll go now.'

Already she was gathering her bag and jacket and Lorcan

was filled with panic. Sometimes Katherine could be so forceful, pushy even, as she reshaped the world into a version that suited her. Lorcan didn't want to leave his wife, not yet, anyway. Despite his occasional infidelities, he was very attached to Fiona. They suited each other. Not to mention that she bankrolled him.

He was appalled at the idea of living with Katherine and – God above – *a baby*. Katherine would have him trapped in suburbia, cutting grass, going to Mass, changing nappies, converting garages, painting bedrooms and the tedious like while she went to coffee mornings, looked at conservatory brochures and contested their neighbours' planning applications. The things that had initially charmed him about Katherine were suddenly choking him.

Besides, he'd got what he wanted from her. The thrill of the chase was over, and now he was scared.

'No,' he said firmly. 'Leave Fiona alone.'

Hearing him talk protectively about another woman was the biggest pain she'd ever felt. She hadn't known it was possible to feel such agony. 'You're not going to tell me you love her?' she choked.

He hadn't been going to, but that suddenly struck him as a good idea. 'Of course I love her, she's my wife.'

'You can't love her, you love me.'

When he said nothing, she demanded, 'You love me, don't you? You said you did.'

'I know I did, but . . . I'm sorry. Look, I'm very fond of you, and you're very attractive . . .' He squirmed. She'd got it bad. 'I'm sorry,' he repeated. 'I've been a bad boy again and –'

'*Again*? You mean, you've done this before? I'm not the first?'

He moved his head slightly from side to side. She wasn't the first.

'But I'm special, aren't I?' Clearing space for him to redeem himself in.

But all he said was 'You're a nice girl and I'm sorry.'

Before she could follow this unwelcome information to its unpleasant conclusion, her brain flitted to another source of horror. There were so many dreadful things happening that she didn't know which to deal with first. 'But I'm going to have a baby.' Hysteria appeared in her voice.

God, what a shambles, Lorcan thought, uncomfortably. He couldn't even tell her to have an abortion because he had no money to contribute to it. 'What will we do?' she begged, her eyes pleading.

'I'm not the one who's pregnant.' Lorcan's face was twisted into an expression of dislike because she was making him feel so bad.

'What do you mean?'

'You're the one who's up the pole. I never wanted you to be. I wanted you to get sorted out but you wouldn't. So do what you like with it. Have it. Don't have it. It's up to you.'

'What are you trying to say to me?' She had a fair idea, but hoped desperately that she was wrong.

'I really think it's best if I don't get involved,' he said, priding himself on how kindly he said it.

'But you have to be involved,' she cried. 'It's unavoidable. You'll have to leave your wife and –'

'Really, Katherine, I think –'

'That's not my name,' she said wildly. At his confused look, she insisted, crazily, 'It's Katherine with a K. It's your special name for me. Say it.'

'Katherine,' he said, loudly and firmly, 'I think it's best if we're not together any more.'

'NO! Don't leave me.'

'It's for the best.'

'The best for you, maybe, but how will I cope?'

'You'll be fine,' he said hastily, turning away from her. 'You'll be fine, you'll get over this.'

'Please,' she choked, 'please.' Then she heard herself say, 'I'm begging you.'

But, as if in a slowed-down nightmare, he was getting to his feet. He was trying to stand up and go away from her. She knew that if he left now it was all over, she'd never see him again.

He was moving away from the table, but she was holding on to his arm and being dragged with him. A stool fell over and he was trying to prise her claw-grip fingers off him. She bumped her hip, wood denting bone, and felt no pain. People were looking up from their drinks and he was saying something. Hard words. Cruel words. Get away. Leave me alone. A clatter as a pint glass fell, its contents frothing silently over the shiny wood. The barman was hurrying towards them.

'But don't you love me?' she heard her voice screech.

'No,' he said.

No.

76

Tara insisted on frisking Fintan like she was a member of the Drugs Squad. She ran her hands over and over him, marvelling at the reduction in his lumps. 'Do you know what I can feel?' she asked, as she caressed his side.

'What?'

'NOTHING!' she yelped, in delight. 'Nothing!' She stood back and took him in – bald, skeletal, leaning on a stick. But the bump on his neck was only the size of a grape. 'You look spectacular,' she exclaimed. 'Good enough to eat. How do you feel?'

'Really good. Lots of energy and I'm eating well. The future is bright. But where's Katherine and my Joe?'

'Hold on to your hat. I've some story for the pair of you.' And she regaled Fintan and Sandro with the dramatic events of the last day.

'Beaker from *The Muppet Show*,' Fintan kept repeating, shaking his head in disbelief. 'After all these years, who shows up? Only Beaker from *The Muppet Show*!'

But when she told them about the situation with Joe, they were aghast. 'She can't do that to Joe,' they wailed, looking at each other for confirmation. 'What's wrong with the girl?'

'I'm terribly worried about her,' Tara admitted. 'I didn't want to leave her. It's like she's concussed.'

'You don't think she's told Joe to get lost because she's bumped into Beaker again,' Fintan suggested.

'No!' Sandro was appalled. 'How could she care for a person who broke her little *bambina* heart?'

'Maybe she wants to get even with him. What do you think, Tara?' Fintan said. 'Maybe she's planning to go to bed with him and at the last minute withhold the goodies and tell him he has a minuscule mickey?'

'I really don't know,' Tara despaired. 'I'm telling you it's impossible to know what's going on with her.'

'God, wouldn't we all love to do that to some oul' louser who dumped us?' Fintan said dreamily. 'Anyway, Sandro, don't worry. She'll be fine. Beaker has a girlfriend, which puts him out of the frame.'

Somehow Tara doubted that Amy was much of an impediment to Lorcan's sexual adventuring.

'And Joe will sort her out.' Since Joe had arranged for Fintan to meet Dale Winton, Fintan had great faith in Joe to fix *everything*.

Tara's worry lifted. 'You're right. She probably got a bit of a shock but she'll be grand in a while.'

'And how was your date, Tara?'

'Eeeee-ooooow, he was awful. Short, balding and plump.'

'But was he nice?'

'He was OK, but I'm saving myself. The next man I get off with has to be completely great, I'm not settling for any old eejit. I'd rather do without.'

'Holy God!' Fintan exclaimed. 'You've changed. What happened to Last Chance Saloon Tara?'

'Yeah!' Sandro interrogated, knowingly. 'Where is gone Tara "I hate not to have a man" Butler?'

'Tara "I'd rather go out with a tosspot who tells me I'm fat than have no one at all" Butler?' Fintan chipped in.

'Wasn't I pathetic?' She winced. 'Last Chance Saloon, indeed! Don't I have my whole life ahead of me?'

'Not unlike my good self.' Fintan overflowed with *joie de vivre*.

'I haven't a clue what changed,' Tara admitted. 'All I know is I'd no confidence when I was living with Thomas. I thought I'd never survive without him, but now I find that he was the *reason* I had no confidence. And it's lovely not to be terrified the entire time.'

'Terrified of what?'

'Being on my own. I thought it was the worst thing that could possibly happen, but now that the worst has happened, it's not so bad. It's nice, in fact.'

'Nice?' Fintan gave her an eyebrow. 'I've heard it all now.'

'Nice sometimes,' she admitted. 'I'm not saying I don't get lonely. I'd love a gorgeous bloke. But I was as lonely as anything living with Thomas. At least now I'm on my own I have some chance of meeting someone. And it really could happen. Look at Katherine. She met a great man and she's even older than me.'

'By six weeks. But I like your attitude. It's all one big adventure. And what about Ravi?'

'Oh, Fintan, *please*. Ravi's my friend.'

'Aha. I think he would like to be more than your friend.' Sandro winked meaningfully.

'Is that a Mars bar in your pocket or are you just glad to see me?' Fintan said suggestively.

'I'd prefer the Mars bar, thanks.'

'But he's mad about you, isn't he?'

Tara blushed and squirmed. 'Maybe. He's never said anything, but, yeah, maybe . . . Although I think he preferred me when I was fat. Mind you, he could be in luck. I'm heading back in the direction of a size twelve again. That's the problem with having no problems. Contentment is a bummer.'

'You're just evening out,' Fintan consoled. 'You were desperate-looking before, kind of sunken. Yes, yes, I know, I'm not exactly a candidate for the Hefty Hideaway myself. But right now you look fabulous. All toned and thin. In fact,' Fintan questioned Sandro, 'don't you think Tara and Ravi would make the perfect couple?'

'He has got a *great* body,' Sandro agreed.

'Oh, don't! I like him so much. But I'm not ready.' She couldn't really find the words. 'I'd like to go out with lots of men,' she exclaimed. 'Keep it light and have fun. I had no freedom for so long, and I'm not ready to give it up.'

'He mightn't wait for you.'

'I don't care, Fintan! I don't care!'

'Marvellous,' he breathed. 'Absolutely marvellous.'

Two and a half miles across London, a violent row was in progress. Amy was screaming at Lorcan. Worn down from several months of abuse, his outrageously flirtatious carry-on with Tara's flatmate had been the last in a long line of straws.

The argument had gone on late into the night and had recommenced at first light. 'How could you humiliate me like that?' Her beautiful face was contorted and tear-mottled.

'How?' he drawled. 'Easy. Didn't you notice? I just flirted publicly with another girl.'

'But why?' she screeched. 'I don't understand. Why are you with me if all you want to do is hurt me?'

Because it's so easy.

Her voice got higher and higher, finishing with a glass-shattering shriek, 'Why do you do what you do? What do you *want* from life? I mean, what do you *want*?'

If he'd been asked that question once he'd been asked it a thousand times. He paused and appeared to be thoughtfully considering her inquiry.

He opened his mouth and with a cruel smile said, 'A cure for Aids.' The last time he'd been asked that question – about two weeks before by a heartbroken pharmacist called Colleen – he had replied, 'What am I after in life? How about a woman who fucks like a rabbit, then turns into a pizza at two a.m.?'

He was running out of smart answers. Granted, the women weren't going to be comparing, but it had always been a matter of personal pride not to use the same one twice. However, it was a smart answer too far for Amy.

'Out!' She drew herself up to her considerable height and pointed with a dead-straight arm to the door. 'Get out.'

Lorcan chuckled indulgently. 'You're beautiful when you're angry.' A patent lie. Amy looked like ten kinds of shit.

'Out!' she repeated.

'Have you shares in British Telecom?'

Her face was both furious and inquiring.

'Because,' he laughingly explained, 'BT profits will go through the roof when you've made your usual number of phone calls begging me to come back.'

'Out!'

He lounged to the door, and just before he left stuck his head back in. 'It'll take me about half an hour to get home so hold off on your first call until then.'

He ambled towards the tube, tipsy with amusement at his

own slick banter. But he hadn't gone far before a type of hangover set in. His soaring high thudded sourly back to earth, the good feelings poisoned with less pleasant emotion. This kept happening. When it came to playing the role of a baddy he'd never been able to help himself. It had always been such fun. But, as the last of his buzz trickled away, he was forced to wonder if maybe it was time to do the decent thing and let Amy go; stop tormenting her and set her free. The more he thought about it the more he became convinced that he was long overdue to move on to someone else – this time to do things right. Perhaps he'd already even met that someone else . . .

The time had come to have a good, long, hard think about the life and times of Lorcan Larkin.

'Hey,' he laughed to himself, 'I must be growing up.'

Amy picked up the phone and dialled a number. But it wasn't Lorcan's.

77

Katherine didn't go to work on Monday. She asked Tara to ring in for her.

'Why? Are you sick?'

'Kind of.'

'You don't look sick.'

'Are you going to do it or aren't you?'

'Why won't you go in? You've never done this before.'

'I can't face Joe.'

'Why won't you talk to him? He cares so much about you.'

'Please, Tara.'

'And why won't you leave the house? You haven't been out since Saturday night.'

'Oh, please, Tara, please,' Katherine beseeched, with a franticness that horrified Tara.

Tara had no idea what was happening to Katherine, but she was very, very frightened. Katherine was presenting a white, dazed face to the world but, clearly, seismic mayhem was taking place below her surface. Tara didn't want to leave her. Anything could happen. Though she had no grounds for thinking it, she was half afraid that Katherine might try suicide. Something was very wrong. It had started on Saturday night and Joe obviously wasn't the cause. He had been an innocent bystander.

'Please, Tara.'

'OK.' The helplessness was killing.

That day Tara rang Katherine almost as many times as Joe did. When she came home from work, Katherine was dressed and fully made-up.

'Are you going out?' Tara asked, desperately hoping she might be meeting Joe.

'No.'

'Oh. Nice of you to make such an effort for me, so.'

'Ha ha.'

'Ha ha yourself.'

They spent a peculiar, tense evening, half watching telly and pretending the phone wasn't ringing every thirty minutes with messages from Joe.

Tara kept looking sidelong at Katherine. The tense, expectant air around her, coupled with her perfect hair and make-up, was saying something. As *Panorama* ended, enlightenment descended, smooth as a lift, and suddenly Tara understood. 'You're waiting for him, aren't you?'

Katherine turned a jerky head. Her eyes were frightened. 'Hmmmm?' she said, edgily.

'You're waiting in for Lorcan, aren't you? That's why you haven't left the house. He doesn't have your phone number, but he has your address and you're afraid of being out when he calls.'

Katherine said nothing and Tara knew she was right. Seeing Katherine's craziness tore her apart. She leapt from her seat and sat right in front of her. 'Listen to me,' she said, with earnest sincerity. 'Oh, please, look at me, Katherine, please.'

Katherine slowly raised hostile eyes to her.

'I'm going to talk sense to you,' Tara said forcefully. 'This Lorcan was your first love. We never forget the first one. You were very young and a bit innocent. And he's exceptionally

565

good-looking, which doesn't help. I'm sure it was a big shock to just bump into him like that on Saturday night and of course you're bound to feel a bit shaky and weird. It's happened to us all. If I met Thomas now I'm sure I'd be upset, I'd be *allowed* to be upset. But only for a short time because life must go on. Especially for you, because you've got Joe.'

Katherine's face flickered at the mention of Joe, then resumed its sullen expression.

'Come on, Katherine, it was a long time ago. So move on and get over it. It's the right thing to do. Hey, even I got over Thomas. If I can do it, anyone can!'

'You didn't get pregnant by Thomas,' Katherine's lips barely moved. Tara let the words dissolve away into silence. The shock was too great. 'And Thomas wasn't married,' Katherine intoned hollowly.

'Are you telling me . . . ?' Tara stumbled, as Katherine's words hit home. 'You got pregnant by Lorcan? And he was married? When you were nineteen?'

Katherine's dead, hopeless eyes said it all.

'Oh, my good God, Katherine! Why didn't you tell us?'

Struggling to find the words – *any* words – Katherine looked mutely at her. How could she put a description on the horror of being young, alone and pregnant? The living hell she'd descended into? The agony of letting Lorcan go and not contacting him?

And the worst truth of all, which had taken a couple of days to dawn on her, that, because she was single and expecting a baby by a married man, *she had become her mother*. The mother that she'd spent her life trying to be as different from as she possibly could be.

Nineteen years of piety, neatness, ironed clothes, completed homework, punctuality and clean-living had made no difference. She was almost exactly the same age, too. Her mother had been twenty.

'Please tell me about it.' Tara coaxed, with terrible anxiety. 'I know it might be hard for you.'

'Not as hard as it was then.' Her back teeth were clamped tightly together. 'You've no idea how much I didn't want to be pregnant. I used to lie in bed and look down at my stomach and feel like screaming. I literally used to feel like screaming my head off, Tara.'

'Why?' Tara could hardly speak.

'Because somewhere in there, so tiny that I couldn't see it, was the ruination of my life. A little alien was growing and getting bigger inside me. I'd never felt so trapped. It was like being in prison, but inside my own body. There was no way to get out.'

Tara nodded miserably.

'I wanted to take away my stomach. I used to wish I could be the girl in the circus who gets sawn in three and who has her midriff moved in a nice wooden section out to the side. I just wanted all the offending parts to be removed.'

She looked at Tara, desperate to be understood, then told her how she'd sometimes plucked at her skin in an impossible attempt to tear away her body, to leave just the unpregnant Katherine, the real Katherine, remaining.

'Did you have an abortion?' Tara, very gently, suggested.

Abortion.

'You know that I don't – at least I didn't – believe in it.' Katherine couldn't meet Tara's eye, as she remembered how, at school, she'd always made mealy-mouthed pronouncements along with the nuns about how abortion was murder, about how no one had the right to deny life to the unborn. But all that had been swept away by the terrible terror that had possessed her. From the moment Lorcan had run out on her she'd wanted to have an abortion. She could see no other way to avoid her life falling apart. She'd known she'd burn in Hell, but she didn't care. She was in Hell already.

If she could only get rid of the baby she'd draw a line in the sand and from that day forth she'd be the best person who ever lived. Redoubling her efforts to live a controlled, careful life. She'd known that other single girls got pregnant, that they had their babies and loved them. But, she, Katherine Casey was different. Somewhere, not so far beneath the surface, she'd felt that pregnancy was a punishment for girls who lived profligate, promiscuous lives. Because she'd always been so well behaved she'd thought it was the last thing that could happen to her. The last thing she'd deserved.

'Katherine . . .' Tara's voice crooned. 'Come in, Katherine.'

'I couldn't tell anyone,' she beseeched, her throat aching from the onset of tears. 'I'd never felt so alone.'

'You could have told me and Fintan.'

'I couldn't, Tara, I couldn't. If I admitted it to you then I was admitting it to myself. I just wanted it to be over, and it was far easier to close the door on the past if I was the only one who knew about it.'

'Jesus, that's dreadful.' Tara was snow-white. 'So you went through it all on your own.' Then she thought of something. 'You could have told your mother, she wouldn't have condemned you.'

'No,' Katherine agreed, with an attempt at being rueful. 'She'd probably have been delighted. Would have organized a termination and might even have tried to make me a test case.'

But Katherine would never have had the moral high ground again. It was bad enough to be the same as her mother, but for her mother to *know* . . .

'So what did you do?' Tara prompted softly, convinced that it was very important for Katherine to talk about this.

Katherine sighed wearily and braced herself for a trip back to Hell. 'I hadn't a clue how to go about organizing an –' even now she found it hard to say the word '– abortion. All I knew was that it was illegal in Ireland and that I'd have to go somewhere in England.'

Tara nodded sympathetically, hoping her distress didn't show as Katherine related the whole story. How – nauseous, tender-breasted and terrified, two hundred pounds in her bag – she'd got the train to Dublin where there was a place that could help her. How she'd hardly been able to believe the enormity of her position or what she was contemplating. How she'd tried to keep her mind fixed on the future when she'd be liberated from the nightmare.

She'd been mortified walking into the centre, sure she'd be spotted by someone who knew her. But they were kind and gentle with her there. She was examined by a doctor who confirmed that she was eight weeks' pregnant, then she was forced to have a chat with a counsellor who tried to point out the alternatives. 'I don't want to hear,' Katherine had choked. 'I just want . . . Please, I just want it gone.'

The counsellor nodded. She'd seen it so often before, these young girls in a blind panic, so frightened about what was happening to them that they couldn't think straight.

'If you're sure?'

At Katherine's nod, the counsellor had said, gently, 'OK,

there's a clinic in Liverpool. I'll go and make the phone call. When can you go?'

'Now.' She'd tried to stop her voice from wobbling. 'As soon as possible.'

The counsellor had left her alone, sitting on the edge of her chair, in the tiny room. After fifteen minutes she'd come back, with a warm smile that she knew wouldn't melt the block of ice in Katherine's stomach. 'It's arranged,' she'd said, quietly. 'I've written all the details here. There's a ferry that leaves this evening at eight. It'll get you in at . . .'

Katherine had heard the information from far away. Trains, maps, taxi to the clinic, return trip, back-up counselling. 'Thanks,' her voice had said.

She'd wandered Dublin for the rest of the day but, thereafter, she couldn't remember one thing about it. With nothing else to do she'd got to the port miles too early. Hanging around in the shed-like waiting room she'd suddenly became aware of a hot, wet feeling. Hefting up her little bag she'd run, breathlessly, to the ladies' where she saw that she was bleeding. It was only then that she'd noticed the pain.

The boat sailed without her and the following morning, no longer pregnant, she'd got the train back to Limerick, still feeling as though she was living in a nightmare.

'So you didn't have an abortion,' Tara attempted to cheer.

'No, but I would have,' Katherine admitted, dully. 'It's as bad as if I did.'

'It's not.'

'It feels like it.'

'And then you came home to Knockavoy and wouldn't talk about it,' Tara remembered. 'You were so bitter. Now I can see why.'

'Then I wrote to my father,' Katherine admitted. In for a penny, in for a pound.

'And what did he say?' Tara tried to remain calm. If her father had rejected her so soon after Lorcan's carry-on, was it any wonder that she was so uptight?

'He was dead,' she said, simply. 'He'd died six months and six days before.'

'How did you feel?'

Katherine wavered, before finding the right words. 'Like dying too.'

Tara breathed out in quiet horror.

'Then we moved to London and I had one disastrous relationship after another, and here we are.' Katherine tried a watery smile.

'But I've had one disastrous relationship after another too,' Tara insisted.

'Not the way I had.'

Tara had to agree. 'It must be something to do with finding out about your father so soon after the terrible stuff with Lorcan.'

'Maybe.'

'Thank God you've told me about it. Obviously Lorcan was meant to walk in here on Saturday night.' Katherine's eyes lit up and Tara's heart descended. 'Because it's blown your past wide open,' she said quickly. 'Now you can get over it.'

'Oh, I see.'

'So, am I right? You were waiting in in case he called?'

'Please, Tara, try and understand. It's never felt finished. It's haunted me.'

'What made you think he'd come?'

'Instinct.'

Tara eyed her shrewdly. 'Desire, more like. But even if he had arrived around here, what would you have achieved by seeing him? It's not as if you'd consider getting off with him again?'

She was appalled when Katherine didn't immediately deny it.

'I don't know what I want,' Katherine despaired, and her confusion was genuine. 'I just don't want to feel this way about my life and my past.'

'And you thought the way to do it would be to get involved with him again? After the way he treated you, you'd have been better off being extra, super-duper *horrible* instead!'

'But I will be.'

Even this made Tara anxious. Lorcan was too good-looking, too charming, too sexy, too dangerous. He would always be the winner. And the fantastical way Katherine was talking, as if he really was going to arrive on their doorstep any minute, was even more alarming.

'What had you planned?'

Katherine thought about all her fantasies, and said vaguely, 'I don't exactly have a plan. It all depends.'

'But it's not going to happen,' Tara said, soothingly. 'And you can still get over everything that happened. We'll arrange for you to get professional counselling, and you know I'll help you and, of course, so will Joe. And, sure, Liv is a *mine* of information about this sort of thing. Although, when you think about it, you're actually grand, look at how great things are with Joe –'

The doorbell rang and they both jumped.

'Who the . . . ?' Tara asked. 'It's ten to twelve.'

Katherine's face flooded with colour. 'I think it's for me,' she said, faintly.

'Who is it? Is it Joe?'

It was Lorcan.

78

'I don't believe it,' Tara breathed, as Katherine buzzed him in downstairs.

The cheek of him! And Katherine hadn't been so crazy, after all.

Katherine opened the door. Her knees began to knock as soon as she saw him, in all his broad, hard masculinity. The appraising expression in his dark eyes propelled her back a dozen years. The arrogant toss of his leonine mane hadn't changed one bit. 'Come in.' She tried to corral the desire for revenge before it all escaped in the face of his mesmerizing loveliness. She was nineteen again and dizzy with disbelief that he was actually there.

He lounged ahead of her into the living-room, where Tara was waiting, her face hard.

'Hi there,' Tara said, coolly. 'We weren't expecting you.'

'I think Katherine might have been.' Lorcan's meaningful, regretful smile intimated to Tara that if only he wasn't saving himself for her flatmate, he'd be making a move on her.

'Where did you get the phone number?' Tara asked, unimpressed. Didn't he know she didn't stand for nonsense from men any more?

'Oh, I didn't ring,' he explained, with another my-God-you're-one-attractive-woman smile.

'I see.'

'Tara, would you mind . . . ?' Katherine tried to be polite.

Tara stomped from the room, surprised at how angry she felt. Lorcan was a tosspot, anyone could see that. For the first time ever Tara had an inkling of how frustrating it must have been for everyone around her when she persisted with unsuitable men.

The living-room door slammed and Katherine and Lorcan sat looking at each other, he on the couch, she on a chair.

'So,' he said.

'Yes,' she agreed, her lips trembling. Beneath her skull, it was lighter than air, unpleasantly insubstantial. She couldn't take in that he was really sitting there opposite her.

'Why are you here?' she asked, with a tartness that required effort. In version one of the fantasies that had consoled her through the years, Lorcan would burst into passionate declarations along the lines of 'I never forgot you, letting you go was the biggest mistake I ever made, let's forget the last twelve and a half years, we've wasted too much time . . .' Which would open up a lovely opportunity for her to tell him of all the ways he could stick it up his bum.

But instead he just said, with confident ease, 'Hey, it's great to bump into you again. We can catch up on old times.' Then he surprised himself by adding, 'And I'd like to know . . .' He faltered, and fixed his sherry-luminous eyes on hers. 'I suppose I'd like to know what happened to the baby.'

Like a slippery eel, her anger kept wriggling from her grasp. She should be furious that he'd waited so long to find out what had happened to his child, but instead she felt semi-comforted.

'Tell me,' he pressed. 'Did you have it? Can I meet him?'

She shook her head.

'Did you have the old Hoover job?' he asked.

She hesitated before saying, 'No.'

'No?'

'I had a miscarriage.'

'But you'd contemplated the Hoover job?'

Shamefaced, she nodded.

So there was no child. Lorcan was relieved. He didn't know what had prompted him to ask in the first place – he'd got slightly carried away at the thought that there was a fine son of his running about the place. But, let's face it, who needed the responsibility?

'So there we are.' Lorcan was keen to move to the business in hand. This wasn't going the way Katherine had imagined in any of her myriad scenarios. He was neither contrite nor cocky enough. She'd visualized throwing his apologies back in his face, like a handful of gravel. Or if he tried to get off with her, she'd practised so many malicious, rapier-sharp ripostes that she thought she'd be able to effortlessly shame and mortify him. (Everything from 'Did I say you could touch me?' to her old favourite 'Sexual harassment is a crime.') But now she felt she couldn't riposte her way out of a paper bag. The shock of his presence was debilitating and she couldn't shake the heavy unreality that accompanied every word she said to him, every glance he gave her.

It was a big effort to regain control of herself.

'I used to see you on telly in *Briar's Way* when I went home to Ireland on holiday.' She forced an arch smile. 'You were just like yourself.'

'Hahaha.' Lorcan's character in *Briar's Way* had been a duplicitous womanizer. 'Hey, we do what we can.'

'You're not in it any more, though?'

'Nah, I outgrew it,' Lorcan wondered nervously if she knew how deep into the doldrums his career had fallen in recent years.

'You outgrow a lot of things.' She gave a sarky smirk. 'What happened to your wife?'

'We went our separate ways.' Around the time he'd started to earn decent money, but no need to mention that.

'Why?'

'Hey. *C'est la vie.* You win some, you lose some.'

'But why? Why did you go your separate ways?'

Lorcan shuffled in his seat. He wished she'd shut up. Even after all this time he remembered how tenacious Katherine was. Once she got the bit between her teeth it was hard to wrest it from her. 'We'd outgrown each other,' he tried again.

'What a shame you couldn't have outgrown each other when you got me pregnant,' she said snippily.

'So it goes. But listen,' he said hastily, 'can I just tell you that you've really blossomed? You were always cute, but you've turned out gorgeous.'

She was just about to ask about his girlfriend when he stretched over and put his hand on her face. The touch of his fingertips on her skin was like a bolt of electricity. Every nerve end in her body began humming and singing, and rational thought was shunted way off course.

'You've grown up into a beautiful woman,' he said huskily. He moved his palm along her cheek and up into her hairline while she sat like a statue, her eyes closed. She knew she was passing up a perfectly good opportunity of acting out version two of her fantasies where she gave him a sharp elbow in the chops for his presumption. But she couldn't move, over-whelmed by the intensity of travelling back through time.

'Sit next to me.' He thumped the couch beside him.

She shook her head.

'Go on.' He smiled wolfishly. His back was hurting from leaning over to her. In fact, his back had been giving him gyp lately, he must get it looked at . . .

He hadn't known how much resistance he'd get from Katherine. On Saturday night she'd have run away with him there and then, he felt. But, in the meantime, she'd remembered her anger, so it was time to send in the heavy guns. 'Do you know something, Katherine with a K?' he said, looking straight into her soul. 'I never, ever forgot you.'

'I don't believe you.'

'It's true.'

She shook her head again.

'I swear to God it's true,' he repeated. 'You were very special to me and if I hadn't been married . . .' The sincerity in his gaze began to trickle light and healing into her heart. 'Would you ever come on over here beside me?' he urged softly.

And she just couldn't help herself. Like an automaton, she jerkily left her seat and sat next to him. She didn't know what was motivating her. Her mind was a snarled mess where desire for revenge was wound tightly around other emotions – the sexual attraction she'd felt when she was nineteen and the need to correct the course of her personal history.

As soon as she sat down, Lorcan clasped her little face in his big, confident hands, as if he was about to kiss her. She knew she should dig him in the kidneys or swipe him across the face, but all of her pre-planned scenarios were strewn on the cutting-room floor. Her anger and desire for vengeance were fatally blunted. Instead the thought that he still wanted her laid balm on her old wound.

But there was something she wanted to know . . . What was it? Then she remembered. 'What about your girlfriend?'

'Don't mind her.' Lorcan chuckled, giving his you're-the-most-special-woman-in-the-world look. 'It's over with her.' Then he prepared to administer a Lorcan Larkin extravaganza. The kind of kiss that destroys women: gentle yet sure, sweet yet macho, firm yet teasing, erotic yet comforting.

Paralysed, Katherine watched in wonder as he moved so close that his face blurred. Just before he prepared for the final descent he added casually, 'She was nobody special.'

She was nobody special.

She was nobody special.

The words echoed in Katherine's head. With a sudden, unwanted clarity, she knew that that's what Lorcan would once have said about her, if his wife had found out. 'Hey, that Katherine girl? Don't worry about her, it meant nothing to me, she was nobody special.'

Out of nowhere she thought of Joe. He wouldn't do that to her. He wouldn't do that to *anyone*.

Lorcan loomed ever closer and finally his lips touched Katherine's. Desperate for breath, she found herself ducking out from under his embrace. 'I have to go to the bathroom,' she gasped.

To her surprise he didn't complain. Until she saw the indulgent look on his face and realized he thought she wanted to brush her teeth before the clinch.

With a watery looseness about her knees, she made it to the door. As soon as she'd closed it behind her, Tara hurtled down the hall, and hustled them both into the bathroom. 'What are you doing in there?' Tara demanded, in an hysterical whisper.

Panic swam to the surface of Katherine's face. 'I don't know.'

'Let me remind you that he couldn't even remember your

name on Saturday night. And he still doesn't remember your surname because if he did he could have got your phone number from directory inquiries. And why is he calling around so late? Where was he before now? Don't tell me he was working because Amy told me he's not.' Tara had spent the previous twenty minutes agonizing, and all her worries tumbled out. 'And speaking of Amy . . .'

'It's all over with them,' Katherine mumbled. 'He told me.'

'And you believed him? God, he must have really gone to town on the apologies.'

Katherine hesitated just a shaving of a second, but it was enough.

'Oh, no,' Tara breathed. 'You mean he hasn't apologized? Hell – o!'

Katherine was snow white. 'I mean . . . I thought . . .' But no matter which way she looked at it, she couldn't justify it. Tara was right.

Lorcan hadn't apologized; she'd been about to let him kiss her and she'd made no protest. How the hell had it happened? *She* was meant to be in control, not him. But she was as powerless and humiliated as the moment he'd left that pub more than twelve years ago. With his good looks and smooth lines, he'd fudged her emotions so much she couldn't think straight – just like old times.

'I'm sorry to be so cruel, Katherine, but you'd do the same for me. You *have* done the same for me, all those nights you stopped me from driving over to Thomas.'

'This is different,' Katherine tried unconvincingly. Away from Lorcan's physical presence her head continued to clear, leaving her demeaned and cheapened at how easily she'd almost capitulated.

'Lorcan Larkin is a bad bastard,' Tara insisted. 'You only have to look at how he treats his girlfriend. And, Katherine, think, please, I beg of you, just *think* what he did to you. And he'd do it again. He was the biggest mistake you ever made.'

'But he was my favourite one.'

'He's a prick. I can't understand how you even let him in the house. I admit he's very good-looking and that you probably still fancy him, but after what he did to you!'

'I thought if I saw him again I'd be able to fix the past.' Katherine was finding it harder and harder to defend her actions. 'My life's a disaster and it can all be traced back to him. I thought that if he was nice to me or if I was horrible to him I'd finally feel OK.'

'Your life isn't a disaster!' Tara said, hotly. 'The past *is* fixed, you just can't see it. In your head nothing has changed since Lorcan legged it, but see yourself through my eyes. You've a good job, you've got a lovely car, you've got great friends, but most importantly you have a relationship that works. Joe and you work! You've been going out with him for five months. He's mad about you. You're mad about him. It's working. It's a *success*.'

'Sooner or later he'll go off me,' she said sadly. 'They always do.'

'He won't. You've gone past that stage with him. He knows you.'

'Why is this one different?'

Tara frantically sought a reason. 'It might be because of Fintan,' she tried wildly. 'You've been so worried about him you haven't had time to be neurotic.'

A stab in the dark, but to her great surprise, Katherine nodded slowly. 'Jesus, maybe you're right.' She lowered herself and balanced on the side of the bath. 'God, I think you're right.'

'And if you don't cop on to yourself really quickly and stop this malarkey with Lorcan, you'll lose Joe.'

'I'll lose Joe,' Katherine repeated, and the thought of being without him rocked her off balance. She couldn't *bear* it.

A film reel of memories unspooled themselves. The night she and Joe had attempted to cook a dinner from scratch and nearly set Joe's kitchen on fire, all the hours Joe uncomplainingly gave to Fintan, the arm-wrestling matches that he let her win, videoing Ally McBeal without having to be asked, buying her a Mac lipstick *in almost the right colour*, his insistence on trying to fix her car when it broke down for the umpteenth time, his unconditional acceptance when she'd managed to tell him about her father. The togetherness of it. And it was mutual. She thought of the compassion with which she'd consoled Joe after Arsenal lost five–nil to Chelsea, the new Wallace and Gromit socks she'd bought because his old ones had holes, the cashew-nut butter she'd tracked down and kept in her kitchen cupboard because he'd once mentioned he liked it, the time and effort she'd put into learning how the Premier league worked for no other reason than she hoped it would please him, the way she didn't mind when Joe hadn't been able to do a thing with her car and it still had to go to Lionel the mechanic, who said that Joe had made things worse.

Before she'd met Joe her life had been a cold, sterile white page, now it was awash with mesmerizing, swirling colours. She couldn't go back, it would kill her. Astonished by the crystal-clear overview of her before-and-after life, she acknowledged how far she'd come, how much she'd changed, how full and rich her present really was.

And to think that she had been prepared to throw it all away for a man who would happily and effortlessly destroy her.

It was like waking up from a dream. A dream where the craziest of things had made perfect sense. But which, with the benefit of wakefulness, were clearly illogical and ridiculous.

'Do you know something, Tara?' Her eyes were full of wonder. 'I think you're right. It's real with Joe, isn't it? I'm not imagining it, am I? It works? He cares about me? Tara, I've got to ring him!'

'Ahem.' Tara nodded politely in the direction of the living-room. 'There's the small matter of a red-haired man expecting to be serviced.'

'What'll I do with him? You wouldn't take him off my hands?'

'I wouldn't get up on him to get over a hedge. Just tell him to leave.'

'As simple as that? Considering he got me pregnant, then dumped me?' Exhilarated with liberation, Katherine demanded, 'Could I not upset him. Just a little bit?'

Tara considered, reluctantly. 'Well, OK, but be very careful. Close contact with that fella would addle the head. If you're not out in five minutes I'm going in to get you.'

Katherine didn't even have to think about what she was going to say. She'd already had nine million mythical practice runs. She slinky-hipped back into the living-room.

'Now, where were we?' she purred at Lorcan.

'Just about here.' He smoothed his big warm palm along her hair and drew her face to his.

He placed his mouth on hers, but just before the kiss got into its stride, she disengaged herself.

'No.' She pulled away from him.

'No?' he hooted.

'Sorry.' She sighed regretfully. 'I just don't fancy you.'

'Wha—'

'You're not the man you used to be. And do you know something?' She looked and saw that it was actually true. 'You're losing your hair.'

He went chalk white. 'This is to do with your dykey friend, isn't it?' he said angrily. 'You were all on for it before you went to the bathroom.'

'I wasn't, and it's nothing to do with anything except your lack of sex appeal.' She smiled prettily at him. 'Sorr-ee!'

'You're a lying bitch.'

'Don't talk to me like that.' She was suddenly icy. 'How dare you?'

She flashed him a grade three look and he recoiled in unexpected shock. She was like an animal!

'How dare you treat me the way you did all those years ago?' A grade four was dispatched in his direction, and his breath deserted him. She was like a *mad* animal. Crazed. Rabid!

'And how *dare* you come back here and behave as if you hadn't done anything wrong? How dare you?'

She took a deep breath and hoped she could pull it off – she'd been out of practice for a while. She clenched her jaw and with monumental effort flung him the Medusa look. From the satisfyingly terrified expression on his face she knew she'd hit home.

He was astonished with fear. She was evil. *Evil.*

'I'm off,' he said.

'I thought something smelt funny.'

'Bitch,' he muttered.

He passed Tara who was sitting in the hall like a guard-dog. 'Bitch,' he muttered, again.

'Prick,' she said, cheerfully.

Roger in the flat below nearly had a heart-attack from the slam Lorcan gave the door.

Tara and Katherine looked at each other. It could have gone either way with Katherine, until Tara started to laugh heartily, then so did she.

'I'm so glad,' Katherine convulsed, 'that I got to use the Medusa look, seeing as I always practised it with him in mind.'

'Very good. Now, are you going to ring Joe or call over?'

'You think I should forget about the Angie thing?'

'Katherine!'

'OK, OK, it's forgotten.'

79

Lorcan strode up the cold, dark road, energized by furious self-righteousness. The outrageous cheek of the woman. How dare she? He'd only came on to her to get one over on pretty-boy Joe Roth and because he'd been bored. Otherwise he wouldn't have been seen dead with her.

He hadn't seriously considered her as Amy's replacement, had he? *Of course not.* OK, he had to admit, she was cute enough looking, she'd have done for a fast fuck and he'd been interested in what had happened to their baby. But not that bloody interested. And what kind of woman would consider aborting her own child? Even worse, what kind of woman would considering aborting one of *his* children? Sick, that's what she was.

Lorcan conveniently forgot that he was a proponent of the locking-the-stable-door-after-the-horse-has-bolted school of contraception and marched priggishly into the night.

A powder-blue Karmann Ghia roared past, briefly distracting him. Lorcan enjoyed a good car as much as the next man. Just as he recognized Katherine behind the wheel, he also saw that she was laughingly giving him the finger!

What was happening?

What was the world coming to?

On he stalked, the shock of Katherine's rejection continuing to assail him with fresh blows. It had never happened before.

It had literally never happened before. He was thirty-nine years old and, in living memory, a woman hadn't ever turned him down. Perplexed, unnerved, he ran his hands through his hair trying to calm himself. And his powerful striding faltered and stumbled as a street-lamp revealed a clump of red tresses tangled up in his fingers. Jesus Christ! I mean, Jesus Christ!

A woman had just told him to sling his hook. His hair was deserting him. He had no job. Suddenly all his angry energy dissipated and he felt terribly old. Old and frayed and past it. Knackered, exhausted, depressed.

Then he thought of Amy. Sweet Amy. Patient, good-natured, loyal Amy. *She* wouldn't turn him down. She'd welcome him back with open arms, soothe away the hurt, boost his morale. What had he been thinking of when he'd decided it was time to grant her her freedom? He'd been out of his mind!

He started to hurry towards her. He must have been mad to have dallied with Katherine. And that girl, Deedee, he'd been with earlier in the evening. Amy was much more beautiful. In fact, once he thought about it, perhaps he . . . perhaps he . . . perhaps he *loved* Amy.

He hurried even more, wishing he had money for a taxi. It seemed urgently important to see Amy immediately, to tell her how he felt. He'd thought he'd never want to get married again. But he wanted a safe haven with Amy, somewhere to lay his weary (balding) head. Perhaps even finally have a couple of kids. Give up on the acting, it was only a mug's game, full of shallow egomaniacs. Get a proper job. An honest day's work for an honest day's pay.

On the empty road a taxi appeared with its light on. Lorcan joyously hailed it. Amy would pay when he arrived.

When the taxi drew to a halt outside Amy's, Lorcan said to

the driver, 'Just give me a minute. I need to get money from my girlfriend.'

'Leave your jacket as insurance.'

'I'll only be a sec.'

'The jacket stays.'

'Oh, all right.'

Amy answered the door on the third ring. She was wrapped in a towel and she'd clearly been asleep. 'Oh, hi.' Her voice was flat.

'Hi.' His smile embraced her. He couldn't stop grinning, so happy was he to see her, his sweetie, his angel, the woman he loved.

She made no move of admittance so, still beaming, he gestured. 'Can I come in?'

'No.'

'Oh, baby, I'm so sorry. About the other night, about that girl Katherine. I was only kidding around, flirting. You know what I'm like.' A rueful I-can't-help-it grin.

'I do know what you're like,' she agreed. 'Benjy's been filling me in.' Benjy had appeared in the hall behind her.

'Hiya, Benjy, man,' Lorcan said absently, then he turned his attention back to Amy. 'You and I need to talk.' His smile held a promise of goodies to come. 'You may, as they say, learn something to your advantage.' Irritably he noticed that Benjy was still hovering in the hall, so he frowned his piss-off-and-leave-us-alone frown. 'Amy and I are just having a little confab here,' he said, with heavy meaning.

When Benjy didn't leave, Lorcan frowned again. 'Would you mind, man?'

It was only then that Lorcan realized that something was amiss. It was gone two in the morning. What was Benjy doing in Amy's? Why were they both wrapped in towels? What was going on?

'We're in love,' Benjy announced.

A honk of mirth-free laughter exploded from Lorcan. 'I know *you* are,' he mocked. 'You've always been into her. But she's mine.'

'I'm not,' she said. 'I'm Benjy's.'

The muscles of Lorcan's face were twitching up and down, in and out, like an accordion. He didn't know whether to laugh or roar, sneer or question. 'But I love you, Amy,' he finally plumped for.

'And I love Benjy,' she said simply.

She didn't *really*. But she was fond of him and she might grow to love him in time. She was too bruised by Lorcan to be bothered with him any more. All she'd ever wanted was a quiet life with a man who worshipped the ground she walked on. Benjy had promised always to be faithful and to love her for ever.

'Not all men are bastards,' he'd assured her. 'Me, for instance.'

And she believed him.

He wasn't good-looking enough to be one.

'Have you actually –?' Lorcan choked, looking from Benjy to Amy and back again. 'Have you actually done the deed?'

'Oh, yes.' They both nodded confidently.

'I don't believe you,' was the only thing Lorcan could come up with.

'Don't worry,' she said. 'You will in time.'

'You're some fucking friend,' Lorcan turned on Benjy. 'After all I did for you. After all the advice I gave you on how to get a girl and this is how you repay me. Nice one, you bollocks.'

'Your advice stank. And I didn't need it,' Benjy said smugly. 'My honest love for Amy was all that was required.'

Amy began to close the door and Lorcan realized in panic that he had yet another problem. 'Hey,' he yelped, 'could you loan me a fiver for the taxi?'

'No.'

And the door was closed in his face.

The taxi-driver had been robbed several times, and now kept a kango hammer under the seat for such eventualities. He was not afraid to use it.

Lorcan Larkin's goose was not only cooked, it was served, eaten, the remains put in the fridge, made into sandwiches the next day, fricassée the day after, curry the day after that, then the carcass was boiled for stock at the end of the week.

At a flat in Battersea, Joe Roth opened his front door to find Katherine standing there.

'Hi,' she said. 'I'm sorry it's so late, but can I tell you a story?'

Epilogue

At the chrome and glass Camden restaurant the skinny receptionist ran her sparkly turquoise nail down the book and muttered, 'Casey, Casey, where've you got to? Here we are, table eighteen. You're the –'

'– first to arrive?' Katherine finished for her.

'No, I was going to say you're the table in the window. Some of your mates are already here.'

Joe and Katherine hurried across the room to Tara, Liv and Milo.

'Sorry we're late,' Katherine apologized. 'Hair crisis. Anyway, happy birthday, Tara!'

'What's happy about it?' Tara grinned. 'How happy were you on your thirty-second birthday?'

'Extremely, actually.' Katherine smirked at Joe.

'So was I,' Liv contributed.

'I can't remember mine, it was so long ago,' Milo said. 'But I'm told I was content.'

'How's the pregnant woman?' Katherine asked.

'She's fine,' Milo answered, proudly. 'Puking like the Exorcist most mornings, but grand by lunchtime.'

Liv gave a benign, earth-mother smile, her hands clasped maternally across her midriff even though she was only nine weeks advanced and her stomach was as flat as a board. Contentment rolled off her in serene waves.

'Are you all right, there?' Milo asked her anxiously. 'Would you like a cushion for your back? Has the urge to eat newspaper gone off you?'

'Newspaper?'

'I ate the television page yesterday,' Liv admitted, shyly. 'He was cross.'

'Don't be telling them that,' Milo chided gently. 'I wasn't cross. All I said was "Next time will you eat the financial pages instead . . ." Oh, here's Fintan and Sandro.'

A taut wire of tension pulled everyone upright. It was three months since Fintan had finished his course of chemo and he'd had his first check up with the oncologist that afternoon. Everyone hoped he'd been told he was in the clear.

His progress across the restaurant floor was observed by the staff and most of the clientele. Tall, gaunt, leaning on a walking stick, his scalp was tufted with a transparent layer of pale-gold duckling down. Baby hair – according to JaneAnn, he'd been blond when he was born.

'Aids,' the Friday-night clientele mouthed and nodded in a frenzy of excitement to each other. 'Definitely Aids.'

'Could be alopecia.'

'Nah, look at how thin he is. And I bet that's his boyfriend with him. A tenner says it's Aids.'

Sandro hovered at Fintan's elbow and they were both smiling. Did this mean that the news was good? 'Happy birthday!' They descended on Tara. 'I know it's not actually until tomorrow, but happy birthday!'

'Never mind that. Tell us what the oncologist said,' Tara clamoured.

'He reckons I'll last the evening.'

'Ah, but seriously. The long-term prognosis?'

'The *very* long-term prognosis is that I'm going to die.' At the circle of appalled faces, Fintan laughed, 'We're *all* going to die.' But his laughter was joyous, rather than bitter.

'But has the cancer, you know, like, stopped?' Milo asked anxiously.

'It's certainly behaving itself at the minute. Gone underground. Keeping a low profile. But they're at pains to tell me that it might come back. Not definitely, but it might.'

'But it might not,' Sandro emphasized.

'We'll just have to wait and see,' Fintan agreed. 'I suppose I'm still in the Last Chance Saloon, but it's not so bad.'

Tara turned to Fintan and heard herself ask a question. 'Don't you mind the uncertainty?'

The words were out of her mouth before she realized; then she wanted to shoot herself for being so tactless. But Fintan smiled, a smile filled with light and life and pleasure. 'No.' Then he surprised her by asking, 'Do you?'

'Do I what?'

'Mind the uncertainty.'

She opened her mouth to protest that her life expectancy had no uncertainty, then stopped and bit her lip ruefully. It was so easy to forget everything she'd learnt over the past year. 'No.' She grinned. 'I'm glad of it, really. When I remember, it makes everything more – don't laugh at me – precious.'

'Who's laughing?'

'Well, this calls for champagne,' Joe announced.

'Now, tell me, Tara,' Fintan asked, eagerly, 'how was your lunch date with – what was his name? I find it hard to keep up – Gareth?'

'Yeah, Gareth. Put it this way, you can hold off on the his 'n' hers towels for a while.'

'Disaster?'

'Not exactly a disaster. But he didn't have much of a sense of humour.'

'Ahjamean?'

'Gareth,' she sighed heavily, 'is the kind of man who'd take you on holidays to the jungle, just so he could point out the window and say, "It's a jungle out there." You know?'

'All part of life's rich tapestry,' Katherine consoled.

'Yes indeed, and my tapestry is very rich at this stage.'

'But so long as you're having fun.'

'Oh, I am.'

'And when you're finished having fun, you can settle down with your devoted Ravi.'

'Jesus, Mary and holy St Joseph, don't go there! Would you all shut up about Ravi?'

There was a contrite silence then Milo murmured, 'Methinks she doth protest too much.'

'Methinks the very same.' Joe nodded.

'Methinks too,' Katherine agreed.

'Speak English,' Liv begged.

'All right, all right, all right!' Tara gave in. 'Have it your way. I'm mad about Ravi and we're going to get married.'

'This comes as no surprise,' Fintan said calmly.

'Would you stop! I'm ready for my presents, Mr De Mille. I hope you all bore in mind that I'm furnishing a new flat and I'm tired of boiling water in a saucepan and sleeping on a knackered sofa-bed.'

'We've heard nothing else for the past month.'

'Excellent. So which one of you got me a bed?'

'Was it me?' Fintan asked anxiously. 'I've to work a back-month until I get paid and I'm job-sharing so I'm only on half pay.'

Tara passed Fintan a parcel. 'No, you gave me this. The day will come,' she said, dreamily, 'when Carmella Garcia will arrive on bended knees and beg you to come back to work for her.'

'Sure, I don't care any more,' Fintan said, tearing off the wrapping paper. 'Good luck to her. What's this? A sharkskin tablecloth?'

'It's a shower curtain.'

'Oh, very nice. Happy birthday, doll. Do you accept butter vouchers?'

As Tara oohed and aahed over her new kettle, inflatable pouf, giraffe CD holder, Aero voucher and shower curtain, Fintan said, 'Do you mind me asking, but did Ravi give you a birthday present?'

Tara looked discomfited and eventually said, 'Yeah.'

'Can I ask what it was?'

'Actually,' Tara's squirmy embarrassment began to be over-ridden by enthusiasm, 'it's this wonderful stuff. You know my long search to find an indelible lipstick?'

They all nodded, slightly wearily.

'Ravi tracked down this great gear called Lipcote that you put on *over* your lipstick. It's just a colourless liquid, you leave it for a minute to dry, and then a world war wouldn't shift it. And guess what – it works! It actually bloody works! Look.' She picked up her gin and tonic and said, 'Watch as I *press* my lips against the glass. I'll give it a good snog. Now, see – no trace of lipstick on it . . . well, only the merest hint. Isn't he amazing?'

'Amazing.'

The champagne arrived. Joe popped the cork, and Fintan and Sandro sniggered and nudged each other as the white spume gushed out.

'Sorry, Liv, none for you,' Katherine said, pouring it into six glasses.

'Now, we must have a toast.'

'To Fintan, obviously,' Tara insisted.

'No, to Tara, it's her birthday,' Fintan said, magnanimously.

'No, no, something a bit more worthy, please,' Tara protested.

'To what, then?'

'To life,' Liv suggested, lifting her tumbler of milk.

'That's a good one,' the others noisily agreed, grabbing and raising their champagne flutes.

'And men with big willies,' Fintan threw in.

'Even better!'

'To life!' Seven glasses clinked in the middle of the table while seven voices chorused, 'And men with big willies!'

MARIAN KEYES

THE OTHER SIDE OF THE STORY

The agent: Jojo, a highflying literary agent on the up, has just made a very bad career move: she's jumped into bed with her married boss Mark …

The bestseller: Jojo's sweet-natured client Lily's first novel is a roaring success. She and lover Anton celebrate by spending the advance for her second book. Then she gets writer's block …

The unknown: Gemma used to be Lily's best friend – until Lily 'stole' Anton. Now she's writing her own story – painfully and hilariously – when supershark agent Jojo stumbles across it …

When their fortunes become entangled, it seems too much to hope that they'll all find a happy ending. But maybe they'll each discover that there's more than one side to every story …

UNDER THE DUVET

Her novels are adored by millions around the world – now read Marian Keyes's collected journalism and exclusive, previously unpublished material in *Under the Duvet*.

Bursting with her hilarious observations – on life, in-laws, weight loss and parties; her love of shoes and her LTFs (Long-Term Friends); the horrors of estate agents and lost luggage; and how she once had an office Christmas party that involved roasting two sheep on a spit, Moroccan style. The perfect bedtime companion, it will have you wincing with recognition and roaring with laughter.